Land of the Well

Sampurna Chattarji is a poet, novelist and translator. She is the author of two poetry books, *Sight May Strike You Blind* (Sahitya Akademi, 2007, reprint 2008) and *Absent Muses* (Poetrywala, 2010). Her first novel, *Rupture*, was published by HarperCollins in 2009. Her books for young people include *The Fried Frog and Other Funny Freaky Foodie Feisty Poems* (Scholastic, 2009). Sampurna's translation *Abol Tabol: The Nonsense World of Sukumar Ray* is now a Puffin Classic titled *Wordygurdyboom!* Forthcoming titles include two books of short fiction and her translation of Joy Goswami's poetry. For more about her writing, visit http://sampurnachattarji.wordpress.com/

Land of the Well

Sampurna Chattarji

HarperCollins *Publishers* India

First published in India by
HarperCollins *Publishers* in 2012

Building 10, Tower A, 4th Floor, DLF Cyber City, Phase II,
Gurugram Haryana – 122002, India
www.harpercollins.co.in

6 8 10 9 7 5

P-ISBN: 978-93-5029-224-2
E-ISBN: 978-93-5029-465-9

Typeset in Sabon Lt Std 10.5/14
Jojy Philip, New Delhi 110 015

Printed and bound at
MicroPrints India, New Delhi

For my dear

Baba, Ma

&

Kiran

Have you noticed that death alone awakens our feelings?

– Albert Camus, *The Fall*

Exposition

One

It was Goa in the monsoon. What did you expect, it was beautiful.

The boy was not alone.

Expensive gliders on his feet, a Hawaiian shirt with too many colours on his back, the boy with the tidy hair tagged behind his mother and father. At seventeen, it made the boy ashamed to be seen with his parents, but what choice did he have? He had done well in the school-leaving examinations, his parents were proud of him and this was their reward. A holiday in Goa, in the monsoon. It occurred to the boy, with an accompanying pain in his chest, that if they really meant to reward him, they could have sent him off alone. But when had they ever let him alone? The boy thought of humiliating metaphors to liken his condition to. A baby duck, walking with small, fast, intently worried steps behind mamma duck. A strolley, attached to an imperious hand, at Papa's well-heeled heels.

The boy knew his parents knew a shameful thing about him. He was top of his class, had been all his life, he was going to Princeton to study engineering or law, no expenses spared, the scholarship was merely about prestige, not money. All this was known, along with the small fact that the boy had no friends. Classmates who borrowed his meticulous, missing-nothing notes, hoping to achieve the same miraculous results as he did by cogging them, yes. But friends, not one. As for girls, the boy knew his parents were relieved that he was a failure with the girls. Enough time for all that later, they must have thought, if they thought about it at all. For the boy, the knowledge of his failure with the girls was sharp, unmerciful. He didn't know what one said to girls, how one could be easy the way the popular boys in class were. He never talked to them, he couldn't. They thought he was arrogant. They gave him openly derisory looks, threw snide comments his way, but most often they completely and instinctively ignored him. If it weren't for the beaming eye of the teacher in every class, shining on him with all the pride and joy in a star pupil, picking him out for all the special tasks, the impossible tasks, pinning on his frame badge upon badge of approval, the boy would have felt invisible.

He knew he was not ugly. It had occurred to him once that the cause of all this avoidance, this social inability might be his unshakeable ugliness. He had studied himself coldly, carefully, in the mirror. He was tall, five feet ten inches. He was lean, sixty kilos. He didn't suffer from acne. His skin was blemish-free, his nose was straight, his eyes dark, his eyelashes manly, his mouth well formed. His chin was nothing special, but it wasn't weak. His torso and arms were not muscular but they were smooth and firm and free of hair. The boy had the idea that girls did not like hairy men. As always, in these matters, he was wrong. He had twenty-twenty vision, in spite of all the hours he spent glued to his books. What was wrong with him, that he should, after twelve clumsy years in school, have not even one friend to tide him over into adulthood?

How could he blame his parents for cherishing his talent, pitying his friendlessness, and bringing him here to Goa, in the monsoon, as a reward?

They stood there—three small humans in a big vault of echoes. The floor was a chequerboard. The boy stared at it. Black and white squares. When he looked away, he saw white and black squares everywhere. The map behind the desk seemed hand-drawn and the proportions were all wrong. It had not been drawn to scale. The boy yawned. They had left Bombay at noon and the food on the plane had been biryani. Where was everybody? Were they in the wrong place? But the hotel coach had fetched them from the airport, the driver had a small placard with his father's name on it, so they clearly weren't.

After a few minutes—during which it seemed to the boy as if in all the universe there remained only the three of them standing on a chequerboard, their small overnighters at their feet like sleeping dogs—a man appeared. He looked like a fish in a coat. His hair stuck to his head and his eyes bulged. The boy watched as if from underwater as his father hectored the Fish-man and his mother fussed about the cottage not having a sea view in her piercing, disapproving voice.

'Short walk, ma'am, to the beach... the cottages closest to the sea are shut for the monsoon... weather warps.'

The words, apologetic, anaesthetic, washed over the boy, who stood distancing himself from them, staring at the lamps hanging from the vaulted roof. Each lamp was a cluster of hanging globes. He wondered what they would look like at night, lit-up. He liked them this way, ghostly white fruit in the semi-dark of the vaulted roof, the huge dark-green leaves. The boy liked the place. He hoped his parents would not make it difficult for him to preserve that feeling.

Another man, not Fish-man, taller, younger, reedier, led the way to the cottage that had been assigned to them. There were four rooms in each cottage, and all the cottages were identical.

'You take the room on the top, son,' the boy's father said, 'we'll take the ground floor.'

The other ground-floor room was occupied. A pair of bright-blue slippers, Crocs, stood outside the door. It occurred to the boy—who was, if nothing else, always fair, even when he acutely disliked someone—that it was nice of his father to have booked a separate room for him. He could so easily have asked for a third bed in their room; they had done this before, when he was smaller. A third bed cost less than a full room. His father was happy with him. This was his way of showing his approval. Grown-up son. Needs space. Separate room. His parents were such nice people. The boy felt deeply ashamed.

Reed-man carried his bag up. The boy could have done it himself, it was hardly heavy, all it had was a couple of shorts and T-shirts, the latest Dan Brown, and his laptop. But hotel etiquette demanded it. The boy followed Reed-man and waited for him to open the door, put on the lights, point out the amenities, turn on the hot and cold water taps and put down the bag, which he had been foolishly clutching all this time. After putting it down, he hovered. The boy signalled downstairs. Reed-man understood. But before he left, he gave the boy a surprisingly direct look into which the boy read the scorn of a newly made, responsible, working adult, so what if he couldn't have been more than two years older than him.

'Still playing the baby, are you?' that look said. 'Shame on you.'

The boy listened from near his door as Reed-man entered his parents' room. He heard his father's loud voice order a beer and two juices, one to be sent upstairs. He saw Reed-man leave their cottage with a spring in his step, his right hand in his jacket pocket. Good, the boy thought. They would get prompt service around here.

He shut the door and slipped the old-fashioned bolt across. In seconds he was sprawled across the bed, asleep.

In no time at all, he heard a persistent knocking on his door. He opened it, groggily wondering who it was, and why couldn't they let him sleep a little longer. His parents. They had changed into holiday clothes. His father was in shorts, his mother in slacks. They looked fresh and young. The boy felt stale. He mumbled at them, not wanting his mother to smell his breath, 'You go down. I'll come.'

What a way to start a holiday. When his classmates talked of Goa they talked of all-night raves, the kick of the little white tab dissolving slowly on the tongue. The energy. The punchy-rhythm of their insides outstripping the speed at which the world turns. The electric light in the eyes of a girl with spaghetti straps slipping off her shoulders as she dances.

And here I am, asleep on my first day in Goa. Asleep. Going to tea with my parents.

Was being a baby duck more, or less, humiliating than feeling like a pensioner in an old-age home? He stared at his face in the bathroom mirror. Were his teeth his own? He flicked them with his thumb and forefinger, and listened to the small, strong sound of enamel against nail before letting the water run.

Where were the other occupants?

As the boy sat by the dead pool full of water, empty of arms and bobbing heads, he wondered if they were the sole residents. Could an entire hotel be run for just three guests? The boy indulged himself in a rare sensation. Open the durbar hall for the evening! Summon the head cook, the prince wishes to congratulate him on his latest confection!

'Let's see the beach before it gets dark,' his father said.

The boy and his mother got up obediently. Down a little path they went, winding brown between green palms. Young palms. One of them was flattened. Strong winds. Most of the cottages were closed. This side looked shabby, as if the hotel couldn't be bothered about housekeeping where no one lived. Low, knee-high lamps were set along the path. Of the ten lamps he counted on his side, three were broken. Great. Snakes in the dark. (Were there snakes by the sea?) Trip and fall in the dark. No, hide away indoors in the dark.

When the little winding path ended and became gravel and sand and wiry bits of vegetation poking out of bumpy little mounds, the boy almost stumbled. The ground tilted upward. They climbed to the top of the tilt and there it lay before them.

The sea.

The boy, who had lived in Bombay all his life, close enough to the sea unlike some of his landlocked cousins, realized that he, like his mother, had drawn in his breath. Breathtaking, this is what the word means, he thought. There was nothing that came between him and the view. No vendors, no bathers, no dog-walkers, flute-sellers, monkey-trainers, tongawalas, no familiar criss-crossing colourful constantly changing bustle. It was quiet, and empty. The beach was very white. The blue water glittered. Little waves ran up and down. Placid and contented, the sea lay there like some big lazy beast, flicking its tongue gently at the sand, as if it was delicious, sweet, fine white sugar melting in its mouth. The boy licked his lips. The family walked down to the sand.

As his father took off his sandals, another word suddenly made sense to the boy. Sand. Sandals. He dilly-dallied behind them, so they wouldn't have to walk together. There was no one else on the beach. Tiny holes pitted the smoothness. He squatted for a closer look. A transparent creature scuttled sideways past his foot. Crabs! Sand crabs. Small, spindly and near-invisible. The boy observed the holes with interest. Nothing happened. No trapdoors opened. He got up and decided to take off his gliders and wet his feet, like his father was doing. The squish of sand turning into mud between his long, slender toes felt good but the crunch of shell under his feet didn't. The boy quickly put on his gliders. *Tomorrow*, he said to himself, *tomorrow I will walk to the other end of the beach, far, far off*. Strangled twists of rope and cloth lay on the sand. The boy found a conch-shaped shell and, conscious of the foolishness of the gesture, held it to his ear. The sound of what he imagined he heard was drowned by the gently increasing sound of the sea to his left.

The sun sank. In seconds, the sea dulled and the sky purpled. The wind picked up. The boy saw his parents turning around. He waited where he was for them to reach him.

Back in the room, he washed his feet. The pretty-pink bathroom tiles ran dirty with sand. So clean out there, so dirty in here. A lesson about everything having its own place, the boy thought, remembering a certain teacher who liked drawing moral lessons from the smallest observation. There was nothing to do here, in this hotel, on that beach. No surfing, no gliding, no speedboats. It was perfect. Exactly what he needed, to recover.

'There's a games room, Sir,' Reed-man said, when he saw the boy wandering aimlessly around. 'If you'd like to play.'

The boy followed his pointing finger. Across the dead pool, he saw an upstairs area, wooden roof, hanging lamp. It was empty.

'What games?' he asked.

'Carom, TT, pool,' Reed-man said enthusiastically.

'No one to play with,' the boy muttered.

However nice and well behaved a boy he was, he was sure of one thing. He was not going to be seen playing carom with his mother. And if he played TT with his father, he would lose. That man was so aggressive.

'I could play, Sir,' Reed-man said, eagerly. 'I only go on duty in an hour.'

The boy looked at him. Reed-man was dying to play.

'Okay,' the boy said.

They walked all around the pool and reached the stairs that led up to the games room. Wooden stairs, narrow, ladder-like. A cool place. The games lay waiting for ghosts to come and strike them into life. The pool table, dull-green with its overhead light switched off. The carom board placed just below the hanging lamp, its polished surface inviting. Four low stools around it. The TT table, the net stretched tight. The boy couldn't bear the idea of sitting down.

'TT,' he said to Reed-man, who hurried to get bats and ball from a cupboard in the corner.

Need to stretch and dance a little, need to come awake.

It soon became clear that Reed-man was scared to make a guest lose. He played the first game stiffly, politely. He lost. The next game he couldn't help it and won. The boy livened up. Now they were getting somewhere! The boy won the third game. Both of them were sweating lightly. Where was the Goa monsoon? The air was hot with unshed rain. The boy won the fourth. He could see Reed-man getting edgy. He had the upper hand now. Reed-man won the next three in quick succession. Breathless and apologetic with victory, he said, 'Sorry Sir, but I have to go on duty now.'

The boy said, 'Cool, we'll play again, whenever.'

Reed-man said 'Thank you, Sir' and left, hurrying, scuttling down the stairs like a crab.

The boy wanted to laugh in sympathy. Who would have guessed he would feel such kinship with Reed-man? Where was the scorn in his eyes now? Maybe he felt bad for that moment of scorn. The boy was glad Reed-man had won, it hadn't hurt his pride, for in such matters too, the boy was fair. He would beat him the next time. He was breathing again, good clean breaths, and he was hungry.

From the bird's-eye games room, the boy could see the vast dining space being prepared. White tablecloths. Here too, the space was half-open, half-covered by the wooden vault. That seemed to be the hotel's architectural motif. The white fruit globes had been lit. The tables nearest the pool were not being laid. *What a pity,* the boy thought. *Could have sat at the edge and lobbed pieces of bread into the pool without being seen.* The metal glint of the buffet dishes drew fresh saliva in the boy's mouth. He was so hungry.

But despite his ravenous appetite, wasn't the buffet too big for just the three of them, and the owner of the bright-blue Crocs? The huge green palm fronds stirred dark and heavy below the boy as he hung over the wooden railing. There was a charmed light around the pool. So what if this wasn't a rave, so what if he was friendless. He was hungry and—strange new sensation—he was happy.

The buffet wasn't just for their family of three plus the unseen stranger. In a sudden bustle, three sets of people appeared. Where had they been hiding? The boy found out that his father had found out there were sixty-four cottages in all. They were like a handful of small stones rattling in a large wooden shell. The boy's father drank his beer, his mother her shandy. The good son had a Pepsi. It wasn't that he didn't drink, he had had beer before and disliked the taste. Rum with Pepsi was more his thing, or sometimes a Cranberry Breezer, even though he felt that was girlish. But he was not going to drink here, with *them*. The boy was clear about that.

He studied the guests.

The first set was a honeymooning couple. Even the boy could tell, as he looked at them mooning over each other. The girl wore a red top and tight black jeans and lots of bangles up to her elbows. She wasn't pretty at all, but when she stood up, the boy noticed with a slight flush, because his mother was next to him, that she had a ravishingly good figure. Her husband was fat and he couldn't stop holding her hand. They ordered some brightly coloured mocktails and whispered and touched.

The second set was a family. Old man, young man, old woman, young woman and kid.

'Son and daughter-in-law,' the boy's mother confided. 'Look at how the mother-in-law spoils the child and how the daughter-in-law doesn't like it but can't say anything.'

The third was a foreigner. He had steely eyes which he mostly kept fixed on the *Lonely Planet* before him. The boy tried to guess where he had come from. Italy? Germany? It made no difference. He was drinking his beer and reading his book and from time to time he smoked. His feet were in a pair of bright-blue Crocs. So he was their neighbour, the one in the other ground-floor room!

So that's us. A nice boy with his parents. A TV-serial-type family. A soppy couple. A lonely foreigner. Dinner is served.

The buffet was good. Goan fish curry and pork vindaloo and prawn rechad. The boy ate everything.

His mother asked the men behind the buffet, 'Where's your famous Goan music we hear so much about? They told us in Goa everyone is singing all the time?'

The men laughed nervously because as far as they knew their job description ended at serving the food. It was unnerving to be asked questions. They all looked as young as Reed-man, who seemed to be everywhere at once. The boy thought Reed-man looked stressed. To reassure him, the boy gave him what he hoped was a friendly smile. And then he ate two helpings of all the desserts, ice cream, fruit salad, orange mousse and chocolate cake. His mother looked contented, his father alarmed.

The bed in the room was turned down so neatly it made the boy want to jump on it and ruin it. An uncharacteristic thought, the boy realized. *Maybe once I go back from Goa I can have some other uncharacteristic thoughts, about girls*. The room was pretty. Too pretty. Girlish pink walls. A white string chair, very comfy. Nice lamps. No wonder his mother stopped complaining about the sea view the minute she saw the room. As the boy fell into sleep with the rapidity of the very young and the very full, it occurred to him that tomorrow would be a wonderful day filled with nothing, absolutely nothing to do.

When he awoke, the roof was pounding with rain.

Two

Raindrops speckled the pool. It looked diseased. The boy felt the bumps on his arms.

'What can we do in this rain,' his mother said, grouchily. As if she had not known she was going to Goa in the monsoon! The flip side of the discounted rates. The stay-at-home boredom that they could have stayed at home for. Why here, on holiday in a posh, deserted hotel.

'Drive,' the boy's father said. 'We can go for a long drive.'

And before mother or son could react, it was all organized. *What a man.* A white Maruti Omni materialized out of the rain, its headlights on.

'Have you been to the loo, beta?' his mother asked him, the habit of seventeen years that she had still not shaken off. The boy felt like a two-year-old being taken to the potty to pee. He grunted what could have been a yes or a no, and she didn't push it. She had freshened her lipstick, and ridiculously, she wore her sunglasses. She looked like a cat in those slanted shades. *How old is she,* the boy wondered. She seemed a stranger in the rain, in her inappropriate white clothes. Speckled by mud soon. The boy got in last and slid the door shut.

The driver drove blindly through the driving rain. The long road was slick, wet. The boy opened the window on his side. Cool stinging spray.

'Shut it, beta,' his mother said. He shut it.

The driver was skinny. His hair curled and his eyes were red in the rear-view mirror. *Drinking, she would say,* the boy thought maliciously, resenting his mother for making him close the window. *Goans!* she would say, the minute they were out of the car. *Drinking in the morning!* What a good idea. The boy felt like drinking. Hard drinks. Spite his parents. Share a bottle of rum with a friend. The driver maybe. Take me to the hotspots, brother. In a blur outside his sealed window Goa flashed past, green and dripping. The green stunned the boy. No one had told him how green Goa would be. He had seen beaches in his mind, yellow upon yellow, stretching into blue. But this! Greenness, juicy as if he could bite it. Black tar gleaming like an oil spill. Red earth slushed up by the rain. And the fields. Vivid young green, acres and acres of it. The rain was slowing down. The boy opened his window again. His mother didn't say anything. The rain stopped. In a sudden streak of sun the boy saw a patch of paddy field reflect a patch of sky.

Who could stop them now! The boy felt exhilarated as they flew to Panjim. Theirs was clearly not the only driver who believed flight was the four-wheeler's true calling. Others whirled past, equally manic, throwing great arcs of water at the Omni, which meant the boy had to close his window again. Everywhere the hidden tangle of houses guarded by lushness. The red-tiled roofs. The post office was a cottage, enchanted in its isolation. Who on earth posted letters there? Suddenly the boy felt a stab of irritation. Who posted letters any more, anywhere? This place was too unreal. Time had slowed down. He felt he'd been here a year already. His body felt terribly impatient. It suddenly made sense why they drove like that. To beat the slowness, the crawl of nothing changing, to get it out, out from under their skins. *I know how to drive*, the boy thought. *If only I could, right now!* He felt like snatching the wheel away from Red-eye and hurtling through space. A missile. Break it, smash the barrier of time holding him back.

The drive was better than the town. A dirty little place, full of scooters. *What's so special about this*, the boy thought sourly. The sun was out and the heat was oppressive. Their driver silently pointed out sights. A sheer white church. An old blue building with flowered balconies. The river. A dolphin trip? Feni? Cashew nuts? Sun hats? The boy's mother was interested in everything. He tagged behind as she bought packets and packets of cashew and his father two bottles of the drink that makes Goa sing, as the shopkeeper put it. Sing? He'd never seen a place more devoid of music. His mother bought a sun hat for him which he didn't want. He wore it. The elastic around the chin was too loose. He let it hang. His father bought 'Life's a Beach' T-shirts for the two of them. Everything looked worn and faded and damp, steaming slowly in the heat. Not a good time, Goa in the monsoon. Everything limped. Photos. Mandatory holiday photos. The boy stood obediently where told and clicked obediently when told. It was like he wasn't there. The glare turned everything white. There were no other young people around. *Get back to our ghost hotel. Sink myself in the pool. The far end of the beach is waiting.* The boy felt sluggish, desperate to leave.

Back in the car, 'Nice, wasn't it?' his father said.

'Hmm.'

'Feeling okay, beta?' his mother said.

'Yes.'

A squashed silence. *Fly brother fly. Who needed Panjim when we had all that green to fly through and that white and secret beach? All ours.*

'Lunch!' his father announced efficiently and the car stopped outside a house. *That's right*, the boy thought, *I could do with lunch. Preferably a big one.* The sign on the gate said D'Costas. Garden umbrella and chairs in the garden. No one there. The boy followed his parents as they went in. A dark room, shadowed with furniture. A shuffle of feet in answer to his father's call. A woman appeared.

'What can we get to eat?' his father said, straight to the point as ever.

'Oh,' the woman said. 'Lunch is over.'

'What? Nothing? Come on, you can't do that to us!'

The persuasion worked. It always did.

'All right,' the woman said. 'Fried fish and pau will do?'

'Will do.'

They sat outside under the garden umbrella, drinking their cold drinks. Red-eye refused lunch and accepted a Mirinda. The air was still. The garden looked bedraggled. At night the strings of lights draped on the trees would be lit. It would be gayer then. Now it looked dull and mucky. A man brought their food. The fish was slightly charred. It was a dry meal, fish and pau. No curry, no gravy on the side. But who cared, the boy was ravenous. He ate huge chunks of fish bathed in lemon juice and gulped down his Pepsi.

'Slow down, beta,' his mother said.

'Where's all that famous live catch,' she continued, accusingly. 'You get better fish in Bombay. Here, finish it,' and she put her piece on her son's plate.

The boy ate it. His father paid the man, blustering over the poor service and dry food. The man shrugged. Vaguely dissatisfied though full enough, the boy got in and slid-slammed the door into the catch.

It felt like coming home. Fish-man had never seemed friendlier. His father fixed another date with Red-eye. His mother went off to rest.

The boy sank into one of the cane chairs in the lobby. Reed-man scuttled past.

'Can you get me an ice cream?' the boy asked.

'Certainly, Sir. To your room, Sir?'

'No, here.'

'Here? No food in the lobby, Sir.'

The absurd protocol of the ghost hotel with the empty lobby! The boy almost laughed.

'By the pool then.'

'All right, Sir.'

And off he scuttled.

The boy heaved himself up and went to the pool. One deckchair, roasting in the sun. He dragged it to the nearest palm. The legs made a screechy metallic sound as they dragged over the concrete. Prone, the heat singed through his cotton shirt and shorts. Above him a glint of sun shot through the fronds. He felt giddy with the light. He held up the camera hanging uselessly round his neck and snapped. The sun would burn out the fronds. The cluster of hanging coconuts would turn black. *It would be a cool picture.*

When Reed-man appeared with his double-scoop strawberry in a silver-coloured bowl the boy thought he was the result of too much staring at the sun. A floating black spot that refuses to go away until you close your eyes.

The ice cream melted faster than he could slobber it up. He drank the last bit from the silver-coloured bowl, certain that no one would see him. If the place had been quiet the day they arrived—*was it just yesterday*—now it was ultra-quiet. You could see the silence rise like desert haze in movies. From the slumbering pool, from the white concrete around it, from the palm fronds, from the back of his hands. It was a hot, heavy quiet, it made you think of a big dog with too much fur. It covered your skin, it clogged your mouth and nostrils, if you sat still under its weight, unresisting, you drowned.

The boy got up, pushing away the sticky deckchair as if it were pulling him down. The sun hat with the loose elastic band had long slipped off his head and was dangling behind his back. Not bothering to tug it back on, he decided to visit the beach. Three, his Swatch said. No one went to the beach at three in the afternoon, in the blazing sun, all alone. He would. Better than retreating to his room with its girly pink walls and sleeping the day away.

The white sand threw the light back at him. The sun seemed incidental. It was as if the white sand had become the source of all light, radiating straight into his eyes. He felt upside down. He walked to the tree that marked the path leading to the hotel and lay down under it. This was the tree he'd identified last evening. He'd need it when he walked to the far end. In that long stretch it would be easy to miss the narrow path. Lost on the beach. Wandering for eternity. *Until my eyebrows turned as white as the sand and hermit crabs burrowed into the deep hollow of my chest.* The boy liked that. It made him sound like Robinson Crusoe, whom he had read about when he was a kid. Who cared about Crusoe now? Certainly not his non-friends. The only thing they read were the guides their tuition classes doled out. Crammers. The boy knew he was a crammer too, how else had he got those fabulous marks. But he was a crammer without tuitions. He was naturally intelligent, everyone said so, he had a fabulous memory. He despised his classmates, their image-addicted, money-fixated, giddy-headed ways. He was different. Engineering or law at Princeton was only a ruse. Of course he would make money, but not in a boring, brainless way. He had this idea, simmering at the back of his mind, hidden from all, especially his parents, that he would write a best-selling book, like Jeffrey Archer or Robert Ludlum or Dan Brown, about a murder or a conspiracy. Or a horror story, like Stephen King. He could, he knew it. But until such a time, he would sit here on this burning Goa-in-the-monsoon beach and let his brains get fried. Bheja fry. Greasy and mopped up with buttered pau. Who needed a pill when the sun could make you high? He was high already. A sand crab as large as a house towered over him. He felt safe inside its pincers, a midget. He was an egg on a Teflon pan. He frizzled at the edges and slid. The pan was flat and slippery. Someone held the pan deftly, that much he could tell, or he would have fallen right off at that angle. The blue-flame sky. The heat full up. Bubbling hot creamy yolk bursting to ooze. Plop onto the plate. The frill of white, the greasy gleam.

A little urchin is watching me. Is he real? He is watching me sit up and register his presence.

The boy suddenly felt like a clumsy old giant in front of such a tiny spectre. The little fellow looked greedy. The camera! It was his father's camera, an old-fashioned one. Was it still around his neck? It was. Would the urchin snatch it and run? *I'm more than twice his size, he wouldn't dare!*

Maybe he wasn't alone. Maybe he was part of a gang of little devils, hiding (where would they hide?), waiting for a signal to leap out and pounce. *But I would defeat them all and they would ask me to be their leader. Me, leader of a pack of little devils!* The boy grinned. The urchin stared at his grinning face, then turned around and ran. His bare feet hit the white-hot sand in little spurts and in a blink he was gone. *Pity,* the boy thought, watching his running form get smaller and smaller. *I could have asked him to show me the sights.* The real Goa, not the pretend-one of the hotel with its blue pool and shiny buffet. Why did they have to stay at such a swanky hotel? Why not in a little place like others did, a cosy little place run by Mama and Papa Goa, warm and red-eyed and smelling of feni and fish? This was the wrong time to be here. The wrong place. *I will walk to the far end of the beach in the blaze and not return. I will spite this whole notion of a happy holiday, so kindly arranged by the parents. I will make sure that when they knock for tea I will not be there.*

The boy felt like an insect crawling across an enormous brass plate of honey. How had the urchin made it so fast? No, it wasn't an insect he felt like. He felt like one of those sticky balls with suction pads. You flung them at a wall and they stuck. Each foot sank into the sand and dragged. His shirt had melted into his skin. Where was the rain? *Could have been sleeping in my room. But no, I had to spite someone, even if that someone was me.* He imagined a helicopter shot of the beach, long, white and empty except for a moving dot. A blip. Him. What was at the far end anyway that was worth walking to? The more he walked the further away it seemed. Would there be a sign saying 'Cavelossim ends here'? Or a village at least with people, real people? The urchin's village. Would it be like Chimbai in Bandra, or Chuim in Khar? Something huddled, smelling different, looking as if it came from an older, forgotten, more fascinating time? He had walked down Chimbai Road after dark, stopped and eaten puris being fried on one side of the narrow road, opposite the man who sold sardines. Everyone seemed to know everyone else in that lane, old friends stood and talked while their dogs sniffed each other. Up a little ladder, he had seen girls sewing. Fatima Tailors. A little further a white cross with marigolds and a red electric diya burning before it. Here there was not a trace of habitation. The ghost hotel with the ghost beach attached. That's what people paid a steep price for during peak season and here they were enjoying it for half. How clever of them.

He walked. He remembered Tintin trying to strangle himself in one of those comic-book deserts. But this was not the desert! The sand had blinded him to the water. The water lay robbed of movement, of whatever peaceful power he had sensed the previous evening. *It looks as tame as the pool I left behind, thoughtfully provided for those too lazy to walk the distance to the sea.* But what if the sea turned violent? All similarity gone! The thought turned turtle. Did the sea have sea turtles? Giant flippers stroking the water gently, almost not moving? Better a sea turtle than a sand crab. Grit caked his lips. He hadn't felt the breeze but there must have been one for the sand to fly up and coat his sticky lips and hands. Still a long way to go. The last time he'd felt like this was when he was in class two and had won a race. It was hunt-the-sweet-in-the-heap-of-flour. *Our hands were tied behind us and we ran. Along the way were piles of flour, one for every runner. (How did they stay in place? Was there no wind? Was each pile neatly in a box?) You had to reach your pile and use your mouth to find the sweets buried in it (how doglike and demeaning). I came up victorious! Mouth smeared with flour, biting the sweet between my teeth I ran to the finish. The others were still rooting in their flour pits. I could hardly wait for my hands to be untied so I could unwrap and crunch up the sweet, mixed with bits of flour. That was all I was interested in. Not in the prize (a tiny cup), nor my moment on the victory stand, poised on the number 1 painted in white on a blue wooden step above numbers 2 and 3.*

What a strange race, the now almost wholly grown-up boy thought as he kicked the sand, white as flour.

He reached the place where the land turned and the beach ended. A natural wall of black tumbled rocks ended his walk. He could have clambered over the rocks and edged around the curve to see what lay beyond. The waves were negligible. But he didn't. No waves were negligible enough for him. The boy fought something he thought had long gone. He had almost learned swimming, the year his father was posted to Calcutta. Along with the trainer he had swum out to the middle of a lake, touched the bamboo pole (or was it a metal wire) that cut through its middle and on the way back he had remembered the many feet of nothingness below him and felt his limbs turn to water. Why did they say that—turn to water? In the water it should have helped, turning to water, becoming the element you swam in. Isn't that what they said when they described someone skilful—he was in his element? The trainer brought him back, panting and flailing. He was amused by his failure, and worse, scornful.

Since then, many pools had tempted the boy. Easy to jump into, manageable blue depths you could see the bottom of. It was not seeing the bottom that scared him.

Not knowing what lay below, how dark, how teeming with nibbling fish or seaweed shapes that stung. The hotel pool he had left behind tempted him, taunted him. *After this long sandy walk, maybe I will swim.* But no. Hotel rules: shower first, then swim. The pool is not a bathtub. The boy turned around. A double row of palm trees swung leftward. They looked painted onto the sky. Where was his marker tree? The boy couldn't see it. He walked forward. Sooner or later, it would appear.

'You're burnt black,' his mother said observantly that evening. 'What made you fry yourself in the sun?'

He didn't bother responding. His throat felt sore. He drank bowl after bowl of soup. So hot it hit his gullet like a fist.

'Slow down,' his father said.

That's funny. I thought he'd stopped noticing what I did. He moved to the noodles. Nice. Soft and slippy down his throat. Why were they serving Chinese in Goa? Not that the boy minded. He loved the tang of salt, borrowed from the sea air, lavishly present in the soya. First soya, then chilli sauce, then vinegar with green chillies. The vinegar was a mistake. He felt as if someone had sliced through his tonsils. The foreigner wasn't eating Chinese. He had asked for an omelette and toast. *Didn't know you could do that at dinner!* The boy felt angry at this small yet important injustice, this vital discrimination. *I thought you ate what they gave you!* There was a sweet-and-sour with the noodles. The boy avoided that. There was a hot capsicum chicken. The boy wolfed that down, even though his throat rasped with every swallow. The couple was missing. Probably slurping at each other in their bed. Better there than here. The joint family looked ragged, as if the day had got on their nerves. They hadn't bothered to dress up like they had yesterday, in silk saris and jackets. The child was hollering for something. The father shouted at the child and the father's mother shouted at him for doing that. The boy looked at them and looked away.

In the morning, Red-eye arrived to pick them up. The boy had realized by then that a host of drivers, including Red-eye, were parked just outside the hotel gate. They could have simply walked out and chosen any car they liked, instead of having the hotel assign them one. But his father liked doing things the grand way. Send out. Call in. Today, he announced, as they found their usual places in the car, they would see Fort Aguada.

It was all the way to Panjim and beyond. They could have seen it yesterday, the boy thought, wondering if his father was thinking the same thing, cursing himself for bad planning, and a needless extra trip. The place was impressive, but where the fort once stood, there now stood a hotel! A five-star hotel, posh beyond poshness, way swankier than theirs. For no ostensible reason, or none that he could identify, it made the boy mad, the hotel behind the ramparts. But the wind and the view from the section in which they could freely walk about whipped his irritation away. The waves lashed against the semicircular parapet where they stood. Was it a turret? No, turrets were towers. A battlement! That's what it was. The waves surged against the stone, and the spray flew at them with unexpected force. *It's brilliant!* the boy thought. His mother gripped his father's arm nervously and took a few steps back. Red-eye stood behind them, angular, not smiling. The boy took a picture, the second one he had taken voluntarily. He went as far back as he could and got it all—the water, the sand, a ship on the horizon, the straight wall, the curved wall, and the three specks, the heads of his co-travellers. They seemed so insignificant against the old stone, the sea, the sky. That was fitting. The boy went down the partially ruined steps and asked his mother to take a picture of him looking up. *Later,* the boy thought, as he posed, keeping his well-formed mouth from the easy and unnecessary curve of a smile, *later I might see some trace of the explorer in this picture, with this brown-walled mossy well around me.* A window cut a square of light into the stone. Maybe cannons were fitted into these windows, firing at enemy ships as they came. *Someone loaded the cannons and I fired. It was precise and ruthless. Boom!*

After the fort, they hit the beaches one by one, father, mother and son. Baga, Anjuna, Colva. Hectoring father wouldn't allow them to spend more than half an hour at each. What was the hurry, the boy wondered. Mother had brought some cashews along and they ate those instead of lunch. The boy had eaten so many idlis at breakfast he wasn't really hungry, but he munched them anyway. At Anjuna his mother grew girlishly eager to buy some brightly coloured bags from a Banjarin. She was from Rajasthan. Why buy Rajasthani bags in Goa? But his mother bought one, as happy with the mirrored thing as if she were a child. At Baga they watched, as if hypnotized, a row of upturned boats, bright-blue, orange, green. Another boat slid in and there was a flurry of brown arms, legs and lungis. *A catch?* the boy wondered, too tired to check. His father hurried forward, looking as if he would like to buy up the whole boat at a bargain, but all he did was stop and stare. Other men mended their nets. It was sleepy, peaceful. Some bare-skinned foreigners sat and drank at the one shack that was open. The boy would have liked to sit there too, but neither parent was keen.

'Back at the hotel we'll have a drink, son,' his father said, as if he were conferring a great favour on him. Man to man, leaving out the woman, his mother. The boy looked back longingly at the shack as they left.

He didn't like Colva at all. The beach was narrow, and dirty. Kids played around. Fully dressed mothers stood in the waves, their thighs showing through wet cloth. The action was obviously at Colva, even in the monsoon. He was glad they weren't living here. By the time they left, the sun was setting. His mother liked it. She sat and watched intently until the last drop of sun dissolved into the sea and then she got up with a sigh.

On the way back, they passed a field where a huge crowd was breaking up. When his father asked, Red-eye said a football match had just got over. So that's what they did on sleepy afternoons! Football! The boy, who had never been into sports, except to watch them, wished he had known. He and Red-eye could have watched the game and maybe some friends of Red-eye would have taken him home and fed him their mother's authentic vindaloo. As they drove by, the string lamps that had been hung all over the field came on, red and yellow and green. It looked like a fair just about to begin. The boy felt like jumping off and joining in.

Without asking, he knew Red-eye had been booked for the next day. His father was a consistent man. That evening they sat at the bar and he drank a mocktail to spite his father's offer of a manly drink. The next day stretched before him. What pleasure in knowing it would be the same, with very, very minor variations.

Three

The next day, everything changed.

The next day changed everything.

He got up early, as if to study for an exam, at six. A single persistent thought which had pursued him through his dreaming sleep jolted him awake like an alarm. Try the pool. Try, when no one's looking. Opening his bag, he realized he had not brought swimming trunks. That was not going to stop him, not today. He wore the rayon shorts bought for him by his father in Bangkok, which his mother had thoughtfully packed. His mother always packed for him. They had a net inside them, around the crotch. The net hung, sloppy along his thighs, getting tangled. He felt foolish, a fish, trapped. When he caught himself tiptoeing downstairs, as if he were on his way to a forbidden assignation, he laughed. No one could stop him from swimming! On the contrary, it enraged his father that he didn't swim more often at the club. At the pool, the boy stopped short. There was a solitary head bobbing in it. Sleek and ripple-less, the body behind it reached the end where he stood, near the steps that led down. It was the foreigner who lived on their ground floor. The water seemed to melt his steely eyes, make him friendly. He smiled and waved. The boy felt cheated. His private pool, destroyed by this foreigner's presence. He wouldn't dare go in now. He barely smiled back. And then the foreigner grabbed the bright-blue rails and began climbing out.

'Nice swim?' the boy said, as if by speaking he would legitimize his being there.

'Great!' the foreigner smiled back and then, 'See you at breakfast!' and off he went, barefoot on the little winding path towards their cottage, rubbing his head with his towel. His body was shockingly pink. The boy waited until he vanished. Then he took off his T-shirt, dropped it to the ground and began climbing into the pool.

He felt sick with fear and excitement. No one was around. Would anyone hear him if he drowned and needed help? He wouldn't know until it happened. He had seen the blue metal pipe that ran along the edges of the pool. He would clutch that and recall his swimming lessons. In Calcutta, they had held a length of bamboo and kicked. Kick! Float! Light! Float! And all the while his body stubbornly leaden, refusing to become light. He would repeat that routine here. The metal pipe felt slippery under his hands. His chin wobbled on the surface of the water and he swallowed a teeny sip of chlorine. He spat it out. His hands firmed. His legs were floating behind him without any instructions from him. Some natural buoyancy that the boy had forgotten about. Now stretch, streamline, kick. He did it. Again. Wildly elated at how well he remembered to kick, the boy released one hand. The whole of him swerved violently. Some current the pool had kept secret from his eyes wafted him dangerously away from the edge. His legs would have hit the pipe in another second. The boy gasped and clutched again. He swallowed, spat. Too rash. *A few more tries before you do anything rash.*

He looked resolutely at the tiled wall before him and kicked. The small of his back hurt. At least he didn't feel like a stone. *That's an improvement. Come on, now try it again. You're so close to the side you won't drown. Just grab the pipe, the railing, and you're safe. This is the shallow end, stupid. It's shorter than you standing up.* But whoever drowned standing up? And whoever remembered facts in the choke and swirl of dying? The boy stuck his head up, angled back and breathed deep. Then he let both hands go. Somewhere behind him his legs were mechanically kicking. He swerved and found himself facing away from the tiled wall. He had turned. Ahead of him, instead of the safe and solid tiled wall lay the whole wobbly watery mass of the pool. He was moving towards it without wanting to. He was headed for the centre from where the blue pipe would be too far. His arms would give out first. Then his legs. Then his lungs. As his head clouded with the idea of biological collapse he couldn't imagine his arms his legs his body any more. Thrashing wildly, gasping, he angled away from the centre and flung himself back towards the blue pipe, made reckless by its nearness. He was sinking, falling. He was choking, grabbing. Both hands clung to the metal.

Winded, the boy, who had in his fright forgotten about observers, hung there, feeling tense and limp at the same time, trembling all over, giving up all attempts to kick-float. After a few minutes he scrambled towards the steps, one hand over the other on that solid blue lifeline, walking through the water clumsily. Let go and grab the step rail. Then one hand over the other, one foot after the other and the concrete ground lay steady under his toes, a miracle. His shorts were in a twist around his balls. He shook himself, the way he had seen wet dogs doing. His hands had a red line going through them. He must have held on tighter than he thought.

It was only then that he realized he had forgotten to bring a towel. As he dripped shamelessly onto the dry white concrete he heard a voice saying 'Sir! Sir!' and saw Reed-man hurrying towards him with a towel neatly draped over his arm.

'Here's your towel, Sir,' and there it was, crisp and rough against the boy's sore hand.

'Thanks,' he muttered.

Had Reed-man seen him flailing around? Or had he simply seen him climbing out, like any normal swimmer? The boy took the towel, not meeting his eyes, and Reed-man, suddenly humorous, said, 'Sir, ice cream?'

The boy knew he meant him to laugh and only so he would be lulled into believing that he was a normal swimmer, that he hadn't flailed and flapped about like a pathetic loser, the boy laughed for Reed-man, and said, 'No no! Anyway, I see breakfast is being served. I think I'll eat at once.'

It was the first day the boy was eating alone. He could tell, by the looks of the waiters, that some breach of etiquette had taken place. His solitary, unaccompanied-by-parents presence was a serious breach. Already the waiters had gotten used to the customs of the guests, the daily habits of people they saw only for a few days, who formed rigid little rituals as if to make their changed surroundings familiar. Just before entering the covered breakfast area the boy remembered to put on his T-shirt. It seemed rude somehow to burst into the dining area clad only in clinging shorts. It amused the boy to see that he was no different from the waiters when it came to monitoring, and guarding against, any possible breach of etiquette of his own. After all, he had been raised to be a good, decent boy.

Moisture clung to him like a slippery second skin. Was it sweat? It felt hot and uneasy after the cool lap of water. The boy sweated and ate. Slowly, and in spite of the fact that he had, in effect, failed, as the food filled him up the boy felt a rush of something like triumph—the triumph over his own inertia.

Later, in the lobby, it was time to go out with Red-eye. Red-eye had been co-opted into the holiday rituals of this little family of three, part of their daily pilgrimage to places of interest, their dutiful appreciation of local sights. The boy was wondering whether to stay back (and commit another breach) when he saw Fish-man, the manager, hustling the male half of the smoochy couple towards his father. He watched with interest. His father listened, first to Fish-man, then to Fatty. Then he nodded vehemently and Fish-man and Fatty broke into smiles. Then father strode towards mother and son and announced, 'We'll have to take them along with us.'

'Who?' It seemed to the boy that his mother was alarmed.

'The couple. The man they engaged last night sent word he cannot come, his mother died, and so they'll come with us.'

Why, the boy wondered. Why not step out of the hotel gate and engage another car? It was easier than smarming up to a man you didn't know. Wanted to save money, Fatty did! Go splits. *That is, if my father let him.* But of course he wouldn't! He tended to be lordly in these matters.

'We were going anyway,' he'd say grandly. 'No, young

man, wouldn't think of it! You can buy your wife some pretty little gift instead!'

Fatty must have figured that out. What a sharpie. His ugly wife had hidden herself in one of the tall-backed cane chairs. As Red-eye drove in, gaily, the boy thought, with an extra flourish, she popped out and stood beside Fatty. She was overdressed for the occasion. She wore some sort of shimmery sari that clung to her. There was some shimmery stuff on her face as well, below her eyes and above them. Had no one ever told her about casuals? The boy found that he already hated her presence, that he failed even to be soothed by the way the sari clung to her marvellous curves. Even the old-fashioned jeans she had worn to dinner would've been better than this wedding outfit! It was a big day for her, the first day she and hubby-dear were going out. After all those days of playing dirty in the dark, she stood there shimmering, her ugly face happy in her own private pleasure.

There was a moment of awkwardness as Red-eye opened the doors.

'We'll get in at the back, Sir,' Fatty insisted.

'What, put your bride in with the spare tyres?' the boy's father boomed. 'Not at all! Both you young men can have that pleasure. The young lady, she must sit beside my wife.'

Clever man, this meant his own seating arrangement remained unchanged! The boy's mother didn't seem too pleased about having Shiny next to her. She was a snob, his mother, and she disliked sharing with perfect strangers. But her manners were impeccable. With a smile that only her son could see the strain in, she patted the seat next to her and Shiny got in. With no such attempt at friendliness the boy opened the back and climbed in, leaving Fatty to follow. There was hardly room for the two seats that had been fitted in for extra passengers. Children might find it comfy, even fun, to be squeezed in there, but certainly not him. Red-eye—who looked as discomfited by this unexpected company as the waiters had been at the boy eating alone—slammed the door on them with what the boy thought was totally justified violence. He had a pact with the three of *them*. They drove, sightsaw, and then they drove some more. They took pictures and stopped for food or drink. It was all done in companionable silence. Silence suited Red-eye, the boy thought. Now already the many bangles of Miss Shiny were jingling and jangling, making the silence jittery. His father felt the need to converse with Fatty. He swung around, uncomfortably, and started an unnecessary diagonal of conversation across the Omni. He asked fatherly questions. They found out Fatty had a fine job with a pharma company. Brand manager, he said with a little self-satisfied smirk. They found out his wife was from Delhi (did that explain the shimmer?) and that she ran a boutique back in Bombay (my god, the boy thought, were the clothes at her boutique as dreadful as the ones she wore?) and that her good name was Lata. As for him, his good name was Alok. Alok Gupta. Why did people still say good name? (What's your bad name then?) The boy could feel Alok Gupta ignoring him at the back. He was, what, twenty-eight? Thirty? The boy was seventeen and he could feel the man trying to repel with every ounce of his good name, his good job and his good wife the hostility being transmitted to him in waves by the seventeen-year-old ill-mannered son of the courteous, generous gentleman. *Because of you and your shiny wife I am sitting here, stuffed at the back like a piece of luggage, a few inches away from your pudgy thighs in polycot pants that no one wears these days.* He had upset the equilibrium (yes that was the word, the boy thought, furiously) of their little drives. He could see Red-eye hunching over the wheel, looking as sullen as he felt.

Their first stop was a tower. St Augustine's? The boy, who had a photographic memory for facts that he read, forgot the name the instant Red-eye muttered it to them. It was an immense black tower, cracked but standing. On the ground lay huge black slabs of stone. They weren't all evenly set. Vegetation grew everywhere, fringing the ridges of the tower like balcony gardens, sprouting in between the stone slabs. The boy stubbed his toes on the slabs, and that's how he discovered the etchings. Markings. Dates. These stones were ancient! He felt a moment of awe as he looked up and saw the sun run a spike through the top of the broken tower. Shiny hadn't deigned to climb over the uneven slabs to the base of the ruin. Her high heels wouldn't allow that. Fatty had attached himself to the boy's father, sensing him to be his only ally in the group. His mother was inscrutable behind her cat-shades. *What a funny group we are.* Red-eye, who normally stepped out with them, had chosen to remain in the car. The boy didn't blame him. As they were leaving—unsure of what they had seen, but sensing it must have been worthwhile—three nuns appeared out of nowhere and crossed the road. The looming black tower and three nuns in spotless white with the sun on their shoulders—it looked spectacular. By the time the boy raised the camera to his eyes, the nuns had vanished. Only the sun glanced through the camera lens, bleaching out the road.

The next stop was the church with the dead man. Saint Francis Xavier. The boy had heard about people coming from all over during a festival when the dead man was brought out so that everyone could touch his feet. How morbid. The church was terribly old. The dark red stone was black at the edges as if a fire had burned it. Inside, it felt empty, even though there were all those benches and carvings everywhere. The boy was conscious that he felt nothing, no stirring of emotion. The ruined black tower had more style. He decided he wasn't into those statues in the niches. They were oppressive. The front part of the church, where everything was carved in gold, was roped off. Not very friendly, was it? Where was the dead man? And then he saw the body.

It was set high up (clever, so no one could check if it were real or a plastic dummy) in a box that looked like a miniature train compartment, or an intricately carved trunk with little glass windows. A light was on in one of the windows. The bulb shone yellow onto a beak-like nose. The boy stepped forward, eyes on the beaky nose and walked straight into Shiny's ample behind. Sorry. He sidestepped, not caring to check if she was furious. *I'm sure she thought I did it on purpose!* What a shrivelled face! Was it a face? He couldn't see anything except a nose and a bump of forehead. The skin was yellow (or was that the light?) and it seemed to stretch painfully. How many years had he been lying like that, mummified for believers to touch him? The boy felt sick. Why did they have to do that? Why couldn't he have been buried decently and remembered quietly, instead of being ogled at and pawed by devotees? Even now, high above in his box bed, with two chubby plaster angels holding a wreath with some Latin words for company, poor old Saint Xavier had inquisitive eyes boring into his skull like termites. The Egyptians did this to their kings but they had the good sense to hide them away in tombs.

The boy felt sick and dreadfully curious. (Was he sick because he was curious?) What would the embalmed saint look like up close? Did skin tear or just fall away? Did they stitch it back? What needles did they use? What potions, to make him stay un-decomposed for centuries? Did they wear gloves to handle him? Did they wipe him with soft wet cloth like they did for his grandfather when he was ill in bed, dying? Turning him from one side to another, his back a rash of bedsores, oozing, crusting. *Why hadn't we known of these potions, these miraculous needles, to keep my grandfather intact? A curio in the family showcase, displayed and dusted with due reverence?*

The boy couldn't tear his eyes away, as if peering long and hard enough would reveal more of the dead man to him. He wished he could float up and see what robes he was clothed in. (Did moths eat the robes? Eat the robes and spare the skin? Did the dead man's wardrobe have to be changed from time to time, like the living?) Perhaps, as he looked, the glass would shatter. *My gaze will make it shatter and a river of shards will fall at my feet carrying the dead man with it.* Would he be light or heavy? Would he be hollow inside? *I will poke him with my finger and he will fall apart like a brittle old sofa. No, I will be more respectful, I will bend down and pick him up, doll-like, and I will walk to the river and float him off to the sea. Free at last…*

'Time to go, beta,' his mother's voice edged in. 'What a dull place, this Goa!'

He couldn't tell what she was more irritated by, the dreary church or herself. The boy suddenly felt foolish. What made him get carried away by the dead body in the casket? His mother was right. No place was duller.

Outside, Fatty broke his reserve and asked the boy to take a picture of him and Shiny with the church in the background. He handed him his own camera, a dinky little automatic, not digital, and showed him what to press. *As if I wouldn't know. All automatics were the same!* Then he gathered Shiny to him and they posed with soppy smiles. The boy, not a hint on his serious face, framed them in such a way you saw the entire building and only the top of their heads. He hoped it would look like they were carrying the church on their heads. Or better still, like their heads were being crushed by the church. Fatty thanked the boy and Shiny smirked. The boy grunted (where were his manners?) and gave the dinky toy back to its podgy owner.

Back in the car, the boy was conscious of a violent cramp in his stomach. First one, then another, then one after the other with no interruptions.

'Stop if you see a loo,' the boy called out to Red-eye, trying to sound casual.

'Feeling bad, beta?'

His mother had caught the gripe in his voice. She turned around and peered at him.

'No just need a loo,' the boy said, angry at the presence of strangers.

'Shouldn't have eaten those baked beans at breakfast,' his mother said, oblivious of his discomfort. 'Too many baked beans.'

(How did she know he had eaten baked beans? The boy's amazement cut through the pain. He had eaten alone. How well she knew him!)

'And this heat! Oof! Where are the famous rains?'

The holiday was wearing her out. She wanted to be back home in Versova, taking it easy, planning her own meals. She had had enough of dead saints and stone towers. The boy's stomach convulsed painfully. The jerking of the Omni didn't help. Luckily Red-eye had caught the urgency that suddenly suffused the air. His father and Fatty had stopped weaving their diagonal web of small talk. Everything was on stand-by, until a loo was found for the crappy son. Red-eye stopped and pointed. A wood-and-metal shack with the word TOILET scrawled on it in red paint.

'There?' The boy's mother flinched.

The boy had no time for squeamishness. He hopped out and almost ran to the shack. The asbestos door wouldn't close. There was a cracked toilet, Indian-style. Without waiting to check for water, he squatted.

Weak and relieved, he walked slowly back to the car. There had been running water, a rusty mug and a blob of soap. He was cleansed.

'Loosies, beta?' his mother asked, as he climbed in.

He pretended he hadn't heard.

Back at the hotel, the boy wondered if his weakened state was inducing hallucinations. The lobby—his lobby—was quiet and cavernous. You could not only choose the cane chair you liked best, you could even shift from one to another, playing a version of musical chairs where you never ran out of chairs. His lobby's only inhabitants (that too semi-permanent) were Fish-man and Reed-man. And now—

The lobby was crawling with people. The boy couldn't see the black and white checks on the floor, there were so many stacks of bulging baggage littered everywhere.

What had happened? Morning quiet as a tomb and afternoon raving. He couldn't see a single woman. They were all men, all loud. Their shirts were open to their chests and their pants bulged. They spoke to each other in blustering voices and seemed inordinately pleased, as if some enormous load had just been taken off their backs or some grand task accomplished. Fish-man was sweating behind the counter, his plastered hair looking oilier than ever. The boy felt bad for him. Who'd want to exchange monsoon siesta for this eruption of people? Who were these men?

And then he saw Reed-man weaving his way through the crowd, in his hand a tray of refreshments. In the lobby! What about his preachy 'no food in the lobby, Sir?' All right, so it wasn't food he was carrying, merely tall glasses of juice, but since when did ice cream count as food? The boy felt mad at Reed-man, as if he had let him down in some essential way. As if he had forgotten they were chums, playing TT, winning and losing the way friends do. What a crummy hotel. For the first time the boy was glad they were leaving the next day.

As if to stake his prior claim, he decided to sit right there. Sit and watch them, balefully. His mother said, 'Beta, why don't you rest? Change your clothes at least.' (His mother's horror of untold germs caught in that filthy toilet!)

'Oh please,' the boy snapped. 'Give me a break.'

She stepped back, stung. Her son didn't usually say things like that. He was a nice boy, even if that meant being silent most of the time. Must be his stomach giving him a bad mood, she decided. He could tell by the way she left without a murmur. Fatty and Shiny had long vanished, back to their bed, he presumed. He watched Reed-man approach a knot of loudmouths near him and deciding to be nasty, he summoned him.

As Reed-man bent to hear what he might have to say, he lifted one of the glasses from the tray. 'Thanks,' he said. *Try and stop me. Just try and stop me.* Reed-man didn't. How could he? Just then one of the loudmouths barked 'Ay! You!' in his direction, and he scuttled away. Who were these men? Why were they here, off-season? Old boys' reunion? No. Whatever linked these men was much more recent, more superficial. That would explain the high pitch of all their dealings with each other. The backslaps, the guffaws. And then the boy had a revelation. He would ask Fish-man. He seemed a little less deluged now. Glass in hand, the boy strolled over to him, trying in every way—his manner, his gestures, his sophistication—to offset the racket of these uncouth men.

'New guests?' he asked sympathetically.

'Yes Sir, a big party.'

'Oh?' he said and waited.

'Company, you know,' Fish-man said, wiping his sweaty brow with his hand.

The boy didn't know, but he nodded.

'Which company?' he asked.

Fish-man named some unheard-of company with a fake-impressive '& Sons' in it.

'Oh, so it's a conference,' the boy said, liking the way he sounded.

'No Sir, incentive. Company incentive to best salesmen of the year from all regions. Every year they send, Sir, but never so many.'

The boy could tell they had destroyed Fish-man's peace of mind too. He ought to have been happy, the hotel filling up off-season, but he sounded harassed, uncomfortable. Poor guy, he thought, and walked away, leaving his empty glass at the desk.

Salesmen! That would explain the loudness. Muscling past doors that you opened only a crack. Bullying pale shopkeepers into keeping stocks that no one wanted. Riding in buses everywhere, singing loud songs while the other passengers tried to sleep. The boy had no reason to hate salesmen, but at that moment he discovered a boundless hatred for their kind. Already one of them had taken off his shirt and was standing in his sweaty banian, as if being in Goa allowed you to do anything. Soon they'd be walking around in their chaddis. He had had enough. He was going home.

And then he saw her.

The clumps of bulging bodies had thinned out. The salesmen had been allotted cottages and were heading towards them, belly-first. The waiters were doubling up as bellboys, scurrying to and fro with bags that seemed too big for a weekend. Maybe the salesmen never travelled without their wares. What were they selling? Vacuum cleaners? Car batteries? *Would they whip them out at dinner, and make us buy?* Suddenly in a gap between a scurrying bellboy and a bellowing salesman, he saw a girl.

She was terribly thin. Her shoulders shone, her collarbones showed sharp and clear through her transparent skin. She wore a strappy white top that clung to her. Her breasts were pointy through the white cloth. Indecent, his mother would say. The boy felt hot and dirty. He needed a bath. She was lost in a book. Her hair was tucked back behind her ears, where it curled. Short, silky hair. Her face was soft, not bony at all. She was the prettiest girl he had ever seen. The boy felt like touching her.

She looked up from her book, straight at him. As if he had been hit, he dropped his eyes and pushing past the last remaining stragglers he ran to the cottage, burning.

Four

The girl was not alone.

At dinner, when the boy emerged gingerly, his insides still raw from the afternoon, he dreaded what he might see. He dreaded what he might not see. She might eat in her room. She might have been on her way out, not in. She might have been a vision he had conjured up. She might have been Reed-man's girlfriend, a local, who went home after visiting her boyfriend, a bad day to visit really, with him running around, and all those salesmen everywhere. She—

She was there. Two tables had been pushed together to make room for them all. The boy, discovering in himself a seamless capacity for slyness, counted while pretending to admire the pool. There were ten of them, guys and girls, all mixed up. Anxiously, but with an outward nonchalance, he tried to see if they were paired. Was there a girl to each guy? No. There were six guys and four girls. They all seemed roughly the same age. They seemed young, but if you looked closer, they were probably around Fatty's age, only Fatty looked older with his wife and his overblown sense of importance. There he was, at the other table, shovelling food into his mouth with one hand, his other hand invisible under the table. Shiny looked apprehensive. The boy noticed her twitching her head in the direction of the newcomers' table. She was afraid Fatty would stray. Four pretty girls to distract Fatty from Shiny. And she was right to be afraid. They were all pretty. But not one was as pretty as *her*.

The boy stuck to the soup.

'Chicken clear soup, beta, good for you. And bread rolls. Don't eat anything else.'

I couldn't, even if I tried. Can't you see I'm devouring the people at the joined-together tables? No, of course you can't. You see me eating my soup, your good little boy looking weak and a little pulled down, poor thing.

The salesmen were thankfully not having dinner with them. The boy could see them standing or sitting around on the grassy square near the pool. In the games room, he saw heads bobbing up and down to the music of the ping-pong ball. A long table had been set up for their 'party', they were drinking and the sounds of their merriment came to him in sudden bursts.

'His' group—for already the boy felt proprietorial about the ten strangers of whom she was one—looked a bit cramped, their elbows and knees knocking. How comfortable and natural they were with their arms and legs so close together. No sleazy gropy stuff like the kind Fatty and Shiny indulged in. And yet there was so much more to touch, if you felt like. Bare arms and legs. The guys wore shorts. So did the girls, only theirs were skimpier. The boy watched, secretly, as they went up and down between the buffet and their table. Only one girl, the plumpest one, wore a long wrap-around skirt. It was bluey-green and patterned with starfish and shells. It was really pretty and when she walked, it heightened how graceful she was, as if her fat was there for the sole purpose of making her fluid, like a dancer. She didn't have the sweaty lumpy look most fat people had. Her bluey-green T-shirt was stretched tight over her full breasts. She looked so friendly and squeezy! Her long hair fell to her shoulders and swung when she walked. She wasn't a girl, she was a woman. A warm squeezy woman. When she sat down, the fold of her skirt fell open for an instant and the boy saw her smooth, beautiful legs.

He went to get his second bowl of chicken clear. The waiters were joshing him, 'Sir, aren't eating anything else, why Sir, the chicken jalfrezi is very good Sir, try Sir.'

He shook his head and smiled a strained smile. *She* was standing next to him, inspecting what lay hidden beneath each of the gleaming lids. She might have heard them coaxing him to eat, the boy thought with a flare of shame. She might discover what a big hog he was. She might despise him for being such a pig, when she, so thin and sensitive, barely touched a morsel. The boy slunk back to his table, neglecting to bring a bread roll.

She obviously touched more than a morsel. As he watched her walking back, in pale denim shorts that showed how long and thin her legs were, he saw she had piled her plate. Pulao, chicken, salad and a roasted papad balanced on top of the heap. Where did she put all that food away? The boy blushed again, just thinking of her body.

He didn't see the others too clearly after that. What he was acutely aware of was their sound, that group-sound he had envied all his life, but never in this way. He heard the lilt and swing of their voices, the sudden sharp laughs that everyone seemed to join in, the little lulls when they ate. The clatter of their forks and spoons was also a kind of conversation. They seemed like one soul with ten different bodies. He heard them eat, talk, laugh and fall silent together and he felt terribly alone.

'Finished, beta?'

His mother's voice.

'Better pack tonight itself. Leaving tomorrow morning, remember.'

What? Leaving tomorrow? The boy started. He couldn't. Not now. Not when…

'Dad, can I stay on till Monday?'

It blurted out of him before he could stop it. He had spoken unthinkingly. If he had thought, he might not have spoken.

'Stay on?' His father looked puzzled. 'What for?'

Before the boy could answer, his mother butted in.

'Let him, na! What'll he do at home on Saturday-Sunday anyway? Let him stay till Monday.'

'I don't know if it's possible,' his father said, pulling his little moustache. *He does that when he feels he's being disobeyed.* 'It was all paid in advance. Three days, four nights. That's how these things work. I don't know what the rates for extension will be, that too on the weekend. Might be full-rate. Might be…'

'Uff-o,' his mother said, looking put off. 'Ask them! What problem will they have extending? More money for them, na? So? We'll ask them right now after dinner. And if you won't, I'll pay!'

Good old mother. For some reason, she had decided it was important his wish be granted. Maybe the cramps and loosies that afternoon had worried her. Maybe she thought he needed to relax some more. All that exam strain and all.

'It's not a question of *who* pays,' his father said, tugging harder. 'It's the modalities. Of course I'll pay! If you had thought of this earlier, beta, I could have organized it from Bombay itself.'

As the boy's parents argued about how it made no difference whether you paid there or paid here, the boy snuck a look at his favourite table. Why was he staying? His father was right. What for? Them? They didn't know he existed. What did he hope to do, mooch about like a stray dog hoping to get adopted? They were way older than him. Unless some of them played TT, he had no chance of getting pally with them. But he couldn't go back. Not until…

'Come on then,' his father said and pushed back his chair with more than usual force.

The boy said, 'You go, I'm coming,' and indicated his half-full bowl.

'Don't take all night,' his father said, and walked towards reception. His mother, torn between watching her son eat and making sure her husband didn't pull a fast one about the payments, hesitated, then scampered after him. He was free to observe them in peace.

They were on the desserts. He watched the squeezy one get herself a huge wedge of caramel pudding on one plate and a slice of ice cream with four gulab jamuns on another. Her friends noticed too and said something that made them all laugh, including Squeezy. She was unabashed. She just wiggled her body at them sexily and sat down to eat. He liked her, the boy decided, she was easy to like in an uncomplicated way. Her face was lovely. Sharp straight nose, large eyes and a generous mouth that curved easily. She had a face that looked like it was born for laughter.

He saw his mother signalling. Dropping all pretence of

eating along with his spoon, he got up. The waiters barraged him as he left, 'What Sir, no dessert, Sir? Gulab jamuns? Ice cream?'

I'm besieged by my own past self, gluttonously gobbling up everything in sight. He fled, smiling crookedly, feeling guilty about letting them down.

It had all been arranged. He was to stay on until Monday afternoon, all expenses paid. If he wanted a meal or a drink here and there he had enough cash, and his mother would probably insist on giving him more. Oh the delights of being a rich kid. Over and over again the boy's heart pounded one word. *Freedom. Freedom. Freedom.*

He declined a joyride to the airport the next morning. It was his mother's idea. Since the coach was anyway coming back, why didn't he come along for a joyride? But no, that would mean precious time lost. In any case Fatty and Shiny were leaving too, so the coach wouldn't exactly be empty. It was the same coach that had picked them up, the same uniformed driver. The boy stood stiffly while his mother hugged him and cautioned him about too many baked beans and avoid the sun, beta. His father just gruffed, saying, 'Make sure you re-book your ticket right away or you'll have to shell out unnecessary amounts. The hotel will have the airline number or you can simply do it online. Don't forget.'

The boy nodded. Big deal. Who cared if he had to pay 'unnecessary amounts'? What was his seventeenth-birthday-gift credit card for? Or had father-dear forgotten that he'd given him one? Fatty seemed glad the son was being left behind, and did a great job of ignoring him. Shiny had a sun hat on over her round goggles. She looked like a cartoon.

He waved dutifully as the coach rumbled out through the gate. The ground in front of the hotel was cobbled, yes that was the word. When you were in a car, the tyres moved differently over the cobbles. He liked that sensation. When you walked, you felt wobbly, especially if your feet were bare inside bathroom slippers as his were.

He walked back, shuffling, feeling stranded, exposed and shy. Where would he hide? Everything led into everything else. Cobbled front leading into part-open-part-covered lobby leading into part-open-part-covered dining space leading into poolside leading into square grass patch if you turned right and winding path if you turned left leading into cottages leading into beach leading into sea. Everyone could watch everyone else, unless you locked yourself up in your room.

The boy realized from the growling hollow in his stomach that he was fully recovered from yesterday. He hadn't eaten breakfast yet, his parents would get theirs on the plane. The salesmen had left a trail of destruction across the now-vacant tables. He could see them jumping into the pool in stripy trunks, each one of them hairier than the next. The pool seethed with thrashing bodies. The waiters had started clearing up. Soon the buffet would be closed for the morning. He had to grab something quickly unless he wanted to starve. Only two meals were included in the package. You could choose which two. Naturally his father chose breakfast and dinner.

As the boy sat down and asked if he could get a dosa, no, two, he felt the previous night's rebuffed waiter cheering up. He was back in form! Too bad he had arrived at the fag end of the meal. But nevertheless, they would aim to please. He asked for a black coffee with the dosas. His mother never let him have black coffee, so now he would. After the dosas he would have four of those mini-uthappams please. And then a ham-and-cheese omelette with toast and butter. No fruit, thank you, my stomach's not up to it. The waiter was beaming.

Fortification. Food was fortification. *With my belly full, my nerves will be steady and I will be up to anything. Walk up and say hello. I'm... And you...? I'll be cool and charming, and they'll like me at once. They? She.*

As he was ploughing into his second mini-uthappam, he saw some of them appear. Squeezy (but of course, she loved eating!), another girl he hadn't looked at carefully last night, and two boys. So these were the couples! (It didn't trouble the boy to realize that he had inherited his mother's soap-operatic bent of mind.) Squeezy's guy was very tall. Six-foot-three at least. He walked with a little spring as if he were on Nike Air. He was thin but he looked tough. He wore glasses and he was yawning loudly as he walked. Squeezy was propelling him forward, laughing.

The other girl was tiny. (Maybe that's why he hadn't noticed her last night. Squeezy and *she* had filled his eyes.) Tiny and snowy white. And he meant white, not pale. She had a heart-shaped face and close-cropped curls that clung tightly to her head. She wore glasses but they suited her. They were rimless. Very chic. Everything was perfectly proportioned. Her tits, her ass (no one was going to stop him saying those words any more), her waist, her hips. Everything was tiny but within her frame that meant big enough. It all flowed and curved very nicely. She wore a little skirt that sat snugly on her. On her pink T-shirt was a single beige flower. It went with her beige skirt, which had pink flowers on it that matched exactly with her top. She looked like a delicate pastry.

Her guy didn't seem like the guy you'd imagine her with. He was young all right, but he was balding! The boy could see it from where he sat, the receding hairline that left his forehead broad and exposed. He had big hands, which he waved about constantly, and he talked the most, rapid-fire, as if he was running out of time.

The boy consoled his heart—*she* must still be sleeping.

Squeezy teased the waiters about running out of food.

'Didn't you know I was coming?' she said. 'Now what will I eat? How will I survive?'

'No ma'am, refills are coming,' the waiters said, blushing. 'Just a few minutes!'

And sure enough they did. Steaming sambar, fresh chutney. Bowlfuls of cut papaya. The boy wondered if they'd have done the same for him. It suited him, though. If they sat and ate, if they sat and ate slowly, he could hang on to the hope that she would come and join them eventually. (She might join the others, who were elsewhere, she might skip breakfast altogether.) Quelling all the other possibilities that made him feel like he might be sick again, the boy watched them, covertly.

Squeezy was the only one who really ate. Squeezy and Baldy, who ate almost as fast as he talked. Tiny had a glass of orange juice and a piece of toast. Squeezy's guy smoked one cigarette after another, until Squeezy mock-bashed him with a plate over his head. He stopped then, but the boy could see his fingers twitching, as if they missed the phantom cigarette. *If it weren't for the shouts of the loudmouths in the pool,* the boy thought angrily, *I could have heard every word they said.* As it was, the fragments that came his way made no sense to him. Close friends spoke in slang no one else understood. He would never understand.

'Anything else, Sir?'

It was Reed-man, who had suddenly appeared at his elbow.

'No thanks. Wait, maybe a plate of papaya. Please.'

'Right away, Sir,' Reed-man said.

Table service at a buffet. What luxury! The boy wished she'd been there to see him being waited on like royalty. He didn't want the papaya, he hated fruit, unless it was in a fruit salad with ice cream, but it would help postpone going away. And then the terrifying, silencing thought came to the boy. Where would he go? The pool was finished for him. The deckchairs overflowed with hairy bodies. The dining room would soon close. His room would be getting tidied. The games room had been colonized by those who were neither in the pool nor beside it. And Panjim was too far away.

The papaya came, cut into bite-sized chunks. He played with it, forking each chunk full of holes before popping it into his mouth. But even that couldn't last forever. They cleared his plate away and he felt naked, as if his excuse for sitting there had just been whisked away. He got up.

He was walking past their table when he heard someone say, 'Pappu!' It sounded like Baldy's voice. The boy kept walking.

'Hey! Pappu!'

It *was* him. The boy turned around. Baldy was looking straight at him.

'Your name Pappu?' he asked, looking serious.

'No.' The boy shook his head.

'Then why did you stop? Har har har!' And he went off into rapid-fire laughter.

The boy felt a complete fool. He turned around and started walking off.

'Hey, Pappu! Where are you going? Now that we've been introduced, don't run away!'

He could hear Squeezy telling Baldy to stop it. But Baldy wouldn't stop. He came running after the boy and grabbed his arm.

'Hey! Cool it, man. Chill.'

The boy stopped.

'There! That's better.'

Baldy looked at him.

'Lost your parents, little Pappu?'

He was about to wrench his arm away and storm off. And then he didn't. *So what if he calls me Pappu and teases me about my parents. It's done. Baldy has done it for me.*

'Smoke?' Squeezy's guy asked as the boy sat down awkwardly in the empty chair next to him.

'No thanks,' he said, his voice sounding unused.

'See! Learn, Ciggy, learn!' Squeezy exclaimed. 'From the mouths of babes! Even this infant has more sense than you!'

The boy felt more embarrassed at being made an example of than being called an infant. It wasn't like he hadn't tried smoking. He had. It was no big deal. He wondered why people did it. It looked cool, that's all. Many of the girls in school used to smoke, just to look cool. They would pose when they smoked, or while they waited for one of their boyfriends to light their cigarettes. They looked stupid. But when the guys smoked it did look cool. Like Ciggy—was that his name?—he looked like he'd been doing it all his life. The cigarette was an extension of his brown-stained fingers. He wasn't posing. He was real. For a second, the boy wished he'd said yes. But with no practice, he'd have choked and that would have given Baldy another excuse to poke fun at him. Pappu. What a ghastly name.

'So, Pappu, what's your story, morning glory?' Baldy said, leaning towards him.

'Stop calling him Pappu!' Squeezy said, laughing.

'Why, what's wrong with it?' Baldy said. 'Pappu, Poka, Lolly, Molly. He fits. Don't you want him to fit, my darling Poka?'

Why was he calling Squeezy *Poka*?

'Of course I do, my darling Cracker,' Squeezy replied, sounding like she was in a play, 'but why can't he have a more sensible name like Ciggy or Tiger or Dodo? Why a pee-word?'

'Why not?' said Baldy.

Pee-word? Dodo? Sensible names? What were these guys playing at? Were they talking about him?

'Pappu!' Baldy said, emphatically. 'You decide. To be or not to be a pee-word!'

The boy nodded, feeling distinctly unnerved.

'He agrees,' Baldy shouted. 'Pappu he shall be! Now, tell!'

'Tell wha-at,' the boy stuttered, hating himself for letting his nervousness show.

'Your story, of course. Why what where when how.'

Squeezy—was he meant to call her Poka? he couldn't!—said, 'Cracker, stop it at once! Give the poor child a break. Listen, don't pay any attention to him. He's lost it. Parents out?'

'No,' the boy said, feeling his courage flooding back now that Squeezy was looking at him so kindly, 'they've gone back. To Goa.'

Yelp of laughter from Baldy.

'I m-mean, Bombay. Left by the morning flight.'

'And you'll join them later,' she said.

'Yes,' the boy said.

'Girlfriend, huh, Pappu?' Baldy butted in. 'Meeting her here secretly with old mum and dad safely out of the way?'

'No.'

Tiny, who had been quiet all this time, said, 'Not everyone's a skirt-chaser like you.'

Ouch. The boy realized he was being held up as an example to these two guys by their respective girlfriends. Not a good idea. For a searing instant, he felt the need to be bad, debauched, exciting, anything other than the good boy he had always been.

'Don't tell me you're a, you know,' Baldy said, winking, 'a v-word. Are you?'

'Cracker! I order you to stop!' said Squeezy, still laughing but with a new firmness in her command. 'Up!'

And she got up, pushing the table away with her nice plump hands. As if that was the signal everyone had been waiting for, they all got up. The boy panicked. Would they abandon him now? He would tag along, unobtrusive. He was good at tagging along. *Baby duck, strolley.*

But unobtrusive was not what Baldy had in mind.

'Pappu-mian,' he said, grandly, flinging one arm around the boy's shoulders (he was slightly shorter than the boy which meant he stretched up and hung heavily against his shoulder), 'come with me and I shall show thee the secrets of Arabia!'

Tiny and Squeezy giggled.

'What a cartoon you are,' Tiny said. 'Don't you dare bully him any more. He may have things he wants to do.'

'Do you?' Baldy turned to the boy, looking up, his face inches away. The boy could see he had brown eyes, jolly brown eyes. They made you forget he was bald. Trapped in that happy brown compelling gaze, the boy shook his head.

'See! He's free as a flea in a bottle of pee!'

'Yuck!' Squeezy and Tiny groaned. 'Listen, just ignore him.'

How can I, when he's locked to my neck, pressed to my side, guiding me unswervingly towards some place I haven't agreed to go to?

And in any case, he wouldn't have ignored Baldy for the world. Baldy was about to lead him to *her*.

'So, Pappu, come and meet our gang. Satisfaction guaranteed! All the wankers and perverts you could want!'

The boy could hear Squeezy and Tiny muffling giggles behind them. He reddened, he could feel it in the way his skin suddenly felt hot, not sun-hot, or Baldy's-pressing-arm-hot, but shy-hot. Why was he calling his friends such ugly names?

'So which way do you swing? No, don't tell me, let me guess. Canines! That's right! Hey guys, listen up! Pappu here is into poodles! Beautiful!'

It looked like he would never stop talking. The boy wished he hadn't eaten so much. The button on his shorts bit into his tummy. Baldy's arm bit into his neck. He was wearing a kada. It hurt.

He was leading the boy to a part of the compound he hadn't bothered to explore. (Which part of the compound had he explored? He had stuck to beach-path-pool-buffet-bed.) It was nearer the beach than their cottage. Almost as if the later the guests arrived, the closer they got to the sea. What about Fish-man talking about weather warp? With the invasion of the loudmouths, the inner cottages must have filled up rapidly. Baldy's gang had one in the second-last row. From here, there was a clear view of the palms he had seen painted against the sky that afternoon at the beach. Were they the same palms or the ones that lined the path leading to the beach, the path with the broken lights? He couldn't tell. He felt disoriented. It was an identical cottage. Two rooms downstairs, two upstairs. Ten people, four rooms. How did it work? Maybe two of them lived in the adjacent cottage.

Baldy dragged the boy into the room to the right of the landing, and shouted, 'Wake up, losers, and see what I've got!'

Five

The room was cave-like in the curtained dark. The sun the boy still carried in his eyes gouged bright patches out of the darkness. For a few seconds the dark stirring shapes (curled, knotted, sprawled) floated into and against the bright spots. Amoeba-like under a microscope. The smear of cells on a glass slide. Seething invisibles.

And then he could see them.

There were five of them. One of the two guys on the bed looked very grumpy. Baldy had woken him up, and he wasn't happy. A girl sat curled up in the string chair and two other guys were sitting on the floor, their backs to the wall. For an instant, the boy felt an overpowering urge to run away and get on that plane to Bombay. But Baldy's arm was locked around his neck.

'Hey!' he shouted. 'Show some enthu! Where are your manners? Aren't you going to welcome Pappu here? Look, he's heartbroken.'

The girl on the string chair brightened.

'Pappu? That's original,' she said, in a voice of honey stirring thick with bees. 'Entirely your doing, I suppose?'

'Well, *he* doesn't mind. Do you, Paps?'

The boy shook his head. His neck felt sprained. He wished Baldy would let go. He felt shy about asking him to.

'Come on, open the curtains, let's see the specimen,' Honeyvoice said.

The boy could have kissed her. For Baldy flung off his arm (at last) and dragged back the curtains.

'Og'way,' snarled one of the two bodies on the bed. 'Trngtosleep.'

'Enough sleep!' said Poka (he had called her Poka!), striding to the bed and sitting down with a thump. 'Geddup geddup geddup.' She bobbed up and down as she spoke and the soft mattress wobbled like a waterbed.

'Fuck,' said the snarly voice and got up, rubbing his eyes. The other body didn't stir.

'Kick Baby,' suggested one of the guys on the floor. 'Make Lolly bite him.'

Baby? Where was the baby? The boy felt deranged. And who was Lolly? Was it a dog? Were pets allowed?

Snarly was a shorty. On the bed he didn't look it, but as he rolled off the edge of the bed and came towards him, the boy registered with something like shock how short he was. Barely taller than Tiny. The hair matted thickly on his bare chest. His breath smelt of sleep.

'So. Cracker's new recruit. Welcome.'

And giving the boy a curious stare he went off towards the loo.

'That was very tame,' said Honeyvoice from her chair. 'Tiger's lost his roar. Hey, you.'

The boy turned towards her. He felt clumsy, as if he might fall over any minute. First, he seemed to have lost the use of his feet, and now, his hands. He sensed them clasped behind him, tight, as if he was in junior school, about to be punished (he had never been punished). Handcuffed in a roomful of strangers.

'What's the E in E equals em-cee square?'

What was this, an exam? How dare they!

'Energy,' he snapped, suddenly feeling as if the handcuffs had been sprung. 'And em is mass and cee square the speed of light squared.'

He felt defiant and vaguely insulted. Did they think he was a fool? Any moron knew this! A microscopic moment of silence followed. Then Baldy burst out laughing. Poka joined him. And before he knew it everyone was laughing, including, for he hadn't stopped looking at her, Honeyvoice in the string chair.

'You pass,' Baldy said, wiping away mock tears. 'Angie, queen of intimidation, is pleased!'

So Honeyvoice was Angie.

'Sit,' said Poka, patting the bed beside her. He sat. The inert body was snoring, the boy could hear it now, little rumbles that vibrated across the sheets. 'Cracker, introduce us.'

Baldy rubbed his hands in glee. Ciggy had draped himself against the frame of the open door. Tiny leaned against the wall, her arms folded across her perfect chest. Poka sat beside him, large and reassuring.

'The log on the bed, dear Paps, is Baby. A spoilt child if ever there was. Nothing—neither an earthquake in Estonia nor an epidemic of elephants—can disturb his beauty sleep. The woman to your right, whom you have already had the good fortune of meeting over breakfast, is Poka. What can I say about her? Woman with the big heart? Largesse Margesse? Indian squaw, everybody's Maw? She is everywoman, Pappu-mian, and everywoman is her!'

The boy was wondering how long Baldy would have carried on like this, hand ridiculously over his heart, if Poka hadn't thrown a pillow at him, which he caught, grinning like Garfield. The boy felt like grinning himself. But he liked Poka too much to spoil it by grinning.

'The tall gent by the door, also familiar over forkfuls of fruit, is Ciggy. Man of few words. Brooding bundle of bad ideas made good. Once an engineer, but now, alas, no more than the humble architect of his own apocalypse.'

Baldy was priceless. Someone should have recorded him.

'The tiny lady there, perfect as a miniature painting, so exquisite on that wall, doubtless marked in your book as enchanting, and indeed truly enchanting, is burdened with a not-so-enchanting name. Lolly, her loving parents called her, and Lolly she remained. In her childhood she was a lover of big juicy lollies, ice lollies, choco-lollies, you name it. Her tiny arms outstretched, she would ask for lollies from all and sundry. Today, in her youth, all and sundry ask *her*, but she, cruel heart, denies them.'

The boy saw Tiny smile in his direction, but he sensed her annoyance, as if Baldy had pushed it too far. She was his girlfriend after all. All this talk of big juicy lollies was in bad taste. It sounded obscene and Baldy knew it. Poor Tiny. Her parents should have known better.

Baldy went on, noticing nothing.

'The queen bee on the string chair is, as you have just found out, none other than Angie!'

Angie gave the boy a languorous smile. The boy, who had been experiencing more new sensations in the last ten minutes than he had in the last ten years, almost fainted. No one, no girl, no woman, had ever smiled at him that way.

She had a smile to die for. He could never have guessed from her proud voice, so spiky with scary-sweetness and hum. It was a smile full of teeth, but what stunning teeth! They were white against her chocolate skin and they filled her face with light. Her smile was better than Julia Roberts's, he thought triumphantly—Julia Roberts was his father's favourite—Julia Roberts was a tube light compared to her. Angie was an incandescent 500-watt phenomenon. Her shoulders were bare, she wore a top that was tied around her neck with two strings. He knew—and the knowledge didn't make him uneasy, because he was no longer sitting next to his mother, he was in a roomful of mature people, all by himself—he knew her back would be gloriously bare. She was grand and queenly. She was—

But Baldy was saying something.

'...Slob one on the floor is Dodo. Slob two is Molly. Now you might very well ask, how do you tell them apart? Listen well, Pappu my man, you cannot. In a fit of inexplicable brotherhood, the two of them swore to be clones of each other. Look closely and you will see. Pants, cargoes. Shirts, tees. Arms, muscled. Amulets, none. Tattoos, unmentionable. Shoes, Caterpillars. Minds, blank.'

The boy could see Baldy waiting for at least one of the guys on the floor to react, but they didn't. They just turned lazily towards him and smiled. Baldy was right. They looked like brothers. Same light-grey cotton tees, same beige cargoes, and brown Cats with the trademark yellow stitching. (Why were they fully dressed so early in the morning?) And yet if you looked again, their faces were completely different. One (which one?) had a long rectangular face, with a sunken chin that seemed like someone had hit him there when he was still soft. The other was the only one in the group with a moustache. It made him look startling, as if he were in disguise.

'And I, moi, myself, am the langotia-yaar, bum-chum, jigri-dost of this here bunch—Cracker the cacophonous crank, presenting Pappu, the papaya-devouring, parent-deceiving boy wonder!'

He was unbelievable. He could have done this for a living. As the general laughter subsided, the boy heard the flush in the loo. That was enough for Baldy. Gesturing theatrically at the closed loo door he said, 'And that, dear Pappu, is the king on his throne—Tiger.' (As if on cue, Tiger came out.) 'Born to lead! Head honcho, kingpinnochio, main man of this here bunch of losers!'

Tiger raised his hairy arms in acknowledgement the way politicians and god-men did on TV. Then, as abruptly as he had raised them, he dropped the act and said, in a flat, cool voice, 'Let's get the hell out of here.'

As the room around him rearranged itself—Molly and Dodo getting up from the floor, Poka sitting on Baby to make him wake up, Tiger throwing on a shirt, Tiny moving to talk to Angie, Ciggy motionless, Baldy blabbing on—the boy felt a terrible pang. *She* was not here. All this time, the tension of knowing any minute she might walk in had kept him on edge, alert. When Baldy dragged him into the room he had half-hoped she might be there. He had dreaded the possibility that she might be one of the two bodies on the bed. He had been overwhelmed with relief when he saw she wasn't. And then overcome by disappointment when he saw she was not only not on the bed, she wasn't there at all. He had held his breath, curbed his annoyance, blurted out his defiance, all for her. And she was nowhere to be seen.

'Where'll we go?' Baldy was saying. The boy's heart was not in it any more. Where a suspenseful bubbling hopeful dread had been, there now was a rectangular hollow inside him, cut out with a blunt knife. He wanted to go back to his quiet room and forget everything. But would Baldy let him? Of course not.

'Pappu, you tell us. Where should we go?'

'Er,' the boy said. He couldn't think of a single place worth going to. 'Out?'

Baldy screamed with laughter.

'Stroke of genius! Out, the boy wonder says. Such simplicity! Out it shall be. Angie, woman of the magnificent shoulders, the boy will take us—out! Ready, all?'

'Er,' he said. But before he could blunder on, Baldy shrieked again and clapped his hand on his mouth.

'Major transgression. Also known as boo-boo. We have left dear Momo lying undisturbed. At once, the wrongdoing must be repaired!'

And he dashed out of the room and up the stairs.

Momo! That was her! Whatever numbness had crept over him a few seconds ago was now transformed into a wild anxiety. What if she hated him? He would, if he were a girl and he met a guy called Pappu. Why couldn't Baldy have chosen a better name? It was better than Cracker. But that didn't console him. Would the name matter? Logic said no. Her friends had the stupidest names on earth. The name would not make the slightest difference. It would be his feet. His feet had always been too big. They stuck out of size 12 gliders, his long twisty toes. The rest of him was fine. But his feet stank. And today he was in rubber chups, of all things, not even his fancy gliders. Everything about his feet in Bata rubber chups was disgusting.

'I'll just,' he said to no one in particular, now that his main audience, Baldy, was gone, 'I'll just (*rush to my room and wear my sneakers*)...'

He was slowly sidling out of the room, when Baldy walked in, saying, 'Not in her room. I tell you that girl needs a leash. Vanishing at crucial moments!'

The boy felt like one of those machines in hospital movies that show the heartbeat going up and then drastically down. He wouldn't have to change his slippers. She wouldn't find his feet disgusting. She wasn't even there.

'Out out, you dirty lout,' sang Baldy as he tugged Baby through the door. Looking at Baby, who would have said he had been snoring so deeply just minutes ago. Wakefulness seemed to him as absolute as sleep. His cheeks were smooth and pink, as if a razor had never touched them. He looked bright and bathed (though the boy knew he wasn't), he had put on a lemon-yellow shirt that made him radiate joy and cleanliness, and he had no trouble at all adjusting to the fact that a newcomer had just joined their group.

Baby. Molly. Dodo. Tiger. Angie. Ciggy. Lolly. Cracker. Poka. Pappu.

And her.

Six

What shocked the boy even more than it pleased him was the fact that they took him seriously. Feeling like he was part of one of those silly dances where boy-girl-boy-girl held each other by the waist and sway-kicked around the room in drunken chains—something he had observed at a party once, sitting on the side and wondering why not a single hand reached out to pull him into the chain—he left the hotel premises with them. All nine of them, a number which made the boy ache, because it should've been ten.

'Which way, boy-won?' shouted Baldy, and the shout was like a charm, a splash of waking cool water. *Must shake off the gloom of not seeing her and rise to the demands of my new group*. Group! The boy—who only yesterday had been solitarily stringing along behind two protective parents and two revolting strangers—was now part of a *group*. The corner of his heart that was still snagged to a rusty nail lifted and came free.

'That way?' he said, and at once Baldy shouted, like someone entrusted with the job of relaying commands to a battalion, 'Thataway, losers!' and they turned left from the hotel gate and then immediately right, down a narrow lane the boy had noticed when Red-eye drove them to the city.

Why were these people going where he led them? Why were they not planning tours like his father did, efficiently seeing the sights? Or hiring bikes like the foreigners did? He would have done that if his mother had let him.

'No beta,' she said. 'Remember what happened to Asha's son? No bike rides for my son after *that*.'

The boy had watched the foreigners enviously on each of Red-eye's excursions, whizzing like metal cicadas in and out of the traffic, going off the road, through the trees, taking lanes that were invisible from the main road. The only thing that softened the blow of not being allowed that freedom, that manliness, was the speed Red-eye drove at. Even the bikers couldn't keep up! But these guys had no parents to stop them from doing anything they wanted. So why?

They clumped along, the flip-flop of their slippers seeming loud in the quiet post-eleven-o'clock air.

'What is this, a ghost town?' the boy heard Baldy say.

He was right. It felt that way. The main road—where the cars stood in a line waiting to be hired—had a sense of urgency. Nothing might happen for hours, but then again anything might, any minute. Things felt on hold, expectant. A pickup truck might go by, music blaring from the radio, the back piled high with plastic chairs for some party that evening. A group of manic bikers might whiz past, scorching the air. A bunch of loudmouths might arrive in a posse of buses, shouting for the hotel gates to be opened.

In the narrow lane off the road, even breathing seemed excessive. It seemed like no one had ever walked down that lane until they arrived. Greenery leaned in, pungent, absorbing all light and sound. On either side were restaurants. All closed. Mama's Kitchen. Pepé's. A little house with a shuttered garage. A woman shaking out her laundry. She looked at them, curious but not friendly. Off-season, the good humour pickling for later. Beach Bums. Goa Karnivale. This one was a funky place with a low green gate, behind which there stood bare blue tables with green plastic chairs upturned on them. The sign was gay, yellows and reds and greens slightly giddy on the board. The restaurant mascot, a larger-than-life plastic man with a mandolin and a painted face, looked more Mexican in his hat than Goan. A kiddy merry-go-round, midget horses with multicoloured coats. The upside-down green chairs had collected water from last night's rain. Why did they leave everything lying outside like this? Why not pack everything away until next season? Any moment the boy expected the signboard to light up and the merry-go-round to start and the plastic man to bob his mechanical head in time to stereophonic tunes.

'Creepy,' Poka shuddered, next to him.

'Why don't we take over?' shouted Baldy, gaily. 'Corporate coup! Bunch of young entrepreneurs takes over Goa Karnivale and turns it into the rage of the West Coast! Or forget such grand plans. Let's just do lunch on those tables. All set and waiting!'

No one responded and Baldy shut up. The quiet was unnerving him, the boy could tell. Even with ample ambient sound, Baldy needed to keep up a constant patter to make himself feel real, and here! He probably thought he would disappear if he stayed in this hush for too long.

'Must rock during season,' Tiger said, suddenly.

The boy jumped a little. Tiger was right behind him. He was so short it was hard to remember he was there. He had a deep voice, the kind that starts in the stomach and gains rumble as it travels up.

'Ya,' the boy said, uncertainly. Was he talking to him or someone else?

'Can't say I'd like it much, during season,' Tiger continued. He had a snappy way of talking, as if he were rushed or angry or in charge. 'Crowds get on my bloody nerves.'

'Mine too,' the boy said, and immediately regretted it. He sounded like a chamcha. It was true, crowds weren't his thing, but it was an irrelevant truth and didn't need to be aired. But Tiger was no longer with him. He was staring at the upturned chairs as if they were cobra's heads. The boy was alone again. Suddenly, he missed Baldy. It was Baldy who had forcefully dragged him in, and without his persistent tug he felt floaty, like a boat that hasn't been tied to shore.

Lesson number one, a small voice said inside him—it is possible to be alone in a group.

'Look! It's incredible!'

Poka's voice came to them from around the bend ahead and broke the spell Goa Karnivale had cast over them. They turned as one and followed Poka's voice. She was right. It *was* incredible.

Right ahead of them, framed between two palms, was a river. It broke through the heavy green lull of the lane with a rush and filled the boy with exultation, the water flowing so freely, the suddenness of open water and sky where so far there had only been trees, closing in. There was a coolness on his cheeks. He could see Poka throwing back her head to let the breeze run through her beautiful long hair. Angie had joined her. They looked like river goddesses, one long-haired and warm, the other bare-backed and grand. A boat bumped against the pole where it was tied. There was a murky patch near the walls on either side and then the clear clean flow of the river.

It was only later that the boy noticed the houses. Modern houses, freshly painted, incongruous in that out-of-time moment. The breach between the row of houses was what let the river into their field of vision, like a window flung open. The house nearest them had a gleaming black Scorpio parked in the front. (Back really, because the front faced the river. Fishing off the lawn, diving off the terrace.)

'Inhabited!' Baldy hissed in a stagey whisper. 'Shall we knock and ask for tea?'

'Don't do any such thing please,' Tiny hissed back.

The boy was surprised by the vehemence in her voice. Why was she angry? Baldy was only kidding around.

'Man! How I'd like to get my hands on her!' said Baby. He was staring longingly at the Scorpio. It sounded odd, coming from him. He didn't look like the kind who was into big cars and mean machines. He looked, the boy thought, like *baby can I hold you tonight*. Then suddenly, Baby wasn't looking at the Scorpio any more. He was looking at the boy.

'What?'

'Nothing,' the boy said. 'It's cool.'

'What's cool?'

From Baby's light but loaded tone, the boy sensed that old familiar situation. He was being ragged.

'The car.'

'What car?'

'The Scorpio.'

'What's so cool about it?'

'Everything.'

'What's everything?'

'F-features, mileage, er…' He was getting flustered.

'Listen, whatsit. Cool is NOT the word I'd use for a Scorpio. Cool is just what someone from your dimwit generation would say. Cool is out. This is post-cool. This just IS. Geddit?'

Why was he being so aggressive? It was like having sand thrown into your eyes, sand mixed with glass. The boy felt himself shrinking. What had he done? He said nothing. He wished Baldy were near him to make a joke about it. But Baldy had gone off to stand next to Poka and Angie, leaving Tiny with nothing but air to hiss at. He knew he had to stop depending on Baldy every few seconds. He had to figure out what each one's trip was, and deal with it. It wasn't *them* he was interested in anyway. It was her. All this was just crap. He was only putting up with it for her. Why was he so scared? He could feel his mind prodding him in small bursts of anger to answer this baby-faced bully. He couldn't. The silence grew longer, and the longer the silence grew the weaker and more ashamed the boy became. He had let Baby rag him successfully.

What was it about these people that made him feel so crushed and worthless? Without meaning to, the boy caught Tiny's eye. With a jolt he saw she felt the same way. But she was Baldy's girlfriend!

Lesson number two, said the small voice inside him—there are rifts in every group, fault lines, even in this one you envied and thought seamless from afar.

'Think someone could get us out on that?'

Ciggy, Molly (with the moustache) and Tiger were eyeing the boat. The boy decided to leave Baby's malignant presence and join them. Dodo, he noticed, wasn't into any of this. He sat on the ground near where Molly stood and stared moodily at the road they had just come down. There was nothing to see but he sat and stared regardless. The boat was covered with a blue tarpaulin.

'Someone's taking better care of that than the restaurant,' the boy said.

'You bet,' Molly said, agreeably. The boy warmed to him instantly. Ciggy he already liked, with his nicotine hands and his un-hassled quiet. Tiger was cool. (NOT cool, he heard Baby say, softly, nastily.) 'Do you row?'

The boy shook his head.

'Me neither. But can't be tough.'

'You'd be surprised,' Tiger said. 'Currents could get you.'

Ciggy nodded.

The boy felt seasoned, mature, standing there with the men, considering currents and boats.

'The owner's bound to be somewhere,' he said. 'Maybe we could ask.'

'Who, the laundry lady down the road?' Molly said, chuckling. So he'd noticed her too! The boy giggled.

'No, she wouldn't help!'

'Ah well, maybe later,' Tiger exhaled, suddenly weary. 'Come on ladies, quit ogling the river, you're making us jealous.'

Baldy, Poka and Angie came towards them.

'What, calling me a lady?' Baldy simpered. 'Gentlemen, you make me blush!'

He was himself again. Poka and Angie rolled their eyes. Tiny pretended not to hear.

'Come on, shall we,' Tiger called to Baby and Dodo. Tiny was a creature hanging in the middle of nowhere. No one spoke directly to her. She was included in the drift of all their conversations, whichever way the wind blew, she was ruffled by it. The boy felt sorry for her. First, a name like Lolly. Then, these weird vibes from her best friends. He decided he wouldn't call her Lolly, not even in his head.

They left the river behind. The lane closed in on them immediately. As they followed it back the way they had come, it seemed as if the river had never been there.

The boy walked with Tiger, Ciggy and Molly. Baldy hovered between their group and Angie-Poka. Tiny hovered between the girls, Baby and Dodo. The boy felt surer now of his place among them. Still shy, but surer. To their left was a low brick wall. It curved away from the lane. They walked along it. Behind the wall was a massive compound and right at the back of the compound was a house. It looked enormous after the little restaurants. Enormous and ancient as if it were part of the land, a rock formation, a giant mushroom. The boy remembered the hint of houses glimpsed in their flash-past through the fields. So this is what they looked like behind all those trees! Perhaps not so large. The once-red tiles on the roof were green with moss. A vast veranda. Rooms which the gloom seemed to swim into. Nothing stirred. Banana trees stood near the wall. No one could be seen anywhere. Could they walk in and look around? Just then the boy saw someone move. Had they been spotted?

'Signs of life on planet G,' hissed Baldy. 'Terrestrial creature, suspicious of intruders, eyes us from afar through a strange eyepiece that flashes from time to time.'

Baldy was observant. All they could see of the person who had moved on the veranda were his or her glasses. Some stray light had fallen on the glasses and exposed the wearer. The boy looked carefully. In the semi-dark of the veranda sat an old man in a rocking chair. He was bare-chested and wore a lungi. It was impossible to tell if he was looking at them or dozing. Baldy wondered if they should check by showing him the finger. Angie suggested they wave instead, might be a bit friendlier. Tiger said, 'Let's move on, shall we.'

The boy would have liked to have lingered. Who lived with the bespectacled old man in that rambling ancestral home? Where were the young people? Did he own Goa Karnivale which is why he kept it unlocked, it was so near? How old was he? Would he be glad of their company, and happy to tell them stories, in Portuguese, which none of them would understand?

The wall that enclosed the old man's house stopped at a dead end. Sighing, as if disappointed, Tiger turned them around and back they went, past the house, past the bend that hid the river, past the Beach Bums, past the shuttered garage on to the main road. Tiger looked at his watch. It was only twelve. It seemed like an awful lot of time had passed.

'Ravenous, aren't we,' said Tiger, as they stood there undecided.

'Not me,' said Ciggy. 'I ate brekker, remember.'

'But I am,' announced Poka, who had been very quiet on the walk, 'and I ate brekker too!'

'Now why am I not surprised,' Baldy said, fondly. 'Look, why don't we forage for food there?'

Almost exactly opposite the impressive iron gates of the hotel stood a wayside eatery. Not a house turned eatery, a real shack. The boy recognized it as the establishment he had eyed longingly over the last three days, knowing full well that with mother hen around to guard his tender insides, he would never put a foot inside such dark unsavoury premises. Although he had eaten a mammoth breakfast only a little over an hour ago, the boy felt a greedy compulsion to eat again. With them.

'Is it even open?' Angie asked, sardonic.

It was all open. A thatched roof created an unbelievably dense patch of darkness in the glare of the midday sun. Everything under the thatch was impenetrable. The tables were stained a deep indescribable colour. The benches seemed to rise directly out of the earth. There was no pretence of a floor, no straw mats, nothing. The shack just *was*, as Baby might have put it. Love it or leave it. They decided to love it.

'Garçon!' Baldy shouted as they shuffled in (Ciggy having to bend from his Himalayan height). 'Guests!'

No one answered.

'Try *munna*,' Angie said, 'it might ring a bell.'

Angie, the boy noticed, had a wonderfully maddening way of suppressing that 500-watt smile of hers. She said these little throwaway things that brought the barest hint of a smile to her lips, where it teasingly hovered, leading you to expect more, and then just as teasingly died.

'Munna!' Baldy obediently shouted. 'Raju!'

A boy popped out of the subterranean hole that presumably led to the kitchen (*oh what would mother say!*) and wiping his hands on his tattered singlet, stood expectantly before them.

'At last! The genie!' Baldy declared. 'Tell me, genie, what can you do for us?'

The boy stood, silent.

'What's for lunch?' Tiger asked.

At the word *lunch* the boy beamed and said, 'Fishcurryrice.'

'Which fish,' Tiger asked.

'Bangdapomfret,' the boy said.

'Ah, a hybrid, how interesting,' said Angie to no one in particular. 'Irresistible.'

While the little waiter digested the mammoth order of five plates of each fish and lots of rice and five beers to start with, Baby took out a book from the pocket of his lemon-yellow shirt and began reading. It was a little notebook. Molly sat next to him, with Dodo by his side, peering gloomily at the table. From this angle, Dodo's sunken chin disappeared totally so it looked like he had no chin at all.

Munna or Raju despatched to the hole with their food orders, they sat back, clutching their streaming cold glasses of beer. Cheaper than Bombay and way, way cheaper than what the boy's father had shelled out at the hotel bar. The boy clung to his glass nervously. He didn't like the taste of beer but here it was important that he should. They all seemed to love beer, this group. Even Tiny, who slugged hers with a robustness he found surprising, and oddly touching. He thought that she, at least, would have preferred shandy, like his mother. A collective aaah followed the first cold frothy sip. Angie had thrown off her sandals and drawn her legs up on to the bench. Some bowls of peanuts had appeared along with the beer. The boy picked a handful. They were soft. He saw Poka bum a drag from Ciggy's cigarette.

'Is that where the name came from?' the boy heard himself saying. 'Coz you smoke so much?'

'No, coz he's a saint,' said Angie, drawling. 'What d'you think? He was born with a puffer in his mouth.'

They sniggered. (Lesson number three—personal questions were not welcome. Yet.) But Baldy brightened.

'You tell us,' he announced, thumping the table with his hand. 'You tell us, Pappu, how you think we got our names. That should pass the time agreeably, until lunch!'

Why did they always have to turn everything into a game?

'Okay,' the boy said breezily, emboldened by the beer. 'I'll start with you! That's an easy one, coz your hair isn't exactly, er, luxuriant. Balding, so Baldy!'

As he said the word out loud, the boy realized his grave and irreparable error. *Baldy is my name for him.* Everyone else called him Cracker. He had blown it. They stared at him, beer glasses forgotten, dripping onto the table. He prayed for Baldy to laugh, to turn it into a joke like he always did. But he didn't. He stared. Those jolly brown eyes that the boy had found so gentle and endearing were dead still.

'Wrong,' he said, coldly. 'Proceed.'

The boy's throat felt like he had swallowed the beer bottle cap instead of its contents. He gulped and turned his gaze to the one sitting next to Baldy. It was Tiny, but he knew better now.

'Lolly,' he said, 'I already know that one. I was, er, told. As a kid...'

Tiny nodded quickly as if to let him off the hook. Move on, get it over with. He felt a rush of gratitude towards her. Poka was next, large, not unfriendly, but neutral.

'Poka,' he thought aloud, blushing to remember what he had called her. (Her squeezy breasts rested against the table.) 'Poka, because you're a Bong and you loved books ever since you were a child, so your Bong friends called you a bookworm, or Boi-Poka, but then that became shortened to Poka and soon your whole family was calling you Poka too...'

Poka puckered her generous mouth as if to acknowledge the laudability of his effort.

'Not bad,' she said, and clapped her cigarette-holding hand against the other.

The boy felt the air unknot. Poka had approved. He

may have been wrong but he had tried. He turned towards Ciggy.

'Ciggy because of all the ciggies he smokes,' he said, in a rush.

Ciggy took his cigarette back from Poka, stuck it on his lower lip and said, 'Bingo.'

They were trying to make up for Baldy's coldness.

'Baby coz he's baby-faced and always will be, and Dodo coz he always wanted two of everything!'

Laughter. The boy quickened.

'Tiger, Tiger coz he burned bright in the forest of the night and Molly, Molly coz he's mollycoddled and Angie, Angie coz she's angelic.'

He stopped and glugged some beer. There! He'd done it.

'Not bad at all,' Tiger said. 'For a greenhorn. Cheers!'

He lifted his glass to the boy and the others did too and they all said cheers, the boy adding his voice to theirs. He was afraid to meet Baldy's eyes. He could tell he was assessing him. What other names did he have for the rest of them, he could imagine Baldy thinking. Takloo motoo lamboo chhotu. Enough freaks in this barrel. Let him. The boy swigged some more beer and chomped a handful of soggy peanut, defiant.

Lunch arrived. With whoops of delight Baldy descended on the plates of fish and rice as if he had not seen food for a century. The boy felt relieved. It meant he was out of the range of Baldy's shotgun eyes for some time. He had asked for bangda. Enormous, it floated in the orange curry. The beer had filled his stomach. He felt queasy. Beer and soggy peanut. He ate a spoonful of steaming white rice and felt better.

'You can share my fish,' he said shyly to Angie.

'The way you say it, honey, how can I resist,' she said, that smile hovering on her lips as she drew the curry bowl towards her. He blushed. She was nicer than he imagined any goddess could ever be.

The silence of hearty eating filled the dark hut. From here the road looked like another planet. The light was shrill. It hurt his eyes. Molly and Dodo shared their fish. Half a pomfret, half a bangda. They looked like a married couple. Ciggy hardly ate, pulling jerkily at the cigarette that never seemed to go out. The boy played with his rice the way he used to when he was little and didn't want to eat lunch because he had eaten ragda on the way home from school. How strange the morning had been. How intense, and prolonged. The last three days were a blur. Today, every second was as sharp as a fishbone, picked clean, marking some mysterious course.

He got to the bill first. Stretching across the table he grabbed the little scrap of paper before Munna or Raju could deposit it next to the saunf bowl. There was a chorus of protest that sounded more like a groan.

'Please,' he said. 'I want to.'

They gave in. Baldy, he noticed, hadn't bothered protesting. He probably thought he owed it to them. Did this mean he would no longer fling his arm around his neck and drag him around like a buddy? How long would he take to recover from being called Baldy by the kid he had christened Pappu, like some benign balding father in a robe? The boy missed him sorely, more than back there in the stifling lane. He wanted him to be like before. The others were still strangers, opaque, he saw glimmers and he was intrigued, but he wasn't sucked in the way he had been by Baldy's brown eyes, by his banter and incessant fooling around. Somehow, he had to make up for what seemed to have hurt him in a way that was almost girlish. Girls minded these things. Silly things they harboured in their minds and nursed and sulked over. He had to apologize. His gesture of paying had really been aimed at Baldy to say, Look, I'm sorry. But Baldy stayed cold, unmoved.

They left the shack. The tar raised an invisible yet solid barrier of heat. They walked slam into it. The boy noticed not one of them wore shades. He had his Oakleys in his shirt pocket but he left them there. His bare toes felt singed as they hurried across. The metal gate stung his fingers as he opened it. Across the cobbles. The moment of dissolution was approaching. Each into their separate rooms, perhaps never to meet again. He searched frantically for something to say that would seal the evening, fold it around them, all in the same place, doing the same thing.

'We could go to Baga in the evening,' he said. 'I know a good driver, he can take us.'

Baldy stopped.

'Us?' he said, cuttingly. 'And what makes you think you're one of us?'

He walked away. The boy stared after him, black spots dancing before his eyes.

Lonely

When does that word become a boil on your chin that everyone can see? When does it get so bad, people can smell it as you approach, alone and obvious? I carried it in my genes, the lonely chromosome. I inherited it with my only-child status, my mother's-ladla-beta status, my reading-pulp-novels-from-the-neighbourhood-library status. If only it had been boy-genius-lonely. Expert-hacker-lonely. Number-nerd-lonely. I was just plain-vanilla-lonely. Skulking at the fringes of playgrounds. What sort of boy are you?

Lonely.

Secretly I dreamt of adulation. Mass adulation. People kissing my feet. Fighting for a glimpse. A rock star of loneliness. A something-sage. A guru of secret sorrows. I had read everything I could find but what I found was not good enough. I had found blood and sex, murder and mortuaries, spy games and sci-fi. I gulped it all down, insatiable. And the greedier I got for the steamy seamy stories, the lonelier

I got. The more pulp I crammed into my brain, disguised from prying parental eyes, the less I cared for the world. I slid between the covers, a compulsive runaway. It made me what I am.

Lonely.

It's not as if I hated it. I loved-hated it. I fed it like a dog snapping at my fingers, whining for scraps. I whipped it into a frenzy of loathing. People! I despised them. The silent loathing I filled myself with to defend myself must have seeped out of my pores and filled the air around me. People despised me. Worse, they ignored me. I was invisible, with my precious unnecessary hurt. No one had done me harm. Everyone had. I longed for someone to dig at the scab and scar me. Peel it away, let the ooze trickle out, fresh again. Heal me. Nobody had wanted to. And so I drifted on.

Lonely.

Seven

Tiger lay sprawled on the bed. He looked feral, his furry chest and arms rude in that pretty-pink room. He gave off a smell of danger. The boy preferred him standing up, fully clothed. Tiger was alone. Next to him lay the note, crumpled.

The boy had returned to his room, head muggy with sun and beer and failure. Sleep, he thought. Sleep it off, and tomorrow everything will be all right. In his room, sleep evaded him like a cockroach under a broom. Every second came back magnified and awful. What made them so attractive? They were unpredictable, they were unkind to each other, and even though they were older than him, much older, they could be so immature! And yet, they had such an indefinable lure, persistent and deadly. An aura that hung over them and made them stick together as if each alone would disappear. They needed each other. Now, *he* needed them.

As he turned uneasily on the bed—having given up, after just a few horribly self-pitying lines in his laptop, the effort of writing it out of his system—Reed-man knocked. He carried a note.

'I'll wait for an answer, Sir,' he said, suddenly servile. The TT champ, the friendly supplier of ice cream and towels had vanished. In his place stood a servant. The boy missed the old Reed-man, even as he relished the fact that his being alone minus-parents had made him a person of some importance. But who could have sent him a note? The boy dreaded it was his father foreseeing his ineptness at organizing his life and choreographing reminder notes with the hotel staff. A conspiracy of control. He felt pissed off as he opened the envelope. It was not his father's writing. In a lazy scrawl the note said—What would you do to be one of 'us'?

And under the question, like in Hangman, there were blanks, waiting to be filled in.

The boy was afraid Reed-man would see through his fake composure. This had to be them. What game were they playing now? Did it matter? He would play. They hadn't shrugged him off after all! They were calling him back. Reckless with joy, the boy picked up the hotel pen and wrote in big bold caps—ANYTHING.

'Here,' he said, folding it and stuffing it back into the envelope. 'Take it.'

He didn't meet Reed-man's eyes. Let him think whatever he liked. Nobody sent notes when they could pick up the phone and talk. Nobody except in classroom romances and ad films. But *they* were obviously different. They had to make everything dramatic.

Some ten minutes after Reed-man left the boy chewing the pen as if demented, the phone by his bedside rang.

'Come,' said Tiger's voice.

What was he, their slave? He could be sleeping. He could be chatting with his girlfriend. He could be busy composing his magnum opus. Right. He sprang up from the bed, wore his slippers and ran down the stairs. The sun hit him on the head like a ton of bricks. When he was small, barely five, his then best friend had hit him on the head with a wooden brick. They were playing and suddenly bang! His head split open and blood poured out. Legend has it he didn't cry. His then best friend did and his friend's mother, who scooped him up in her arms and raced him to a doctor, his fresh blood leaking all over her pale silk sari. All accounts pointed to his being a heroic little man. But the sun was a different matter. He cringed, and plucking out the Oakleys from his pocket he clapped them on. Ah. A little better.

It was the same ground-floor room where Baldy had dragged him that morning, a morning that already seemed light years away. The boy knocked and when Tiger said, 'Enter,' he was seized by a strong desire to run away. He entered.

Tiger lay sprawled on the bed, shirt off. The debris of morning had been picked up and tidied away. The room glowed like a new thing. In the middle of that glow lay Tiger. Furry and alone.

'Rash, don't you think?' he said, as if continuing a conversation they'd broken off a minute ago. 'But done, committed—to paper. No backing out now.'

'No.'

Tiger meant the word he had written on the note. ANYTHING. Inwardly, the boy shuddered. Such a large, dangerous word. What would Tiger make him do?

'Rule one, hide nothing,' he snapped. 'Everything out in the open.'

A long pause.

'So. Fear. What d'you fear most?'

The boy's hands were a little clammy. Tiger obviously liked the heat. You could hardly tell the air conditioning was on. Fear. Why did he want to know? He had committed. In writing.

'Water,' he said, his voice sounding thick. 'I fear drowning.'

His armpits were streaming. It was the shame of admitting this to an adult.

'Ah!' Tiger said. The boy thought he saw his deep-set eyes spark with interest. 'Then come.'

Come? Already Tiger was swinging off the bed, slipping into his chappals. Where?

Out into the blinding sun. They were mad. Where to now? The boy followed Tiger, cursing silently. They stopped by the pool.

No one was around. All safe from the sun and snoring in bed except them. Even the loudmouths had vanished.

'Go on,' Tiger said, indicating his head towards the water. It was a prim gesture, sparrow-like. He hadn't bothered putting on his shirt. He looked serious.

'But,' the boy began and stopped. No use. He had committed. He took off his shirt, put it on the ground, carefully placed the Oakleys on top of it and began climbing down. The hot metal rails stuck to his hands. He wouldn't have been surprised to see bits of skin left behind as he climbed. Down, down. He clutched the long blue metal pipe. It was like the repetition of a nightmare. He kicked his legs. He must make an effort. When he looked up he saw Tiger was wearing his Oakleys.

'Let go,' he shouted, or so it seemed with the water splashing into the boy's ears.

'Can't,' he said, 'can't swim.'

It was a lie, he could, but only in theory. It was all bull about how you never forgot. What you never forgot was the fear.

'Let go.'

Tiger was on his haunches now, peering at the boy through the boy's sunglasses. What if he drowned? It would serve them right. Police case. Drowned body in the pool. Reed-man, lurking unnoticed, the witness who saw it all. Ragging the poor boy, he would say. Against his will. Tiger behind bars. Prowling. The boy felt light-headed. Beer, sun, too much food, no sleep, now this. He let go.

He didn't swim. He didn't drown. He thrashed about, flapped, heaved, swallowed, gasped, and found himself miraculously on the other side. Another blue metal pipe there. He clutched it and wheezed, feeling asthmatic and blind. His muscles were tearing open. He had a stitch in his side.

'Bravo,' he heard Tiger's voice float across to him. 'Now come back.'

Was he joking? Even in his *feels-like-my-windpipes-are-full-of-water* state the boy could tell that Tiger wasn't joking. Somehow, beating logic, he had to get back. He let go, again.

Halfway across, he found himself turning into a stone. His legs were stone, his arms were stone. Stones don't swim. Slowly, relieved of the responsibility of behaving like a human in water, he stopped. His head pointed downwards. Everything was splashed with light. Fear made him heavier. Even if he tried to command them, his stone arms and legs would refuse to obey. He would die on a Saturday afternoon in a swimming pool in Goa. Hit the bottom head-first and crack open like a nut. He was hitting something. He was—

Tiger had him by the shoulders. Swimming easily, he dragged the boy across the water to the steps and hauled him out. He crawled up and collapsed on the hot concrete. His lungs were on fire. He gagged, again and again. The chlorine taste was everywhere. His eyes stung as if they had acid in them. As he wheezed, sucking in lungful after lungful of burning air, he realized it wasn't just his chest or his side. Everything ached. He would never walk again.

Tiger slapped the boy on the back a couple of times. To make the coughing stop, the boy thought, gratefully.

'Not bad,' he heard Tiger say, when he finally stopped gasping and retching. 'You almost did it. Get up.'

Reluctantly, the boy obeyed. Never had he clung to solid ground so desperately, never been so grateful for concreteness, even as it roasted his bare flesh. The ground would not dissolve, molecules separating and rejoining endlessly in some vicious, viscous dance. It would stay firm under his feet. As he stood up, the air around him seemed treacherous, bottomless, like water.

Tiger's fur lay matted to his skin. He still had on the Oakleys.

In the room, he wordlessly flung the boy a towel. He rubbed himself, shivering, and then wrapped himself in it, like a blanket. How had his shirt got wet? Tiger took it to the bathroom. The boy crouched on the carpet, fearing damp circles on the bed and more, fearing proximity to the man who had flung him in and fished him out. Such a short man. He was powerless and he had chosen it.

'Wasn't so bad, was it?' Tiger said, as he settled back on the bed. Bluff. Like an army colonel. His father must have been in the defence forces. They learnt these things there.

Tame the body, break the will. *I am not a soldier.* The boy looked at him, silently.

'Now. That was the first. We will each pose a little test for you. A little ritual, if you like. A rite of passage. Pass them all and you can consider yourself one of us. Though frankly, why you should want to be part of a bunch of old losers like us baffles me.'

She. But where was she?

'Of course, I'm not saying we don't have our charms,' Tiger said, and smiled.

Suddenly, the boy saw Tiger for what he was—a suave sinister little man. It rattled him. He wanted no part of this dangerous man's schemes. He would walk out right now and tell them to stuff their little rituals. He would spoil whatever game they had planned for him, he wouldn't go along. He had that choice. This was not a college hostel where ragging was the norm, unavoidable unless you killed yourself. What power did they have over him? None. He would leave and that would be that.

The boy sat right where he was.

Tiger punched the phone next to him.

'Come,' he said.

His favourite command, snappy, like him. Who would be next? Despite himself, a little prickle of excitement ran down the boy's legs. His arms were wrapped tight around his knees. He would soon find out.

It was Baby. Of all people, it had to be Baby. Baby was openly hostile. He took the string chair where Angie had been sitting that morning, and said, 'So?'

The boy knew better than to reply. He stared at him, hoping his fright wasn't showing. He felt a strong dislike for Baby, and he didn't care if that showed.

'So,' he repeated, 'was it cool? Your little escapade with Tiger?'

He's mocking me. Escapade! What words these guys used.

Baby cleared his voice (not that it needed clearing, it was as soft, unthreatening and smooth as his baby cheeks) and took out the little notebook the boy had seen him reading at lunch.

'Listen, you.'

He read as if to himself.

'"The will exhibits itself as organized body, and the presence of disease signifies that the will itself is sick."'

He looked up.

'Who said that?'

'You,' the boy said, feeling insolence rush back like warmth into his cold jelly-bones.

'Ha-ha,' Baby said, softly, not smiling at all. 'Very clever. Let me rephrase. Who wrote that?'

'Who cares?' the boy answered.

'Oh, is that so?'

He sounded ironic, but the boy could tell he was annoyed. The insect was refusing to be squashed. *What was it about Tiger that made me obey him instantly?*

'Illiterate, are we?' Baby said. 'Could you at least divulge your understanding of the said statement, or is that too much to ask?'

The boy was not going to let himself be browbeaten by such withering sarcasm. He had survived a sarcastic father, and now he would survive Baby. He wished he could ask him to read that line again but that would be an acknowledgement of inattention. Something about the will itself being sick. If you're ill that means you want to be ill. But that's crap!

'It means if you're ill you want to be ill. But that's crap,' the boy said, not bothering to censor his thoughts for Baby's sake.

'Ah-a!'

Baby sounded triumphant. Obviously he had goofed up.

'The insect has a brain!'

He used my word. He called me insect. He's telepathic.

The boy felt hunted.

'And how refreshing to be told by an illiterate insolent insect that Schopenhauer is crap, don't you think, Tiger?'

Tiger was smiling. The boy couldn't tell whether it was a smile of pleasure or derision as his eyes were still obscured. *Behind my precious Oakleys. Cost a bomb. Give them back.*

'Next,' Baby said. '"All disease is only love transformed." I won't bother asking you who wrote that, as you obviously will not know. But what I will ask is this—how does this relate to the first statement I read out?'

All disease is only love transformed. Like being sick with love. Like having loosies thinking of final exams or a girl you didn't dare speak to. But what about the will? Did one will oneself to be sick with love or did it happen, without warning? It happened without warning. The way *she* had happened without warning. His will was helpless.

'They don't relate,' the boy said. 'The first statement talks about willing yourself to be ill. The second talks of love as a kind of illness. The will has nothing to do with love, love happens, just like that.'

'Ah-a!' Baby said again, but differently. He was listening. He was impressed. He couldn't scorn him any more. 'Insect has been applying himself. Next. "He who desires but acts not, breeds pestilence." Blake, William Blake.'

He's showing off. He wants me to know how well read he is. He needs an audience, a helpless ignorant listener like me.

'Do you agree with Mr Blake or do you violently disagree?'

Pestilence. What a curious word. Like escapade. This guy was obviously a lover of words found in books which he plucked out and put in conversations so that his conversations sounded like talking books. Despite himself, the boy was getting interested. How had Baby found quotations that were all somehow making sense to him? He who desires but acts not, breeds pestilence. That made sense. Like an itch. You're dying to scratch and you've been told not to, so you try to avoid it but finally you can't take it any more and you scratch so bad you bleed. Would have been better if you'd scratched a little in the beginning, when you first felt like it, instead of waiting till it became a tornado. But was that what Mr Blake meant? Perhaps not. Desire to act. Like me wanting to go up to *her* and say something, anything. But unable to, paralysed. So what next? *I obsess about her. I can't eat sleep drink. I get madly jealous of anyone who talks to her. I hate her for talking to everyone but me, forgetting that I'm the one who hasn't talked to her so she doesn't even know of my existence, and so I decide to harm her. I harm the woman I love because I am afraid to act on my desire and so I breed a pestilence of hate, and harm her (or myself) instead. Yup. That made sense.*

'Makes sense,' the boy said, aloud. 'Makes total sense.'

'Insect and Mr Blake see eye-to-eye, Tiger,' Baby announced, softly. 'There's hope, yet. "He alone will die who wishes to die, to whom life is intolerable." Comment.'

Was he an English teacher? The way he talked, like exam-paper questions. That would explain it. He'd done the whole range, hadn't he? Wanting to be ill making you ill, love as illness, lack of action as unhealthy, now death. Something gnawed at the boy about the first statement, the one he'd wanted repeated. It said the will itself is sick. How could that be? The will wasn't a body-part like a liver or a toe. How could the will be sick? That was like saying love is blind. Love wasn't real, just a feeling, nothing solid. How could it be blind then, like a person? But wait! *That's* what he'd missed! The will is seen through the body! The body expresses the will... Like when you're embarrassed, your ears turn red. And when you're scared, the hairs on your neck stand up or you get goosebumps. That's what he meant! Whatever your will felt, the body exposed it. It was hopeless at keeping secrets. This last quote was linked to the first one! If your will itself is sick, it shows as disease (the body being as transparent as water). And if your will wishes to die, your body follows (being an obedient little dog that goes wherever the master goes). To whom life is intolerable. Suicides. That's what made people commit suicide.

The boy didn't realize he'd said the last bit to the room. It's only when he heard Baby say, 'Pray elaborate on that cryptic comment,' that he realized he'd been thinking aloud.

'I mean, why live if you don't want to,' he said, not sure any more what he meant, just talking, hoping he wouldn't get flustered and start stammering again. 'That's what it says, when life is intolerable you want to die. Some people live even when they can't bear to, some people don't. They kill themselves. Suicide. Makes sense.'

They were both looking at him, not saying anything. Without knowing how, he felt he had leapt over some last, invisible hurdle. Baby was almost looking tender. Tiger took off his glasses (*my glasses*). His deep-set, curiously shaded-from-light eyes were crinkling. *He's assessing me*. The boy looked back, assessing him. Baby's voice broke in.

'"Mutate, like a virus." Could you do that, insect? Since you seem so sage about matters of love and death, surely you could mutate? Do you know what mutate is, you of the cool-generation (his mouth twisted when he said cool), or should I explain?'

'I know mutate,' the boy blurted out, unnecessarily loud. 'Everyone knows who's ever seen Teenage Ninja Mutant Turtles!'

Tiger and Baby burst out laughing. The boy stared at them, ready to get offensive, defensive, whatever it took to save his honour. But they weren't laughing at him.

'Teenage Ninja!' Tiger wept. 'My god!'

Baby, whom the boy had found so distant and scary, was slapping the bed as he laughed, rocking, howling with laughter. The boy was impressed. It hadn't been *that* funny.

'You're priceless, insect,' Baby said at last. His pink cheeks were red with laughing, even his neck. He wiped his eyes and shut the book. 'You're priceless. I'm done!'

The boy, and how strange that was, felt a little nudge of disappointment. He wanted to continue talking. Mutate like a virus. What a cool statement (thank god he said that only to himself). Who wrote it? He wanted to know. Viruses interested him. Mutate like a virus. That's what hackers did. Invented newer and newer viruses that no one would recognize, so that when they came to destroy your files from the inside, you were clueless. Was Baby a computer geek? A hacker? No. Though it wasn't as exciting, he'd settle for him being a teacher. He had it in his mix of scorn and persistence, and the way he spoke as if he knew everything. Suddenly, the boy felt a flare of admiration for Baby. His good opinion mattered. *I want him to like me. Hell, I want to be like him.* But Baby was leaving the room.

'Good luck, insect,' he said as he left.

The boy felt a thrill of delight. The way Baby said 'insect', it sounded so friendly! He had survived Baby and Tiger! Why should he be afraid of what else lay in store?

Eight

Angie and Poka came in together. The river goddesses, cloaked in mischief. They seemed full of suppressed hilarity, like two naughty girls who've just done something they shouldn't have and are dying to tell someone how terribly wicked they've been. The boy felt silly sitting on the floor with the towel around him. With Baby it hadn't mattered, but with these two women... He scrambled hurriedly to his feet, trying not to look too conspicuous.

'Where to, child,' Angie said, that honeyvoice of hers sweet with entrapment.

'Just...' He pointed at the loo. And then in case they thought he meant something else, he blurted, 'My shirt.'

'Oh no,' laughed Angie, 'allow us a glimpse of your nubile charms!'

Now he'd done it. He should have continued to sit quietly on the floor and they wouldn't even have noticed he was shirtless.

'Go on, it's only us, Mama Bear and Mammy Bear!'

The boy felt like giggling. Angie and Poka as bears was a bit much. He let the towel go.

'Mmmmm!' they chorused.

'Very nice!' Angie said. 'Are you real? Poka, he's as smooth as a baby's bum! He'll give Baby a complex!'

The boy wanted the earth to open and swallow him up. He was unhappy about his hairless arms and chest. Something girlish about it, infantile. Grow some hair on your chest, beta, his father would say in those early days when he was still trying to make him into his son. Rough, ready, a sportsman, a loud voice, a managerial manner. He meant, Be a man, be manly, but at age seven (or was it eight) the boy thought he meant it literally. Every morning he would examine his torso for signs of hair growth, and every night he would go to bed wracked with disappointment. He grew into adolescence cursed with smoothness. And now these two luscious ladies were cooing over that cursed smoothness like pigeons in heat.

'Let him go, Angie,' Poka said, 'he's blushing and not just on his face!'

Grateful, ashamed, the boy ran to the loo where his shirt hung over the tap. It was damp and wrinkled. He shook it out and wore it. He scanned his face in the mirror. It was the same face he had in the morning, but it felt like someone else's.

Back in the room, Angie and Poka had settled down. Angie sat luxuriantly on the string chair, and between her legs, on the floor, sat Poka. The boy was shocked by the casual intimacy that they indulged in so carelessly before strangers. He should have been flattered but instead he felt uncomfortable. He could see the outline of Angie's thighs under her white linen skirt. He could see the flawless shape of her calf as she stretched out her leg through the slit. She was hot and she knew it. The two of them were annoying Tiger. Excessive hirsuteness is a sign of mental deficiency, grizzly goes to war clad in fur coat, some Bengali joke about a jungle boook with lots of Os in it, that sort of thing. The boy was glad. They might even forget about testing him and then they could simply chat.

'All right then,' Angie said, 'shall we?'

She looked gleeful.

'Right. You're going to tell us a story.'

'Not just any story,' Poka said. 'A story with a horse, a fish, a cloud and a fruit in it. You get two minutes to think about it and then you start.'

'Forgot the crucial bit, sweets,' Angie drawled. 'It has to be erotic.'

This was worse than Tiger's test. Erotic? The word loomed over the boy like the fruit Poka wanted in the story. Red and poisonous. Did they mean a dirty story? How could he? He had looked at enough pondy to know it wasn't about storytelling. Pictures yes, gross and shameful, but not words. Surely these two didn't want him to tell a story with nasty words in it? He couldn't.

'Listen,' Poka said (always the gentle one, his rescuer), 'do you even know what erotic means?'

'Let's see what he *thinks* it means,' Angie squealed. 'Don't you dare help him!'

His lifeline snatched away, the boy stared at his toes. Still sitting on the carpet, he could feel three sets of eyes on him. They were waiting. This was supposed to be his thinking time, not sitting-blankly-and-wilting time. Let's see what he thinks it means. A fruit a horse a fish a cloud. How weird.

'Thinking time up,' said Angie efficiently and pressed a knob on her watch. A manly watch, he'd noticed that earlier, a solid knobby manly watch, out of synch with her hot-bod vibes. Well, such observations wouldn't do him any good now. His time was up.

'In a far country without any rain,' he began, 'a horse wandered, riderless. It was a white horse, sacrificial, waiting for the spurt of blood at the tip of the golden knife. It was the aswamedha horse and it dreaded the moment of its death. But it had to keep running, running through countries, claiming each land that it galloped through for its king. Forward was the only way it knew, that white horse. And so, driven by thirst and dread, it ran.'

With an electrifying gladness the boy knew he had caught their attention. Angie's hands had started braiding Poka's long silky hair, fine braids which she wove nimbly with unseeing hands. Her eyes were on him, listening.

'At last the horse came to a place where instead of open fields like the ones he'd left behind, there stood a wall of wire. Twisted wire woven into a wall. The horse felt the stab of something unfriendly against his muzzle and he neighed. It was too high for him to jump over. His body would catch on the twisted wire and he would die like a fly in a metal web. He would die anyway, but that was later. It was now that he was concerned with. As far as he looked to right and left—the wall stretched, nasty and invincible. The horse pawed the ground. He could not go back. He thought of all the brave horses of legend and how they would have leaped, but he could not. He loved his white mane too much, his perfect silver hooves, his bright eyes that the queen used to kiss with her soft mouth. He loved himself too much and he wanted to live, if only to feel the queen's warm thighs astride him as she rode him every morning, undetected by the king. He would have to return to her, but not the way he had come. That path was closed to him.

'He pawed the ground again. The ground was sandy, the loose earth came away easily under his sharp hooves. He remembered a dog he had once seen in the royal compound. Digging the ground, nosing in and coming up triumphant with a bone. Memory flared in him like a bright fire and he snorted hot air and began. The earth flew. A hole had appeared at the white horse's feet. He would dig until the light came in from the other side, that's when he would know he could pass safely through.

'And then he saw it.

'It was a golden light, nothing like the blue air around him. The blue air was pale and nothing shone in it, not even the sun. The golden light from the hole at his feet shone like the ring that pierced the queen's nose. He felt weak with longing. He bent his face to the light. It shone golden and smelt sweet. His knees trembled.

'"Devour me," said the light. "Devour me and throw my seed back into this hole. I will grow into a tree taller than the wall of wire. My roots will spread under the earth to the other side. Immense roots, they will break open a hole in the wall, large enough for you to ride through without the wire catching your perfect white mane. And once you have crossed, I will throw one fruit down to you which you must carry between your teeth, uneaten, until you return. Give it to no one, least of all yourself."

'The horse understood. He devoured the light and it was heavenly. He had tasted apples from the royal orchard, sweet and crunchy between his great white teeth, he had tasted sugar from the queen's powdered, perfumed hands, but never had he tasted anything this sweet. It melted him, it melted inside him. He ate it all, and when the softness and wetness gave way to a hard centre, only then did he remember about the seed.

'Regretfully—for he yearned to suck the seed until it yielded everything, yearned to bite that hardness until it broke—he threw the seed into the hole and pawed the earth back into place. He would have to wait. The light had said it would grow. Out of the flat dry earth a tall tree, erect and bursting with hidden fruit. He could hardly wait. He scanned the sky. Not a cloud. When would the rain come that would flower the seed into being? His own thirst came back to torment him like a goad. The blue air pressed down on him, hard and shiny. He broke into a sweat. What if the light had lied? What if he was doomed to stay here forever, next to this impassable wire wall, unable to go backwards or forwards, trapped and doomed to die friendless and alone? The soft strangling of the silken cloth that awaited him was far better than this death. Big drops of sweat fell on the ground where the horse stood and darkened the sandy earth. It was the sweat of fear and desire, it reeked of lost hope, and it fell off him in drops as stinging as tears.

'The horse was so afraid of dying there, alone, that he didn't notice when the green shoot poked through the ground like a tongue. The ground where he stood was damp, and still he wept tears of sweat and still the pushing plant grew. It grew and grew until it towered above the horse, and only when the green shade softened the hard blue air did the horse look up and see what had happened. The ground trembled as the immense tree's roots pushed their way under the hem of the wire wall and rose groaning on the other side. It lifted the wire wall with it as it went.

A hole appeared where there had been a mesh of thickly intertwining wire. The horse could not believe his eyes. Snorting, he trotted forward, and delicately, fearing a snag on his splendid white mane, he eased himself through the hole.

'He was through! He raised his hot eyes up to the towering tree and he thanked it. "Here," said the tree in answer and it dropped one single fruit at the horse's waiting feet. Gently the horse held it between his great white teeth and began the long journey home.

'Briskly, he trotted. Silvery, he flew. And all the while, between his teeth, the golden fruit. His lips quivered at the thought of the sweetness so close, so denied. He trembled at the thought of his teeth bruising the fruit's fine skin. Riderless, the horse kept on running. It was flatland still, but turning green. The yellow sand was left behind and now he saw before him a river. It was a timid river, running shyly at his feet. He would cross it in a minute. But as soon as he put his foreleg into the river's cool water, he heard a voice.

'"Wait, silver horse," the voice said. "I cannot let you pass until you have answered my riddle."

'The horse felt impatient. Who was this? Who dared to bar his way, he, the aswamedha? War would be waged on that impudent being! But where was it?

'"At your feet, silver horse," the voice said.

'The horse looked down. Near the leg that was still in the water there swam a tiny fish with scales as silvery as his hoof. He could have kicked it out of the way! But something stopped him. Gently he placed the beautiful unbruised fruit on the riverbank and said, "What is your riddle?"'

Angie had stopped making braids. Her hands lay on

Poka's shoulders. Poka's unbraided hair lay spread across Angie's lap.

'"What tastes sweeter, the flesh of a fruit or the flesh of a fish?"

'The horse snorted. What sort of question was that?

'"The flesh of a fruit of course," he said, huffily. "Now let me pass."

'But the fish would not let him go so easily.

'"How can you be so sure?" it asked. "What about the fruit you've placed on the riverbank? How do you know it is sweet?"

'"Because I have tasted one just like it," the horse said.

'"But no two fruits are exactly the same," the fish said. "How do you know this one is not bitter?"

'The horse was filled with rage. The sweet flesh he had carried all this while, trying not to think about it and yet unable to think about anything else. How dare the fish suggest this divine thing was bitter?

'"Try it yourself and see," he snorted, forgetting what the light had told him.

'"I cannot," said the little fish. "The fruit is my sister. I cannot eat my own sister. But you can. Eat it here in front of me and tell me if it is sweet, and if it is, I will swallow the first hook of the morning and die for being so impudent, and you can cross in peace."

'The horse forgot everything. Give it to no one, least of all yourself, the light had told him. But his mouth was mad with the smell of the fruit nestled so long against his tongue. He bent his face and delicately picking up the golden unspoilt fruit, he ate it. He felt the juice burst inside him like a shower. He felt the pulp slide down his throat like a caress. And when he crunched the tiny seed barely bigger than an almond, he felt an excruciating pain that sliced him along the belly and brought him shivering to his knees.

'The fish had gone. The water of that timid river was bursting the banks. Roaring, wet with fury, it rolled over him and he drowned, dreaming of the queen's juice-stained lips, her perfect golden hands.'

His story was over. He had spoken as if in a dream. He had forgotten about Angie and Poka and Tiger and the reason for being in that room and their reason for watching him as he spoke.

Now, coming back, the boy waited, shivering slightly, even though it was stuffy in Tiger's overheated den.

The two women were looking at him, wonderingly. It was as if they were not themselves either.

Then Angie broke the spell.

'You... are a poet,' she said, 'and you did not know it. That was gorgeous. Which book did you steal it out of?'

The boy laughed. Joy.

'The one in my head,' he said, cheekily.

It had worked! He felt light, feather-touch.

'Liked it?' he asked, amazed at himself.

'Loved it,' said Poka exhaling, as if she had been holding her breath all along. 'Super. You should write that down. Full marks.'

The boy felt like dynamite. Any minute now he would explode. The two goddesses loved it. If only for that it was worth it, this foolish game they were playing, like kids. He wanted to jump up and hug somebody. He hugged his knees to his chin.

But what was this thing they had for leaving each time they finished? He didn't want Angie and Poka to go. He wouldn't mind now if they stayed and watched him flounder through the next test. He felt as though they were on his side (hadn't they always been?). Wanting to detain them, to delay their going, he asked, 'But was it erotic?'

They looked at each other. Poka made that crazy-cute gesture with her mouth, as if she was kissing someone you couldn't see.

'It was for me,' she said.

Angie just smiled. As she turned to go, the boy saw that her bare back was criss-crossed with the pattern from the string chair. He imagined the way it would feel under his fingers and shivered.

'A drink!' Tiger declared as soon as they were gone. 'Call in, shall we?'

Cursing about the prices on the menu, he called and ordered a beer with two glasses. The boy would much rather have had a cup of chai, strong and sweet. What time was it? He'd forgotten to wear his watch in the morning. Inside this room, time seemed to have become meaningless. It stood outside the framework of what a day meant. On other days, time followed the rules, hour upon hour. Today, it was jumping tracks. Speeding, slowing, stopping. He liked it.

Before he could flex his cramping thighs, Ciggy appeared, silent and smoking. The boy found it hard to imagine Ciggy making him do anything or say anything. It didn't fit his idea of this tall, gangly, boyish man, whose spectacles always seemed to be slipping off. The boy stood up. He had pins and needles in his right leg and he couldn't bear to sit. But neither could he bear to stand or walk. Aargh! Zillions of pricking points all down his leg.

'Smoke?' Ciggy asked him, as if he hadn't already asked

earlier that day and been refused. It was his way of saying hello. He said it to everyone. The boy shook his head.

'All right then. Let's see how long you can stay silent. Absolutely mum. Okay?'

And he parked himself against the door, like he had in the morning, only now the door was closed. *One makes me swim, the other makes me squirm, another says 'talk', and yet another says 'be quiet'*. Had they planned it in advance or were they just naturally coordinated? The boy was glad though. Staying quiet would be easy, especially after all the talking he'd done in the previous session. Session! It was beginning to sound like visits to a shrink. Or a series of dentist's appointments for root canal. Only less painful. His pins and needles stabbed. Moaning might have helped but he couldn't. He was being studied for silence. A study in silence. Like a painting. An empty white room. On the table a telephone, black and dead. A study in silence featuring a telephone, that instrument of speech transferral over long distances or short. It was the kind of thing Baby might have been interested in. The boy hoped Baby wouldn't ignore him when he saw him again. He longed to be friends, real friends, with Baby. Exchange ideas, share his deepest thoughts, ask his advice. Maybe read his mysterious notebook. How he'd like that! Perhaps Baby would let him, as a special mark of distinction. Perhaps...

There was a knock on the door. Ciggy opened it. It was the waiter with the beer. Ciggy raised his eyebrows.

'Which two of us is this for?' he said, looking at the boy.

He almost replied, 'You two can have it,' but remembered just in time. Silence. Absolutely mum.

'Us two,' said Tiger, 'but I think I'll pull rank and deprive junior of his due, what say?'

The boy mimed *sure, go ahead* with his hands. He felt a bit ridiculous. They poured and clinked their glasses. Aah! Their cold-beer thing. And then Tiger began talking to Ciggy and Ciggy began nodding and hmming in agreement. They talked about the women in their group. What a slut, found out she's been sleeping with him for a year now. Bitch. And what about her, little miss high and mighty, playing hard to get and making eyes at every available male. They're all the same. Ice maidens for show and hotpants below.

The boy's cheeks blazed. He could guess who they meant. Each 'she' was as clear to him as if she were present in the room, naked. He felt hot and bothered. How dare they? Ciggy's own girlfriend, being bad-mouthed by his friend! How could he stand there so calmly and take it? Kind, generous Poka! He didn't believe a word of it! She was so... the boy almost blurted out his indignation and fell back. *Test, remember.* They're testing you to see if you can sit through a slanging session without opening your mouth in someone's defence. Very clever. So Ciggy was as devious as the others. All that quietness was just a cover for meanness. How sly they all were! Except Angie and Poka, they were the only two upfront and honest ones.

The boy felt like drinking that beer. Getting up (they hadn't said he couldn't move) he poured himself a glass of water. The two of them ignored him. They described some of the disgusting things Tiger had caught them doing in Angie's room. *I refuse to listen. I object.* And then they talked of Momo. Momo, meaning *her*. What a horrible name. What was her real name? Surely she had a real name. If they said anything bad about her he would shout at them and leave the room. So there. But they didn't. Instead, Tiger's voice turned sympathetic and he said, 'Poor girl, I wonder how long she'll take.'

Take for what?

'She's too fragile for such stuff, it isn't fair,' Tiger said and Ciggy hmmed and nodded in agreement.

What stuff? Tell me!

'It isn't as if she hasn't had her chances,' Tiger continued, sounding like a bitchy aunty. 'It's just that she blows it every time.'

'Ya, poor thing. And ever since the death—*whose death? my heart was impossible to control*—she's withdrawn into a shell.'

'Maybe another shock would bring her out of it.'

NO! Too cruel!

'That's what the shrinks say—*shrinks? she was seeing shrinks?*—but what do they know.'

Questions bubbled on the boy's lips like a raving man's froth. And yet he stayed quiet. Now more than ever he had to survive this lunacy, pass this test and the next one and the next one, every last one of them—for her. She needed his help. He would stay silent for as long as it took, as goddamned long as it took to finally get through to her, to find out what was wrong, and save her.

Nine

She walked in with Baldy.

The boy almost fell off the carpet. Ciggy and Tiger stopped mid-sentence and looked meaningfully at him. Baldy had come unsummoned. He had just pushed open the door and come in. And with him there she was. Twenty-four hours had already passed since he saw her first. He had worked hard at getting used to her absence. Where he had hoped to see her, he had seen instead an empty *she-might-have-been-here-should-have-been-here-wish-she-were-here* space of longing. It hurt him physically now to see her fill that space with her body, real and inescapable.

The boy looked for some place to hide his feet his hands his eyes. She was sitting on the bed and leaning against Tiger. His hairy arms were touching hers, exposed in her summer dress. The boy felt revolted by Tiger's hair. His obscene hair making contact with her helpless skin. He felt like he might get loosies again. His stomach gave a sudden jab of pain.

'Not through yet?' Baldy jostled Ciggy. 'Come on, move over. Give a guy a break.' *Did he mean me, enough ragging, let him go?* 'Bad enough you've been hogging him all this while.' *He didn't mean me.* 'Now it's Cracker's turn.'

And he looked ironically at the boy, daring him to call him Baldy again. *Baldy, baldy.*

'Awrigh',' said Ciggy past his cigarette, which he was just lighting (which one the boy wondered, fiftieth?). 'He's all yours. I'm done. He's in. A man who can keep quiet is a man worth talking to.'

And with that utterly weird statement, Ciggy left.

Baldy rubbed his hands. He was always rubbing his hands, like a greasy man in a play.

'May I?' he asked Tiger, as if asking his permission to dance. Tiger nodded, the kind king who allows his daughter to waltz with the prince. Ridiculous.

She sat where she was, leaning on one of Tiger's two pillows. Why hide for so long and then suddenly appear when least expected? Was she a sadist too, like them?

'Okay Paps!' Baldy said *Paps* like it was a bad word, spitting it out. 'Watch me.'

The boy looked at him, dutifully. He took out a small vial. In it was a clear colourless liquid.

'What you have here is two parts hydrogen and one part oxygen, in other words what is known in common parlance as etch-too-oh or water. Pani. Jal. Miraculous liquid without which continents would shrivel and populations die out. Nectar to the thirsty, heaven to the unwashed, blessing to the farmer, business tool to the professional car washer. A liquid unparalleled by any other in the history of liquids. A liquid that's fluid enough to be everywhere, adulterated or original. Found in perfumes and car batteries, tear ducts and tender coconuts. Protean and passive, non-flammable and necessary.'

He paused as if expecting applause. His eyes shone with excitement.

'So, Paps,' he continued, 'on one hand a vial of water. Distilled water, mind you, sterile, hygienic. Pure as Adam's thoughts on the day he was born. On the other hand (like a conjuror he pulled it out), a syringe. Nasty needle, this,' he said, shaking his head at the syringe in his right hand like a disapproving mother. 'Most feared weapon this side of vaccination. Feared by babies whose tender flesh it pierces like an instrument of unwanted benevolence, providing protection against their own virulent futures, but in what a malevolent disguise! Feared by grown men with rotting teeth, whose gums it enters like a sting of terror, leaving numbness and woolly tongue in its wake. Feared by mothers whose children stab themselves with it willingly, pumping new life into their veins, altered and addictive. Feared by patients wondering if the needle that approaches their skin is contaminated by the illnesses of another. Never was a needle more maligned and more malignant!'

He relished the pause of his own making. His words were gushing over the boy in thick and slippery waves.

'And now, my dear Paps, I will proceed to fill the syringe in my right hand with the distilled water from the vial in my left. (He did, efficient as a nurse.) Pure harmless innocent water. Max it will do is cause a little bump under your skin. But... (and here he started looking crafty) BUT. Is it pure, harmless, innocent? You only have my word for it. And that is all you will have before I plunge it into a carefully selected vein in your tantalizingly smooth, amazingly unmarked forearm.'

The room was quiet. The boy could hear her breathing, a little wheeze in the pull and push of her lungs.

'I see it has finally sunk in, dear Paps,' Baldy said. 'The idea of sticking this innocuous needle into your arm isn't exactly heart-warming. To be precise, it is even, perhaps, alarming. You only have my word, and my word may not be good enough! What if… (he held up the syringe until it was level with his eye) what if this isn't water at all but sarin. Have you heard of sarin? A toxic nerve gas. It's lethal. Not only because of its innate qualities but also because it's colourless, odourless and dissolves in water. Nothing could be easier than to pass off sarin as water! Do you see my meaning? You can't tell the difference. Which means I could be playing a terrible trick on you. But you'll have to trust me, won't you? That's what being friends means. Trusting one another. Corny, but true. Trust me when I tell you it's harmless, and we're friends for life. A little snicker of doubt and out you go, out through the door never to return! Which will it be?'

More than when Tiger threw him into the pool, more than when Baby threatened him with his baby-voice, more than when Ciggy let Tiger slash his girlfriend to pieces without uttering a word in her defence, the boy felt like leaving. He would have if she hadn't been there. He couldn't chicken out with her sitting there. That was Baldy's cleverest move. He would know about guys not wanting to chicken out before girls. He was using that knowledge like a weapon. That's what he was using, more than the needle that he said was filled (maybe) with a liquid he had never heard of. *Baldy wants to poison me with doubt and fear. What if it were neither water nor sarin, but something much worse, something that might give me AIDS, or hepatitis, or some other awful incurable disease? Would he do a thing like that? It would be murder! But why should they care, they know I am alone, they could do it, and take me to my room, and leave me there to die. No one would know. Except Reed-man. Reed-man brought the note I was foolish enough to answer. Reed-man would know I had been with them. But would he tell? Would the sight of my dead body drive him into silence, afraid of the police, afraid of what they might do to him, his job, his security, if he said anything? It couldn't be! It's Baldy we're talking about, the brown-eyed funny man. I offended him, true, but he'd gotten over it, he must have! No one killed people because they made fun of the way you looked! Anyway I hadn't meant to make fun, I was just going with the flow. It was his fault, not mine, being such a sissy over such a silly thing. He couldn't still be nursing a grievance over an unintended insult! Or could he?*

'To use the right jargon,' the boy heard Baldy say, 'you're about to play a trust game. Corporations spend good money teaching their employees to play them. You're getting it for free. Ask Tiger. Trust is the first principle of teamwork, to quote one of the many things we learnt when we were busy being successful. (*He's forgotten about me, he's mocking himself, he isn't doing his spiel. It's as if he's looking at himself looking at himself. It's freaking me out.*) So, will you won't you will you won't you, won't you join the dance?'

Tiger tittered in the background. The sound of that suppressed little laugh brought the boy back to reality. What was wrong with him? He was thinking like a cheap crime flick, like one of the best-sellers he read. Murder indeed!

'Yup,' he said, and extended his arm. He was getting theatrical too. It was infectious. He had caught it from Baldy and he didn't care.

'Wah!' Baldy shouted, sounding almost like his old self. 'Taaliya! Bare your left arm, Pappu-mian, and let me do the dreadful!'

The boy bared his left arm. It was like a blood donation

camp, only there they asked you to clench your fist and bare your elbow. Afterwards they gave you biscuits and juice, just in case you fainted. *I hadn't fainted, but I had taken the biscuits and juice anyway.* As he watched Baldy tap the syringe with a professional air, the boy wondered if he did drugs. Or had in the past. He looked so professional. Was there a drug mixed with the water? Maybe there wasn't, but how did he know that injecting water was safe? How did he know it was a new syringe? Baldy hadn't opened it in front of him. A violent fright clutched the boy's insides. It was too late. Baldy had found a spot on his upper left arm. Did he have a swab for before and after, to rub the spot, to hold it there? He was being a fool. Dread, black dread. He would die. He should have gone home with his parents. This was madness. He needed no friends if this was how you made them. Talk was fine but needles! He felt his stomach cramp. He wanted to rush to the loo and puke his insides out. But the stuff was already in his blood. He couldn't puke his blood out. He was dying. Please...

'Relax,' said a gentle voice. 'Can't you tell when someone's joking?'

Inside the boy there was a terrible shivering. He looked at his bare, goose-pimpled arms expecting to see that trembling erupt in a million ripples on his skin. But his skin looked flat and calm. Only his insides shook. His feet were ice. His tongue was thick and parched. He couldn't breathe. He was dying. *It was her voice.*

Baldy was kneeling in front of him on the carpet. One hand was on his shoulder.

'Relax,' he said. 'Didn't you hear Momo? It's a joke, man. Chill.'

The boy opened his eyes which he had shut tightly without knowing. She was standing next to the bed. He had scared them. *What was in the syringe?*

'I'm fine,' he said. His voice came from another place. 'I'm cool. I just need to...'

'Yes, just splash some water on your face, buddy, and you'll be as good as new.'

Baldy was helping him up, his arm flung around his neck like before.

'Here. Now wipe.'

He felt like a bewildered child. *Had my fear been that obvious, for her to notice?* He walked back into the room, and felt silly. What a fuss. He smiled.

'Bravo!' shouted Baldy. 'Pappu pass ho gaya! Graduated with flying colours! Pappu comes out top of the pops! Pappu is part of the pee-clan! Join the Pappu-parade!'

It was hysterical. He was just as he had been that morning! The boy felt a burst of affection for Baldy.

'Scared you, didn't I?' he said, quick as a cat on his feet. *Turn the thing around, fool them.*

'Never, not for a second,' said Baldy, but he was lying.

What was in the syringe? Where had he thrown it?

'You *were* scared!' the boy said, grinning.

Baldy grinned back. She was sitting down again. The boy was acutely conscious of her every move.

'Oh but you haven't met our fairest maid,' said Baldy, catching the boy's eye, the blush still hot on his cheek (how clever he was, how keen-eyed). 'Momo was absconding this morning. This evening I gave her no such chance! Momo, this is him. The young one. An innocent if ever there was. And this, dear innocent, is Momo of the maddening moods,

Momo the mystery, Momo the miraculous. She may not look it, but she rules us all, and we love being under her delightful despotic thumb.'

Momo said nothing.

'And because she is the first lady, she will be the last to test your mettle. Momo, test on for testosterone!'

He's back, my funny crazy friend, spinning words like coloured tops!

She looked straight at the boy, as if she had known him forever and said, 'Listen, just reply honestly to whatever I ask you, okay?'

The boy nodded. The trust game, the truth game.

'Have you ever been in love?'

What was this—Miss Universe? Was this the question that won you the crown? The boy felt unmanned. He couldn't answer that question to her face. He nodded.

'And does she love you in return?'

He shook his head.

'Do you think she might, one day?'

'I don't know,' he said. 'I hope so.'

'If she asked you to die for her, would you?'

He was silent. Why this death thing again? So morbid.

'I guess so,' he said.

'You're not sure.'

'No, I mean yes. I am.'

Was he being truthful? Or did he merely want her to think him heroic?

'If any other woman, say me for instance, if I asked you, right now, to die for me, would you?'

His heart lurched. How had she guessed?

'Yes, if you were the one I loved.' *Oh thank you god for making me say that.*

'Excellent.'

The boy looked at her. She was observing him carefully. Not unkindly, but intently. Would she see what he was trying to hide? Girls were very clever at these things. But if she did see, what then? He couldn't hold her gaze. He looked away. He saw that Baldy was beaming at him. Tiger was swinging his hairy legs off the bed.

'I hereby call this session to an end,' he said, adopting Baldy's speechy style. 'It is now my official pleasure to consider you, Pappu, as one of us.'

And Tiger came over and shook the boy's hand, as if he were a general congratulating an officer. Careful, the boy thought, next thing you know, you'll be saluting your NCC salute. But what about the others? Tiny, Dodo, Molly? Would they not quiz him, make him do things to prove his mettle? They wouldn't! These seven were it! Relief washed over him. It was over! What an elaborate way they had of choosing their friends. Is this how they had chosen each other? No, they couldn't have. This was for outsiders. He was the first outsider. He had won his friends. He was in.

Momo smiled from the bed. Baldy was on the phone.

They came pouring in. Poka, Ciggy, Angie, Molly, Dodo, Baby, Tiny.

'We hear wondrous tales,' Baby said, smiling, 'of valour and wit!'

Angie winked at him. Poka hugged him (her breasts against him, glorious!) and Molly gave him a conspiratorial grin. They were wonderful. He loved them all.

'In celebration of our newly extended fellowship, we are now all going to the beach,' Baldy announced, assuming the role of tour operator. 'Kindly follow me, please do not lag behind and please do not leave your belongings here and there.'

They left the room not bothering to lock the door. Outside, it was night. The boy stumbled in disbelief. How many hours had he spent in Tiger's room? Impossible to believe how scorching the afternoon had been. The sky looked purple and black. He remembered his first evening in this place, alone in the games room. The same spill of happiness was in his heart. He tasted the night, cool and salt, against his cheek. It was windy. He was in love.

Ten

You never saw so many stars in Bombay. In Bombay you never saw the sky. You saw the sodium glare, the smoke haze of traffic under unfinished bridges, a daily armageddon, something nuclear in the heat and troubled light. The sky was a neon billboard, back in Bombay. Here it hung low, a breathing thing, touching them as they lay on the sand.

The sand felt moist against the boy's bare calves. His arms were crossed under his head. The stars were huge. The only constellation he knew shone bright and clear, reassuring. The one useful thing his father ever taught him. Orion, beta, the hunter. See his belt, see his head? Everything else he had learnt from Daadi, as she read to him from the books she wrote for children in beautiful Hindi, mixing folktale and mythology, each word sparkling like a jewel. Today she had come to his rescue. That story he told Poka and Angie was her gift, inherited by him. How else could he have spoken the way he had?

His new friends seemed moody and thoughtful. *It suits me, this closeness of being together without needing to talk. It gives me time to fill out, to fill my skin to bursting, as if I were a grape, or a balloon.* This was the true nature of joy then. The boy had never felt his whole being rise to the surface like this, eager and alive. There was no hollowness in his stomach now, no shivering under his skin, no anxiety inside his bones. At that moment he could have done anything. Every pore was wide open for the cool night to come streaming in. He was Orion the hunter, he was the sand under his legs, he was the muted crash of the waves.

He tilted his head so he could see the others. There was no moon, but the white sand was lit by the stars and he could see quite clearly, now that the glare of electric lights no longer hindered his vision. The lamps that were meant to light their way to the beach were, as he had suspected, useless. Only one shone faintly through its grimy glass. In season, they would all be fixed. They were debris, monsoon debris, and they could drift where they liked in the dark, cutting their feet on shells. Baldy, who thought of everything, had brought a torch. He looped it in front of them, hooting to scare away owls (so he said) and keeping up a patter like a tour guide. But once they settled down on the sand he had become absolutely quiet. The boy could see him lying on his back, looking straight up at the sky. Tiny sat next to him, a small figure of doubt. The boy hoped they had made up since morning. Poka had her head on Ciggy's bony lap (the other way round would have been nice!) and she was humming. Ciggy was smoking. The boy could see the tip of his cigarette glow and dim, dim and glow as he smoked. Baby and Dodo sat cross-legged, two statues. Tiger, Momo and Angie had decided to walk, three dots along the white edge where the sea began. From time to time Angie laughed out loud and the sound travelled back to them, sharp and disconnected. If he had been alone on the beach that laugh would have frightened the boy. Molly had become inconsequential, now that the boy knew he wasn't one of the seven. And yet he had been so openly warm towards him. The boy felt guilty. There he was, doing some funny exercise with his legs. Lift curl lift curl. All by himself.

There was something sad about these people. It was only now, brimming with gladness, that the boy could see it. They were boisterous and manic. They had a funny way of making new friends. They were cool (though Baby might have disagreed), the way they talked, smoked, teased. But now, in the star-quiet on the sand, they were sad. It was as if they had suddenly given up pretending and were allowing some unspoken sorrow to rise up and engulf them, tidal, beyond control.

He was imagining things.

He sat up. His neck hurt from the funny way he'd propped it on his arms. He felt gritty at the collar. Far off, beyond the curve of beach where he had not gone, a travelling beam pierced the dark. The lighthouse! They had driven to it the day they went to Fort Aguada, but it had been closed. How he had wanted to go in, climb up to the top and see the enormous lamp that threw its light across the water, warning of rocks and danger. It had been a childhood dream, to live in a lighthouse. There was a book his mother had read to him when he was a boy, about a lighthouse keeper and his son. Home was at the base of the tower, through a little red door, cosy on stormy nights. And work was above, climbing spiral stairs and lighting the lamp each evening. It was a romantic job. It suited his idea of himself, a lonely boy in another country, comforted by the sight of the ceaseless waves and the birds that flew by. At night, certain of the bright flare above, he would read by a smaller light inside, perfectly safe and sound. Stories of shipwrecks and mermaids. It was a beautiful, juvenile dream. And now here was a real lighthouse, the first he had ever seen in action, hidden but for the beacon it shone into the night.

The boy wished Momo was next to him, so his thoughts could travel into her by the sheer closeness of their bodies sitting silently together on the sand.

She seemed terribly far away, walking by the sea with her friends.

Poka was whistling now. It was some old song, from one of those black-and-white movies his mother liked to see. It made the boy nervous. These people were from another era, another time zone. What was he doing with them? How could they have anything in common? They were old... but the way they behaved! It sometimes made them seem younger than the people in his class, the ones he had only watched and not wanted to be friends with. It was as if they didn't care how they behaved or what anyone thought of them. They were beyond all that. They just *were*.

There should have been lights here. And food. A classmate had been to a place like that in Madras. Wild, he said, a disco on the beach. Just a bare wooden dance floor, huge speakers and the sea. The boy tried to imagine it here, on Cavelossim. It didn't fit. He couldn't imagine these melancholy people around him dancing at a disco by the sea. Throngs of people, shiny with sweat. Bare knees bending, hips twisting. Chilled beer, spicy food, everyone shouting to be heard above the music... It was better this way, kind of secret. His secret initiation into a group of ten mysterious strangers. He shook his head. He needed food.

'Insect,' said Baby's voice. 'Shall we forage for sustenance?'

The boy's heart contracted. Baby was telepathic. He had done it before in the room and now again.

'Yes,' he said, 'could do with some sustenance.' He said the word carefully, not wanting to sound fake. 'If everyone else wants to, that is.'

'Everyone?' Baby asked.

'No, I'm not hungry,' said Poka. 'I'm staying here.'

Baldy suddenly sat up and burst out, 'What! Poka not hungry? This is an epochal earth-shattering moment! Bring on the nautch girls!'

The boy heard Tiny sigh, a small, tired sound.

'Come on, people!' Baldy called out to Tiger, Angie and Momo, cupping his hands around his mouth. 'A feast is in order for the One Who Will Not Eat!'

One by one they shook off their stupor and slowly got up. Ciggy yanked Poka to her feet. She complained, but not too much. 'Not eating, I swear,' she insisted. Tiger, Momo and Angie looked mussed up and distant, blinking irritably when Baldy swung the torch at their faces as they came up. The boy felt his euphoria evaporating, as if he needed to be surrounded by sad and silent people to feel it. He looked back at the foaming sea before running over the ridge towards the hotel, and for one fleeting second it seemed to him like a warning.

It was the merriest dinner ever. Poka forgot her honourable intentions (as Baby described them) and ate as heartily as expected. The boy was a close contender which gave everyone reason to crow and whoop with laughter. 'Where do you put it, in your wrists?' Poka asked him enviously. Baldy dared the boy to eat ten gulab jamuns and he took the dare and won. The prize was an eleventh gulab jamun, fed to him by the delectable Angie. Ciggy introduced a burn-holes-in-the-tissue-stretched-over-the-glass game that made no sense but was played anyway with great seriousness by those sitting at his end, everyone borrowing his cigarette to burn the holes. The boy was delirious. Only last night (last night!) he had been sitting at another table, watching them eat and laugh and talk. Now he was sitting at their table, eating and laughing and talking *with* them. It gave him a weird sensation, as if there were two of him. He glanced at the table where he had sat with his parents. It was empty. He imagined the waiters' amazement. Reed-man seemed positively obsequious now that he knew he had friends. Not mamma's boy any more. The boy astonished even himself with his appetite.

There was music along with dinner. A live band. His poor mother, she had missed it. The boy felt strangely bad for her, now that she wasn't around to annoy him. She had hated the trip made in his honour. The music would have cheered her up. They sang Hindi songs though, and only when Angie walked up to the musicians and asked them to sing Goan songs did they break into the melodies that are supposed to be so special. They *were* special. Lovely hummy songs with lots of guitar and soft-sounding words. The family (still there!) was dancing. The father held his little kid by the arms and dangled him across the floor, the mother was itching to join them, he could tell, but she felt hampered by the presence of her in-laws. None of their group got up to dance, except Angie, who danced on her own. The others tapped their feet and swayed their shoulders. The boy felt horribly self-conscious. He was a miserable dancer. He hopped. He stepped on toes. He flung his arms into people's eyes. He could tell that Poka with her fluid fat was a good dancer, her flesh was rhythmic from the inside. So, surprisingly, was Baldy, who suddenly got up to join Angie. Angie's shoulder-shakes felt dramatically Brazilian. The boy had a vision of her doing a samba at the Mardi Gras, clad in very little. And then he was mortified, thinking about Angie like that with Momo sitting next to him. When they had dragged their chairs out, pure chance led to him getting the chair next to her. On one side Momo, on the other Molly. Over the music, over the gulab jamuns, over the bustle at their table, the boy was intensely aware of her. Her breathing, with that little wheeze he had heard in Tiger's room, alarming because it was unexpected. She ate very little, which frightened the boy. Tiger's conversation came back to him. Was she starving herself to death? But only last night he had seen her with a piled plate! She was not hungry, that's all. This close he could see a circular patch of tiny red marks on her forearm. They weren't pimples, nor scratches. He kept looking at the marks, secretly, as if willing them to vanish. Was she ill?

Finally, they got up. The loudmouths had wandered in and taken every available table (the foreigner was missing, must have left that evening) and their noise drowned the band, to whom they flung requests loud as insults. The band, sweating, stopped for a round of cold drinks and then resumed their music, bravely agreeing to please the loudmouths. The Goan songs stopped and they went back to the latest Hindi songs. Some of the loudmouths sang along. It was mayhem. The little family fled and they followed suit.

The boy had forgotten he had a room of his own. But the others hadn't. One by one, they trickled away, until Baby and he were left alone. Around them the sound of the band and the shouts of the men grew infernal.

'Can't hear myself think,' Baby said. 'Why don't we go to my room and chat?'

The boy's heart thudded. Baby wanted to chat with him, the insect! He nodded, hoping he didn't look too eager.

'There's some stuff I've written that might interest you,' Baby said, as they started walking towards the cottage.

The notebook. Baby meant him to read it!

'I'd love to,' he said, keeping his voice level.

'No one else will be there,' Baby said, as if he hadn't heard him. 'Tiger's joining the other potheads. When they're done they'll call us. We'll come back here, what say, near the pool, once the din subsides?'

The boy nodded, overcome by the thought that he was privy to the group's micro-planning. *Baby's friend.* His head whirled. They were in the room. Baby was switching on his laptop. And then he was talking, telling him the most unbelievable things...

Maybe an hour, maybe several hours passed, but it felt like mere minutes before Baldy's voice cut in, shouting outside the cottage, 'Come out come out, wherever you are! Deckchairs ahoy for miladies and lordships!'

As Baby obeyed and the boy followed suit, he wished, for a brief treacherous moment, that they didn't have to go just yet.

Eleven

It was as Baldy said. The loudmouths had managed to make a whole lot of deckchairs appear and had hogged them all day. Now that they had retired to their rooms the empty chairs lay scattered all around the pool. Ciggy and Molly were dragging them together when Baby and the boy arrived. Angie avoided the chairs and dangled her legs in the pool. The boy was sorely tempted to join her but he felt shy. Besides, the pool was a reminder of his humiliation. The water shimmered blue in the lights. So different from the dark swirling mass they had left behind at the beach, crashing and frothing. This was pretty and tamed. It was like looking at a sheet of glass with the light shining through. He had been so happy. He could have stayed that way forever, reading, listening, agreeing, asking, bursting with the awareness of Baby's faith in him, his openness... What would they do now? Without thinking, he said it aloud.

Baby heard him.

'Now,' he said, looking at the boy intently, 'now we tell you everything.'

'Do you believe in guilt?' Baby began. 'I do. Guilt and retribution. Crime and punishment. The great opposites that any moral man must face. Unless of course, he is blameless.

'I was a climber those days. A climber and a hiker. Pindari, Rohtang. Ice picks, ropes. Smelling ripe, not washing for days. Euphoric and unshaven, scratchy and smelly, we climbed. The world in our backpacks, provisions, stove, cigarettes, chocolate. In a hut far above humanity, we'd run into a man from our tribe. A Bengali, offering us boiled eggs in return for sugar. A Lucknawi, genteel and soft-spoken, as if he were receiving guests in his own home. For us, it was like distilling life into elementals. Air, water, stone. Food, drink, survival. It went to our heads. The air thinned, tempers frayed. We suspected each other of murder, of hiding bars of chocolate. We wept with exhaustion. We fought with each other, we fought against the rock. Some gave up midway and turned back. But every year, addicted to walking the knife-edge of endurance and sanity, we climbed.

'Then one year, one of us died. I was the one Yanky should have been roped to. Angry at something I had said about his girlfriend, he unhitched himself and shouted unprintable words into the air. To our left there was a drop of many hundred feet to a frozen river. To our right, a sheer wall of rock. We clung to the wall like spiders, roped and inching forward, spiked boots skidding. When he unroped himself, I tugged to make the one before me stop, and he the one before him. But before I could bring our inching cavalcade to a halt, before we could stop and persuade the fool to tie himself back on, we heard the scream. It echoed and died as he fell. Later, much later, the helicopter jittering in the gusty wind, almost slamming into the rock, the body recovered, frozen, broken at the neck. I never climbed again.

'Back in Delhi, ordinary life. The monotony of classes,

studying, pretending to. And then one morning, I woke up and found I couldn't get out of bed. When I tried, I fell and my roommate had to pick me up and put me back on the bed. I had slipped a disc. Two vertebrae were jammed against each other and would need to be stretched apart with an iron weight on my leg. I was moved to a hospital. In a white bed that winched up and down, washed, turned and cleaned by stout nurses with rough hands, I lay prone for two months.

'You see, dear insect, the only time I really loved a woman, she loved someone else. She was small, with a dimple in her chin and hair that frizzed madly around her little face. We had nothing in common, not even love. She wasn't into trekking or climbing. She'd laugh at us as we prepared for our trips. She'd wrinkle her nose at the thought of no baths for days. She was too delicate for such things. I could have carried her all the way up without tiring, she was that little. But she wouldn't let me. To her I was just a baby-faced boor, and though she was fond of me in the way that women are fond of pet dogs, love was out of the question.

'The one she loved was Yanky.

'And Yanky, big mutt that he was, didn't love her in return. He had his heart set on a big-boobed babe with a brain the size of a full stop. She had her own reasons for hanging around with old Yanks. She would shimmy up to him, waggling those enormous mammaries of hers and nestle against him as if she was a bird seeking protection, and Yanky would turn totally moony.

'When we teased him for betraying his intellectual self with that big-boob fixation of his, he would flush crimson and lose his command over his otherwise impeccable English.

'"You...big...*jerks*!"' he would finally manage to splutter. "You..."

'And giving up totally he would get up and walk off, leaving a crimson trail of anger behind him. It was one of our favourite entertainments, to tease Yanky about Jogita. Only, my teasing was shot through with a sensation that was strange even to me. It infuriated me that Yanky couldn't see how fortunate he was. *She*—beautiful darling fragile she—loved him and he didn't notice. Or he noticed and he didn't care. It made me want to break his face, knowing how much grief he caused her. And that's why it felt strange. That I should be willing to batter my friend because he couldn't love the woman I loved the way she loved him. Since when was I such a martyr? I should have used Yanky's inattention to make her fall in love with me, readily available, ready-to-please me. But I couldn't do it. Giving up all hopes of my own, I discovered in my heart the violent desire to make *her* hopes come true at least. It was humiliating. And that was another strange sensation. To discover in myself an infinite capacity for humiliation.

'"Tell me what you want me to do," I would beg her mutely every time the whole lot of us met on the lawns or in the canteen. "Just say the word."

'She never did but everything was clear to me from the bruised look in her eyes when she saw Jogita coming up to join us, her entire being braced against the moment when Jogita's hugely soft and perpetually moving body would come to rest, quivering, against Yanky's. She would say hi to Jogita in her usual sweet, slightly sing-song voice, but that didn't fool me. I could detect the tremor in that greeting, the effort that almost drained her, turning her pale even at the height of summer. I would stare directly at Jogita then, brazenly, daring her to feel ashamed. But, bimbette that she was, she saw nothing but another man crazy for her all too obvious charms, and the look she returned would always be brazen in return, and complicitous. It made me feel foully angry. How dare she assume I was interested in her!

'But all that was a mere distraction.

'The real thing was her anguish, so poorly concealed. The real thing was Yanky's *blindness*. If only I could tear him away from that cow, if only I could make myself heroic and loved for one instant by giving her what she wanted most, and then crawl off somewhere to die.

'I know, I can tell that even you think my thoughts those days were more befitting a schoolboy than a man. That's what happened when you were starved of the companionship of women. You turned abnormal. Either too cocky or too chicken. You could do nothing sanely, soberly. You wanted to marry the first girl who looked at you or you wanted to go to bed with as many of them as there were hours in the day. And when neither happened, you turned into a sort of nowhere man, taking what came your way, turning caddish without knowing it, slippery at the edges so that no girl could grab and get to keep you and turn you into a despicable prized possession.

'After my failed love for her, I never thought much about what women meant. They were functional, I used them perfunctorily and moved on. I certainly had matured.

'Sometimes I felt spiteful towards Yanky for doing that to me. For making me the one who had to cope with telling her, "Yanky's dead." For having to be the one who sat with her and consoled her and rocked her like a baby, only to know that now, when there might have been a chance for me, I had well and truly lost her forever. After a while she said I reminded her too much of him, we had been such good friends, always together. She wanted to forget. She drifted out of our group and I only saw her sometimes, passing by amidst drifts of chattering girls or walking easily and happily with a guy, slowly repairing her life.

'If she had married me in the first place, the day I asked her, the very first day I met her, everything would have turned out different. Yanky would have been alive, and so would I. Life would have been beautiful.

'Sometimes, insect, the strangest things are beautiful. The hepatitis B virus, for instance. Like the palest coral, clumped in patches, tainted only by our knowledge of what it is. Have you ever seen a picture of it? I can bet that if you showed it around without saying anything, you'd have women cooing over how pretty it was.

'Or say a picture of acute lymphocytic leukaemia. Floating pebbles, vivid purple and lovely lavender. I recall thinking when I first saw it how it could easily have been an art student's exercise in abstraction, modern but not cold. Could have been anything but the picture of a cancer eating away at the very substance of life...

'Yanky and I had been roped together at the waist minutes before he fell. In hospital, I felt as if he had pulled me down with him after all. And then I felt guilty imagining that my plight was in any way comparable to his. He was dead. I was alive, even though it didn't feel that way. My leg grew numb and heavy like the weight at its edge. With the traction removed, I still felt limbless, a pillar of congealed flesh from the waist down. I couldn't scratch myself. I couldn't turn unless someone turned me. I had to pee and crap into a ceramic bowl that stank under my bed. My body was open to inspection, injections, sponges, vitamins, examination, cross-examination, but not to human contact. No one touched me because they wanted to, but because they had to. It was touch based on duty, a duty filled with revulsion. I withered. And, in my desperation, I picked up a book my roommate—the one who picked me off the floor—had left for me one endless sultry afternoon.

'It was a slim volume titled *Doctor Brodie's Report*. It was by a guy I had never heard of. Jorge Luis Borges. It made me crack a smile, that rhyming long name I didn't know. The cover was macabre. A skeleton gazing philosophically at a skull. Was it my roommate's idea of a joke, chosen for thematic similarity to my present doctor-riddled existence? At least it made me smile, the first smile in as far as I could remember. I opened the book and started reading.

'The book had nothing to do with doctors. In fact, it was like nothing I had ever read. I didn't understand it. I read it at one stretch, the eleven very short stories one after the other, and I felt swamped by something big and strange and infinitely complex. This might amuse you, insect, to know that I wasn't, in those days, a reader. Not of books at any rate, just magazines and the mandatory daily news. But it wasn't my status as a non-reader that made me feel overwhelmed. It was something else. The language was simple, the characters described in a few crisp and clear words, but the intent! The intent was profound, as if below those crisp words lay an abyss I only had to lean forward a little to see into. There was a secret at the bottom of that abyss, and you had to risk your life if you wanted to glimpse it. It terrified and bewitched me. I started reading the stories again, this time in reverse order. I had grasped by then that just because they were short didn't mean I had to race through them. This time, I wanted to savour each one separately, slowly, try and comprehend the meaning. Each story was an enigma and reading closely was the only key.

'My roommate did more than pick me off the floor. He picked me up out of the real world and set me down in unreality.

'Doctor Brodie wasn't a doctor. He was a missionary who found himself among a strange tribe he called the Yahoos. Their king was a blind limbless torso, covered in dung and deeply powerful. After counting to four, they went straight to many. Sometimes one of them became a poet and he was feared like a god and shunned. The whole story was written as if it were a real report, made by some scholar. It was intensely weird.

'There were others as weird, insect, some more, some less. But the one that really psyched me out was called The Gospel According to Saint Mark. A young guy, a medical student, visits a cousin in the country. While his cousin is away, a storm destroys the foreman's hut, and the foreman and his family move into the main house. They're illiterate, can barely speak properly. Out of sheer boredom the student decides to read to them from an old Bible he finds. They listen to him like children. They grow more and more respectful towards him. He enjoys his role, and one night when the foreman's daughter enters his bed, he enjoys her too. Next morning, he realizes the banging he has been hearing since the previous day is not for repairing the foreman's roof. They've been making him a cross. He's going to be crucified.

'I shuddered and asked my roommate to get me more. He did, scrounging them from the second-hand bookshops in CP. I read as if in a trance. This Jorge Luis Borges wrote as if in a trance. Nothing really happened in his stories, no action, or what I had, until then, thought action to be. I should have been bored stiff. But instead I felt as if my mind was being peeled open. There were tigers in his stories, imaginary tigers, there were old men obsessed with objects that ruined them, there were young men killing and being killed with knives, there were knives becoming the people who had used them.

'Suddenly it became clear to me. I was merely a symbol in someone else's universe. I was being dreamed. Everything that happened to me was happening to my double whom I had not met, yet. Or maybe I was the double. I was the double of the man who fell off the cliff because of me.

'It should have scared me. Instead, in my medicated haze, I felt comforted being inside that labyrinth of words.

'I lost the use of my legs for two months. When it was over, I had to learn how to walk again. The soles of my feet were crusted with scabs. My legs, transformed by disuse, felt like ropes that would coil noiselessly onto the floor if I stood up. I whimpered like a baby getting out of the wheelchair. They had to make me. After hating the bed, the smell, the nurses, the room, I was afraid to leave them behind.

'I didn't leave everything behind. I took one thing away, for good.

'"Spondylitis," my doctor told me, cheerily. "Sometimes happens to slip disc cases. Lifelong caution, mind you. Wear the belt and the collar when travelling. No sitting in bad postures for long stretches, no lifting heavy weights, no aerobic exercises, only a bit of yoga, supervised. There's only one thing you can do with spondylitis—learn to live with it. Good luck."

'And he shook my hand as if he were congratulating a particularly bright student.

'A collar for my neck, a belt for my waist. I felt like that rope had never been untied.

'I went back to my hostel room. My roommate was happy to have me back, from now I could do my own book-scrounging. My friends threw a welcome-back party in the college canteen, keema and scrambled eggs and toast and tea. The girlfriends I climbed with were glad at my recovery, but not overjoyed. They had found new climbing partners. They talked excitedly of the next trek. My other girlfriends talked of the play they were doing. My male friends ate prodigious amounts of food in my honour and slapped me on the back so I choked with fear of yet another dislocation, cursing myself for not warning them in advance, cursing them for not knowing. When I told them, sharply, not to be so rough, they looked at me as if I was paranoid.

'I *was* paranoid. I gave up volleyball. I gave up riding my roommate's bike at breakneck speeds. The word *breakneck* frightened me. I was afraid of buses, what if a sudden jerk led to another slipped disc? I tried to walk everywhere, which meant I didn't get very far. The university grounds became my prison. The only trips I took were to CP in one of the girlfriends' cars. There I would get off and scrounge to my heart's content. I picked up anything that looked interesting, or odd. Jorge Luis Borges had put the bug into me. I had become addicted—to reading. My male friends guffawed at me. I had never been intellectual. My intellectual friends guffawed at me. Secretly, at another time, another place, I might have guffawed at myself. But right then what I was doing was too serious to be funny. If I were the double of a dead man, I would need a new skin to disguise myself in. New skins didn't come easy. They took time, and diligence.

'I pored over my finds like one of those obsessive men in the stories. I realized as I read that the more morbid and off-centre they were, the better I liked them. Death enchanted me, the way slippery rock faces once had. Death and disease. At first, that led me to the obvious titles. *Death in Venice. Illness as Metaphor. Cancer Ward. Coma.* But then, as the reading became an end in itself, I picked up any title that intrigued. I was a traveller without a map. All the careful planning that my climbing days had taught me I threw away, so much unwanted baggage. I let chance lead me. And so, my trail grew stranger. Death lurked still, but in devious ways. The curious titles beckoned me in. *The Sailor Who Fell From Grace With The Sea*, that's one I will never forget. Like Doctor Brodie, it fell slim and mysterious into my hands. It was a twisted world of Japanese boys, for whom killing was an act of friendship, an act of restoration. The writer was a Yukio Mishima.

'A new trail was laid. I rooted out every Mishima the pavements of Delhi had to offer. And there were many. *Thirst For Love. Forbidden Colours. After the Banquet. The Sound of Waves.* They sounded like romantic pulp novels. The only thing they romanticized was death. Who was this man? Every introduction informed me that he had killed himself after finishing his most famous work. Why? Consumed by a desire to understand this morbid man with the magnificent pen, I looked everywhere for *The Sea of Fertility*. I found it, four books in one hardback volume, the print tiny and exasperating. That didn't stop me. If my back was shot to pieces, my eyes were in mint condition. Hammer and tongs, I read, forgetting classes, friends, company. My girlfriends had begun to look at me worriedly whenever they ran into me at the canteen, shovelling toast into my mouth, not looking up to say hello.

'"Are you all right?" they'd ask.

'"Yup, absolutely," I'd say and plunge back into my teeming silent world. I knew they thought Yanky's death had affected my brain, not my spine. I could tell from the way they suddenly stopped talking when I passed, or came up to me looking sorry and doggy-eyed. But I had other things to think about. Shunsuke, an aged professor, corrupting a beautiful young boy. Etsuko, delicate and lovely, cutting off the head of the man she loves because he spurned her. Kioyaki dying, white as the snow outside his window. I felt fragile and battered, as if all those things had happened to me. And incredibly, I felt safe.

'It's hard to believe I stayed in that other world for so long. I have no recollection of my last year in college. I know I passed, but not an exam do I remember writing, not a single lecture do I remember attending. Conversing with me became impossible, as I would only talk if the subject was a writer I was reading. I was irritated by the others' lack of interest. I was even irritated by their interest, as if they were encroaching on my precious terrain. I scorned writers who wrote in English. It's all elsewhere, I became fond of announcing, English Literature is dead. I read Robbe-Grillet and Marguerite Duras. I read Adolfo Casares simply because he was Borges's friend. I read Manuel Puig. I read Jean Genet. Overnight, I wanted to become the most well-read person on the planet. And I took notes, copious notes, as if I were a scholar preparing for bigger things.

'Bigger things meant normalcy. Emerging from my reading trance, I found I was all alone. My friends had long abandoned me. My roommate, comrade, mentor, saviour-in-time-of-sickness had gone abroad. My family? I couldn't remember the last time I had spoken to them, except to ask for money. Suddenly I had no room to live in any more, no dining room to eat at, no canteen where I could drink endless cups of tea on credit. I needed to find a job. I walked into a publishing house and offered them my services. My commerce degree had nothing to do with 'suitability for the post'. I could see the puzzlement on the face of the woman who had, by some miracle, agreed to see me. She was in marketing, was I looking for an opening in marketing? Before I could answer, another woman walked into the room without knocking, perched on the table and asked me casually, "So, who are your favourite authors?"

'It was a dream question. It led to a conversation that left the other, puzzled woman completely out. It was a duel of tastes, like something in a Borgesian tale. She hated Mishima, but was sold on Puig. She adored Borges, and what do you know, she had read Adolfo! I got the job that very day.

'I was the lowliest of the low. I was given every task that no one else wanted to do. I had to check manuscripts for typo errors, or I had to put in and remove commas. Sometimes I had to key in the manuscript myself. The manuscripts were nothing like what the woman and I had raved about. They were self-help books and alternative medicine and Chinese cooking for Indian housewives. My brain frizzled. I was paid a pittance. But I hung on for that rented room, that bed, that lamp by the bed throwing its circle of light on my book before I slept.

'It's only now that I realize, insect, what I was doing. I was trying to lead the life Yanky might have lived. Yanky was Eng. Lit., so bright only a couple of professors matched up to him. Yanky was my best pal, in the way only two diametrically opposite people can be best pals. I had coaxed him into climbing. He had taken to it with the ease of a natural. It killed him. That was the big picture. The small picture was that if I hadn't irritated him on the rock face that day he would never have unhitched himself. So I killed him both ways. I broke his neck as surely as if I had done it with my own bare hands.

'It's taken me ten years to figure that out. Ten bloody years of becoming a nowhere man. And always, hanging over me like the Damoclean sword I only learnt of in my twenties, my unreliable body. Not mine any more to rappel effortlessly over rock. Not mine to heave and heft a bulging rucksack onto a waiting buddy's back. I became an old man, fussing over every twinge. I moved up from being the lowliest of the low to assistant editor, then editor. I sat at meetings discussing whether ayurveda was already out. My book collection grew exponentially. In the office I was considered a bit of a guru on all matters literary. Young trainees looked at me wide-eyed, hoping I would teach them some useful literary lingo to help them job-hop-skip-and-jump. I took some of them home, hoping my *erudition* would rub off on them. It didn't work. Instead, they rubbed off on me and I began listening to remixes and saying "awesome". It was ghastly.

'And then I met Yanky's brother at a publishing party. I didn't even know he had a brother. Just back from the States. A best-selling author. A couple of prizes under his belt. Very debonair, very in. He struck me as shallow and disgusting, but I swallowed my dislike for Yanky's sake.

'"Awful, tragic," he said, shaking his head at imaginary

gnats. "He was always the star in the family, my kid brother, bright, but frittering it away, no focus. I told him, Yanks, you need to focus, but he always knew better. Great potential. What a waste."

'I could have knocked him to the ground. My mourning was not even halfway done, and here was his brother with a mouthful of platitudes. Feeling sick, I accepted the invitation to his house.

'By then I had a new foe to deal with. As if a spinal problem wasn't enough, my bones went brittle.

'"Osteoporosis, my boy," my new south Delhi doctor affirmed. "Nothing that can't be handled with vitamins and a diet. And lots of sun."

'Lots of sun! In Delhi summers that meant sunstroke. Dehydration. Gastro. I stared at my doctor, uncomprehending. He patted my back cheerfully and saw me out, clutching an arm-long list of medication.

'When I walked I feared bumping into things. I had read Firdaus Kanga. I knew how bad it could be. And though the doc had assured me I was nowhere in that league, I felt my bones crumbling at the very thought of collision. My most dreaded office calamity was bumping into someone around a corner. I never hurried around corners. I avoided corners, preferring to stay static, a locus of immobility. I feared the edges of doors, cupboards, tables. I feared everything at hip level, as if furniture had a malign will of its own, waiting to crash against my weakened skeleton. I had become the skeleton on the cover of *Doctor Brodie's Report*, contemplating my own mortality. If earlier I had walked slowly, my waist constricted underneath my orthopaedic belt, now I crawled. I was senior enough to be granted some eccentricities. I was left alone.

'I went to Yanky's brother's house, drawn by a morbid desire to make myself suffer. He appalled me, but that too was right in the scheme of things. It was a modern home, muted and abstract. His wife was an artist back in New York. She wore black and looked like a spider with fingernails. It was a wine and cheese party as if after an art opening. The works on the walls were hers of course. And Delhi was *so* refreshing after New York, *so* unaffected. The laughter in the room was as tinkly as spoons tapping against glass. I felt suffocated. A bomb would be nice, I thought, murderously nursing a Médoc. A bloody bomb to wipe them all out. Apart from a whole swarm of strangers, the entire publishing fraternity was at that party. I ought to have circulated, networked, made some fantastic deal or another by the end of the evening, but all I did was seethe. It was as if Yanky's brother had burst the soundproof bubble I had encased myself in ever since the accident. Nothing had penetrated all this time, except the books. And now the world was pouring in through the gash he had unknowingly made with his sudden appearance. My bones felt brittle with rage.

'I entertained myself by imagining what horrible illnesses the people in that room were concealing beneath their designer clothes. Eczema. Rectal cancer. Ringworm. Pustules. Scratchy loathsome vile diseases in the vilest places. It made me feel a bit better. And then the calamity I had been dreading in office happened right there. A woman walked full-tilt into me. My rib cage impacted, my wine glass tumbled out of my hand onto the carpet and I almost followed it.

'It could have been a lot worse. The woman who walked into me was so well cushioned she softened the blow. I almost didn't mind the idea of a replay. She was all apologies. She picked up the glass, wiped the stain on the carpet with her napkin and made it worse, held me by the shoulders as if checking for cracks, giggled breathlessly and introduced me to her friend.

'That's when I realized what a narrow escape I had really had. If I had bumped into her friend, I might just have splintered all over. He was tall and bony, all angles and elbows. He had a cigarette stuck on his lower lip and his eyes glinted when he saw his girlfriend blow over me like a hurricane. He grinned a little and said, "Smoke?" I hadn't smoked since my climbing days. But I took that cigarette like it was a lifeline. As I inhaled that familiar taste, that smell, I felt dizzy. It had been so long. In the room with me were two other people. Real people. I held out my hand and introduced myself.'

Twelve

'Naturally we took him home, he looked so hopeless standing in that room all by himself,' said Poka. 'Ciggy and I were not an item then, as Baby had imagined, just friends. Home was where Angie and I stayed. Angie was amused by what she called our pickup and we made a night of it, talking until dawn. Not surprisingly, Baby became one of us, and we went out often, the four of us. Or increasingly, we stayed in, pigging out on beer and pizza.

'It was uncanny actually, Baby's arrival in our lives. We ribbed him to hell about his notebook entries, but I wasn't sure we thought they were funny. I, for one, was in a mess. My friend's younger sister had just died in a car crash. She was nineteen. Her much older boyfriend had been driving, drunk. I loved Kimi, her ardent face, her sensational voice. She played the piano like a diva and when she sang, rooms lit up. I remember going to her place after her death and walking in on her parents sitting numbly in the dark, staring at the television, which they had not put on. They had nothing to say. She had been in a coma for nineteen days before she died. One day for each year of her life. I never met her boyfriend, but even the thought of him made me feel murderous. Why couldn't *he* have died instead?

'I'd already met the Old Lady by then. I had a cough that had lasted for three months. Nothing worked, ginger-and-tulsi tea, honey, pills, syrups, lozenges, nothing. Sick of feeling sick, I visited her. She sat in the ground floor of an old house in Gujranwala. On benches pressed against three walls sat lines of patients. There was no separate chamber. The Old Lady met everyone in that room, everyone's problems were discussed out in the open, no matter how private or shameful. She was dreadfully old, ninety-three, the regulars told me, and she was formidable. She took one look at you and told you what was wrong, and not just with your body. She treated everyone like a child, no matter how old you were. Naturally, for her own immense age gave her the aura of an unquestionable, impregnable deity. I suspected some people came, travelling long distances, merely to look at her. Here was a person who had lived a whole century, almost! They gazed at her, as if by looking hard enough they could make the secret of her long life reveal itself. She didn't appear all that ancient, though. Her skin was mottled, her hands shook as she poured the little white pills into the glass bottles, and patients had to lean towards her and shout out their troubles, but her eyes were clear, her mind was sharp and her tongue was sharper.

'I had a ringside view and it almost made me forget why I was there. I watched in rapt admiration as she took on her patients. A dark lady with inflamed skin turned out to be a policewoman. She had to stand for anything between twelve to eighteen hours at her post. She was single and had giddy spells. Her skin erupted. The Old Lady asked about her periods. The dark lady blushed livid and said her periods were painful.

'"Don't worry," said the Old Lady, giving her a wicked all-knowing smile, "I'll fix everything else, you just go and get married."

'The man who was with the policewoman looked embarrassed. Was he her lover or her father? Father, I thought, embarrassed at having to hear about his daughter's monthlies before a roomful of strangers. They left, thanking the Old Lady profusely.

'An old man had ulcers. Another old man constipation. One woman was too fat, her sister too skinny. Discreetly, pretending the room wasn't greedily eavesdropping, drinking in every sight and sound, women confessed, raised their saris to show their cracked, spotted, bleeding, oozing feet. Men untucked their shirts and lifted them up, showing chest, back or stomach. Children stuck out their tongues, said aah and clamoured for the sweet sugar pills which they were given handfuls of and which they strewed around the room like Hansel and Gretel's trail through the forest. It was a community theatre of ailments. Everyone participated, everyone watched. And the Old Lady directed it all, a grand old mistress of ceremonies.

'It was the Rajasthani family that brought out the maestro in her. A very young wife with her child, her husband, and a supremely confident, slightly older woman, who, it turned out, was the young mother's sister. The young wife-and-mother looked stricken. The child sat passively, uninterested in sugar balls or the other kids. The confident woman took the lead. Her sister had come all the way from Udaipur. It seemed the little boy was not developing. He was underweight, one side of him flopped when he walked, he had fits, and he ate next to nothing.

'"Bring him here," the Old Lady commanded. He was

brought. She examined his chest, a pitiful bony little chest, and tapped him on the back. She found out his name and made him smile. Then she turned to the mother and said, "*You* are a very timid person and the result is your son!"

'It was like a prophecy. The older sister nodded her head vigorously and said, "Yes, she's very timid, she's always scared he'll fall down, he'll fall ill."

'The husband who had been sitting modestly in the background, suddenly became animated and said, "Yes, even I tell her but she doesn't listen!"

'He was a good-looking man, tall, with clean features. He looked gentle, innocuous in this drama of discovery and diagnosis, but I had the feeling his wife was afraid of him. She was afraid of him and afraid of being a mother so young. Given a chance she would weep. The Old Lady was so overpowering. She hectored her, "Let him grow! Do not stifle him with your timidity (she said this phrase in English which made me wonder how much the mother understood, poor creature, pale with fright), it will harm him for life! Let him run and play, let him fall down and get hurt. Push him forward, don't pull him back!"

'The husband nodded vigorously.

'"And you," she had spied the nodding husband, "you better give your wife some courage! Don't frighten her even more!"

'He looked sheepish, like a chastised schoolboy. He was not blameless, as he had imagined. The Old Lady turned back to the sister, obviously having identified her as the only sensible one in the group, and said, "Make her understand. I will give medicines for the boy. But the real medicine is a mother's courage!"

'It was virtuoso. I almost clapped. The Old Lady was not just a medicine woman, she was counsellor, psychic and shrink. I felt giddy at the thought of what revelations she might make about me.

'Hoping to be told deep dark secrets about myself that would change my life forever, I leaned forward humbly, expectantly, and let her feel my pulse.

'"What is the problem?" she said, after listening with closed eyes to what I hoped was a strong and healthy pulse. I told her about my cough. She listened and said, "How are your periods?" as if they were my pet dogs or potted plants. She asked all the women about their periods and she warned all the men not to eat yam.

'"Perfectly normal," I said, "no cramps."

'"Good," she said and, without explaining another thing, made a note of my medicines in her fat ledger, keeping accounts of half of Delhi's sick in her crabby handwriting. This close I could see the discolorations on her papery skin. She wore a lovely crisp cotton sari and a microscopic bindi glittered between her eyebrows. Her hair had dwindled to a wisp, but was pinned carefully to her head. She took pains with her appearance, it was important not to let go. I felt deeply let down. Where was the insight, the utterance, the prophecy like the one she had made to the petrified young mother? Or at least, where were the admonitions about unhealthy diets and bad modern habits? Why did she think I was well adjusted and sensible enough not to need her advice? I resented being taken for a stable, sensible adult. I wanted the Old Lady to draw deep from the well of her ninety-three years and comfort me with something more than little white pills. I wanted revelation. I left, swearing she was a sham.

'She wasn't. My cough began to ease out. I went back. Something new had started happening, and I told her about it. A lump on my eye, a pain in my side, for every little thing that happened to me, I went to her, that's how much I believed in her powers. The cough had long gone, and still I returned to that poky room as if compelled. The theatre had now worn thin. I could see she wasn't a saint. She lost her temper with the older kids who talked too much. She scolded the women who forgot their bottles. She bullied the thinnest, quietest ones and told them to stop being sissies.

'"Look at me," she said, "I lived rough and tough, and you see the result!"

'She revelled in her old age, her lucid mind, her lack of complaints. She sat, more like a frog than a queen and held court, wielding her ninety-three years over us like a sword. I decided I didn't like her, but I returned. Everything I came for got cured, only something new appeared and so I had a genuine reason for being her devotee after all.

'I felt better and better. But one Sunday, after a lovely lazy morning at home with a crate of beer and the usual suspects, around evening, I felt as if I was dying. It was a physical sensation. Talking about it cannot begin to express the dread, the helplessness that crept through me from my feet up to my heart. I was laughing uproariously at something Baby had said, and suddenly I was struck down.

'"My feet are getting cold," I told them.

'"Why, scared of what Ciggy might do if you're alone?" they joked.

'Then they saw I wasn't kidding.

'"Sit down, breathe," they said, gentle and a little scared. "It'll pass."

'"I can't feel my hands," I said, "I can't feel my feet."

'"Wait, I'll rub them," Angie said, and she did. It didn't help.

'"My heart," I said, "it's beating too fast. Here."

'I took Angie's hand and placed it on my chest so she could feel the tremor ripping through me like a storm. She said she couldn't feel anything. I felt dreadfully alone. I crossed my legs and did the mudras Angie had taught me. Deep breathing, stillness. I came out shivering like a leaf. It seemed as if any minute my limbs would scatter in different directions. I sat on the cold floor, hoping the ground would earth me. It wasn't the beer. It wasn't the grass. I hadn't smoked, and anyway grass only made me giggle. This was coming from inside me, and it was taking over.

'"Try salt," Baby said, "a pinch of salt, it could be low blood pressure."

'I licked a dab of salt off my damp palm. It didn't help. Sugar. It didn't help.

'"I know," said Angie and brought out a chocolate from the fridge. I ate it. It didn't help. I wanted to weep and thrash about on the floor. My heart was uncontrollable. I kept putting my hand on my chest as if I could catch hold of it and slow it down.

'"Wait, be normal," said Angie. "The more you panic, the more you panic. Let's eat dinner."

'We ate dinner, me not tasting anything. They talked and laughed around me, trying to make everything seem normal. I loved them for it, but it didn't help. They put me to bed like a baby. I was afraid to close my eyes. What if I never woke up again? I closed my eyes. I could hear my heart racing, speeding up, sprinting past the last barrier and dropping dead.

'I woke up and it was gone.

'"It's gone," I said at breakfast.

'"See, I told you," smiled Angie.

'But I had spoken too soon. It leapt out at me during lunchtime in the office. I was sitting down to eat out of someone else's lunchbox, when it grabbed me by the knees. I recognized the familiar lurch, the creeping cold, the weakness. It's here, I thought. Ignore it. I broke a piece of paratha and ate. It crept up. Ignore it, it'll go away, I commanded myself. The more you panic, the more you panic. It had reached my heart and I was trembling. No one saw me trembling. Numb with disaster, I sat, eating tiny pieces of paratha as if that alone could save me. My brain seemed to shut down. It clogged and everything around me receded into greyness. The one whose paratha I had burgled was talking to me, and I was answering but she was far, far away. Sound died. I was trapped inside my body which was letting me down, closing down one part at a time with me trapped inside, unable to get out. I got up and walked away. In the loo I sat down and cried. Great heaving sobs, not caring if anyone heard. What was happening to me? My feet were cold. As I cried hot gushing tears, I felt warmer. The exertion of crying so hard heated me up. I felt the life-giving warmth and stopped crying. *You're okay, all right?* I whispered to myself. *You're okay.* I got out and washed my face. It had gone.

'It kept coming back. I dreaded the good moments, knowing that just around the corner of every happy moment lay the grey beast, waiting to pounce and bring me down. I was constantly alert. I loved the safe times so much I started weeping thinking how soon they'd be over, ambushed by the bad ones. It could hit me any time. Waiting for an auto. Eating an ice cream. Sitting next to Ciggy sharing his smoke.

I couldn't explain what it was like. "I feel sad," I'd say, looking at their worried, puzzled faces. But it was more than sad. It was anguish. When I lay down, trying to ease its passage out of my body, helping it escape by lying down, I'd feel the suffocating weight of not knowing what it was.

'"Everyone is going to die," I found myself keening once, knees dragged up to my chin, rocking myself. "Everyone is going to die."

'Angie held me hard, but I shuddered and shrank, as if from a fiend. It seems like such a melodrama now, but then it was all too real. Go see your doctor, they said, my sweet friends. I went. My heart was perfectly okay, the doctor said. My reflexes. My blood pressure. I asked him if I should get a brain scan and an MRI but he laughed.

'"You're perfectly fine!" he said. "Now go!"

'I didn't tell him about *it*. I was too scared he would think I was mad.

'It was like learning to live with a ghost. I constantly sensed its presence and dreaded its coming, but I couldn't shake it off. I had forgotten what life was like before this *thing* happened to me. One weekend when I was alone, I felt a terrible pain in my heart. It's an attack, I thought. The more I thought about it the more I knew it was true. I had had a terrible presentiment that this would happen on the very weekend the three of them were away. I went to the phone. Not to call my doctor but Angie.

'"Listen, I'm feeling very bad," I said, when I got through at last. My mouth was metal. "I just needed to tell someone. I hope it'll pass."

'"It'll pass," she said, "just keep talking to me." And so we talked, long distance, racking up enormous bills, because I knew if I didn't, I'd die. The pain passed and I slept. They came back the next day, ruining their weekend. I almost wept when I saw them, and I was so happy that it hit me at once, starting from my toes, creeping up.

'I constantly thought about death. I had never been afraid of dying until then, never. I had never even been afraid of death. When I was fifteen, my grandfather died and I had gone alone to see him in the dead of night in that old haunted house where he lived after my granny's death. I sat by him and kissed his cold forehead without an iota of fear. I had done everything. Not needles, but everything else, shored by an absolute, idiotic and never-breached trust in the goodness of strangers. And now, cleaned-up, secure, content, safer than ever with a job and a circle of friends, I was deeply, inextricably afraid.

'There was one good thing that came out of it. I realized I was in love with Ciggy. The extent of my terror about losing him confirmed it. I had dreams of waking up to find him dead, knowing that I had killed him. I watched him like a hawk, certain he had concealed some debilitating illness from me. I began counting his cigarettes, dreading that he would get lung cancer and die spewing blood. I felt heartbroken when he grinned at me in that loopy way of his, certain that was the last time I'd see that grin. Of course I couldn't tell him. I was dying, I was a psycho, I had panic attacks like other people had dal-chawal, he didn't need that in his life! And so I died a little every day, watching him, wanting him, and never wanting him to know.

'I took a train home to Cal, too afraid to fly. In the train, it engulfed me. Hurtling through the night, cut off from everything, I was at its mercy. I called Angie Baby Ciggy from my cell, thanking my stars there was a signal, and told them. I calmed down. I reached Cal and after spending two days there, I flew back. I was afraid my mother would find out. She knew her daughter. She would catch me having one of my attacks, and it would multiply, a terrible infection swamping families and cities as I fled.

'Back in Delhi I visited my doctor.

'"I'm having panic attacks," I said, feeling foolish. "I'm getting palpitations. My feet and hands freeze and I can't breathe."

'He didn't laugh or tell me I was imagining things. He heard me out and said, in that wonderfully gentle way of his, "Are you on any medication?"

'"No," I said. "Nothing but vitamin capsules and the Old Lady's pills."

I told him all about my visits to her, how miraculously she cured everything.

'"Stop them at once," he said, more serious than I'd ever seen him.

'"But—"

'"That can be the only reason," he said.

'I nodded my head, not believing him.

'"And what if it strikes again?" I said, oddly relieved to have got it out in the open, not hidden away inside me like a tumour.

'"Take one of these," he said, and he wrote me out a chit.

'Restyl, the chit said, in his neat undoctorly hand. What an appropriate name. Rest. Still. I bought a leaf of Restyl and just looking at the little pink tablets made me calm. I thought of a painting by Matisse. *Luxe, calme, volupté*. It soothed me.

'I never got the chills again. Once, on holiday, I felt it, like a passing tweak on the cheek by a teasing friend, and I panicked for a second, but that was all. I don't know if it was stopping the Old Lady's medicines that did it, or the knowledge of Restyl in my purse, waiting like a magic potion to rescue me. I never had to take it. Not once.

'Later, I realized it must have been the Old Lady's pills after all. She was trying to fix something I hadn't asked her to fix. Maybe she saw in me a malaise too grim to be told and so, surreptitiously, under cover of coughs and colds and sties and aches, she went about tinkering with my insides. She was shifting tides inside me, resetting the clocks. She was ambitious and she was dangerous. She held too much power in those crabby hands of hers, in her imperious voice that no one dared to argue with, in her reading of symptoms from a throb in the wrist, not waiting to be told, but deducing stealthily like an investigator of the soul. Maybe if I had survived her course, I would have been cleansed of all past, present and future ills, but the price was too high. She had been wringing me out like a rag and I hadn't been able to bear it. I threw away her little glass bottles, still half-full, and I smiled at how she would have scolded.

'And so, after the worst time in my life, came the best. Ciggy moved in and Angie complained about noise levels going up at all the wrong times in all the wrong places. We were very happy. I loved Ciggy, and he me.

'"Hitch up with Baby-face," we teased Angie, making Baby blush like a nun.

'"Any time," Angie said, sitting on his lap, crushing him, knowing they would always be dearer to each other than life and never ruin it by becoming lovers.

'When Ciggy got transferred to Bombay I asked for a transfer too. It came through and we left together. Baby moved in with Angie, to save on rent. We missed them sorely in Bombay, city of nameless souls. Then, like an avalanche, they all moved. Angie first, then ten months later, Baby. Our little gang was together again. It felt like a fairy tale. But somewhere, circumspectly present, like a bruise on the underside of a pear, I felt inside me a dark spot, a stain reminding me that I was capable of dwindling to nothing. It was a reminder of chaos lurking just below the surface. Maybe in my family, hidden from me by my wise parents, there were cases of madness, dementia, instability. Something had come unhinged when I took those little white pills. The word *unhinged* disturbed me. I felt like a door gone askew, refusing to shut tight. I had to watch over myself. If I sensed myself slipping away, I would have to raise an alarm and be saved. If I felt myself wanting to repeat compulsively a certain action until the action built into a frenzy, I would have to stop and walk away. I would have to be happy, but not delirious, because with delirium came madness. I would have to try and achieve a kind of calm, but not the dead calm of a pond choked with waxen lilies. I felt like I was many people. Inside me, many people, packed into one small place. Many terrains, bumpy, hilly, treacherous, uninhabited, swarming. I would have to enter them carefully. I would have to be gentle with what floated up and what lay buried. I would have to want neither too much nor too little. It was uncanny. I was talking like one of Baby's notebooks, filled with notes on illness, insanity, death, degeneration. Maybe what I needed was a notebook of my own, where I could write down the few wise things that would help to keep me sane.'

Thirteen

'Lolly had told me about this new friend of hers from work,' Baldy said. 'Poka, she called her. With a name like that how could I not want to meet her at once? The Institute had teemed with Bongs. Bongs and Mallus. I considered myself an honorary member of both tribes. So this Poka, what was she, a boi-poka, a gubrey-poka or a chhar-poka? I insisted Lolly call Poka and her friends over to her place (naturally my own place was only fit for the cockroaches that crawled out of the sink every night) and make them—poor Dilliwallas—feel at home. I knew all about Poka's boyfriend Ciggy and their other friend Baby. I spent five minutes laughing silently, a sort of slow hardeehardeehar of cosmic proportions. What names they had, these Dilliwallas! Lolly gave me a look. She was—had been—a true-blue Dilliwalla. And what about you, *Cracker*, her look said pointedly. "What about me?" I laughed back. "I'm just getting ready for some fun."

'You see, Pappu-mian, Lolly believed in living as if she were the imperious mother of a large and noisy brood of hormonal teenagers, blasting acid rock in their rooms. To spare herself from their (purely imaginary) assaults on her sensitive need for peace and quiet, she had found herself a house that was vast. There were *five* bedrooms, and each door sealed you away from the rest of the house into what could have easily passed off as one normal-sized Bombay flat. As a result, her house could be bursting at the seams and you would be blissfully unaware. The living room was the only place where congregation was permitted, where many soft stratagems appealed to your better nature, reminding you to refrain from noise. A miniature fountain with the gentle murmur of mechanically regulated water. A bead curtain that whispered when you walked through. A muted lighting scheme. A soothing CD on the system, something suitably soporific, trance or chants.

'"All you need is incense, Loll," I'd tell her, "and this could become the hot new shrine to peace in the midst of modern-day stress. You could be a millionaire!" She already was, but she was too well bred to point that out.

'So into this haven of Lolly's, I suggested she invite the girl with the wormy name and her friends. I had decided I wouldn't like them, even though one of them *was* a Bong. It was just one of those things. I was allergic to Dilliwallas. Loll was the only exception.

'"How about inviting some of my drinking buddies too," I suggested brightly to her, just to watch the look of horror on her face. "It'll be fun!"

'"*No!*" she said, and that, as always, was that.

'On the designated evening, they walked in, looking shy. I almost cracked up. Nobody I knew still wore that old-fashioned look of hesitation and pleasure. They hovered near the door, a bottle of wine in Ciggy's hand, a bunch of flowers in Angie's arms. How civilized, I hooted to myself. Lolly did the honours and introduced us. I did my bowing-scraping clown act, just to get them out of their awkwardness. If anything, it made them more awkward. I was going to get my money's worth.

'I don't know, Pappu-mian, if you are psychic. I'm not. Never was a more down-to-earth, rooted-in-reality banda than yours truly. But that evening, below my I'm-the-life-and-soul-of-the-party exterior, something stirred. It wasn't long before I found out what it was. Not psychic shit after all. Just the weird way someone you've just met invariably knows someone you've known from another life. They were all utter strangers, and already one of them had reason to hate me.

'I did the hostly honours at the bar. Ice? And what can I make you, are you sure it's okay to call you Poka? I mean with a delightfully Bengali wonderfully literary name like yours, why Poka? And so on and so forth. Lolly was delighted to see me getting along so well with her new friends. She glowed like one of her brass lamps. She decided to leave Poka and Ciggy to me and took Baby and Angie on a guided tour of the house, an honour I had never seen her bestow on anyone. She was going all out.

'So was I. It's funny, but I was having trouble disliking them. Poka was all warmth and light. Ciggy was relaxed and laconically charming. We were hitting it off wonderfully and then I put my foot in my mouth. I mentioned that I had fled from Delhi to Bombay. Start anew. That kind of thing. It was the beer talking, or simply their guileless presence. Whatever it was, it led to interested questions from Poka. Oh! When did you leave? *That's* where you used to work? Funny, a friend's sister worked there too! Really? What was her name?

'"We called her Kimi."

'I will never forget that moment. I fell a thousand feet

into darkness and when I surfaced, I saw them looking at me strangely. "Smoke?" Ciggi said, in the way he has of offering the nicotine stick as the panacea for all ills. I shook my head. Poka was eyeing me. In the way that two people can suddenly read each other's minds just by the look in their eyes, in that split second I knew she knew.

'I was the one. Kimi, all of nineteen years old, had died because of me. It was my car we were in that night, twenty days before she died. It was late and we were high as kites. We always were, and not just on the things we drank. Being together had that effect on me. She was intoxicating. One smile from her and my veins would pop with adrenalin. She had joined as a trainee in the production house where I worked, and we had fallen for each other. It was insane. We would work nights, just to be together in the semi-surreal space of studios and editing rooms. She stopped going home. She stayed in my barsati, and wore my clothes. We never slept. I had never felt so young, so alive. And she, leaning towards me, her oval face bright with love, had never looked more wonderful. She never did those usual girlfriend things of nagging me about drinking too much or wearing the wrong clothes or cleaning up my house. I adored her for that. In her black polo neck and little red boots, her lips soft and swollen, she just laughed as she watched me wear the same old crumpled T-shirt that I had worn all day to the party. The party we should never have gone to.

'I drank too much. It hadn't always been like that. At the Institute we drank like there was no tomorrow, and with it came the inspired clarity that made sense of everything we did or saw or learnt. We were invincible and the alcohol just proved it. We were intense and argumentative, brilliant and blistering. We fuelled our directorial dreams with the cheap hooch we swilled. We walked on ether. In Delhi, when I found myself in a job I didn't like, I found myself wanting, more than anything else, to walk on ether again. That hard rough pleasure of knowing you're a man, capable of anything. I drank rough and hard, but instead of clarity all I got was tiredness. I drank to kill the tiredness and then I drank to spite it. I drank alone in my barsati and then, disgusted at the wimp I had become, I drove out roaring, looking for mates. I found them, old Insti-types, trying to find work, working, creating little circles of failure, success, bitterness, and I joined them with a dying thrill. We drank better stuff now, all of us had more money, no matter how disappointingly earned, and we drank it all down, defying it to destroy us.

'Kimi was a sting of ice-cold water in that world. She walked in, her face bright with friendship for all my buddies, no matter who they might be, and I knew she affected them all. Her face was a stab of *what might have been*. They teased her, big-brothered her. They accused me of not looking after her as she deserved. They told her stories about the Institute that would have made any other girl faint. But not Kimi. She was made of something far stronger. It was as if she had decided the greatest proof of her love for me would be to love all these hard-drinking, furrow-faced men with signs of bellies and wobbles of insecurity. I was the one she was reassuring through them and I was the one she stung the most.

'That night she made me feel more reckless than I had ever felt. I was challenging something unsaid, my growing old perhaps, my thinning hair. This will never last, something inside me screamed. She's young, she's lovely. You're old, you're decaying. I drank myself blind. My buddies noticed but I threw them off when they came to steady me. I could see Kimi's face and it hurt me terribly. When they offered to drive us home, I raged out, dragging her by the hand as if they had threatened to take her away.

'If only they had. I drove without seeing. She sat taut as a wire beside me, not saying a word. She held herself hard against the seat as if to keep herself from bursting into tears or a terrible rage. I drove. And when I woke from that slam of dark and screeching tyres and grinding pain, they told me she was dead.

'My last image of Kimi was her face quivering with all the things she might have said, and didn't. She was willing to die with me, but she left me behind. Later they told me she had been in a coma for nineteen days. I couldn't imagine her destroyed. That face, never. And so I imagined her the way she looked when sleeping beside me, radiant with an inner light I could never get enough of.

'I couldn't live in Delhi any longer. I fled, carrying with me the terrible burden of having escaped. I should have been in jail. But friends in high places, powerful forces I hadn't appealed to had worked to save the life I hadn't asked for. In Bombay, I would make a fresh start, that was the understanding when I left. I didn't believe I could, but I did. I got a job, a house, a girlfriend. I started living a little, and then that evening, at Lolly's place, it all came flooding back.

'Pure hate is hard to describe, Pappu-mian. I hope you never have to face what I did the day Poka looked into my eyes, and knew, without my saying a word, what I had done. Her eyes slammed shut, the same great thud of darkness as on the day of the accident. All the light went out. Instead of two dancing bright eyes, two spiralling pinpoints of steel were boring into me, pitiless. I could sense Ciggy stiffening, alarmed by the sudden coldness in the air. For a few seconds nothing seemed to function. And then Lolly walked in, house tour done, beaming at Angie and Baby's compliments.

'Poka showed her mettle, that evening. She got up, and enveloping Lolly in one of her trademark hugs, she said, "Now will you sit down and talk to *us*, for a change?"

'The girls were wonderful, they talked, teased, flirted. Baby stayed a bright shade of pink the whole evening. Ciggy—grateful that whatever 'it' was had passed—eased back into his happy quiet. I didn't dare look at Poka again, and without making it obvious, she never once looked at me or spoke to me the rest of the evening.

'I felt a hundred years old when they left. Lolly was so happy at the success of her party and the surprisingly low-key behaviour of her otherwise unmannerly and unmanageable boyfriend that she just steered me gaily into her bedroom and recounted everything Poka and Angie had said until she fell asleep from sheer fatigue. I stayed awake, remembering things that turned my flesh to lead.

'I knew I had to speak to Poka alone. Would she agree? And what would Lolly think? And Ciggy? I needn't have worried. She called me, a few tortured days later and she said, "Look, we need to meet." She fixed a place and I went there after work, trembling like an alcoholic off the wagon. I had quit hard-drinking. I had quit meat. Everything that made me remember Delhi I had quit, but that evening I could have done with a few stiff ones. And of all places she chose a pub. Toto's Garage. Enough quiet there, I figured, and enough privacy, hardly anyone went there that early. I walked into the reddish dark of Toto's and looked around for her. There she was. In the corner, against the wall. My heart sank.

'She was drinking beer. I ordered one too. She didn't mince her words.

'"I've hated you all this time, not knowing who you were," she said. "She was my friend's baby sister, and..."

'Her lips twisted as she fought to keep her calm. My mouth was dry. No amount of beer would help. And then she began weeping. To my great and dark horror, not caring if the waiters saw, she wept. I would have given anything to weep with her. It would have absolved me. Tears, shed in the company of another. I didn't dare. I clung to my slippery cold glass and watched the drops slide down.

'It was only later, when she wiped her eyes and said to me, half-crying, half-laughing, "Don't be a goose, they're staring," that I realized I *had* been weeping after all. That's what saved me, Poka told me later.

'"If you hadn't wept like a silly goose, your nose going red in front of all those waiters trying to pretend nothing was odd about two adults blubbering in a corner, I would have continued to hate you. Seeing you cry, something gave," she said, "something slipped loose and broke the vice around my heart."

'She did the unthinkable. She forgave me.

'We never told any of the others about it, this is the first time. Somehow that made us closer than I've felt with anyone in a long time and not in a romantic sense. She was my co-traveller, the keeper and sharer of my grief. It was as if I had given her custody of that part of myself no one knew of, the place inside me where I had sent all the things I couldn't bear to see in the clear light of day, things that came out and haunted me every time I felt anxious and alone. It was funny, but thanks to Poka my memory of Kimi became something I could take solace from, could draw into the light, and hold carefully in my hand like a precious thing. It was no longer one long, wracking scream.

'And so, Pappu-mian, thanks to my dearest Lolly, Poka and Ciggy came into my life. Baby and Angie too. For all my bragging about Bombay being the place for me, it wasn't till I found myself part of this group that I felt I might actually manage to *live* here. What had happened in Delhi had filled me with a peculiar dread. As if I were some sort of ill omen. A death wish forced on those who didn't wish it. I was unlucky. It sounds like old wives' tales, I know, but I felt it in my bones, where the trauma still lingered. It made me wary about expressing my love for Lolly (there my dear, now you know it), as if the minute she saw in me the same flare of emotion I saw in her, something would mar it all, a big black plague would fall on us with cruel suddenness. Because, and this is what even Poka didn't know, it had happened before.

'I was in school then. She was in our sister school across the road. We had met at one of those typical social events that schools believe are so vital for fostering healthy relations between the sexes. She was my other half. Never before, or since, have I felt so in tune with another person. We completed each other's sentences, each knew what the other thought without a hint or a word. We had a plan, a sensible, practical, grown-up plan. We would wait until we finished our studies and then we would marry and live together. Only, she never finished school. One day, too impatient to wait for the signal to change, she raced across to where I stood on the opposite pavement and was killed on the spot. There was no way the car could have braked in time. I stood rooted. They had to slap and shake me to bring me back to my senses. No one, not one single boy in that class of forty-one dared to laugh or tease me. Even then, just fourteen years old, they knew what had happened was an adult love, an adult loss, too real to be scorned.

'So that has been my secret. The one I have carried around all these years, saving it undoubtedly for this telling, for the ears of an innocent who has agreed to hear us all. It is my disease, and the only way I can cure it is by dying. The death-bearer. Something medieval. Baby would know. All I know is that it hurts, knowing it might happen again, and not knowing if I can survive the guilt a third time, not with you, my love, whom I have been scared to acknowledge, because I love you too much.'

The night shrank around the sound of their breathing. Tiny's face was wet. She looked at Baldy and Baldy looked away. The boy felt like weeping. The funny sad man. It was true. The clown-face with the dripping eyes. It was not fair. He would not let Baldy be so sad. He would protect him from his curse. It was foolish to believe he was cursed.

Angie kicked her feet in the water and the blue light shimmered in response.

Fourteen

'It wasn't till Momo joined us that we understood what was going on,' Angie said. 'I can't remember who introduced her to us but once she came it was hard to imagine her not being around. Our first instinct was to protect her, she looked so frail. But Momo didn't want to be protected. On the contrary. Momo wanted to be left just as she was, defenceless and destructible. Her body, we realized slowly, was her accomplice. It betrayed every weakness in her, and she watched, curiously detached. When she became one of us, we watched too. It was as if she were transparent, and we could gaze freely at whatever forces ravaged their way through her, leaving behind a battlefield of scars.

'I know! It sounds theatrical. Even I feel like smiling, almost. But if you had watched her those first few times, you would not have smiled. You would have been troubled, like we were, and fascinated. It was never a very serious reason that triggered it, or at least it didn't seem that way. Maybe she had a nasty new boss, maybe she had split up with her boyfriend. And Momo knows I don't mean to trivialize what must surely have been important to her, and us, her friends, her sympathizers. What I mean to demonstrate is this. The reason was *inconsequential*.

'The loss of a loved one or the loss of a favourite book—her body made no distinctions. Perhaps, inside, neither did her mind. The slightest hint of distress was enough to trigger an avalanche of reaction. Remember that first time we saw Momo under attack? It was her skin. The skin on her arms mottled into an army of angry red blotches. I saw it first. We were both in the kitchen trying to make coffee to wake us up for our tedious working day ahead, when I saw her arms. Stupidly I thought, oh my god, it's measles. But when I told her, she just looked down as if her arms belonged to someone else and said, "No it's him." The boss, the boyfriend? What did I know in those early days about her barometric body? Momo must have seen the look on my face. She must have explained. But all I remember is waking up more effectively than coffee has ever woken me as I stood against the kitchen ledge and stared at her thin pale arms erupting. Momo looked away, as if bored by her body's shameless exhibitionism. I wondered if I should make her sit down. Or hold her by the shoulders and show her around. Look at Momo, she's erupting. I did neither.

'Instead, I made silent observations. It's only on her arms. Not on her bare legs, not on her face and until I pull up her T-shirt and prove myself wrong, certainly not on her stomach. Why this predilection for the arms? What controlled this eruption, choosing a site so specific and so random? I could have been a scientist, standing there and recording my observations in my little mental notebook. I think Poka was not the only one infected by Baby's notebooks, each of us had our own version. As I looked, I felt myself overcome by the need to scratch the itch that was surely rampaging through the big red bumps. Why didn't she scratch them? Would she let me? She certainly wouldn't.

Already in our short acquaintance I had figured out how much—or how little—she would let people get away with. She guarded herself against other people, but never, never against herself.

'As I watched her that morning, so calm and unaffected by what must have been an uncontrollable desire to scratch, I realized that Momo was a message not from the gods, that would have been too creepy, but certainly from the demons that tormented us. Only, we didn't know it then.

'We all reacted the same way to Momo's irrationally bumpy arms—with utmost seriousness. Not even Cracker cracked an "oh-how-rash-of-you" kind of joke. Poka, I sensed, wanted to either embrace Momo or flee crying from the room. Ciggy went quieter, if such a thing was possible and forgot to say, "Smoke?" Baby's eyes widened, as if some theory of his had just been confirmed. Lolly was the only one who dealt with the occurrence in a practical way. She opened the fridge, took out ice cubes, and wrapping one, then another, in her little hanky she slid them down Momo's arms, while we watched, as if some ancient ritual was being carried out before our heretical eyes. Momo didn't move or protest. She sat there and let the ice cubes cool the bumps, not having said whether they needed cooling, not saying either if the cooling soothed her. No one mentioned a doctor. Not Poka who had developed a fanatic dread of them ever since she discovered what she liked to call her 'unstable quotient'. And certainly not me. The bumps lasted four days. On the fifth day, Ciggy bought wine from his bootlegger and we celebrated their disappearance, without mentioning what it was we were celebrating.

'Momo made us a gentler bunch. With her amongst us, we left our irritations at the door. We eased out of our work-skins the way we eased out of our shoes. We were afraid of being the ones to cause what we had now begun to take for granted, like a mole on the face, or a stammer. We didn't want to make her body allergic to us! There were enough irritations and incidents and people out there for that. We were the witnesses. She privileged us by letting us observe her body's rebellions.

'Soon, I saw a pattern. When she was mildly upset, her arms would erupt into splotches or bumps. When she was sad, her breath would turn wheezy and she would cough. When she was tense, she would get a nasty rash on her hip, on the right side, or behind both her knees. When she was violently angry, her lip would grow a sore. It would burst with pus, and then it would scab. We would pray she got well by the time the scab appeared, because otherwise she would pick at it—the only time I saw Momo actively engage with a disorder—and it would split open and pus all over again. It was horrible, that crusty thing on her lip, a hideous excrescence, to use Baby's words.

'When we girls changed in front of each other, as if we were sisters or hostel-mates, we saw a tiny pink patch on her chest, in between her breasts. One day I asked if I could touch it. It was smooth and warmer than the rest of her skin. Is it a birthmark, we asked. Momo shook her head. It had simply appeared one day, and stayed on, constant, overshadowed, dormant. However close we got to Momo, we never asked her how the patch reacted when something more dramatic was happening to her. I would have liked to have discovered some synchronicity of mood between that passive patch of pink and whatever active incursion she was currently enduring. But I couldn't. I didn't dare.

'Momo's fevers became legendary. One minute she

would be sitting with us looking perfectly normal, the next minute she would turn pale, and find it hard to swallow. She would stagger to her bed, the mercury rising rapidly in the thermometer as if to scare us all into uncharacteristic behaviour like calling a doctor. And then, just as abruptly, after a night of cold compresses and peeled oranges and relentless tossing and turning, she would be all right. Feeble, but feverless. We never quite understood what caused the fevers. They came and went randomly. I suspected they were important in some peculiar way to Momo. She had an air of fulfilled expectation each time a fever passed. She was proving something to herself, only we didn't know what. Did they make her weaker? I couldn't tell. For me Momo's biggest strength was her willingness to be weak. She didn't believe in immunity and resistance and fighting back. She was the most peaceful among us, and that was strange, for her body gave her no peace.

'That taught us something. At least, it taught me something. The more defensive you got, the more hopeless it was. I had seen it in Poka's case. The more she fought the idea that what was bothering her had a name that needed to be uttered, the less she was able to overcome it. I was fighting something unmentionable those days. A weird and smelly female thing. No one knew, not Poka, not sweet little Loll, and certainly not Momo with her aura of unbreakable inwardness. It worried me each morning when I went to the loo, hoping the night would have miraculously wished it away. Morning after morning, I was disappointed. I had visited rounds and rounds of doctors, male and female, and offered my orifices for searching, probing, testing. I had taken courses and courses of foul-tasting medicines that left my tongue feeling like a dishrag and replaced my appetite with something close to revulsion for anything resembling food. I hated my insides. I hated my female parts. I hated waking up. I hated not knowing whom to tell, or what to do that I had not already done.

'And then Momo came into our lives. I watched her, I can now confess, a little enviously, as she let wave after wave of affliction wash over her. What gave her this serene distance from the things that disrupted her system? And then it hit me. She didn't hate what happened to her. She embraced it, and after embracing it, she detached herself from it. So her illnesses came and went, leaving her stronger, even as she readied herself for the next assault. In her attitude, I found my solution.

'I bought myself new lingerie. Frilly satiny things. I decided to forget I had an unsightly, seemingly incurable ooze, and decided to live a little, love myself a little. Forget what I could have so aptly called the curse if the curse hadn't already been taken. I decided not to hate myself for being a victim, I decided to *forget* I was a victim.

'It worked. In a month, the problem was gone. I was no longer at the mercy of a bodily fluid. I had shrivelled it up with my sarcastic gaze. Hah! *You?* I can survive you! And it worked. Sometimes, when I got all anxious and tense from some other part of my life, it would come back and worry me like a nagging partner. But then I would remember Momo's detached and unruffled face, and I would tell it to be gone and it would obey. Momo, who suffered more than anyone I have ever met, taught me how to be well.

'That's when it fell into place, what the bunch of us was all about, why we hung around together so compulsively. We were all sick and trying not to admit it. We were unable to deal with our sicknesses, ailments, problems, maladies, call them what you will. I felt more like a scientist than ever, dissecting, analysing. With cheeks so soft you just had to squeeze them, Baby was suffering from brittleness. His bones rebelled against the babyness he had been gifted, a genetic present he didn't have the option of refusing or throwing away. That's why hard rock faces drew Baby so strongly. He needed to set them against his own unwanted softness and prove something that didn't need proving. He was unable to take Yanky's plunge to his death. So he blamed himself for his softness at not being able to take it, for being the one who lived.

'The more I thought about it, the more I made sense of our mysterious affinities. Hard facts. After the accident, Baby delved for facts that he could tap his nails against and say, this, this exists. But his mind was more devious than him. And so he wandered into territories soft and unyielding as himself, the temptress worlds of fiction. I saw it all so clearly, and it was all because of Momo.

'We were being eaten away by our own unwillingness to see. Poka had understood some of this. But that's because she had gone under and surfaced. Her malady had been mental from the start. It made it easier, though it felt harder, poor thing. Cracker had always baffled me and only now I figured out why. Too many burdens. Cracker the jester, Cracker the death-bearer. Once again, the opposites I saw in Baby. Once again, the symmetry of irrevocable contrast. I know! I sound like Baby's notebooks, but then Baby has always shared them with me. In me he found no resistance to his theories, and so I became his disciple, his truest believer. I wish I could cure your brittle bones, babe, just by believing in you.

'I thought I saw it all, but still some veil obscured what

made us stick together, what made us tick. I felt Momo held the answer in her transparent body. It floated there, in her veins, her bones, her lungs X-rayed into palpable existence. I thought if I looked hard, I would find it. Amoebic and formless, mutant and wise, Momo became her illnesses, and her illnesses became her. If she were ever to get completely well, throw off the protean cloak of her reactive self, what would happen to us?

'We needed Momo, we needed to study her closely, and derive some clues about ourselves. She would teach us how to live with our illnesses, *despite* our illnesses. But if she transformed herself one day and emerged unmarked and invulnerable, what then? Correct me if I'm wrong, people, but I think that's why we came here to Goa in the monsoon, to this remote hotel with its deserted beach. To devote ourselves to this research—on ourselves. To isolate the specimen for closer observation, as if we were in a lab, in controlled conditions, minus any other distractions. But what we didn't realize is that our eyes wouldn't change! We needed to see both Momo and ourselves with new eyes, if we wanted this to work. That's when *you* entered the picture. We all had the same thought that night we saw you sitting so fretfully with your parents, longing to be like us. We picked it up, the yearning you sent out in waves. We've been together so long, honey, we sense these things and act on them, instinctively, without discussion. Cracker threw the bait to you next morning, and we pulled you in, a fresh pair of eyes, another heart. What if you had left? That thought never crossed our minds. We were certain you would stay.'

Fifteen

'That doesn't mean we didn't like you for your own sake,' Tiger said. 'We did. Wouldn't have drawn you in otherwise. Momo felt you had a good vibe. Something straight and unspoilt. Momo's never wrong about these things. But she couldn't have drawn you in. Only Cracker with his easy camaraderie could have done that. And then, just to see if you were a sport, we planned the tests. Ice breakers, really. Though Baby called them mythic trials, the stuff all would-be heroes have to pass through. Gave the game a classical slant, didn't it? Made us feel less like third-year hostellers getting our jollies from frightening some fresher. We all agreed you came out well, not cocky but confident, thinking your way through, fighting whatever fear you must have felt. Good show.

'Wouldn't it have been simpler if we'd just walked up and said hello? It would, but complex is more fun. It's the simple stuff that gets you down. The everyday workaday stuff. That's what kills you in the end. You're too young to know it, but there's poison in what we do every day to make a living. We wake up and zombie-like we go to work. There, with other zombie-like people, we do business. We become suits. The ultimate insult to oneself is to become a suit.

Bright mental-types that aptly come out of institutions—management, engineering—we are the ones who slowly morph into what we once hated most. Can you imagine what that does to your insides?

'You try to lighten up, you play squash maybe, with the boss. Or TT with the juniors, trying to remake yourself in hero mode, the boy with the blazing backhand. You play computer games, juggling life and death, cosmic regeneration and upheaval, a sort of virtual King Kong, destroying everything in your path, especially competition. Your game scores do the rounds in awed whispers. You are buoyant for a few exhilarating moments and then you sink again, back to who you have become. A corporate blob. You think about long-term impact on company policy. You don't crib about the tie or the endless kowtowing to power that will one day hopefully be yours. You dream of money, bigger money than imagination can cope with. You will never be a shark on the stock market, or a hoarder of illegal stashes. You want to do it right, above board, clean. You believe in corporate raiding. You will be a pirate of the boardroom vendetta. You will bare steel at the throat of someone weaker and younger and you will climb on, trampling his face under your feet. The day your blobby despair changes to razor-sharp exultation, you know you will survive.

'To some, that exultation never arrives. Or it does, exacting a price too big for your little ambition to cope with. All your hair falls out. Your teeth go rotten. Your breath curdles with every extra hour you slave. Your armpits exude a scent no perfume can hide. It is the scent of fear. "Someone is watching me. Someone is behind me trying to get ahead of me. Someone is already ahead of me." Fear stinks up your snazzy, wrinkle-free shirts. Stomachs give in, lacerated by quick meals, oily with haste and deadlines. Ulcers pop up. Eyes get inflamed, red with computer fatigue. Wrists and necks sprain. Feet swell. Appendices burst. Lungs spot. Kidney stones shoot with pain. Hearts attack.

'I should have gone into the forces like my father. At least there I would have known what to expect, nothing more, nothing less than the blatant tyranny of regimentation. Instead, I chose the disguised tyranny of corporate life and died a little every single day.

'It hit me out of the blue. One day, I was the blue-eyed boy of every boss in sight, the next day I was the outcast, reviled. It wasn't family problems, unavoidable circumstances, regrettable incidents. Nothing of that sort. One day I got up and walked out of a roomful of very important clients. I had just dug my own grave. Stress, too much, too young. Take a sabbatical. Detox. The smiley-mouthed stone-eyed bosses shook my hand and wrote out my cheque. I was, officially, released.

'What a polite way of saying fired. How corporate. As I left that glass-fronted building, humming with air conditioning, I felt I would never be able to face another human being again. But outside, in the sweat and glare of noon, I realized that the only human being I needed to face was me. If I survived my own contempt, I would be fine. No one else mattered.

'I didn't try to get another job. I let time swim aimlessly by. I had enough money, oh more than enough. I could easily survive for a year, two years. I could repair my insides, and calm the panic that set my heart fluttering in anticipation of my next big mistake. Faulty valve, the doctor told me, when I couldn't ignore the pain that I thought was purely psychological. Slow down, I told myself. Think. Or better still, don't think. Vegetate.

'I returned to infancy those first few months after what I now call the Big Break. I slept for hours. I pulped fruits and drank huge sludgy glasses of them, milk, fruit, cornflakes mushed together. I put on weight. I went walking every evening on the promenade, easy in the knowledge that none of my compatriots would be back home that early to bump into me and look away, sympathetic and gloating. I read myself to sleep every night, all the books I'd bought and never had time to read. I zoned out.

'Until reality started creeping back. Rent, bills, letters from home, a growing restlessness with eating, sleeping and reading. But at the thought of entering another company, glass doors sliding noiselessly open as you approached, deep-pile carpets and muted lighting and looming atriums with abstract sculpture and modern cafés in primary colours and open-plan offices and shining whiteboards and sleek laptops flicked open casually to display rows of numbers and cunning pie charts—at the thought of every little detail of my past, I felt my faulty valve twitter in alarm. I couldn't. I would have to find a job *outside* that monstrous monolith all corporations had become in my mind, one gigantic soul-flattening dehumanizing bulldozer. I would have to look elsewhere.

'I wasn't maverick enough to open a coffee shop or a gaming arcade. I wasn't reckless enough to start a company of my own. You could start small, but who knew what it would grow into and then I would have a Frankenstein on my hands and no one to blame but myself. No, I would have to think harder. And then I got it. I would be a counsellor. How to cope with corporate stress.

'It was so easy, I would have laughed, if I hadn't been scared of upsetting whatever divine forces smoothed my path for me. I did everything myself. The mailers. The aid material. The structuring of what I called my 'Bust Stress Before It Busts You' workshops. One by one, doors opened and the many forms of corporate damage poured into my hands, waiting to be de-stressed and sent back, ready for more damage and then back again into my healing hands, an endless flow of returns. It would have been evil if I hadn't been so earnest about it. I *wanted* to save those young burning-the-candle-at-both-ends executives before they combusted. As for the corrupt, haggard and powerful older men and women who came my way, them I wanted to flog publicly as some sort of cathartic experience for all participants, myself included. But all I did was suggest, extemporize, actualize. I generated simulations, hostilities, face-offs, showdowns. And always humour—laugh your way through stress. Distance. Deflate. I have to say I was very good at it. I was making more money outside the system than in it. I had found myself.

'But all of me refused to dance with joy. All of me refused to whoop with delight at the way my future seemed assured, as no one would ever run out of stress. One part of me was already taking stock.

'I noticed Ciggy at that session because he seemed so tranquil. Surely they needn't have sent him, I thought to myself. In an attempt to create a relaxed atmosphere, participants were allowed to smoke. This was a rare group with only one smoker, Ciggy, who seemed to have smoked ten cigarettes since stepping through the door. That was my only signal that all was not well with this tranquil man. I imagined what would happen to him if he was forced to stop smoking. For him, the only air worth breathing seemed to be the kind inhaled through his filter-tip. More and more offices were becoming no-smoking zones. You had to stand on the balcony and smoke. Or get into the car, drive to the gate and smoke. I decided to make him my guinea pig.

'"All right," I said to him. "You've joined a strictly no-smoking company. Nowhere, not in the loo, not even near the lifts. Let's see how you cope with it. Starting now."

'He looked bemused, as if to say, "Is this guy serious? Do I have to listen to him?" But he stubbed out his cigarette and came forward. I felt intimidated when I saw how tall he was, how purposeful behind that friendly tranquil air. I felt short and weaselly. When he sat down, I relaxed. I was the ringmaster again.

'"Right. Now while the rest of us go on with our discussion, you will sit and enjoy the smoke-free atmosphere of your brand-new office."

'I know, it sounds like deliberate torture. That, too, was part of my scheme. It always worked. Ciggy shrugged and slouched down comfortably in his chair, his long legs sticking out at the semicircle of participants. The women looked sympathetically at him. I could tell some of the guys wanted to laugh. I went on with my spiel, set exercises, allocated roles, led group-chanting. Ciggy sat behind me, a silent rebuke. It was a two-hour session. He was going to bear up after all. Excellent!

'And then I heard the sound. A tiny crack-crack. It was almost drowned by the buzz of the session. I threw a glance at my "subject". He was sitting, slouched, like before. He was cracking his finger joints. Tugging, snapping, pulling. Lots of people I knew did that. I hated it. Made me feel queasy. I pretended I hadn't noticed. But I was feeling tense, as if I was the one who was nicotine-deprived. I rushed over to a knot of four people who seemed on the verge of coming to blows. All part of the game. Give in to aggression and get it all out. But at the back of my head, the sound persisted, the tiny crack-crack of finger joints being kneaded. His face, I'd noticed, was still tranquil. Good. Nothing to worry about.

'It was one of the women who noticed.

'"Sir!" she yelped. "Something's wrong!"

'I whirled around, abandoning all pretences of cool, calm, in-control, and there he was, Ciggy, serene, uninvolved in the bloody mess his hands had become. My faulty valve went haywire. He had broken his own fingers. He had broken them as if they were pencils. I don't know how many he had broken but I wasn't waiting to find out. I rang for the ambulance, dismissed the session, and bundled Ciggy's hands into a towel. He just sat there, refusing to move, cooperate or make eye contact. His face had the same gentle expression as before. I wanted to weep over his broken hands. How large and bony his hands were. What about the pain as he cracked his fingers? Not a whimper. When the ambulance came they looked at us queerly. I went with him and it was only after the clean-up and the scan and the finding that two fingers in his left hand had been broken, it was only after all that and seconds before he was moved to the OT, that he acknowledged I was there. A small flicker of acknowledgement and then it died and he was trundled away.

'I don't know when he got word to his friends or how. Certainly not through me. But they rushed in, looking distraught, as if Ciggy was the last person they expected to visit in hospital. They eyed me queerly too. What had I done to him, they silently accused. What was I doing there? I waited with them, feeling useless and guilty.

'Lolly was the only one who didn't treat me like a murderer. She said, "I've heard about you, you're the stress-busting guy, right?"

'I nodded, dumbly grateful for the conversation, any conversation.

'"What happened?"

'I told her. Her eyes went wide when she heard how quietly he had sat there, smokeless, breaking his fingers one by one. The others listened too, even though their faces were turned away. Poka burst into tears. Cracker came over and shook my hand, as if conveying condolences. Not your fault, mate, he seemed to say. Angie ignored me. I realized I should leave. I left.

'It was Lolly who initiated that visit to my place, weeks later. Who knows how she found my home address. Probably some corporate HR file which listed such details as a matter of course. Maybe we shared the same tax consultant. Who knows. I was blown away to see them at my door. Ciggy, slouching, bony, smoke curling out of his nostrils like some gentle dragon, Poka, looking nervous, Cracker and Angie determined to be talkative and friendly.

'"Good to see you... well," I faltered as I shook Ciggy's hand. "Thanks for coming."

'I didn't ask them why or how come or anything. Just seeing them was enough to know they didn't blame me for what had happened. For one chilling moment the thought struck me that they had come for my professional help. Somehow, seeing them rush to be with Ciggy at the hospital that day, I had acutely felt the lack of my own friends. Not one friend. Only acquaintances. No one who would drop everything and come running to my side. Funny considering what a mister popular I had been in the office. But the minute I fell from grace, my office friends dropped me. I was left alone, to sink or swim, they couldn't care. I felt a flash of hate when I thought how fake all that bonhomie had been. And then I felt a flash of relief that I had seen it for what it was. Here were people who looked like they made friends for life.

'For some reason, they decided to adopt me. I needed befriending and that was that. Soon, it was like I had known them all my life. By day I stress-busted for others. By night I busted my own stress, chatting, laughing, relaxing with my new friends. It was like going back to college when no night is long enough and no subject too trivial. I was a new man and I had them to thank for it. Maybe now at least that niggling part of me that loved playing spoilsport would shut up.

'It didn't.

'By then we knew each other well enough to know our weak spots, our individual Achilles heels. But like Angie said, it wasn't till Momo came that we realized what bound us. We were all weak. Inside, where we should have felt strong and able, we were either whimpering children or doddering oldies. Twenty-seven going on eighty-seven. It scared me. Together we felt strong, healthy and cheerful. Peel us away from each other and we weakened. At least I know I did. Even when we groaned and moaned and complained about our physical ailments, major or minor, like a bunch of crotchety old people, it wasn't necessarily because we felt gloomy, but because it made us feel better. We took a perverse pleasure in talking about our defective, troubled selves. It bound us together. We cracked jokes about ourselves. The Gerries, Baby called us, short for geriatrics.

'"Golden Oldies," said Cracker.

'"Hypos," said Lolly, short for hypochondriacs. She was the only one who never had a problem.

'"Hypochondriacs with a death wish," said Ciggy.

'"Self-absorbed dysfunctional spoilt brats," said Angie, with a gleeful grin.

'"Loonies," said Poka.

'Only I said nothing, because I was not sure. Was it normal for young people to be so consistently ill? What about our fathers and their fathers before them? No complaints and all of them sixty-plus. Ate like horses, led unhealthy lives, didn't exercise unless they were my dad who was a fitness freak, watched mind-numbing TV, the original couch potatoes who never counted their calories, stayed hale and hearty and never lost an opportunity to scoff at this hopeless younger generation's imaginary ailments. What about our mums who worried about our thinning, greying hair, our fragile digestion, our ruined eyes, our weak spines, our feeble hearts and said it's all in the diet, all those vitamin supplements and foreign foods. Or suggested archaic recipes involving ghee to restore health and vitality. Or simply sighed and looked resigned as if we had let them down in some unforgivable way.

'Why was being young and ill incompatible? Unacceptable?

'"They're jealous," said Baby. "We've stared into the abyss and the abyss has stared back."

'"It's unnatural, that's why," said Lolly, ever the realist. "We've had easier lives, better nutrition, we should be healthier than our parents."

'"No, we haven't," Molly would say, "we've had *tougher* lives. More pollution, more adulteration, more tension."

'"Stop sounding like my mom," Cracker would say.

'And so it would go on and on. We constantly thought about our insides, our stomachs, our backs, our bones, our hair. For all our intellectualizing, it seemed we hadn't proceeded beyond the animal stage of being one endless bodily process, an unresisting conduit for disease. It infuriated me. I wanted to stop obsessing about the body that carried me around, the heart that pumped blood to my brain and my bile duct. I wanted to shrug off the whole mess of me-ness and just live, free of this disgusting unglamorous angst. Was it middle age?

'That brought on the biggest laughs, though I asked it seriously. Middle age! We were in our late-twenties, twenty-seven, twenty-eight. Baby and I turned thirty this year, and only Momo is older that both of us. We were young and virile, with due apologies to the ladies, we were bursting with vim and vigour. And yet we felt like we were... dying.

'There it was again, that word. Dying. Death. It came back again and again. It didn't scare me, but I was tired of having to ignore it, as if it wasn't there inside me, that niggling worry that refused to be named. I wanted to confront it and say, "Listen, now that we've met, will you shut up and leave me alone?" But honestly, I couldn't ever be that flippant, even when we were fooling around, laughing at ourselves and our incurable worries. Death was serious business. I wanted to be prepared.

'"When you are sick of sickness, you are no longer sick." Baby had written this in his notebook of little quotes and he read it out to us triumphantly one day. Old Chinese proverb. When you are sick of sickness, you are no longer sick. Weren't we all reaching that stage? Did that mean that now we could truly be well? If it were that easy, why were the hospitals and loony bins full? Who enjoyed their problems?

'I did. I enjoyed the significance my faulty valve bestowed on me, like a blessing or a knighthood. Rise, Sir Weakheart! It made me feel fragile and special and set me above the rude healthiness of the unimaginative. My problem was a sign of my evolution. I was a balanced, sensitive, bright young man who was once under great pressure, and look what it gave me—a weak heart. Poka was—beg your pardon—*is* a warm, caring, intelligent woman who loved with her whole being, and look what that did—it frightened her out of her wits. Tranquil Ciggy? Oh he just broke his own bones.

'We were ill because we had willed it on ourselves. Our unique and enviable individuality had given rise to each unique and unenviable defect, each impairment, each curse. We were chosen, hand-picked, an elite. We were destined... for what?

'There could only be one answer. And the search for that answer brought us here.'

Sixteen

They're looking at me.

The wind had completely died. They were suspended in an enormous stillness, they, the pool, the palms, the sky, the stars, space. The boy felt like he was at the tip of an enormous pendulum, throttled in mid-swing. It seemed unreal that the hotel lights should be kept on all night, with no one to see them. All these previous nights he had slept in his room, unaware that outside his four cosy walls the hotel was awake, deathly quiet, light-struck and staring. It was as if the hotel had two lives. One curled up, hidden, asleep, the other exposed, awake. There was something obscene about the staring flat blue of the pool, glassy-bright in what by now must surely be the middle of the night. And all those motionless shapes around him, strangers, even though they had spoken so long and intimately to him.

What did they expect of him?

It wasn't just the silence, it was the stifling heat. The boy felt the sweat trickling down his chest under his thin T-shirt. He could see by the light of the pool the sheen on Momo's neck. Her thin neck, her crystal face. He imagined his fingers resting themselves against the slope of her cheeks. When Angie had spoken of Momo's body so openly, he had wanted to disappear. She was chiselled thin. She was a mystery even to her friends.

Her friends. They were looking at him.

It felt foolish to speak. To blurt out the questions that hung in his mind like the stillness they were suspended in. What could he say? They had called him many things. New eyes. New heart. An innocent. They had spoken in riddles about finding answers and making observations. What had that got to do with him?

They hadn't taken him in out of friendship. He was part of some elaborate scheme of theirs. The boy felt a spurt of pain. He was merely part of a plan. What if he had not been there? Would they have chosen someone else? Reed-man, for example, his shyness overcome by Baldy's warmth and bluster? How easily Reed-man might have been sitting here instead of him, his collar open, off-duty, overwhelmed.

They were expecting him to say something. They had given him the facts, or at least some version of the facts, and now they expected deductions, as if he were a detective. But detecting what? No one had died—yet. Why their obsession with death? His arms prickled. That tiny wheeze in Momo's breath. She had found him straight and unspoilt. She at least had reacted to *him*, not what he could or would not do. For her, he would speak.

'I'm sorry,' he said, his voice too loud in the still air. 'But what do you want from me?'

The silence, if anything, worsened. It wasn't like a house in the dead of night, where you might hear a tap drip or a lizard fall to the floor. This silence was soundproofed. The wet, dense heat grew heavier.

'You haven't told me who you really are. Your real names. Your childhoods. You've talked about how you met. You've told me about your illnesses. You've said what binds you together is illness. If you know so much, and yet tell me so little, how can you look at me now and say mysterious things like the answer is here. Which answer? To which question?'

The boy sounded defiant, and a little sulky. That was all wrong. He had meant to sound aloof and indifferent. Disdainful. Yes, that was the word. He didn't want to sound like a little boy who's dropped his ice cream and whose mother won't buy him another.

'But that's the whole point, sweetheart,' Angie drawled. 'We're waiting for you to tell us! Who are we, really? And what should we do?'

What was he, a prophet?

Under his defiance and uncertainty, a new emotion stirred. The boy was flattered. They needed him, his fresh eyes, his keen intelligence, his non-judgemental heart. They were older and wiser but they needed *him* to interpret them to themselves.

Take the facts and deduce. Comprehend. Conclude. Things he had always been good at. The only things he had ever been good at. Hadn't they tested him, and hadn't he passed? He was not just good enough, he was better! Okay, so maybe there were no facts, merely confessions, emotions. That was a good enough place to start.

'All right then,' he said, suddenly flooded with the kind of joy only a burst of confidence can bring. 'Listen.'

Seventeen

They called it the Land of the Well. In that land no one knew what illness was, which wasn't strange because no one ever fell ill. And no one paid any attention to how lucky they were because they thought that was how things were everywhere else in the world.

Right at the centre of the land stood the Well. It had always been there, deep and brimming with cool water. But strangers could not drink from it, not until they had answered the question asked by the Deity of the Well. They could drink from the streams, and the rills and the rivers, but not from the Well. You couldn't fool the Well. Even if you veiled your face, the Deity would know it was an outsider's face looking into its waters. The Well was ancient and the Deity that made its water sweet-tasting was older than time.

No one had seen the Deity, but everyone knew it was there. And so, before they drew water, the people of the land folded their hands respectfully, bowed their heads and breathed a prayer of thanks. They had no idea that it was the Well that kept them free of pain, disfigurement and disease. They were simple folk, they took their health for granted. The only thing anyone ever died of in that land was old age, and that too a very, very old age. The only symptoms were a silvering of hair, a thinning of the body, a slight shake in the voice and hands, and sometimes, a fading of memory. But otherwise, the sparrow-eyed old people, both men and women, stayed alert and active until the end, and when their time was up they left the world peacefully, dreaming in the early hours of dawn.

As the words left his suddenly parched tongue, the boy was conscious of a pressing need to drink water, and an equally pressing need to keep every pair of eyes on him. He could have asked them to pass him a bottle, Baldy had one right next to his chair, but he didn't want to stop, didn't want to risk losing the sweet sensation of having every pair of eyes on him, especially hers. He licked his lips, which tasted of salt, and spoke.

This land, like all lands, had a king. The kingship was not hereditary, it had to be won. The reigning king was called Tiger, because of the furry pelt that covered his body, in which they said stripes of gold lay concealed, stripes that you could only see when the king walked bare-chested in the wind.

Tiger had fought and won the kingship—some said with his hands, some said with his mind. He didn't have a palace like other kings. He lived in a house as plain as his neighbours', he wore no special robes, he did not carry a sceptre. He had no court, no courtiers, no durbar to sit in every day or once a week for petitioners to meet him. In fact, he had no duties at all, except to be, at all times, kind, kingly and stern. The Land of the Well ran itself and the king was its gesture of greatness, a promise made to itself.

Some said he had a secret throne under the banyan tree

near the Well. It was made of glass, they said, and in it danced the purple-gold feathers of a thousand peacocks, unfurled for rain. Some others said his throne was made of cloth dyed the deep indigo of an illusionist's mask. The cloth throne hung from the branches like a child's swing, the glass one stood heavy and silent, rooted to the ground. Most people said both thrones were true, the king chose one or the other depending on his mood.

The king's greatest power was this. Nothing about him proclaimed, loudly and visibly, 'Here I am, the king', and that was why he was surrounded at all times by a strong and magnetic aura. The children watched him striding by empty-handed, and made up stories about how his sceptre was invisible, and how if you went too close to him, he would swing it at you and turn your head into a turnip. Their mothers watched him striding by, an ordinary man, no different from their husbands, and spun stories of the crown they never saw, hiding their envy and longing. These were the stories they told their children at bedtime. About the king's crown that shot blue and red-hot sparks when he was angry, sparks that could burn you if you failed to receive his anger with humility. But—and this was the part the children loved—if you bore his wrath in silence, the red and blue sparks turned into jewels which he offered you with a smile, letting you pick them off his palm where they lay softly glowing. The men watched and listened, and wanted to be part of the storytelling too.

'His robe is made of the skin of ten tigers,' they said. 'You cannot see it because you are not his enemy. But if you were, instead of seeing a small man with empty hands and ruffled hair, you would see a crouching wall of black and gold—ten enormous tigers waiting to pounce and tear you open.'

The children shivered with fear and delight, and the conjuring went on, giving the king his greatest reason to be.

> *Under his breath Baby began murmuring. 'Tiger, tiger, burning bright, in the forest of the night.' There was an edge to the murmur, as if his teeth were clenched. The boy felt a flare of irritation. Why did Baby have to butt in? Baby's voice was like a pebble in the flow of his thoughts. For a second, he felt like stopping, ruining everything. But the words kept coming and so he let them carry him along.*

The king had no obligations, except one—he could never marry. If the king had a child, the child would claim the throne that existed only in the people's imaginations. And if there was more than one child, there would be bloodshed. No wonder this king, like all the others before him, was single.

That didn't mean the king was lonely. He had friends, if that's what you wanted to call them. *Baldy's laugh cut through the air.* They were a strange bunch and they seemed to have nothing in common but their strangeness. The people had their own names for them. They called the man with the baby face the Wise One. His face seemed too young to be considered wise, but they had seen the book he carried everywhere with him.

Some said it was a book of spells.

No, a book of chants.

No, a book of faith.

Everyone had a different idea about the book the Wise One carried. In the old days that book alone would have been enough to make him a sorcerer. Now, it made him a man of wisdom, of words that were the true source of knowledge.

Then there was the Silent One. The children were always trying to find ways to annoy the Silent One, daring each other to do something awful enough to make him shout at them. But they never succeeded. As he approached, tall, friendly eyed but distant, the dares died away. The children sensed that if they crossed the invisible line that guarded the Silent One's privacy, they would feel something much more dreadful than the king's imagined red-and-blue wrath. A burning stick perpetually lit at the tip of his fingers or the corner of his mouth, the Silent One was untouchable.

At least the Silent One and the Wise One had gravity to recommend them. What about the Funny One? He talked as much as the Silent One didn't! He waved his arms about and made faces and laughed loudly. What a strange companion to a tiger-king, a wise man and a silent man! But there he was, undeniably close.

And then there were the River Goddesses. They were magnificent! Both were big, as goddesses should be. One was the personification of warmth. The other wore a slight disdain wrapped around her regal shoulders. One wore her long and silky hair braided. The other piled it up and left her proud neck bare. They were always together, and in the early mornings when the sun was still weak, you would find them at the river. They waded in up to their knees and stood gazing at the palms on the far side.

Some said they were two of the Seven Sisters—'The young daughters of the sky, who do not eat and cannot do harm, do not dress and are not naked.' Some said they were women by day, and great golden fish by night. The people of the land wrote songs to the two River Goddesses, but they never heard those songs. They did not know they were goddesses.

And what would she think, as he laid these offerings at their feet instead of hers? The boy would have given anything to look in Momo's direction. Instead, he looked at the pool as if he were reading the story from its clear blue surface.

And last of all, there was the Small One and the Two Who Looked and Walked Alike. In the people's eyes they were the lesser companions. *There. I've said it. So shoot me.* In the hierarchy of the king's invisible court, the Wise One and the Silent One came first, the right and left hand of the king. The Funny One came next, the River Goddesses were above them all, and the Small One and the Two Who Looked and Walked Alike were last. Their functions were not clear to the people, because they carried no signs of who they might be. And so, depending on the numbers that people thought were holy, the king's companions numbered five, or eight. Together with the king they were the Six or Nine.

What they loved best was talking. Every night, they talked to each other, sometimes by starlight, sometimes by a fire near the Well. They never talked about the times when they were children growing up somewhere else in that blessed, unmapped land. They felt their childhoods were not important. Or perhaps, too important. Too secret, too precious to bring into the light, even if it was only the dim light of clouded stars or the flickering light of flame. They believed they were preserving their true selves by not talking about the times when they were little. Bound by this secrecy, they spoke only of their present and how they came to be wise or silent or sad.

Sometimes, as if the Silent One had cast his spell over them, they said nothing and sat gazing into and away from each other. Something was missing in that land where everything and everyone would always be well. But what?

If only the Deity of the Well would answer questions instead of asking them! But for that they would need to find another well, another deity. And so they stayed on, the king and his five or eight companions, slightly discontented, harbouring unanswered questions.

The boy paused for breath. What made this listening different from the one in Tiger's room, where he had been, at first, so acutely conscious of the two women sitting in front of him, and later, so forgetful of their presence? At what point had Baldy pushed the bottle of water towards him? The boy drank swiftly, spilling most of it on his T-shirt, and continued.

It was around this time that the newcomer arrived. Newcomers were as rare in the Land of the Well as illness itself. The newcomer was a girl. The people were amazed at how quickly she became part of the king's circle. What was so special about her? They studied her from afar and found nothing. No book, no staff, no ring, no robe, no scar, no reason. Like any of them she was unmarked and ordinary. She was not as small as the Small One. She was thin, like the Silent One, and short-haired, unlike the Goddesses. As they watched her, it became clear that when the king's companions walked, they surrounded the newcomer, as if to shield her from the people's prying eyes. How had this outsider moved to the heart of the king's circle?

Disturbing rumours began.

'The newcomer has brought a new word with her and

let it loose into our land, like a crazed rat. The word is Disease!'

'The newcomer bears a scourge! She has been seen with red welts on her arms, as if whipped or bitten. She brings danger!'

Unsafe and affronted, the people started calling her the Scourge. It was a cruel name, returning from the memory of a time before wellness became the air they breathed. Old men who had never taken ill grew rheumy-eyed with the fear that some malignant thing would mar their last days. Women shut their children behind closed doors. Men threatened revolt.

'The king is losing his kingliness!'

'Time for a new king!'

But that could not be, for in this land the only way a new king could be made was if the old king said so. That is how it worked. The old king would call for a fight, a tournament, and all the men who wished to be king would gather in the tournament ring they had built in the desert and there, behind great walls, they would fight with swords or words the people never knew, for the men were sworn to secrecy. After hours, or minutes, the new king would emerge, and the old one would prepare to be a subject like those he had once been king of. It was a fair and honourable system and no evil could disturb its workings. But what about the Scourge?

The rumours multiplied.

'The River Goddesses do not fear her!'

'The River Goddesses walk everywhere with her, and hold her by the hand.'

'Surely she cannot be harmful if they have taken her as their own?'

'But what of the wheezing we heard like a creature in her lungs as she passed?'

'What of the twenty days she lay in a fever, locked in the king's house, where the companions have all moved in, whether to tend to the Scourge or kill her, we cannot tell.'

'It is unseemly of the king to let them into his house. He is, after all, our king!'

The people forgot how proud they had been of their king's ordinariness. Now they wished he were openly tyrannical and wreathed in ceremonial coldness. They forgot how much they had enjoyed the liberty of creating him in their minds in any way they pleased and longed for a single fearful image. Deaf to rumours and suspicion, the companions and their king looked after the Scourge, day in, day out.

No one remembers who suggested she drink from the Well, or who told the people. But the day the king and his companions walked her to the Well, children buzzed around them like flies. It had been so long since they had seen their favourite Silent One and their magical king with the invisible crown! But their mothers would not let them follow. They came after them shouting and scolding, and dragged their children away. Only one child, whose mother was dead and whose father was in another town, managed to follow them right up to the Well. He was the one who told what happened there.

'The River Goddesses took her up to the Well,' he said. 'They stood beside her as she held on to the edge of the cold stone. The Two Who Looked and Walked Alike, the Small One, the Funny One, the Wise One, the Silent One and the king made a ring all around the mouth of the well. A ring of people around a ring of stone. They folded their hands and bowed their heads. The River Goddesses splashed the bucket deep and pulled it up. The Scourge dipped her hands into the bucket and brought them cupped full of water to her face when the Deity said, "Wait! You cannot drink until you have answered my question!"

'I heard the voice, I tell you I did! It was a big voice, coming from somewhere deep, and everyone, even the king, leapt back a little. The Scourge let the water drop back into the bucket.

'"Ask," she said in a small voice.

'The River Goddesses looked at each other over her head. They were worried. But the king looked very angry.

'"No!" he said, stepping forward and shouting into the Well so his voice echoed. "She is no stranger, she is one of us! This is her home! You cannot ask her questions as if she were an outsider!"

'"Then she cannot drink," the Deity said in a voice that seemed bigger than the king's shout, though it was as soft as a whisper. "Then she must turn back."

'"So be it!" the king said and he turned around and began walking away.

'The River Goddesses looked at each other again. Then they held the Scourge by her shoulders and walked after their king.'

Never before had the boy felt as exposed as he did now. His heart fluttered. This fear, he said to himself, this fear is silly. She will not hate me just because I changed her in my story. Keep talking.

In a matter of hours, every person in every household knew that the Deity of the Well had refused the Scourge. No one mentioned that this was the king's fault. The fact that he had shouted at the Deity was quickly suppressed, as if it was a guilty secret. The newcomer had been rejected, and that was good!

The companions felt differently.

No one in recorded history had ever shouted at the Deity before. The fact that his behaviour had been unthinkably rude didn't worry them half as much as what that behaviour revealed. The king had got involved.

Until that day, he had been much more than a symbol to them. He had been audience and counsellor at their nightly sessions, a confirmation of their own strength, their ability to be in control. Now he had betrayed himself, put himself in a place of weakness. It worried them because it was a warning of what was to come. Wasn't the newcomer unsettling what they considered fixed? Wasn't every rash of anxiety on her arms, every wheeze, every feverish sweat, every ache binding them closer to her? She was changing the patterns they had been so content with all these years. She was affecting everything.

What could they do but bring her back tenderly to the king's ordinary house and look after her? The truth was—she didn't need looking after. She ebbed and flowed and dimmed and glowed regardless of what they did, or tried to do. It was as if inside her there sat a little deity of her own who controlled her internal tides and currents, so that sometimes they rushed and roared and brought fever into her cheeks, and sometimes they died and shrank until she turned pale and wasted. The companions felt the little deity mocking them, their troubled eyes, their constant probing, their anxiety and their dread.

Poka stirred.

The truth was—the king's companions didn't worry only about the newcomer. Ever since she became part of their circle, strange things had been happening to them. At first they kept it hidden from each other, but then, in the way of people who have been together too long, they found themselves unable to pretend. Long into the night, after the king had gone to sleep and the newcomer had taken refuge in her room, they whispered their troubles to each other. A lot remained unsaid on those whispering nights, and a lot was guessed.

The Wise One had started doubting the wisdom of his little book. The words were the same, written in his own hand, unswerving sense-givers for all the years he had learnt to be wise. But their meaning escaped him.

He read out the fragments that he cherished and obeyed, and his voice became bleak with doubting. His look seemed to say, 'What does this mean?' His tortured eyes seemed to say, 'Why do they not soothe and comfort me, these dark pronouncements that helped me look at life and death with the carefree ease of a boy? Why do I find them craven and deceitful, like words written on air? There are philosophers here, there are poets. There are madmen and geniuses. Each speaking with the clarity of one who knows what true misgiving means. Of all the books that I have turned to, this book is the repository. I have held every nugget until it gleamed under my breath, under the daily rub and shine of my attention. All the wisdom I need is here. On death, on life, on all the mysteries in between. Then why this fading and slipping away as I storm through the pages, angry with myself for doubting? It shakes me, I feel weak, my bones feel brittle with despair. I cannot walk any more without fearing I will break.'

His own eloquence shocked him. How could he know what Baby felt? Had he overstepped? Baby was silent, his shoulders tense. Momo was looking down into her lap.

It unnerved the others to see their Wise One tremble. All the companions and even the king had drawn courage from his words. They heard him voice his doubt, and they did not know what to do.

What happened to the Funny One was perhaps even worse. The Funny One had never taken the companions' anxieties seriously. In his gesticulating hands they had become hilarious apparitions, things to scorn and laugh at. But one night, soon after the Deity's rejection of the newcomer and the king's rejection of the Deity, he broke his vow of clowning and shattered them all.

'Any woman I love dies,' the Funny One said to them. 'I have done it before and I will do it again. I dream of the women I have killed. They return to me whole, beautiful, and then as I reach out to touch their faces, they crumble beneath my fingers. I dread my dreams, even though they give me a glimpse of the women I have lost. In the mornings I see the curse of death in my hands. My caresses are like twisted silk, tightening around the trusting throat. I dare not love, and that is why I must stay away from the Small One, with whom I have fallen in love despite my curse. I must not love her if I want her to stay alive.'

The companions were startled. The Small One! She was always on the periphery, peaceful and tiny, not intruding, not clamouring to be one of them. They had known that she stayed for the Funny One. But they could never have guessed that the Funny One had wanted her to stay. A shiver passed through them.

Love would be the death of them yet.

Why were they all so silent? Why didn't they move, get angry, tell him to stop it, to shut up? Why were they torturing him? If he didn't speak, everything would turn into dust.

The River Goddesses were falling apart because love had entered their lives. The one with the braided hair had long wanted the Silent One to be her man. She had not known it until she felt shaken by a tremor every time he passed with a smile on his unspeaking lips. The tremor was more evident of late. Ever since the newcomer came, she sensed the ground beneath her quaking. Life was slipping away, swift as the current she stood in. The Silent One was slipping away too. He and the newcomer sat together for hours, not speaking. Why did the Silent One never sit with her on the riverbank? It pained her and the tremor grew and grew until it became a wild bird flapping in her chest, in her throat, in her hands that shook uncontrollably unless she twisted them together and held them hard.

Was the newcomer infecting the Silent One with her mysterious illnesses? Was the Silent One about to die? The world turned faint. Odourless, colourless, soundless, the world went far away from where she sat, stranded, denied the warmth and joy of life.

The other River Goddess was the first to see what troubled her. She of the Magnificent Shoulders clasped Her of the Braided Hair and tried to hush the tremors. She pressed their bodies together, hoping the warmth would travel from her enfolding arms and pounding heart into the other body, suddenly so frail inside her bigness, so small.

It was no use. The braided one shivered uncontrollably. The other companions saw that something was wrong. Together, they enlarged the circle of arms that held the ailing River Goddess, who flapped and flailed as if she were really a fish left to die on dry ground. They all soothed her, but the one who soothed her most was the Silent One, for in his comforting she found that he returned her love. Colour seeped back into her grey world, and now when she shook, she clung to the Silent One's bony fingers and felt safer.

Poka's soft body nestled against Ciggy's lean legs. No one nestled close to Momo. The boy saw and did not see. Why was Angie looking at him that way? Was she angry? Was she hurt?

The other River Goddess felt oddly hurt by the desertion of her soul-twin from the riverbank. They didn't stand in the water any more, gazing at the palms. The braided one would rather sit with the Silent One, not saying much, as if she were training to be his disciple.

She never guessed that it was her resentment that caused the ooze that stained her sunny temper an evil shade. Every morning when she woke, it fouled her mood and made her grim, unapproachable. The more she tried to forget it, the more it came back to nag her. She wanted to stand waist-deep in the river and let the current wash it away. Her magnificent shoulders stooped with the shame of it. But she was proud, and so she never shared her trouble, not even when the whispering nights grew longer and everyone else's troubles lay bared.

It was the newcomer who made it easy. *This, my love, is for you.* Of all the companions, She of the Magnificent Shoulders had watched the newcomer most closely, and been the most protective. To her, the newcomer was like an open landscape, now ravaged by yellow forest fire, now bristling with ice, now parched and cracked with despair, now green with hope. She saw changes sweeping through her, sparing nothing. She thought of the newcomer often. Her open willingness to be watched. Her lack of shame or guilt or apology that she should be the centre of their concern, the upsetter of their ordered days.

She bore no signs of being a victim, even though she was one. This gave the River Goddess courage. She decided to be stronger, and so, all by herself, inspired by the newcomer's strength, she triumphed over her affliction. While all the other companions fretted about the newcomer's influence, she the magnificent-shouldered admired her.

But what about the Silent One? And the king? The companions couldn't tell. The Silent One never spoke. And the king was never present. The newcomer could have told them a thing or two about what was going on in those two hearts. But they didn't ask, and so, she didn't tell.

You see, the cracks had always been there. With the newcomer in their midst, the cracks became visible.

There was a breeze like a short sigh. The boy was sweating. Would it finally rain? His calves felt as if they might suddenly cramp. He drank a swig of water, and noticed Baby beginning to smile.

It was the Wise One who came up with a solution.

'She must answer the question the Deity of the Well wants to ask,' he said.

'What if she can't answer?' said the magnificent-shouldered River Goddess. It troubled her to think they might expose the newcomer to harm.

'Let her at least try,' said the Wise One. 'If the Deity is pleased with her answer and lets her drink, she will be well again.' *And so will we...*

He did not say the last four words aloud. But everyone heard them as if he had.

'Let the king decide,' said the Funny One. 'He was the one who stopped her when she was willing.'

The companions nodded. The king would have to be told.

All this time, the king had chosen to stay away. No one knew why and no one dared to ask him. It was time to call him out and let him speak. The River Goddesses went to him.

'Come and join us tonight,' they said. 'We need to settle the doubt that has spread throughout the land.'

The king could not refuse the two women, which was why the Wise One had sent them. He nodded. To the River Goddesses it seemed he had grown old.

That night, they all sat by the Well under a bright starlit sky. It was cool and breezy and it lifted their hearts. This was the way things had been before the newcomer came into their charmed circle of nine. Even the Two who never spoke, who kept themselves to themselves, felt included in the warmth that night. The Small One sat close to the Funny One. The Funny One sat very close to her.

'We need to cure the newcomer,' said the Wise One.

A long silence followed. It was as if even the Deity of the Well was listening.

'There is a way we haven't tried,' said the Funny One,

whom the king trusted the most. 'She can answer the Deity's question.'

They held their breath. Would the king flare up again? He sat, eyes dark, thinking. 'She is one of us, is that not enough for the Deity?' he said at last. No one spoke.

'And what if she answers? Will the water truly make her well?'

'We cannot say,' the braided one said. 'But it would put a stop to the awful lies they spread about her.'

'What lies?' the king said, with a quick, pained look.

'They call her the Scourge,' the magnificent one said. 'They think she brings disease where there has never been anything but wellness. They fear her and what she might do to them.'

And to you and to us, the companions thought. We fear it too.

Only the magnificent one looked scornful of such an idea.

'What if she cannot answer?' said the king at last. 'Will that not double the mistrust and the malaise? What then?'

'That is a chance we will have to take,' the Wise One said. 'I think she will answer, and answer well.'

There was reproach in his voice, for not allowing her to speak that first time. The king must have felt it, for he said nothing more. Towards the end of the long night, he spoke.

'Let us do it. Even if it does not cure her, at least it will cure the people of their hatred for her. Tomorrow morning, we will bring her to the Well.'

'Stop, stop, stop!' said Baldy, making the boy jump out of his skin. 'Not another word until I have returned

from the loo! Hold your horses, everyone, hold your breath, hold on half a tic!' And he raced off to the side of the lobby where the washrooms were. The boy could have done with a break himself, but something made him reluctant to get up, as if the minute he did, so would the others and the night would be over, the spell would be broken and he would be alone again. He drank some more water, grinned feebly at Molly and looked at his toes. What did she think of his story? How would he ever know?

'All done!' sang Baldy. 'Tell on, tell on!'

And as if activated purely by the sound of Baldy's too-loud voice, the boy told on.

The next morning dawned cool and clear. The newcomer always woke early. When the companions told her of the plan to take her to the Well, she agreed, simply, without fuss. They didn't tell her that the earlier they went, the less the chances were of being spotted, followed and abused. It was a foolish precaution. It was summer and the women went early to the well, but the companions didn't think of that.

They walked swiftly. The Goddesses walked on either side of the newcomer, the king walked ahead and the rest behind. The breeze skipped lightly at their heels. Any minute now the sun would rise. If they felt any nervousness, they did not show it.

The Well was silent, as usual, this Well that never dried, no matter how cruel the summer. The Goddesses peered into it, hoping to see themselves, but the dawn had not sent its fingers into the well, and so only the dark looked back at them. They made a circle. The king cleared his throat.

'We are back,' he said, a shade louder than he need have in that quiet dawn. 'She will answer and then she will drink.'

He needn't sound so proud, the companions thought. The Deity is not to be treated lightly.

But they said nothing.

The bucket hit the dark water with a splash. Up it came with the grind and creak of the pulley, worked by the strong arms of the River Goddesses. They swung the full bucket out. The newcomer cupped her hands and brought the water to her lips, knowing it to be an empty gesture. And then the Voice said, 'Wait. You cannot drink until you have answered my question.'

Water trickled out from the newcomer's pale hands. She lifted up her perfectly shaped head, and said in a small, resigned voice, 'Ask.'

'What is worse than death?' the Deity said.

'Disease,' the newcomer said.

'What is better than disease?'

'Dying.'

'What is the best way to die?'

'Peacefully.'

'Which would you choose—life or death?'

'Life, because it includes death.'

'Is disease a symptom or a cause?'

'Both. It is the symptom of our lives and the cause of our deaths.'

The companions and their king were listening carefully. The Deity had never asked more than one question before.

'When do you feel most alive?'

'When I embrace death.'

'What is your greatest sorrow?'

'Not being able to immortalize each joy.'

'Why is joy so important?'

'Because it is the reason to be.'

'What is eternity?'

'A palmful of water reflecting the sky.'

The Deity fell silent. The breathing of the king and his companions was the only sound that broke through the surface of that silence like bubbles.

And then the Deity said, 'You have answered well. You may drink deep!'

The king sighed out loud. No one looked at him. The newcomer brought up another handful of water and drank. It was like a bird drinking. The Goddesses urged her to drink more. Succumbing to their will, she drank and then she wiped her face with her wet hands and said, 'Can we go home now?'

She was like a child at the mercy of those who believed themselves older and wiser. She trusted them completely. It made the companions feel guilty of unacknowledged crimes. The king, on the other hand, looked radiant. He cast a triumphant glance at the unseen Deity and turned away. As he turned, he grasped the newcomer's hand.

'Come,' he said.

The king and the newcomer—who was not new any more—walked on ahead. The companions, shocked by what they had seen their king do, followed. The people were waking up, coming out of their houses. At first they watched them pass without saying a word. Then the murmurs began.

'The Scourge has smitten the king.'

'The Scourge is a witch!'

And then new murmurs.

'The Scourge has drunk from the Well!'

'She has answered the Deity and drunk the water!'

'She is accepted! The Deity has blessed her!'

Before they knew it, the crowds following them were huge, a low singing had begun and still the king had not let go of the newcomer's hand.

The boy could feel his heart pounding in his throat. If he swallowed hard, would it go back to its right place? Please god, please let her not hate me.

The newcomer needed a new name. She was now neither the Scourge nor new. But the companions couldn't think of a name and so she remained nameless, except among the people, who, swinging from one extreme to another, decided to call her the Blessed.

The companions, with all their book-learning and uncertainty, hesitated to call her the Blessed. The king's weakness, they called her in their minds. The Girl who weakened their fellowship. The image of the king grasping her hand hung before them like a taunt. The king was weakening.

And so was the newcomer. How stubbornly the old name clung to her, refusing to be shaken off! There was no reason to rejoice in being called the Blessed. The water she had drunk had not cured her. Far from it. As if making up for lost time, her body flashed through a series of ailments, each worse than the other. One day she was whooping with coughs, the next day she was pitted with bumps. She sweated, bled, spotted, shook, shivered, retched, bloated, shrank, blistered, prickled, panted, choked and babbled in delirium. Nothing spared her. She rejected nothing. And all the while, the king stood by, helplessly watching the girl whose hand he had caught, feeling inside him the first stirrings of the weakness the companions had witnessed by the Well.

It was the king's heart. As he stood and watched the girl convulsing through disease like a translucent doll, he felt a valve in his heart flap open. It was as if he were seeing it before him—first a strong and beating heart, then the sudden stutter, the missed beat, the rush of too much blood or too little. He didn't clutch his heart to dramatize his little discovery. He just stood there, feeling the palpitations that signalled the beginning of the end.

He would have given anything to marry the girl whose hand he had caught. Marrying was forbidden, and that is why the mere longing to do it made him feeble. It would mean losing the kingship, shedding the mantle of his Self. He would have to call for the tournament right away, years before he would have if she had not arrived. But he would call it, he would play and willingly lose, and then he would walk out a free man and marry the girl who lay dying.

The companions read his thoughts as plainly as if he had uttered them. With the king gone, the fellowship they treasured so dearly would be lost. Destroyed as surely as the afflictions were destroying the girl he wanted to throw everything away for. All that the water had done was restore her to purity in the minds of the people of the Land of the Well. Suddenly she was blameless.

But was she?

The companions resented the king's weakness. But because they were loyal to him, and because they wanted to save themselves, they looked after her night and day.

Let her not die, the magnificent one begged. Let her live. Without her how will we ever understand what our own bodies are trying to tell us? Only she knows, only she can help.

This wish of theirs was accompanied by another, more devious one.

Let her live, they prayed, but let her not be changed too much. If she emerges completely cured, what will happen? Will she and the king go off and leave us to our own damaged fates?

As they watched her, tended her and bathed her, conflicting thoughts raced through their minds like fevers of their own.

The king sat vigil every night. One night, too exhausted to protest, he let the companions take him to the farthest room and put him to bed. He fell asleep at once. After what seemed like ages, he slept soundly. When he awoke, forgetting for a second where he was and why, he found the doors of the house flung wide open. The companions were nowhere to be seen. Nor was she, the dying one. Wild panic seized hold of the king who had fought many battles alone and unarmed. What had happened while he slept? Why had he slept? Where was she?

He ran to the open doors and saw the companions coming down the road. Behind them walked a multitude of people, the people of the entire land. What was going on? What were the Two Who Looked and Walked Alike carrying in their arms?

He reeled when he recognized her body. It looked smaller in their arms than it did when she was lying down. She was wet through. She hung limp and wet on a rigging of bones. Each bone seemed to slice through her skin, the air, his eyes. He couldn't run to her as he would have liked to, the people of his entire land were watching and he would have to be kingly, for them. He waited, every nerve straining, his heart missing beat after beat after beat. They had reached the open doorway where he stood.

'The people found her when they went to draw water this morning,' the Funny One said, looking straight into the king's eyes as if to steady him. 'She had thrown herself into the Well.'

The king's heart struggled to pump the blood that would carry this message to his brain. He stayed uncomprehending. The Two who had never had any function before now had one. They carried the dead girl between them, their strong arms holding her as if she weighed nothing. The Wise One's baby face was grey. The River Goddesses' faces were wet. He looked and looked and still he couldn't see what they showed him.

But he was their king. Now what was the use of calling for the tournament he wanted to lose for her? Would he stay their king till kingdom come? He mocked himself, and only because the people stood there, a sea of waiting faces, did he know what to say next.

'The Deity took her,' he said, surprised to find his voice steady. 'She was wise, like the Deity, and they belonged together. Eternity, she said to the Deity, is a palmful of water reflecting the sky. She who was mortal is now part of eternity. Each time you, my beloved people, cup your hands to drink she will be part of that gesture, repeated through the ages. And her memory will grow as long and as deep as the shadow of the Well in our hearts.'

Every word cost him. But the crowd was thrilled. Some burst into tears, others raised their voices and hailed him. He had spoken well, even if he felt ice streaming into his blood, freezing him as he stood. He turned away.

'What shall we do with her,' the Goddesses asked, the only ones who dared.

'Give her to the water she so longed to be part of. Give her to your river, let her be carried down to the sea.'

He said this and closed the doors.

The companions turned away, towards the river. The crowd surged behind.

'The Blessed One!' they chanted. 'Eternity!'

The magnificent one wanted to rage at them and at her companions. When they came to the river it was she and her soul-twin who took the girl's body, light as a broken branch, and waded waist-deep before letting her go where the current was swift and would carry her far, far out of their lives.

When they returned to the house, the king was gone. No one had seen him go, for they had all been by the river. They rushed to the Well, but he was not there. He had vanished as surely as if he had been spirited away. What about the tournament? What about the new king? Who would take his place? How would they choose the new king without the old one? How could he have left?

Heedless of what the land demanded, he had gone.

The companions had no words to soothe each other. She was gone, and so was he. It was all her fault. First she had brought with her the jitter of doubt and disease, now she had taken with her their leader, their king. And she hadn't even answered their questions! Why hadn't she, when she knew so much? What made her speak to the Deity and not to them? Why did she have to kill herself?

The companions felt betrayed, and they left the land too, looking for a place where they might forget.

Injured and ageing, they left, knowing in their hearts that they would never return.

Eighteen

No one spoke. No one moved. What did he expect, a standing ovation? The boy looked away towards the far end of the pool, wishing he could dive into it. Wherever his words had taken him, he had followed, trusting completely. Hadn't he felt the same warmth and sureness when he spun his tale that morning? But now that it was over, he felt hollow and embarrassed. His left hand was resting on the still-warm concrete, the weight of his body on it. His wrist felt ready to snap. Weak and useless.

'So. The little myth-maker has spoken,' Baby said at last. 'And spoken well.'

The boy's heart gave a little leap of pleasure.

'But curious,' Baby continued. 'Very curious. While turning us all into archetypes, you left yourself out. The innocent, as you would undoubtedly have called yourself.'

No, the boy felt like snapping, pleasure turning to bile so swiftly it made his head spin, *as you have already called me!*

'Why such modesty?'

He had gone back to that earlier version of Baby near the hidden river. Nasty for no reason. The boy didn't reply. It wasn't that kind of question.

'But,' Tiger broke in suddenly, as if leaping out from under cover. 'What happened to me? You can't just say I disappeared and expect me to feel better, can you? Where to?'

It was meant to lighten the air, but all it did was heighten the chalk-dust taste in the boy's mouth. They were not nice, they were barbed and twisted, and anything he said or did could lead anywhere except to feeling more like one of them. They were unstable, deranged.

'And why were we all so villainous, darling?' Angie's voice drawled. 'You made us sound like a sinister sect of fetishists.'

The boy wasn't sure what 'fetishist' meant, but he didn't like the way it thickened and sharpened on her tongue. A tool to poke someone's eye out with.

'At least you were the compassionate one, Angie,' Poka said, 'praying for her life and all. I was one of the bad guys. And Tiger, poor Tiger...'

That wasn't what she should have said. Ciggy coughed uneasily. As if that were a signal, Baldy's voice rose as he heaved himself off his deckchair, 'Enough malingering, you maniacal morbid misfits! Midnight makes towards morn!'

The boy couldn't help it. He giggled. Baldy had punctured the venomous bubble they all seemed to be trapped inside. The spite leaked out as they laughed. But something unpleasant lingered—inside the boy.

Why did they insist on him being such a sport when they themselves weren't? Why was he here instead of in his room, plugged into his music, plugged out of the world? Why had he thought they were people worth knowing when they couldn't even take a little made-up story, which they themselves had asked for?

Maybe not having friends wasn't such a bad thing after all.

And yet, despite his annoyance, how he still longed for them to like him! How he yearned for an approving smile, an arm around his shoulder, a hug. All those things they had given him, just this evening, and now they were withdrawing like anacondas engorged with prey. The boy wanted to rewind to the morning. His hope had grown with every hurdle he passed. He would return to Bombay with them. He would now have places to go to on weekends, hang out with the gang, doing cool adult things instead of walking bleary-eyed in the morning to buy pau for mother. The high point of Sunday, bhurjee-pau at eleven, and the TV on, parents going off for lunch at the club, happy in the belief that their boy was having friends over, good to let him have the house to himself sometimes. Now he could truly have friends over. They would come, and he would get Usha to cook for them, or they would call in, pizzas or Chinese, and spend the afternoon lazing, and then blaze off in the evening first to one haunt and then another, driving for the sake of it, maybe even to the beach where they would have bhel and gola before going home, not his home, theirs, to talk and drink some more.

'Moronic muffins, more like it,' said Angie. 'My god, how we've scared the little lad. Cheer up, cherub, don't take everything we say so seriously!'

The boy looked tentatively in her direction. The night was black but the bright blue glow from the pool hid nothing. She was smiling, she seemed friendly. He wanted to lighten up but you never knew with these people. They were as predictable as the monsoons. *If only it would rain and drown us all.*

'Wait, where's Momo?' Baldy asked.

All his anxiety, hurt and uncertainty fused into a flash of pure dread. Where indeed was Momo?

The boy got up, forgetting his sprained wrist and the crick that had been creeping into his neck. She was nowhere to be seen. He had been so snuffed out by their rejection of his story that he hadn't even noticed she was not part of it. She had been sitting across him all along, on one of the deckchairs. He had been content knowing she was there, listening to him. Then the story had absorbed him, and once it was over, the blow of their reaction had blotted out everything except his disappointment. When did she leave? Where did she go? Inside his chest, the hammering began.

'She must have gone back to her room,' Poka said. They were all up. They were like leopards, the boy thought. One moment lethal and lazy, the next moment alert, sniffing the wind. They cared for that girl, no matter what he had said. Why did he make them dislike her in his story? Why did he make Tiger disappear?

Suddenly the boy felt a blinding hate for Tiger. He had seen it and that's how it came out in his story. Tiger loved Momo. The way she leaned back on the pillow in her summer dress, touching Tiger's bare and furry arms. The way he didn't draw away, nor give her a normal buddy hug, but sat still, as if holding his breath. The way she never teased him. *But she never teased anyone, she never spoke, except to ask me strange questions.* Tiger and she were trying to avoid each other and he had lifted the veil and seen it all.

Panic and hate. Not an easy combination at any point. Even less when you're with people you've only just met and who are out to make you look bad. Not easy when the panic is for the one you love and the hate for the one you've discovered loves her too. The boy stood as if robbed of all thought, all ability to move or act.

And then he was walking behind them, scurrying to catch up like a child whose strides don't match the adults'. He was caught in the cross-current of their alarm, and he felt it strong.

'Her cellphone's here, but she isn't,' said Poka, who had gone up the steps faster than you imagined she could with her bulk, calling out from the balcony of the empty room as the rest of them stood below, staring upwards. They could have been a bunch of Goan serenaders, if the mood hadn't been so grim and the girl on the balcony so agitated.

'Must have got bored with Pappu's story and wandered off to the beach,' said Baldy, with a half-laugh. 'Too polite to interrupt. I tell you, these convent-educated girls!'

It was thin, his attempt to lighten things up.

'Come down and we'll go look,' Ciggy said.

Poka raced down. She was the only one who mirrored what the boy felt. He wanted to run to the beach, screaming out her name. That dark path with the broken lamps. Those salesmen, probably all drunk, but maybe not all asleep. Snakes in the grass. A twisted ankle. Her ankles so delicate. They hurried towards the edge where the cottages ended and the path began. Had it only been this evening *last evening* that he had walked down the same path, his heart singing? It seemed gross and untrue. The one functioning lamp was out. Switched off in a fit of economy. No one goes to the beach this late. How dare they! The boy was furious with the place, the monsoon negligence, the implied insult in not respecting the hotel guest's slightest whim, like walking to the beach at any unearthly hour. Baldy, so well prepared before, had left his torch somewhere and he scolded himself loudly for it. They must walk blind. The others might link up, take refuge in each other, hold hands, but he couldn't. He dreaded them again. Touch was to be dreaded. He stumbled over the lip of the path onto the slope leading to the beach. Already his eyes were getting used to shades of dark. The huge glittering stars he had rejoiced in so stupidly were gone. Clouds, monsoon, his brain informed him, dully. Storm approaching. The steady roar at the edge of the lighter dark that was the sand, it could crush them, that roar. It could sweep them away. Was it high tide? Was there less beach now than before? It was hard to say in that many-shaded shifting dark. They ran down the slope. How could they see if she was there or not? Surely she wouldn't have gone walking in the pitch dark? If she wanted the rush of sea in her ears, she might as well have sat here near their marker tree. Or left her sandals at least, as a sign.

Nothing. Baldy shouted. Her name was snatched away by the roar. Then Baldy and Molly and Dodo and Ciggy and Baby and the boy shouted. He, shouting her name, that silly nickname of hers that had nothing to do with the bone-woman she was, ivorine and perfect. Tiger did not shout. Even as the boy yelled, foolish, unwanted, he noticed that Tiger did not shout.

There was no answer. They didn't expect an answer. They were shouting to keep the fear away, flinging it like a dare at the roar of the water they saw in fits and starts, a brief gleam, sullen in the light of an abruptly exposed then concealed star.

They stopped shouting and stood still, uncertain. If he had been alone he would have raced down the beach, whatever of it was still sand, first in one direction all the way to the turn of the rock, and then the other. If he had been alone he wouldn't have needed to run. He wouldn't have known them. He wouldn't have been in love. He wouldn't be here at all, wishing he had the guts to run up and down calling her name, hoping to save her and win her, the way they did in stories. *Not mine.* But he wasn't. He was at the outermost fringe of a strange group and he would take his cue from them. She was their friend first.

'Where where where where,' Poka moaned. 'Where could the fool have gone?'

The boy could tell in the dark that she was close to tears.

'Let's search the grounds. She's so mad she might be sitting in the lobby, thinking. Or in the games room, fast asleep. With Momo you never know!'

It was Baldy, trying to making things sound silly, and therefore less frightening.

'You girls! What would you do without us to look after you!'

No one rose to the bait. Neither the big women nor the little one. They walked back the way they had come, their feet surer now. The only thing about them that was surer.

They searched the grounds. In between the sixty-four cottages the paths were thankfully well lit. There were little grass triangles everywhere. They peered at them for any shape that looked like a sleeping or sitting body. They climbed up the wooden steps of the games room, steep and ladder-like but for its banister, and switched on the shaded swinging lamps. It was foolish to think of her here, among the carom boards and the pool tables. They switched off the lamps and climbed down. They went to the open bar where a cartoon mural of Goa took up an entire wall. They tiptoed through the lobby, the tall-backed cane chairs looking like alien furniture in the almost-dark. A thin man, unknown to the boy, slept with his head on the reception counter. The sound of his hoarse breathing seemed immense in the vaulted lobby.

'Shall we wake him up and ask?' Poka whispered.

'No use, he's out like a light. Wouldn't have seen an elephant pass,' said Baldy. They were standing in front of the hotel where the neatly laid cobbles stared up whitely. Above the arch, a light shone and on either side of the gate were bright globes of light. The gate was closed. In the watchman's box, the night watchman dozed. Cradled across his knees was a rifle.

'Fat lot of good these jokers are,' scowled Baldy. 'One snoring, the other singing lullabies to his gun. Useless. What if the hotel were raided? Or bombed? HEY!'

The boy jumped, Baldy's shout was so unexpected. The night watchman leapt up, dropped his gun, bent to pick it up and waved it around before he saw the only threat was a bald guy peering angrily into his cabin.

'Are you on duty or what?'

The man mumbled.

'Did you or did you not see a girl leave the hotel?'

Baldy spoke slowly, saying each word clearly and loudly as if speaking to an idiot. The man mumbled incoherently and waved his gun about.

'Well, remember that you saw us,' Baldy said fiercely. 'We are going out to look for our friend and if we are not back soon I want you to send reinforcements. Understood?'

The man mumbled.

They squeaked open the big iron gates and slipped through.

'*You!*' Baby rounded on the boy. 'It's your fault!'

The boy stared at Baby, too astounded to speak.

'Do you remember the story you told, or is that too much to ask of a boy-genius?'

The boy didn't let the sarcasm dripping from Baby's words bother him. He couldn't. Baby was worried too. This was his way of showing it…

'Why did you have to make her throw herself in the well?'

The viciousness in Baby's tone frightened him. He found himself answering, 'B-but why should she do what *I* said?'

'Why indeed! Maybe she thought you were psychic. You wouldn't know, would you, boy-genius, that for the last two years Momo has been systematically trying to kill herself?'

Whatever heartbeat was left in the boy died, then surged.

'And then you tell her a story where she does kill herself and it's all very romantic and timeless! For two years now we've been trying to prevent something like this from happening and you come waltzing in out of the blue and make it sound like the only perfect prophetic ending there could be!'

You're the ones who picked me out of the blue, one part of the boy wanted to protest. The other part of him went silent and stunned. What was Baby suggesting? It was outrageous.

He should have been angry, violently angry, but all he could feel was stunned. *He* had made the woman he loved go kill herself? The words unfolded in his brain very, very slowly. Then he should be the one to know where she went.

'The river.'

The boy wasn't aware that he had spoken, but evidently he had for they stopped looking away and stared at him.

'In that case, it's the river.'

Someone, was it Poka, drew in her breath sharply. It cut through the air and made him wince.

'The boy-genius has spoken!' Baby said angrily. 'His words have driven her to the river. Bravo!'

He was already walking away from the gate, towards the little lane.

'Wait,' said Baldy. 'Let me find the damned torch. That lane wasn't too cheerful even at midday,' and he slipped back through the gate. They waited, their silences knocking against each other. When Baldy came back he held an enormous ancient aluminium torch, not the tiny but powerful Maglite he had carried earlier.

'At least some use that old fool was,' he said, shaking the torch to make the light flicker on. 'Come on!'

They slipped into the lane. At night, it had none of its charm and all of its creepiness. Inside the hotel, dead and heavy though the air had been, it carried a hint of faraway movement, some undertone of the sea roar and movement that made you remember you were at the cusp of land and water. Here, there was nothing. They were enveloped in a thick soundless sludge, throats tightening as they breathed. The feeble torch-beam flickered eerily over the bright furniture. Ghost town. Ghost carnival. The giant guitar-strummer. His shiny blue knees were caught in the travelling beam of the watchman's torch that Baldy wielded like a stick. Would the mascot drop his guitar and send his hands after them, would his head swivel as they passed? The boy was behind the others, he would be snagged first, and even if he screamed they would never hear it in this lane that sucked up all sound. The boy hurried up and bumped into Molly.

'Sorry,' he said, feeling sorry that he had ignored Molly so openly. Maybe Molly at least would have been on his side now, if he hadn't ignored him and sucked up only to the others. The old Goan house looked impenetrable. The boy remembered the old man. Was he an insomniac? Had he spirited Momo away? Was he watching them now with an old man's sleep-deprived murderous eyes, looking for another victim? The boy hurried.

They had come to the turn. Here in the gap where the white houses guarded the river, the air eased, as it had before. He felt shivery and hot as he remembered the boat. Would she be lying in that boat, asleep?

'The boat's here,' Baldy said, 'but not her.'

He flashed the torch impatiently at the river, which lay still. Not even a little splash against the moored boat. All sound, all movement was gone.

Nineteen

'Guilt and retribution, insect,' said Baby's softly menacing voice. 'The stuff I believe in, remember?'

In the sweltering air of the lane the dark inched closer. Would they throw him into the river? They couldn't! Such things didn't happen. Not in real life. But what had been real about his life since the morning? Since the evening before? The boy's shirt stank from sweat or fear or both. Shower and bed. He needed a shower and that soft hotel bed.

Of course he remembered. Baby had been so guilty about his friend's death that he threw himself into books. Funny way of showing your guilt. Very convenient. It's not as if he pined away and died. He lived, brittle bones or not, and he made defenceless people squirm. That was no way of showing how bad you felt!

But it was all in his head. Baby hadn't really killed his friend. It was an accident. He just assumed the guilt. He was arrogant about that too. *I made it happen. Now he was keen to foist this 'I made it happen' guilt on me.*

He didn't have to try very hard. The boy's insides were churning. He wanted to bite off his tongue. Black tongue. How crazy he sounded! A crazy old woman gabbing about black tongues. A curse on his words that made a human being disappear. A curse...

But Baby was saying something. The borrowed torch was dimming and brightening as if it were run on sound frequency, tuned to the jab and jitter of Baby's voice. *Let's go before it dies. Don't leave me alone in this airless lane without light.*

'We could leave you alone in this airless lane to find your own way back,' Baby purred. *It's uncanny the way he picks the words out of my thoughts.* 'But that would lack imagination, and imagination is not what we lack, as you might have gathered by now.'

Why had the others shut up so completely? Were they even there? The boy peered, sweat falling into his eyes as he blinked. Why did no one but Baby speak? Why didn't they run screaming to the hotel and call the police and rouse the sleepy place and send out men with dogs and drums? Why stand stone-stiff and look away as Baby needled him? He would do all the running and screaming and hunting. If he was guilty, he was willing to pay. *Let me go*, he suddenly felt like yelling. *We need to find her, you stupid fucks!*

He was in a comic strip. The action slowed as debris fell and the hero and his antithesis scorned each other with words while buildings flamed. It was a pause before the action kaboomed into chaos again. *Think of it as a comic strip.*

'She was our barometer, insect,' Baby continued, as if he had all the time in the world. 'If we were believers of the religious kind, we would have said she took our anxieties onto herself, that we might suffer less. And we did suffer less, looking at her. We suffered for her, and so we suffered less for ourselves. See? It's almost theological.'

What a pompous ass he was, what a complete maniac. Showing off, even now when she might simply have tripped somewhere in the dark and was this very minute waiting for her dear friends to come and untwist her bent leg from under her and carry her home. What power in that soft voice shut him up so completely, made him unable to utter his disgust? The boy was watching himself in mute. His head moved, his mouth opened, but no sound emerged.

'But now *you*, insect, *brilliant* storyteller with your unsheathed words, you have done away with her. Which leaves *us*. We'll talk, we'll show each other our scabs. Great. We'll count the remaining years. But we might want to die too, do you realize that, insect? Better the clean cut than the festering wound. Die young, for somewhere I believe we still think of ourselves as young. You don't, do you, insect? You—what are you, seventeen, eighteen?—you think we're old. When you're seventeen everyone who's over twenty is old. We have grey hair at the temples, do we not? We have bad livers, bad consciences. As you said so poetically—we are injured and ageing. Thank you very much. We are. Maybe we won't be for much longer. Maybe we'll give up the ghost right away.'

The torch-beam was pointing the boy away from the river towards the lane. The boy turned. Conscious of the spot of light aimed at his back, he found himself walking back the way they had come. He was the first now. If anything suddenly reared up, white-faced and black-mouthed in the middle of the path, he would be the first to see it. He was their shield against the horrors of that lane, their prisoner. Silent black shapes, the others followed him. They could all have been ghosts but for Baby with his quiet, insistent voice.

'And then again, maybe we won't live those long festering lives after all. Maybe we'll go back to the hotel, lock ourselves in our rooms and slit our wrists.'

And Momo? the boy wanted to scream. *What about her? Why don't we rescue her? Why talk?*

'Because Momo, undoubtedly, is dead. As sure as a body washed up two beaches away. We failed to save her. You know that, don't you, insect? It's all exactly as you said. With only one slight, but vital, difference. In my version, you don't get away. In your version, we left, never to return. Tiger was never heard of again. And you were never there. That's the part that needs a slight correction. You, so cleverly outside the ring, watching, passing judgement, you too will reach your end with us.'

They had reached the end of the lane. The road lay before them, the border of some impossible fairy-tale land where nothing like this ever happened. They crossed like a procession of mourners. They opened the gate. Baby dropped the torch on the table near the watchman's sleeping head. Baldy didn't yell. They scrunched across the cobbles. Baby was still talking.

'So now we go to our rooms and we do it. You're old enough to shave aren't you, insect? So you have a razor and you know how to use it. Don't tremble. Think of her and die well.'

He paused dramatically. They were past the cane chairs.

'Or wait, I forget my own ingeniousness. Or rather the ingeniousness of my friends. Nothing so messy for you, insect. Privileged not to be blood-smears against a wall, stains all over your clothes, blood all over the floor, the bathtub. It's already been done, insect. You're it.'

He started walking away. The rest shuffled after him, zombie-like. Not one person's expression could the boy see in that murky dark, the pool a glow just outside his field of vision. What was Baby talking about? What had already been done?

And then the hair on the boy's arms prickled. He felt the pinprick stab of that clear liquid-filled syringe. He had trusted Baldy. He had been a fool and let Baldy plunge the needle into his veins. *He was it.*

What had been in the syringe?

If sleep is what the boy had longed for, it now seemed like a cruel joke. In his room, that girly pink room that his mother liked so much, sleep fled from the boy as if he were a leper. He put on the lamps. The turned-down bed seemed snide, a tongue stuck out at his stupidity. Why were there no normal lights, big overhead lamps that would flood the room with unsparing brightness? Why these mood-making useless lamps you could barely see a corner by? He tore off his shirt and flung it to the floor. His solitary stink engulfed the room. He had forgotten the room had an air conditioner. He rushed to the bed and knelt in the circle of light the lamp threw on the bedside table.

His arm looked like it always had, hairless, and newly tanned after all those noontime trips. But there—on his left forearm below an old vaccination mark was a barely noticeable red bump, microscopic. He felt it with his right hand, one finger gently pressing. He had allowed his body to be opened up through this microscopic portal, and his body had accepted what went in without a murmur. Why had his body not protested? Why had he not foamed at the mouth and bled from the nose? Why was he not a barometer?

It had gone inside, that clear colourless liquid. What was it? It was in his blood now, not now, hours ago. Rushing around, being busily circulated. The boy remembered his biology drawings, the intricate heart, the efficient pumping machine. Where had his efficient heart sent that colourless liquid? Why had he not fainted or felt nauseous or giddy or any other kind of pain? *I did faint.* What was it? Would it kill him overnight? Or would it take years, some strange virus that would attach itself to his cells and reproduce until it killed him from inside? The body-snatchers. His own cells, by his own foolishness, attacked and taken over.

The boy dropped his head on his bent left arm and wept.

After what seemed like a long time, he realized his left arm was numb. He was still kneeling. The room was suffocating. He got up, slowly. He walked to the air conditioner and put it on. Should he wake the sleeping man at reception and ask him for the bill and a taxi, he was leaving right away, very early morning flight? Should he wake his parents with a frantic call? Should he tell them...what? That he had allowed some guys to inject him with an unknown liquid and now he thought he might die?

It came slowly, the sinking realization that he could tell no one. That's what made their plan so brilliant. It made him look so dumb he would have to stay dumb, just to prevent anyone from laughing at him. He was their best alibi. Signed, sealed, switched off. Mute as if he had a gag in his mouth.

But what about Momo?

Was she dead?

What madness made him stay on after no more than a glimpse of her? If he hadn't stayed on she would be alive and he...

His head throbbed painfully. His whole body ached. His eyes felt scratched and bruised. He wanted to weep again but the tears wouldn't come. He walked into the bathroom, clambered clumsily into the tub and opened the shower. He stood under the shower. It was a long while before he thought of soap and shampoo. He just needed the water to run over him, endlessly. He stood and stood and maybe he shampooed and soaped himself and maybe he came out in a towel or maybe he just dripped naked all over the carpet and collapsed onto the bed.

He was dying. She was dead. They would all be dead by morning.

A cold soberness fell on him like a winding sheet of ice. He was not shivering any more, as if ice was his true element. He was as cold as a corpse, only he wasn't dead, yet.

He towelled himself dry. He dressed. He opened his laptop, and began writing, faster, faster than he had ever written before.

He wrote:

This is not the first time. They have killed a boy before.

Accusation

This is not the first time. They have killed a boy before. His name was Abhimanyu but they called him Christmas. They told me everything I write in these pages for you to find when you find my body. Every murderer needs to confess. They confessed to me. Every word is true. They thought I would be dead enough, or stupid enough, to stay silent. How wrong they were.

Abhimanyu was a boy even younger than me. He was fifteen and they killed him. No, Baby killed him, but the others were accomplices. All of them, Baldy, Poka, Angie. No, not all of them. Not Momo. She was a victim too. She was their guinea pig, their lab rat. Angie told me this herself. They tested Baby's theories on her. Baby was twisted inside. He was a psychopath, the kind you find in movies. He had a pet theory on illness and disease and he made Momo his lab rat and Abhimanyu his victim. He told me everything. No, he SHOWED me everything. He took me to his room after dinner, making sure no one else was around, and he showed me. His notebooks, where he copied things down. His laptop where he wrote reams and reams of notes, his ideas, his experiences, his dark deeds.

'Speed-read them, insect!' he told me, sneering. I did. I speed-read them, and I committed them to memory. Baby didn't know that about me. But even if he had, he wouldn't have cared. And you know why? Because he thought I wouldn't dare talk. No, because he *knew* I wouldn't live to tell the tale. And even if I did who would believe me? You. You must believe me, you must, no matter how outrageous it sounds, it is the truth. He took the risk, he exposed himself, he told me everything because he had already planned my death, my silence. I fooled him, didn't I? And he thought he fooled me! Making up aliases for each one in the gang, cover-ups, nicknames, smokescreen. I saw through them all and here I am, putting it all down in black and white before I die.

Baby's real name is Pravin.

Baldy's real name is Abhinay.

Angie's real name is Chitrangada.

Poka's real name is Bonolota.

I know the other's real names too, but the others weren't as guilty as these four. Shall I write them down, anyway?

Ciggy's real name is Shantanu.

Lolly's real name is Lavanya.

Tiger's real name is Mukul.

Molly's real name is Amulya.

Dodo's real name is Aniruddh.

There it is, their alibis blown, so that they can be nabbed, nailed, condemned. They shared the guilt, even if all the guilt should have been Baby's alone. Shall I tell you their gang names too? What good would it do? Between my private names for them and the names they told me were theirs, between their gang names, their nicknames and their real names, what were they hiding? A trail of blood.

Murder, with the victim as accomplice. I was both victim and accomplice, until now. Now I have added a third role to my persona—accuser.

Baby had a fixation for death and disease, did I tell you that already? He kept notebooks, the old-fashioned kind, the kind you wrote in with a pen. Notebooks on Illness. Death. Degeneration. Mutilation. He copied his favourite quotes into those notebooks and used them to brainwash his gang. Everything was diseased for him. Even cities. A city is like a tumour, he wrote in his book. We carry our illnesses inside us. A hepatitis virus can be beautiful. This is the kind of thing he tripped on. He was crazy about the insides of our bodies. The fluids, the stink. Only he used fancy words like 'contagion' and 'allure'. He wanted to *be* a book, that man. He wanted to play god. The God of Death. That's why he came up with Who Dares—Dies. You know what was so evil about Who Dares—Dies? It wasn't what the name made it sound like. It wasn't about daring to throw yourself off a cliff or jumping in front of a speeding train. Nothing so honest and upfront. It was devious and dirty. Baby liked to work in devious ways. He liked to make you do all the dirty work. He infected your mind with thoughts of illness, with fear, with an extreme loathing for life. He wanted you to kill yourself slowly, disgustingly, not with poison you drank out of a Baygon bottle or a chunni you hung from a fan and tightened around your neck. That wouldn't do for him. He wanted something intellectual!

That was his biggest problem. He was an asshole trying to be a genius. He was fucked up to begin with and then Yanky's death drove him completely mad. Yanky was his best friend. (He didn't tell me his real name, and I never thought it might be important.) He told Yanky rotten things about his girlfriend while they were climbing a cliff and Yanky got pissed off, unhitched himself from the rope and fell to his death. And then Baby got a slipped disc and stayed in hospital for weeks and that's the time he started reading crazy morbid books like *Doctor Brodie's Report* and *The Atrocity Exhibition* and thinking about death. If he was so guilty why didn't he go kill himself? As if he had the guts! Instead, he started this cult, pushing others to kill themselves while he watched and laughed at how stupid people were. He described that book to me, the Atrocity one. It had a naked girl on the cover, only her skin was peeled off so you could see the meat inside, and all the nerves and lumps of bone. It wasn't a sexy picture. Inside there was another girl inserting things into her vagina. I hated the words Baby used. Nasal pit, urethral groove, hymen. Lactiferous duct, gland of Montgomery, parenchyma of breast. Comminuted fracture, posterior dislocation. He was obsessed with breasts and cross-sections of anatomy. He was obsessed with fractures, the names of bones, patella, fibula, tibia, he thought he was so cool. The chapter that had the illustrations Baby was raving about was called 'The University of Death'. Even if I don't write another word, that should be proof enough.

You had to harm *yourself*—that was his greatest trick. You had to find what hurt you most, what scared you most, and press and press until you bled and shat and broke down, internally, physically, emotionally. And if you didn't know what your problem was, why Baby would help you find it! He took pleasure in discovering what was wrong with you, he was great at that. And if you didn't have anything wrong with you to begin with, by the time he was through with you, you would. He had a radar, the minute he spotted the chink in your defences, he zoomed in for the kill. But mostly he let you do it all by yourself.

'Find the means to target the weakest spot in your psyche, your system, and work at it, day after day, relentlessly, until the whole of you crumbles around that eroded place,' the great guru told his followers. If you had a weak stomach he encouraged you to feed it all kinds of garbage. If you had a weak heart he advised you to tax it, alarm it, jolt it. If you had asthma he suggested you inhale dust and smoke. If you were afraid of heights or closed rooms or spiders he made you go looking for heights, closed rooms, and spiders. He told me how the gang went into friends' garages, turned on the engines and inhaled exhaust. How they drank tap water from anywhere, especially when illnesses were floating around. How they tore their own skin, just to see it bleed. How they kept food outside the fridge in summer and ate it when it had turned, gone sour, the rice, the potatoes. How they kept cats because they had heard cat owners ended up with fur balls in their stomachs which they thought was a fascinating way to fall ill. They never took tetanus shots if they got scratched by one of their cats or by nails. They searched for mangy dogs, so they could nuzzle against them, especially the girls. The boys in the gang looked out for men at the barber shops with skin conditions and waited to be shaved after them. They had heard that barbers who shaved the old-fashioned way with the strop razor caught nail infections from the foam they wiped off the edge of the blade each time. They believed a head massage might pass on such an infection, and so they went for old-fashioned shaves and more head massages than they needed. They met at the strangest places to share their adventures, at defunct bus stops, in public gardens in the middle of the afternoon, even sitting on road dividers until the cops came to shoo them away.

'It's not about immediate results, folks,' he said to his gang, 'it's not like instant coffee. This one will take a good long time to brew. We're doing something very important. We're breaking the taboo. We've dared to cross the line that separates acceptable behaviour from unacceptable behaviour. We've plunged the syringe in, we've let the blood flow out, we've swallowed the rot, we've braved the blade. It isn't courage that we lack. But do we lack determination, resilience, sheer bloody cussedness? We can only find out by taking the path we've chosen wherever it leads us, no matter how vile, no matter how harmful, no matter how destructive of our selves.'

These are the kind of speeches he gave! He was a raving loony, but so were the others to go along with him. Why did they listen to him? They were all so close to him, all of them, Baldy, Tiger, Ciggy, Angie, Poka and Momo. Momo. I loved her so much my stomach hurt, I wanted to throw up. I ran to my room and clutched the basin and retched and nothing came. I was sick with love for her. But she didn't give a damn. She looked at me just once, when I fainted after they injected me with the needle, and she spoke to me just once. If it weren't for her I wouldn't be here, I wouldn't be writing this, I wouldn't be dead tomorrow. But she's not the one I accuse, never. She was harmed too. She was dying because they were killing her. They were pushing her, slowly, fatally, over the brink.

Baby started Who Dares—Dies on the net. He was ecstatic about the number of people who thought like him and agreed with his bizarre ideas. The first virtual meet was so good they decided to meet in person.

'You know, insect, that week of waiting and thinking about the kind of people who would turn up almost killed me,' Baby told me. I *hated* being called an insect. But I was too awed by him to protest. 'I was excited and agog, I was tripping on the thought that there were people sick enough to want to be sick.'

He said it, not me. A bunch of sickos, for whom illness was something they *wanted*, like sex. I was disgusted by what Baby told me, and still I listened. I couldn't stop listening, and I'm glad glad glad because now every little thing makes sense.

He hated innocence. Ageing is a form of corruption, he said. Innocence is criminal. It's shocking, he said, to pretend that life is beautiful. It isn't and the sooner you face that fact, the closer you come to the truth. It's shocking to be so self-centred and blind, so protective of your own equilibrium! He gloated as he insisted that Who Dares—Dies was not guilty of *that* sort of wickedness. Who Dares—Dies was honest! Its aim was the end of pretence. Stop pretending that life is interesting enough to live. Put an end to it, but for god's sake, do it interestingly. It was the exact opposite of the kind of unthinking innocence that he hated so much. It sought to tear away the surface, replace the blankness with seething. It was a form of corruption too but it was blameless, as it was directed inward, harming no one but yourself. Too much was being said about living, he said, too little about kicking the bucket. Lots of spiritual mumbo-jumbo about heaven and hell and inner tranquillity and afterlife, but nothing about the infinite possibilities of air and water, unclean hands and expelled fluids. Contagion, my friend, the allure of contagion, he said.

He was a nutter and every word he said to me proved it, each one a nail in his coffin.

Wellness is vacuum, he said, with that smug, superior look of his. Wellness is boredom.

According to Baby, illness was where the action was. Illness made you important, got you attention, took you away from reality, put you in bed, allowed you to dream and play-act and be special and looked after. The more terminal the better. The more unmentionable the better. For Baby illness was performance, the sick room was his theatre. He wanted all of us to be part of that theatre. If you were well, you were a nobody, worth nothing. Illness was the only accomplishment worth gloating about. The more disgusting the better. Sores, oozes, pus, vomit, intestinal, rectal.

'You are no one in the land of the well,' Baby wrote in his notes. No one. A non-entity. A blob. A Thing. Not a person, not a human being, just an insect. More than his descriptions of the three teachers who killed themselves in his school, more than his ravings about his mother who had only one breast, more than when he talked of turning his own little dog away from his door—that one line of Baby's drilled through my brain and scared the living daylights out of me. My god, that line terrified me. Even then—speed-reading as if my life depended on it, as if I were cramming for the biggest exam of my life, the exam that would make me Baby's trusted confidant for life if I passed—that line made me feel like I was witnessing my own death. It was horrible. I felt as if all my accomplishments—my marks, my academic excellence, my seventeen-going-on-eighteen years of preparation for my brilliant successful future—all of it added up to zero. Zilch. Nothing. It was the heartless certainty of that line: *You are no one in the land of the well.*

It ruled you out. It made a blank space, a black hole out of you. It said being well, being happy, being successful meant nothing. No, it said something a lot more twisted. It said that *unless you were unwell you were of no earthly consequence*. You were less than a bug being squashed under someone's feet.

Baby believed it, and he made the others in the gang believe it too. They fell for it and carried out all those experiments on themselves, and thought they were so special, so brave, but what Baby never realized is that it was all a grand failure—his cult, his attempts at engineered self-destruction, all of it failed, not one of them died the way he would have liked them to, they lived on and on, and so he got impatient and started looking elsewhere.

He was a very sick man. Sick in the head. Insane. He spoke to his reflection, and he wrote down everything 'the man in the mirror' said back. He raved about cuts in the feet and leptospirosis from rat urine in water, and ulcers in mouths, and stutters, and itches, and headaches, and little lumps under the chin, and pains in the calf, and every little thing that was not a little thing at all to Baby and his double, no, they were indications of the bigger illnesses, the sneaking bastard illnesses waiting to catch you off-guard, the big daddies, blood cancer, diabetes, tumours. He mistrusted everything, the air, the water, his skin, his body, his spit, his blood. The only thing he trusted blindly were his books, they were his gurus, and he swallowed them whole and regurgitated them in little pellets to impress us all. He was a con man and they all fell for his con. I fell for it too. I actually thought he liked me! All he liked was the idea of another sucker to take the place of Abhimanyu whose name they destroyed like everything else they touched.

When I was little, my favourite character in the Mahabharata was Abhimanyu. I wept and wept when he died. Daadi explained why he had to die, but that didn't help. It was his destiny, she said, but that didn't make it any less cruel.

From the moment Abhimanyu also known as Christmas joined their gang, or wanted to join their gang, Baby hated him. Hated him because he couldn't control him. Hated him because no matter how abusive and rude and demeaning Baby was to him, Abhimanyu never reacted. Baby wanted to humiliate him by ordering him to design that video game.

'What can you do?' he asked Abhimanyu, sneering. 'What's your *thing*?'

'Computer games,' Abhimanyu said, suddenly looking happy, and confident (Baby's *exact* sneering words so that 'happy' and 'confident' sounded like shit).

'Well then, don't just stand there, design one. Your elder brothers and sisters want to play,' Baby said to Abhimanyu. He imagined this was the perfect way to get rid of the boy forever. Obviously someone as stupid as Abhimanyu would fail! But instead, Abhimanyu did it. He actually did it! He designed a fabulous game that was the opposite of most games in which you were trying to avoid getting killed. In this one you were desperate to kill yourself and everything and everyone was trying to stop you. You picked a persona—male, female, old, young, name, alias, and you picked your modus operandi—shooting, hanging, choking, pills, drugs, poison, jumping from buildings, slitting wrists, drowning. It was a highly evolved, intelligently designed role-playing game, and you cannot imagine *how* sarcastic Baby sounded as he mimicked Abhimanyu explaining the game to them.

The worst thing about Baby was that he could not tolerate the idea of anyone else's intelligence. He couldn't bear the fact that a mere boy was more talented than he would ever be. It was pathetic.

And then when he found out that Abhimanyu had called his new game Who Dares—Dies, Baby didn't know whether to be shocked, annoyed or flattered.

'He was trying to impress me, insect,' he said to me. 'He was trying to win my approval.'

Secretly how delighted he must have been! Baby loved being worshipped. I worshipped him too, after I'd gotten over my fear. Fool that I was I wanted to impress him, hell, I didn't just want him to like me, I wanted to be like him one day. But outwardly Baby pretended he didn't give a damn. He hated the fact that Baldy and the gang loved Abhimanyu's video game so much they forgot to be cold and cutting to the boy, like Baby wanted them to be. He wanted to break Abhimanyu, spoil his happiness, crush the success of his game, destroy the proof of his skill.

'Still only a game, no matter how fancy,' Baby told Abhimanyu. 'It doesn't prove a thing. Doesn't prove that you've understood one goddamn thing. Death is no game. But of course *you're* too stupid to see that.'

Abhimanyu stood there, saying nothing, his head hanging down. Two days later, two whole days during which the gang hadn't stopped raving about the game which Baldy was already making plans of selling worldwide and making a killing on, Momo brought them a note from Abhimanyu.

It said, 'Tell Sir I understood.' He had thrown himself off the thirty-fifth floor of a building in Gurgaon. That was his proof.

Abhimanyu died, and the only thing that Baby could think of was what a waste it was. Not a waste of a life, oh no, but a waste of a disciple. Baby had wanted Abhimanyu to be his Ekalavya, he wanted to take from him a gurudakshina that would cripple him forever. Instead, Abhimanyu took his life into his own hands.

But that didn't make it suicide! It was murder. Clear and simple murder. Baby murdered him by challenging him to prove his faith. Baby knew which buttons to press. He had seen Abhimanyu's desire to belong, he had seen how insecure and unconfident he was. He pressed and pressed until Abhimanyu broke. Baby killed Abhimanyu just as surely as if he had pushed him off himself. It was his taunting voice that was the hand that pushed him, it was his sneering face. Baby hated Abhimanyu more than he hated me. He hated his shyness, his awkwardness, his eagerness to please, his obvious need to be liked. He had brought presents all wrapped up in shiny paper for everyone in the gang the first day Momo brought him to the meeting.

'What's the occasion, Christmas?' Baldy said to him as he shyly handed them their presents. The name stuck. No one called him Abhimanyu after that. He was rich and overprotected and ridiculous and when he spoke of how he wanted to be with them because he hoped to understand what to do with his *life*, Baby and the rest could barely stop themselves from laughing in his face. Why had Momo brought him to them? She shouldn't have. But how could she have guessed such a horrible thing would happen? She was Abhimanyu's cousin, Baby told me. She was losing hair those days, clumps and clumps of her long beautiful hair, and one day she turned up with all of it shaved off and a scarf around her head. Nobody dared ask her anything, they were scared, Baby most of all. What were they doing to themselves? What if Momo died? Did it matter? Of course it didn't matter! He was only pretending to care when he told me how much it hurt him to see Momo's hair gone.

Why, I should have asked him, isn't that exactly what you wanted? But instead of being thrilled, he was unsettled. I know why. She was succeeding where he had failed. Who Dares—Dies, this private little whacked-out experiment about daring yourself to fall fatally ill was a failure, and so it was no longer enough. Now you had to hurt others. Go public, in the underhand way that only Baby could teach them. Here was a bunch of people who were sick to begin with. I mean mentally. Each of them had a deep dark problem. That problem made them want to do harm to themselves, serious harm, so that instead of hating themselves they could be sorry for themselves. They wanted to become actually, physically ill, so they could sit around and pity themselves. Act like martyrs. It was totally warped, and the way Baby wrote about it in his notes was totally psycho. But when it didn't work, except for Momo, he went berserk and started spreading the net wider, flinging hooks in as many directions as his crazed mind would go.

'Go out and infect the people!' he announced, like some modern messiah of doom. 'Infect them with rumours and juicy malicious lies, start scandals, provoke riots, incite mobs, and do it all through words, carefully dropped poison in people's ears.'

They did it, and it spiralled. Schoolteachers were beaten up because someone planted a story about child molestation.

Supposed AIDS victims were harassed and thrown out of neighbourhoods. Baby showed me all the press, all the links stored carefully on his laptop, as if it was something to be proud of! At that time my heart was bursting with joy at the thought of how much Baby trusted me, confided in me, I thought I was the recipient of his confession of all the dark deeds that he expressed so much false remorse for.

'We were young, insect, we were foolhardy, we had no empathy.'

Empathy! As if he even knew what the word meant.

Now I know all his confessions were bogus, he was laughing at me all the time, knowing his secrets would be safe with me, not because I was his friend, his chela, no no no, but because I was soon going to be dead. And do you think they stopped at rumours? Of course not. Each one outdid the other at *real* schemes, and Baldy was the one who started it.

His pet scheme was to get girls drunk and then drop them off on deserted Delhi roads. Dizzy was the first girl he picked up. She sang in a nightclub, and afterwards he bought her drinks and charmed the pants off her. Naturally when he offered to drop her home, she agreed. But when she unexpectedly threw up all over his new upholstery he got so pissed off, he opened the car door and pushed her out. It was two a.m. Next day there was news of a girl raped and that girl was Dizzy. But it was Baldy who was the real culprit. Soon, what had begun (so he said) as an accident became an addiction. He took to frequenting bars and clubs, the seedier the better, so that he wouldn't meet people from his own circle. It was easy for him to pick up girls, he was funny and charming and different in an interesting way, in short he was everything I was not, and each time he would play the same game, offer to drive them home, then abandon them at the worst, loneliest unlit spots he could find. I never thought Baldy had so much evil in him.

That was Baby's greatest power. He understood how inhuman human beings could be. He was a great judge of character. He kept telling me Abhimanyu had let him down, had misunderstood him, had disappointed and angered him by his foolish, rash death, but he was lying. Abhimanyu's death was what he had wanted all along. He knew someone like Abhimanyu would do exactly something that drastic. He made up for his own failure, the failure of Who Dares—Dies by killing that harmless boy.

I am a *hopeless* judge of people. I thought Baby was my hero, I thought Baldy was the nicest funniest kindest man on the planet, and I thought Poka was an angel. Have you any idea what she did? How could you, I haven't told you yet.

She was a doctor who tinkered with people's insides. She prescribed medicines for small ills but all the while she kept introducing new and much bigger problems into the bodies of her hapless patients. She dressed in a cotton sari and dished out medicines in a little room filled with people, all of whom she destroyed, gradually, secretly, internally, changing them from inside, the way Baby had taught her to.

'We carry the root of our illnesses inside us, insect,' Baby told me, just as he must have told her. 'The root, the cause, the root cause.'

Poka held her patients' wrists, hating their *smelly oozing* bodies, her exact words, full of disgust, not wanting to look at the scars the scabs the boils, just touching their wrists and feeling their pulse in order to know exactly what she must do to unlock the trouble that was dormant. She was like a witch doctor, only worse, because she never really cured anything, she only planted things, like the creator of a poisonous garden.

'Here,' she said, lifting a little blue book with a plain hard cover and waving it at me across the pool. 'Here is where it's all written down.'

And without any warning she dropped it into the pool. I would have dived after it had I been a great swimmer. But what would have been the use! It was so clearly intentional, her dropping the book into the pool. She wanted to obliterate all the evidence. All the names written in her neat and rounded hand. Arsenic. Belladonna. Mercury. It was her bible, that little blue book with the plain hard cover. In it were the names of the poisons she fed her unsuspecting victims. And she didn't spare Momo either. The medicines she gave Momo started giving her panic attacks, as if all her other problems weren't bad enough.

'Momo's real problem was so deep-rooted, she needed to purge herself of it,' Poka said to me, as if what she was doing was the most natural thing in the world. 'She needed to come out of her passive acceptance of everything that had gone wrong with her life, her avoidance. She needed to face the fear, taste it, be overwhelmed by it before she could start living a normal life again. No one understood this until I felt her pulse. It was like a bird with broken wings, that pulse of hers, beating erratically below her scarred skin. She needed to be healed...'

...and I healed her.

She didn't say it out loud, but she implied it.

How could someone like Ciggy be in love with such a wicked woman? Ciggy never did anything, at least I don't think so. He was too busy smoking himself to death. Molly and Dodo were always just the chelas, trailing at the back. And poor Lolly, what was she doing hanging out with them? She was there for Baldy and Baldy didn't deserve her. Baldy was eyeing Angie. I heard him sing to her that night on the beach. *Angie.* Was there a song like that, or had he written it for her?

That was what was wrong. Everyone was in love with the wrong person, and for the wrong reason. Lolly wanted Baldy, Baldy wanted Angie, Angie wanted me, I wanted Momo, Tiger wanted Momo too, and Baby wanted Yanky's girl who wasn't even there. I think they loved each other not for who they were but what they were suffering from. Tiger wanting to kiss Momo's wheeze out of her mouth. How had I failed to see right away that Tiger was madly in love with Momo? I should have known the minute I saw him go stiff on the bed when she came and sat next to him in her pretty summer dress. Her bare arms next to his hairy ones. He didn't hug her, or relax the way he did around Poka and Angie and Lolly. That was the first time I realized and it came out in my story. They didn't like my story. Because they didn't like the truth. Why did I make her kill herself in my story? Because I wanted her to escape from them. I wanted her to run away, away from their tricks and treachery.

Angie said it straight out—they were harming Momo, deliberately. She brought plants into the house that aggravated Momo's asthma. She created tense little situations around little things like who left the coffee cups unwashed knowing that was the kind of thing that made Momo break out in a rash. She cooked the stir-fried veggies in the same kadhai in which she had just fried the prawns, knowing Momo had a borderline prawn allergy. She told me the story of a person who had died instantly from prawn allergy in a restaurant. As she spoke, she had a *look* in her eye that terrified me. She sprayed too much perfume in the bedroom they shared, knowing strong perfumes made Momo feel nauseous. She changed the soft yellow lights to white tubelights under the excuse of economy, but really because she knew the flicker of the tubes gave Momo migraines. She played her music way too loud, boosting the amp and the bass, because she knew the thump of it affected Momo's heart, just a little flutter, but enough to make Angie happy. She gave the maid acid to scour the bathroom so that the smell would linger long after, stinging poor Momo's nostrils, making her nose run, her eyes water.

And Momo said nothing, not because she hadn't noticed, but because she was willing. She was willing to be a lab rat. *She* was Baby's truest disciple, not Angie, because she understood what he wanted from his victims. She was willing to be the one on whom the long, lingering, self-destructive Who Dares—Dies experiment would be successful at last. And she was willing because she was in love with that man.

Why couldn't I see it until now? It hurts horribly inside. What was she in love with? His baby face, his soft voice, his warped mind? Momo wanting to make love to Baby's brittle bones, like wanting to walk into a wall of glass and hurt herself all over. I wanted to save her, send her a message, SOS. Get away, I wanted to tell her, come away, come away with me. As if I could! In all that time, all those hours that I spent with them, longing to see her, fainting like a girl in front of her, answering her questions, sitting next to her, telling my story for her, wanting to run around like a loon looking *everywhere* for her, wanting to cry and shout because she had gone, because she might be dead, because she was, for sure, dead, in all the time that I had, that was mine to use as I pleased, what did I do?

Nothing.

Not one little thing. Not one little word. No one was a bigger idiot than me. I was an idiot with girls. Only one girl in my whole life ever spoke to me. Her name was Rohini, and she wasn't ugly or stupid. She was pretty, and popular, and she topped her section every year. She spoke to me like it was the most normal thing, and then she went off with her gang of male admirers and girlfriends, all of whom were full of contempt for me. She told me once that the others thought I was strange. The girls thought I had no sense of humour, no social skills, no ability to charm, and the boys thought I was too interested in classes, too good at studies and not at anything else, that I was different but not in an interesting way, that I was arrogant, always carrying a big fat book around, never talking to anyone. Arrogant! Me! They should have met Baby to know what arrogance is all about. And those big fat books? Best-sellers each one of them. Nothing heavy like what Baby read!

If only I could meet Rohini once and tell her everything. If only I had asked her out once, or bought her a birthday card. She was straight and unspoilt and I really liked her. Maybe she was a Saraswati girl. Baby talked about this in his notes. The three kinds of girls. He classified them as if they were a species! The Kali girls, wild-haired, full of passion, activists, feminists, marching on morchas, killing the guys if they said anything sexist, wonderful, crazy, scary girls. The Lakshmi girls, pretty, ultra-feminine, sweet as roses and hard as nails, interested only in boys with cars, never spending their own cash even if they had it, wanting nothing more out of life than rich, good-looking husbands who would be their slaves. And the Saraswati girls, talented, warm, comforting buddy-girls who slept with the boys out of affection, who cooked for them and made them do all the work like cutting and washing which they never minded, who warned them about their girlfriends but never in a nasty way, who drank with them and never threw up and said stupid things or got into fights like the boys did, girls who sometimes went into blue fits and wept copiously, only to recover their cheery selves again, girls you could actually love and live with. Baby had a Saraswati girl in his life once, but he ignored her for a Lakshmi girl, Yanky's girlfriend, who ignored him for Yanky. He lost her forever after Yanky's death. Serves him right. He deserved no one, least of all someone as beautiful as Momo.

What a horrible name, as if she were a chicken dumpling. Tejaswini. I will now and forever call her Tejaswini, never that awful nickname again. But Baby couldn't see *her*, he only saw his slides with microbes floating on them. Instead of writing love letters he wrote raving notes on how beautiful the Hepatitis B virus was, like clumps of palest coral, how wonderfully purple and surreal acute lymphocytic leukaemia was, how beautiful the strangest things could be, if people were only intelligent enough to see them. He loved viruses just as much as he was petrified of them.

'Terror is not being able to see it,' he told me, a strange light in his eyes, 'not being able to grasp it or know it until it takes your shape, enters your blood your saliva your urine your spit your secretions. You only see it when it's too late, and by then it looks like you. Your eyes turn bloodshot, your skin turns yellow. You are not yourself. Suddenly the virus is you.'

He wanted to *be* a virus, that crazy evil man.

He even read out a poem to me that he said a girl had given him, a poem about how a virus could be beautiful. No girl wrote that poem for him! He wrote it himself, down to the last word. And the 'she' in it was probably Yanky's girlfriend. The one Baby was so hopelessly in love with.

He couldn't talk about love without bringing in viruses and blood. He couldn't talk about friendship without bringing in pity.

'You can only truly like someone you feel sorry for,' he wrote in his notes.

When I realized that Baby actually *liked* me, that he wanted me to be one of the gang, the inner circle, I felt as if my heart might explode with happiness. When I thought that thanks to Baby's acceptance of me into their group, my access to *her* would become so much easier, I was delirious with joy. And when I realized that he told me everything not out of remorse, or friendship or even pity, but merely because he had already planned my death, I wished I had killed him first.

He thought he was king. And sadly, so did Tejaswini. He was her lord, her master, she did everything he wanted his followers to do, and still he did not, he could not love her. I should have killed him for that. He was obsessed with germs for god's sake, with microbes. And I? I was obsessed with her.

Was it her transparent arms? Was it her bone slicing through her skin, painful to look at, even in the kindest light? Or was it her hair, curling emptily at the edges along her slender neck, the sweet hair that grew back, each tendril waiting for someone's fingers to curl around? Was it her spine, each vertebra single and visible like pebbles down her back? She looked as if she would snap if you held her too hard. I wanted to snap her hard against me. Her feet were obscured in that rush of bodies in which I saw her first. I imagined them pale and lustrous, crossed one over the other. Her toenails would be midnight blue, and around each ankle would be a finely braided rope of silver. Delicate, those silent anklets, no tinkling bells, no warning as she crept up and threw her arms around me. Her breath would be moist in my ear and her body breakable beneath her clothes. But her face! Her face would be soft, pressing into my cheek like a kiss. I would hold that face for hours. Stroke it gently, afraid to leave on it the smudge of my fingers, like bruises. And then after touching her, soothing her, I would dig my fingers in until she split, tear her open like a mango and suck her down. I would mangle her face to a pulp between my teeth and break her body, snap it against my knees, over my thighs, crack her open and strew her on the ground. Hard splinters would pierce my bare feet as I walked bleeding over her bones. She would be kernel skin pulp nut, an ecstasy of damage, a butchery of teeth and nails, a savagery of howls. I would destroy her with my bare hands, until her neck snaked into the sky and her legs contorted into the earth and her arms grew wings, brittle and shiny with light.

It must have been her arms.

She alone among them hadn't befriended me out of spite, as part of a cruel game plan. She had found me unspoilt, she said I had a good vibe. The others were just looking for someone they could have fun with like they did with Abhimanyu, and they happened to find me. I was their bakra, their second short-term victim. And I believed that was their way of making friends! All those bizarre tests, their complicated ragging! I did it all, all for her, and she didn't even notice. The only woman who noticed me was Angie.

Angie had the hots for me. Even a guy who is hopeless with girls and knows zilch about them can tell when a woman has the hots. It was her idea, the erotic story. She was an older woman, she liked me, but just seeing me with my shirt off was not enough for her. The fact that I had a brain, that I could talk, even if I blushed more than any man should, the fact that I could spin stories, all of it increased her attraction for me. I could feel it. I should have jumped for joy. Here at last was a woman, not some sex-crazed teenager with spots on her face, but a real hot woman interested in me, and all I could do was obsess about Tejaswini. That's how stupid I was.

I wasn't innocent as they kept calling me, I was just plain dumb. All the kids in my class had done it already except me. All they thought about was sex. One couple had even got caught doing it in the public loo near the bookstore. They had forgotten to lock the door. But not me. No one would come with me, even if I asked. I'm seventeen, I'd be eighteen next month if I weren't dying tonight, but the only woman who ever touched me was my mother.

Baby told me how horrified he felt about being touched during his illness. The harsh hands of nurses. The hatred he felt for those hands without whom he would have reverted to an even more loathsome, unwashed state. He needed so badly to be touched, like me. He wrote of the indifference to all sensations that is the greatest proof of illness, a revulsion for food, a distance from your own lifeless fingers. He told me about the time he fell ill with typhoid and had the most terrifying dreams. I'm convinced those dreams drove him nuts. The way he described them, the way he made me feel the pain he felt inside his head, as if he was possessed by demons armed with terrible weapons of torture...

Don't get me wrong. I am NOT sympathizing with him. Poor little Baby, so ill, it made him sick in the head. No way. That hypochondriac megalomaniac dysfunctional monster, that obsessive-compulsive psychopath has damaged too many people already. Someone has to stop him. That someone is me.

They lied to me when they said they would kill themselves tonight. Of course they won't! They'll be alive in their rooms, laughing. But not for long.

They thought they were immortal. 'Immortal animals,' Baby wrote in his notes. They moved in a gang, a cluster, they hated the couples who fell away from their cluster, they hated the need for two lesser mortals to be alone together, separate, they loved the gang so much.

They were demented and it was all thanks to their demented little leader with cheeks so soft all the girls wanted to squeeze them. His father was ashamed of his babyness, he wrote about that in his notes. Ashamed that his boy played the leading girl in all the school plays. Not ashamed of his athletic victories but not proud either. Baby had turned away his puppy once, from his door. It had run away when he was in boarding school and when he came back home on vacation, one night the pup returned and cried and scratched at his door. He was awake, he heard him, but he didn't let his puppy in. What kind of a *person* was Baby?

'Obligations make you a victim,' he told me. 'I wasn't interested in being a victim, I was interested in finding one.'

'There are always reasons for murdering a man. On the contrary it is impossible to justify his living.'

This was one of the many quotes in his notebook.

'I swear, gentlemen, that to be too conscious is an illness—a real thoroughgoing illness.'

This was another.

He wrote about the precise way in which carbon monoxide kills you, the way it had killed the three teachers in his boarding school.

He wrote about how when he was ten he discovered if you dug your elbow into someone's thigh it would hurt more than if you punched him. He wrote how he discovered that if you sat on someone's chest and twisted his ears, the person you sat on could neither breathe nor hear nor scream.

He loved the term 'oedema'.

He made lists of writers with dreadful diseases. Oscar Wilde: Meningitis. Flannery O'Connor: Disseminated lupus. Richard Wright: Aerobic dysentery.

'The thing that makes you live can kill you in the end,' he said to me. 'A printer died of ink poisoning. The inks he handled every day to make the books he loved entered his bloodstream and killed him.'

I hate to say this, but he was right. I had never felt more alive, more aware, than when I fell in love with Tejaswini. But if it weren't for her, my absurd desire to be brave in front of her, my ridiculous acceptance of a syringe in my fucking arm for god's sake, if it weren't for her, I wouldn't, this minute, be dying.

They told me she was suicidal. Who wouldn't be, in her place, suffering so much, being tormented by her friends, with not one good day to hold on to? They were driving her to it, the beasts, it was they who made her kill herself, not me, I am not that powerful, how could I be, when all I told them was a story and not even the awful truth of my love which I knew she would refuse. Everything, *everything* that Baby had spoon-fed them—all his theories on illness being mental, each of us carrying our own death wish inside us, each of us already infected with the germ of our own destruction, the body the ultimate barometer of our psychoses—all of it they tested on *her*. And they told me they were trying to save her. I never heard a bigger lie. They brought her here so it would be easy for her. The sea is a good place to drown. And then they had the cheek to accuse *me*. And I fell for it! Guilty as charged, I bowed my head, slunk back to my room like a whipped dog, a condemned criminal, and got ready to die.

This is what happens when you have never had a girlfriend. You simply don't understand anything, until it is too late.

But I have found a good way to spite Baby. If he thought he could terrorize the shit out of me by telling me I've been infected by whatever was in the syringe, something incurable and irreversible, something so dreadful it might knock me off before dawn, or creep up on me minute by minute over an unspecified, perpetually panic-stricken time, I will not give him that satisfaction. I will follow Abhimanyu's example. I will end it my way. Better still, I will follow Tejaswini's example. If she had the guts to walk into the sea, so do I. But remember—this changes nothing. Whichever way I die, they did it. They are to blame. The fact that I chose a quick death over a lingering horror that would make my whole life miserable is only a sign of my own strength, my determination.

My arms hurt, my back feels like it might snap in two, my

neck feels like it has wires running through it, my calves are cramping, my mouth is so dry I can hardly swallow. Inside my body I can feel my heart pumping, pumping madly, pushing the blood into my fingers as I watch them fly over the keys, I can feel my nerves, they are all short-circuiting, if I stand up to stretch, they will explode with pain.

I wish I could have said goodbye to Daadi. She is the one who taught me how to speak. She was unhappy about my going to Princeton. Now will she be happy that I am not going, after all?

'You were meant for better things, beta,' she told me before we came to Goa.

'Like what?' I asked her.

'Like writing, spinning words like the finest silk, telling stories that generations will remember.'

'You mean, like you!' I laughed and hugged her. She was the only one in my family I could bear to show physical affection to.

'No, much better than me.'

'What stories would I tell?'

'The ones that are inside you, waiting to be born.'

'But what if they're not there?'

'They are.'

'How can you be so sure?'

'I have not lived eighty years for nothing,' she said, and her grey eyes twinkled.

It bothered Daadi that the only books I read were my course books and English best-sellers. She never said anything. But I know it would have made her very happy if I had read some of the books on her shelf, the Hindi books, the books of poetry, the tomes of mythology and literature. If only I had. The only books of hers that I read, again and again, from cover to cover, were the ones she wrote for kids.

'Why don't you write for adults, Daadi?' I had once asked her.

'But that's what I do!' she answered. 'I write for the adult each of those children will grow up to be.'

'That's not a straight answer, Daadi!' I said to her. And then, 'Don't you get bored writing for kids?'

'Never!' she said. 'The day I get bored is the day my death begins.'

She has arthritis in her fingers, she can't write any more. That's why she feels so restless and angry with herself. What a fool I am. I should have asked her to tell me her stories, line by line, scene by scene, and written them down. I could have been her Ganesha. She would have been so happy. If only this idea had come to me before. I could have smuggled out some time somehow from all the cramming and done it. If only she could have heard me tell Angie and Poka my story. But I know her. She would have listened and she wouldn't have been as surprised as I was.

'You had it in you all along, beta,' she would say, with that shockingly youthful grin of hers. 'The right moment needed to come along and get it out of you, that's all.'

So Angie and Poka had been my right moment. How I had loved them both in that room as they listened to me, forgetting to breathe as they listened.

And then everything crumbled, turned to mud, to poison.

My head reels. I have never written so fast before, never remembered so much so quickly. Too much has happened too fast. *Too much of a muchness is too much for me. My fire is on fire and I'm sick.* I saw those lines in Baby's notebook on Illness. They sounded like a slogan we could all have used. If all of us had lived, and stayed friends, real friends, we could have sung those lines like an anthem, around campfires on beaches, around beer mugs in city bars, around empty maidans and crowded cricket stadiums, we could have stood as one indivisible teeming crowd, wave upon wave of people, and chanted *My fire is on fire and I'm sick.* We could have shot videos of our chanting, we could have posted them online, we could have lived to celebrate our illnesses, our excesses. Instead of wanting, like Baby, to die, to make others die, we could have lived and listened to the chant in twenty different languages, *Aami oshustho, bolo shobai, oshustho.* These words were written in someone else's handwriting below the English lines. They sounded like Bengali. It must have been Poka. Did she have the same idea? A subculture of sick people, young enough to mock death, old enough to be terrified of it, reckless enough to hurry it on? And all the while, as we chanted, the truth of our most intimate illnesses—the things we had brought upon ourselves by the simple power of our weakened, pressured, stressed-out, pushed-around, trampled, angry, sad and fearful wills—all the while that truth would be simmering below the chant, below the dance, below the singing.

I'm sick, people, say sick.

Yes, I was sick, with love. Sick in the head, sick in the heart. I had never had such a physical reaction to any girl before. I could suddenly *feel* every part of me. And everything felt extreme. The extreme heat in my ears, the extreme cold in my feet. I was already weak when I saw her. That was the afternoon my stomach was bad. My insides felt scraped and raw. When I breathed I felt as if I was a hollow pipe being waved about by a pair of too-rough, clumsy hands. Maybe that's why my love felt so close to something I would never recover from. Some terrible infection. A queasy feeling in the centre of my empty stomach that was directly linked to the way she tucked her hair behind her ears. When I rushed away to my room as if I couldn't stand the sight of her a second longer, I held the basin in the bathroom and leaned over it, retching, even though nothing came out. I was breathless, and the empty retching made me wheeze and cough and tears rolled out of my eyes. I felt so ashamed, even though there was no one there who might have laughed to see me that way.

Everything important affected my gut. Stomach, viscera, gut. I had no guts when it came to girls. And Tejaswini was no ordinary girl. If Baby had been the one standing in my room, laughing and calling me 'gutless', he would have been spot on.

When did my accusation become a confession?

When I first saw Tejaswini, on that afternoon when everything changed, I couldn't tell the difference between what it meant to be in love, and what it meant to feel it. They always say you fall in love. That's not what happened to me. Love fell into me, into the waiting hollow pit of my stomach, where it seethed and spun, as if I were the sea being churned and any moment now the poison and nectar would separate. Love clung to the walls of my intestines, and wouldn't let go.

I felt sick and desperate. And, though this makes no sense,

I felt happy. I felt like standing on a rooftop and yelling. That's how happy I was.

There was no way I could have survived it without *doing* something. When I saw her with her gang, when I did my feverish counting to see if there was one boy for every girl, when I saw that she didn't seem to be part of a twosome, did it make me feel any better? No. It made me jumpy, it made me want to shovel food into my system, too much food, too quickly, so I would have a real reason for feeling upset. Everything seemed to be jumbling up inside me that morning when my parents left and I was alone, ready to make my move or die. Everything that had seemed separate and opposite and extreme the previous afternoon was, that morning, jostling and pushing and spilling against each other, so I didn't know if my liver was in my leg, or my lungs in my mouth. I was a mess. I knew I was going to get the jitters every single millisecond if I didn't do something that made it possible, even remotely possible, that I should soon, very soon, talk to her. If Baldy hadn't called me Pappu and dragged me into their centre, I would have sat in that ghost hotel, petrified, sick to my stomach, frozen, unable to move, unable to say a word, until the time came for me to leave.

That's how gutless I was.

Baldy made it easy. Baldy gave me a chance. And in the hope of meeting her, of impressing her, of talking to her, I did everything they asked, I behaved like a pathetic performing dog, jumping through hoops, I stretched myself, I endangered myself, I made my body and my brain function in ways I had never imagined possible, and at the end of it, did I even get a chance to say one private word to her?

Of course not. All the time, while talking to them, while

being insulted by them, while walking around with them, while lying on the beach looking at the fucking *stars* with them, while sitting by the pool listening to them, while telling them the story of their lives that they were too fucking stupid to see for themselves, all the time I was sick to my bones with a feeling they should have found another word for by now.

Nothing—not the thought of dying because of an evil twisted prank that will make me walk into the water as soon as I am through writing the words that will condemn them for life, not even the thought that I will never see Daadi again, never again hear her voice reach deep into my heart, never again feel the warmth that would fill me when I told her the stories I found inside myself, just like she knew I would—nothing in the world makes me feel as sad as the thought that I got and missed my chance to tell Tejaswini those three little words that look so easy when you write them down. I know she will never read them, yet I need to write them down, once and forever, the three frightening little words I have never said aloud and never will.

I love you.

Interrogation

I can't say I *knew* him. I only met him that weekend. Though met would hardly be the word for it. Baby and the rest were playing one of their games, and they dragged me into it. It was in Baby and Tiger's room. I beg your pardon? No, that's what we called them. No other names. He was on the floor, not Tiger, the boy was on the floor and the others were on the bed. I can't remember if he had his shirt on or not. He looked terribly shy. I think the girls had ragged him before I came in. No no it wasn't what you think. They had asked him to tell them a story, that's all. No, I did not hear the story as I was on the beach at the time. We were in Goa, we had a whole private beach to ourselves. Why would I waste it sitting in the room? Yes, I was alone on the beach. The others were in their rooms, which is where they were most of the time.

Anyway that's the first time I laid eyes on him.

He was a sweet boy, that much I can say, even without knowing him at all. We only had one conversation, if you could call it that.

'Go in and ask him some unanswerable questions,' Cracker told me before dragging me into the room. How could I refuse? No one could refuse Cracker. Besides, I had spent the whole day on the beach. Even someone like me needed to hear some human voices by then.

What do I mean by 'someone like me'? Isn't it obvious? Someone who likes being alone.

I don't remember what I asked him, all I remember is that he fainted. No, not at my questions! Why would he faint because of my questions? He mustn't have eaten anything all day, maybe he had low BP, maybe it was the heat, how do I know why he fainted?

I'm not getting defensive.

Maybe if you listened instead of trying to push me into a corner, it might be easier for me to tell you what I remember.

Everyone got a scare when he fainted. Even Cracker, who never took anything seriously.

But someone, I forget who, splashed water on his face, and he was all right. He blushed, and that was sweet, I haven't seen a boy blush for ages, and then he answered my questions, which proved that I had obviously not asked unanswerable ones like Cracker wanted me to. And then we all went out.

To the beach, of course. Where else?

We all had dinner together that night. We had a lot of fun. The boy had a huge appetite! Cracker made him eat a mountain of gulab jamuns and everyone died laughing. No, of course not. He didn't force the boy. It was a dare, the kind of silly thing guys do, bet you can't eat twenty gulab jamuns, bet I can. That kind of thing. I don't think it was twenty though, maybe a dozen. Is that important? Well if *everything* is important, we'll never get to the end of this, will we? No, I'm not in a hurry, but I don't see the point of asking whether it was five or twenty-five gulab jamuns!

Fine.

What I'm trying to say is that by dinner, he seemed like one of us. He wasn't blushing any more, he laughed and joked with us, he was perfectly okay. They had live music that night, and I think he and Poka danced. Or was it he and Angie? Or did Angie dance alone? I can't remember. Anyway, all I know is we laughed so much we had stitches in our sides.

Then we went and sat by the pool and talked.

How late was it? I have no idea. I never wear a watch, I have metal allergy. I break out in rash. That's right. It must have been pretty late. Even those awful guys had gone to bed. The sales guys, a team of loud and hairy men. No I don't have a *problem* with sales guys, it's just that they were all over the place, making far too much noise. For god's sake, we had come to Goa to get a little peace, can't you understand that? Those guys just wrecked the place.

Thankfully by the time we finished dinner, went to our rooms and returned to sit by the pool, no one else was around.

We talked about ourselves, mainly. The boy wanted to know about us, and we told him. That's what friends normally do, right, tell each other about their lives?

No, he didn't tell us anything about his life. We hadn't got to that point yet.

No, all of us didn't talk. I didn't. I prefer to listen. But Baby talked, and Cracker talked, and even Angie and Poka talked. Tiger? Yeah, maybe, I can't remember. Ciggy never talks anyway, and poor Lolly was sulking because Cracker must have been mean to her. Lolly and Cracker are a couple, yes. Not married, of course not. And Molly and Dodo were, as always, the taciturn twosome. Are Molly and Dodo a couple as well? Not in the sense you mean. No, Molly is a guy. Molly and Dodo are both guys. Why do they all have such funny names? Why don't you ask their mothers?

So they were talking and I was listening. They didn't say anything I didn't already know. I've known these guys for years. No, I don't remember how many years, but long enough. I have an asthmatic condition, and I couldn't sit out in the night air too long. I left after a while. Maybe the others talked too, after I left. I don't know. I was tired and I could feel my asthma coming on, I just wanted to lie down on a mountain of pillows. I went to my room, and went to bed.

I have no idea where he could have gone.

No, I really have no idea.

What?

How do you know it's him?

Oh. Oh god. Oh dear dear god.

I'm sorry about that. Can I have a glass of water?

Thanks.

Is there anything else you want to ask me?

No, I wasn't going back with the others. I had already decided. They knew that. Why? Because I had had enough of Bombay. I was going to find a nice little home-stay in Goa and stay put. I needed time to think. About my life. Where it was headed. No, my parents separated years ago. My father lives in Delhi. No, that was not an option. I needed to be absolutely alone, can't you understand that? How could I be alone in my dad's house with his wife and his new baby and his pet frigging poodle?

I'm sorry. I'm not getting hysterical. What I'm trying to explain is—they did *not* leave me all alone and go off, they knew I was staying back. They had an early morning flight, they had jobs to go back to Monday morning, they left, period.

How do I know whether they went to say goodbye to the boy or not? Why don't you ask them?

My mother died soon after the divorce.

What business is that of yours? And how is it related to the case? What if I refuse to answer? Are you going to *make* me answer?

No, I do not have a boyfriend.

That doesn't mean I don't love someone. The two don't necessarily coincide. The one you love may love someone else. Can't you understand that? What? No, I have not read the boy's notes. How could I? They're in your possession. Should I steal them and read them?

I am not being offensive.

I was very sick when I got to know Baby and his friends. It felt like heaven, having friends. People I could trust, people I could let my guard down with. People who looked after me.

I cannot explain the nature of my illness. No, it wasn't some private shameful female disease, as I can see you imagining. Nothing like that. Even the doctors could not tell what was wrong with me.

Why is it important? Oh yeah yeah yeah, I know. You already told me—*everything* is important. I was ill *all* the time, all right? And the nature of my illness kept changing. And sometimes it didn't even look like I was ill, at least not to the outside world. Yes, I know, they call that kind of illness lunacy. Pagal ho gayi. I felt like that before I met Baby and his friends. By then I felt I really would go mad if I had to have one more doctor tap my chest, take my blood, sniff my urine, press my stomach, bend my knees, X-ray my brain, examine my stool, puncture my skin. One more doctor's visit, one more lab report that didn't show anything, one more echocardiofrigginggram, and I would have gone mad.

They saved me.

No, I don't think they had anything to do with this *incident.*

Yes, I had already made my plans. I had spoken to one of the waiters in the hotel, and he said I could stay with his aunt and uncle near Baga. That sounded perfect. I didn't even care about seeing the place, like he suggested. As long as the bed had clean sheets and the bathroom had running water, I was fine.

Yes, that's the one. You can ask him for the number. Now can I go please?

Tejaswini
aka Momo

When she left the cop station she was trembling so hard she thought she was having a stroke. There was no one she could call. Certainly not them. So she did the only thing that occurred to her. She sat down. Right there, not twenty metres away from the foul cop station with those damning eyes boring through her clothes, she sat down under a coconut palm and shivered uncontrollably.

All my life, she thought, words scattering inside her, *all my life I have been trying to fight pain. And now this.*

This this this.

Monstrosity.

And we had done it. Not just them. We. I was part of it too. Just by being with them, I was guilty.

The cops thought they could break her with their questions, wear her down with their whys and wheres and whats. They did not know she was an old hand at answering questions that probed right into her most private parts, questions that stuck their fingers into every possible opening, ripped open every freshly stitched wound, every healed and ancient scar. The questions came dressed in clean clothes, wearing sanitized gloves that concealed the prurient, ugly interest in what they could never begin to understand, let alone heal.

Where does it hurt? What did you eat last night? Why did you wait so long before coming to see me? How have your periods been? When was the last time you had a similar infection? Who treated you? Do you have the old prescription? Are you on any other medication? How long have you been taking this? What's your normal schedule? Have you been drinking? Late nights? Are you under a lot of stress? When was the last time you checked? Do you prefer warm weather or cold? Do you sleep well? Do you feel dizzy only when you get up suddenly or all the time? Is the fever highest in the morning or in the evening? Can you promise me you will come back next week? Are you nauseous? How long has this been going on?

Too long, doc, she wanted to say, too frigging long.

She hadn't always been like this. This combative, this *hostile*. Spitting out words. Wishing she could kill someone. That's the last thing she should say, at such a time. That's just the kind of thing the cops *want* her to say. Maybe they were wearing her down after all. Maybe she would end up saying 'I did it', just to shut them up. She should be calm, calm.

When she got angry she couldn't breathe. Everything tightened up. Her eyes fogged over. She couldn't see, she couldn't breathe. She never shouted when she was angry, because she didn't have any breath left over. Instead, she went tighter and tighter inward until all of her was a little spring coiled deep inside where no one could reach.

It always took a long, long time for that little spring to loosen up, unwind, spiral out and finally leave her.

'You need to vocalize,' her last counsellor had said to her. 'Get it out of your system. Talk. Shout. Scream.'

I would, she thought, if only I had the breath to do it.

She had been turning everything inward for as long as she could remember.

Maybe this new combativeness, this open, outwardly directed hostility that the cops inspired in her was not such a bad thing.

Would it cure her?

That was the question she asked every time she tried something new. Aroma therapy, crystal therapy, journal therapy, water therapy, yoga, ayurveda, homoeopathy, naturopathy, allopathy. And every time she wanted 'yes' to be the answer, she was more than willing to settle for 'I hope so' but it always slid towards 'maybe, let's see' and then finally it stopped and died in a little, lethal 'no'.

Cure her of what?

That was a good question. The kind that made you want to hold your stomach and laugh until you cried.

Cure her of everything. Maybe the cops had a point. Everything was important. Everything needed to be understood.

One day she woke up and felt really old.

That was the day she started noticing that even nine-year-olds said 'When I was young' with utmost seriousness and absolutely no awareness of how comical they sounded. Everyone had a concept of age, of ageing. When she started working at the age of twenty, she thought everyone else in the office was ancient. Those ancient people couldn't have been a day older than she was right now! Thirty-two. A few more days and she'd be thirty-three. That's why they came to Goa, to celebrate the coming of the next big number.

It was strange how she had never noticed it before—the fact that all her friends, her peers, a few years younger, a few months older—all they ever talked about any more was their bodies. Not their celebratory amatory fecund fine-limbed bodies. No. Their decaying creaking malingering mischief-mongering bodies. What is going *on*, it made her want to ask. What happened to us?

Life happened.

That's the kind of smart-ass answer Cracker would have given. Cracker, whose real illness was that he could not forgive himself for the death of his childhood sweetheart. *If*, he kept telling himself, so silently you had to be deathly quiet to hear it susurrating inside him, if I hadn't been standing across the road, if I had crossed the road and waited for her near *her* school gate instead of mine, if she hadn't noticed me waiting, if I hadn't waved at her to *make* her notice me waiting, if she had looked right and left, if there had been a traffic signal there, if if if.

How many years did it take him to look at another girl again? And when he looked, and loved again, why did it have to be the same kind of girl, the same small girlish build with budding breasts, the same complexion and hair?

Because we only ever keep looking for the same person all our lives, the one we originally loved.

Poor Lolly. Poor tiny girlishly perfect little Lavanya.

Cracker was so afraid that she would die too, this third avatar of his long-dead undying love that he didn't dare tell her anything.

Until that evening around the pool, thanks to the presence

of that boy who listened with the raptness of a child being told a fairy tale.

The boy unlocked something. I had never heard them talk so much, so openly. Nor had I ever seen them befriend a perfect stranger so quickly. Baby was picky, choosy, Baby set very high standards for those he chose to mix with.

Why was Baby so keen to get the boy into the group?

Suspicion is like the first drop of spilt coffee on a clean white paper napkin. The moment it touches the soft tissue, it spreads and spreads and spreads.

She had been away the whole day, and when she was climbing the steps to her room, Cracker accosted her and said, 'Come and see our new acquisition.'

'Don't tell me...'

For a moment she thought the guys had been stupid enough to buy a motorbike instead of hiring one, like everyone else did.

'Baby's got a new toy. We've been breaking him in all afternoon. Now it's your turn to think up something suitably nerve-wracking for him to do!'

'Him?'

'Just come on in, and see for yourself.'

'Why are you carrying a syringe?' she asked, suddenly noticing.

'Because I have a little guinea pig!' Cracker sang, waving the syringe about.

'Don't tell me...'

But by that time the door to Tiger and Baby's room was

already open, and before she knew it, she was sitting on the bed, and Cracker was talking about trust games, which meant the boy had to trust him and let him plunge the needle into his arm.

Why hadn't she rushed across the room and snatched it out of his hand right that minute? Why *hadn't* she? She should have. Her body was abhorrently familiar with needles. Injections in the spine, in the hip, in the gum, even once, god god god how awful, in the eye.

Why hadn't she snatched that syringe away?

Because never for a second did she believe any of it. She knew these guys, all talk. They were testing him, they wanted to scare him, they were getting their jollies scaring some poor little boy who should have gone home with his mamma. A joke. Clearly a joke. And even if the thought of rushing and snatching the syringe away had crossed her mind, she would have quelled it, because she wouldn't want to seem like a hysterical old woman who couldn't see a practical joke if it hit her on the nose. That's what they thought she was—hysterical and old. That's the last thing she wanted to be, especially in front of an entirely new person, a boy who might find her hysterical too.

He chose, didn't he? What right did he have to make her feel as if she had anything to do with that choice?

Then, when he fainted and they all panicked, even then, what was she thinking? Why did she do nothing more than stand and watch?

Because the boy didn't matter to her at all.

Baby had that effect on her. If she entered a room where he was, or where she thought he might be, her heartbeat would accelerate. By the time she was breathing the same air as him, painfully aware of his presence, no matter where he was in the room—and he always took great care to be far away—she would have to fight hard to reclaim herself, the way she had been on the other side of the door, every organ in place, an eternity ago. If, as happened that evening, it turned out he wasn't in the room at all, and all her anticipation had been in vain, things would be no different. In the jolting awareness of his *not-being-there*, she would still have to fight hard to reclaim herself. The simple idea of proximity to him would make everything in her rise to the surface, as if her blood were a stream of iron filings rushing towards the true north of her skin. And because her blood-hot reaction to his cold indifference or his chilling absence shamed her immensely, a great upheaval would follow. As she watched her brain pull back, and felt her body resist, then realign itself—snapping, crackling, slowing, responding to the brain's commands to be still, retreat, return, lie down—she would be overcome by exhaustion.

Seconds after she was all together again, the wheeze would start, or the intolerable scratching, or the razor-sharp pain in the lower belly.

How could she focus on the boy and the needle, when so much was going on inside her?

Was she the only one affected by this nagging guilt? Molly and Dodo had returned when they heard. The others were being questioned in Bombay, that's what the cops told her. She couldn't bear to call anyone else apart from Molly and Dodo, and they came, as she knew they would, even though it was fruitless, their being quizzed by the cops, their waiting with her.

They told her about the morning in the lane with the boy,

then at the shack, where he had paid for lunch. They told her about that night at the beach, how frantic the boy had been when they realized she was missing. They told her how it ended, with Baby telling him he was doomed to die with them, that the injection was lethal. That they were going to do it the messy way, cut their wrists, slit their throats, that he was luckier than they were.

It had all been a joke, except the boy took it seriously. They told her how later, in their rooms, Baby and Cracker had laughed until they cried, congratulating themselves on what good actors they were, and Poka, she was the best. Of course they knew Momo would be safe somewhere, but her disappearance had seemed too good an opportunity to miss. Molly and Dodo had not wanted to be part of the charade, but did they have a choice, did they ever? And so they went along, accomplices in their silence.

In his story, the boy made Molly and Dodo the bearers of her corpse.

She thought about every small detail and she was revolted. How could she overcome that revulsion and ask Baby, point-blank? And even if she did, how could she be sure that he would not lie?

None of the never-ending questions posed by cops, by docs, by gods, would ever make any difference, because she would only ever be able to hear just one.

What had Cracker put in that syringe?

She couldn't bring herself to believe that Cracker would have been foolish or reckless enough to do such a thing. There were other ways to die than by hanging for murder. Besides, Baby would never agree to something so blatant. It was a joke, a joke, a joke...

Except that no one, not one person, was laughing.

Being ill made you susceptible to everything. Moods, weather, the static from a plastic chair against your dry skin. Green sunlight in palm fronds, the smell of smoke from an early morning fire, paint. Something someone said ten years ago. Something someone didn't say ten years ago.

She remembered the time a notice came around instructing residents to save enough water for the day as the overhead tanks in their building were going to be cleaned. The next morning, when she stood under the shower, a frothy white spume fell on her. A pool of suds swirled near the grating. She closed the shower and stared at the froth with horror. Was it the remnants of the soap they had used to wash out the tanks? Had they used acid? Was it some detergent that would lift her skin away, or god no, was it DDT? The air in the bathroom smelt chemical. Her nostrils stung. She felt afraid to touch, soap, cleanse or even towel her body, wet from that first burst of possibly toxic water. All through that day she felt uneasy under her clothes, even after she had had a second shower later in the afternoon, testing the water first before stepping under it. For days after that, she was susceptible to white froth, brushing her teeth, being served a fresh cup of cappuccino.

Being susceptible to everything made you ill. And these were just ordinary, everyday versions of 'everything'. When the big things hit you, that's when you saw how alone you really were.

There was a time when she wrote poetry. She even wrote a poem for Baby once, on a subject close to his heart. Odd how she remembered it, word for word, remembered the way he had read it out to their gang, her words in his mouth, an unbearable intimacy.

A virus can be beautiful,
she said.

Outcry revulsion rage.
Do you know what you're saying?
Are you sick?

She smiled, stern, and said,
Think.

Think of the way it touches people,
blind, indiscriminate,
loving them all,
plunging into their bloodstreams
with the heedless ardour of a saint.

Think of the way it spreads
faster than a blush
faster than kohl under sleepless eyes
faster than fire gossip fear.

Think of the distance it travels
as if the world were porous like skin,
borderless like thought.

Think of the faces it shines out of,
every hue under the sky,
a fever of red and yellow and white,
a delirium of black and brown.

And think of the words 'to die for'.
Could anything be sadder,
more beautiful?

He probably threw it away.

She never relaxed, not even in her sleep. While she waited for sleep to come, she lay rigid, feeling a steel rod driven through her shoulders, her fists clenched. She woke up feeling tense, exhausted, embattled.

When she understood that the only person you can never get away from is yourself, it horrified her.

That was the time people in the house began hiding the knives from her. Knives, forks, screwdrivers, blades, kitchen scissors, office scissors, harmless baby scissors with plastic blades. Then they hid the clothes lines, the spools of thread, the balls of wool, the string that tied the laundry wrapped up in brown paper from the dry-cleaners. The one pair of stockings that an aunt had given her, that lay unused and twisted in a ball in her cupboard, scarves that she never wore because they slipped off unless you tied them tight, dupattas in every conceivable material and style, silk, chiffon, crumpled cotton, crepe, sequinned, embroidered, plain. The medicines, the pills above the basin, the cleaning liquids below the basin, the insect repellents in the store room, the rat poison, the plant spray.

She saw what they were doing, and she wanted to laugh in their faces. How would they hide the bridges, the overpasses, the railway lines, the blind curves, the piped gas that came into their kitchen? How would they hide the buildings that grew taller and taller, so your head reeled and your eyes watered if you tried to see to the top of them? How, if she went away from the city, would they hide the wells, the rivers, the sea?

And even if they sent her away, kept her locked up in the safest place of all where nothing presented itself as a means, even then, how would they hide what they couldn't see, the inexpugnable unreachable source of harm that she had hidden inside herself?

'She has jaundice,' Sonali's son told her over the phone. 'Yesterday she went into rigor twice.'

That night she thought it was she who was dying. There was no pain, just a spreading cold, an almost lethal failure to draw breath, and a restlessness in every inch of her that no amount of tossing, turning, getting up, lying down on her back, on her stomach, on her side, thrashing about, getting up, lying down, curling into foetal position could cure.

She sat glued to her inhaler as if it were an extra mouth, wanting to kick and flail, wanting ten blankets on top of her, a crushing warm weight, a body, someone breathing with her, slow, calm and steadying.

That night she wished there had been someone next to her, someone she could have woken up and held on to.

The next day when she visited the hospital, Sonali was sitting up, her eyes glittering, talking too fast. Her skin was yellow, her breathing difficult, her breath sour.

They talked about poetry, about Sonali's poems, which she had sent a week ago to the publisher, about *her* health, as if that mattered!

Sonali had wanted to know if she had eaten anything.

'There are idlis, and very nice chutney,' she had said, wanting to tempt me into the voracious hunger she knew me to be capable of, especially when I visited her house to be pampered and fed like her third child.

Even there, on that high hospital bed, her stomach obscenely swollen below that bilious green gown, her desperately fatigued husband trying to doze on the uncomfortable sofa, her younger son trying to strum his guitar, her older son wiping the table where something yellow had spilt, even there Sonali was the lady of the house, the caregiver, the hospitable host, the big-hearted woman she would see for the last time that evening.

She refused to see Sonali's bloated dead body, crushed by garlands, cotton up her nose, her yellow face made up for the last viewing, the bright silk sari they must have dressed her up in before they took her away to the crematorium.

She wanted to remember her alive, upright, glittering eyes, racing mouth, her cancer galloping so rapidly her organs could not escape and collapsed one by one. She did not want her last visual memory of her friend to be a corpse.

When she walked into Sonali's house the morning after the cremation—filled with strangers, family whose faces she had seen in the many photographs Sonali surrounded herself with, no one crying except her, coffee being served, Sonali's husband in a clean white kurta, asking if she had eaten—she knew she would never visit that house again, never have the strength to face the vacancy left by Sonali's death, the bone-chill she had felt two days before, as if in preparation for this irreversible frost.

It took her months to be able to say, 'Sonali's dead.'

Every time she thought of bringing those two words, never seen in combination before, to her mouth, she felt a stab inside her heart, as if a little assassin sitting right in the centre of her chest had woken.

For months after Sonali died, night after night she was sure she was dying too, and yet every merciless morning brought her back.

Their group was beginning to break apart. It happened to the best of friends, and it was happening to them. Each one of them had gone secret on the other, as if nursing irreparable grudges. Vast silences fell between them when they met. If a good thing happened to one of them, a promotion, a raise, a new house, a car, it was hard to tell if the others felt glad or envious. There were times when she thought they even loathed each other. When Angie suggested they come to Goa to celebrate her birthday in advance, she almost said no. If she was going to feel alone, she'd rather do it by herself. Not in the midst of a group of people she had once held dearer than life.

Instead, she said yes.

She had this foolish idea. In Goa, away from everything the city did to separate them, she would get a few moments alone with Baby.

She dreamed of them walking along the moonlit beach, she dreamed of his fingers brushing hers, she dreamed of declarations.

She, thirty-two-going-on-thirty-three, dreaming like an adolescent.

And there in front of her, a real adolescent with melting eyes and dangling hands, listening to a bunch of ancients telling him their tale.

The boy was susceptible to Baby. How evident his hero worship had been as he sat beside the pool! That was the first time she really saw him, not when she entered Tiger and Baby's room earlier that same day. Saw his clean cheeks, his long legs, his neat hair, his bony Adam's apple. Saw the boyish adoration that coursed through him like an electric charge. He reminded her of a friend's little dachshund whose sleek black body would quiver with a burst of joy when his owner came home, the uncontainable demonstrative love of a very young dog.

She had wanted to warn him, signal to him the danger in

placing his adoration so openly at Baby's feet. But then she thought—it's different between men.

For one blistering second she had wanted to *be* the boy.

They needed an outsider to keep them together that night. That's why Cracker and the others coerced him into the gang. He would be their glue.

With him in their midst they reverted to their earlier selves. The boy made them want to be wiser, wittier, merrier. He made them want to confess, unburden, confide. It was they who talked, and yet it felt as if her unspoken words were part of what they said. She felt linked with them after ages. As she listened to them talk, first Baby, then Poka, then Cracker and Angie, and Tiger last, it was as if she too, like the boy, was meeting them for the first time. Discovering new things about the beloved. Discovering their gift for invention.

They made things up. Not about their illnesses, but about how they had met each other. And most of all, about her.

She was never the one who wanted the boy in their midst. But that's what Tiger told him.

'Momo thought you had a good vibe.'

Momo never thought about you at all, sweetheart. She would have liked to, but the truth is, she had other things on her mind.

'Momo's never wrong about these things.'

Which things? Knowing which boy will be fool enough to trust a bunch of complete strangers, including one who stuck a syringe in him?

Not her.

And then there was Angie. Claiming to be Baby's truest disciple! Going on about how Momo was their barometer, the key to their condition, a message from the gods or did she say demons? Waxing eloquent on her being transparent and accepting, mutant and wise.

Clues, Angie kept saying, as if this were a murder mystery. We needed to study Momo, she kept saying, as if Momo were a schoolbook. For god's sake, she even described her as a specimen.

'Isolate the specimen for closer observation.' What was she, a scientist? Did Angie even remember that she was sitting right there, or did she think she had, as usual, preferred to stay away?

Who knows why she kept silent, listening as they spun yarns in which the truth kept brushing against its opposite.

Because she could not vocalize. Could not speak, shout, scream, could not say, 'No, that is not the way it was.'

There was another reason. She knew something had happened between the others and the boy while she was away at the beach. Some energy had been exchanged that now bound them to each other. She was extraneous to this new relationship that had as its focus the boy. Baby had instigated it, this game in which camaraderie and insult went hand in hand.

Besides, the boy loved it.

He was enthralled, he sat like a person under a spell as they spoke to him, weaving fact and fiction, about themselves, about her.

How could she have broken that spell?

In such a beautifully confident voice the boy uttered the words that began his tale—'They called it the Land of the Well.'

If the first time she looked at the boy carefully was by the artificial light of the pool, the first time she looked into him was when he began his story. Looked past the childish body language, the boyish adoration, into the place where those words came from.

How had he hidden it so well?

And how had her friends been clairvoyant enough to pick just the right boy for that evening's important ritual?

He spoke as if stories were what he had told all his life. Stories that felt as if they were part of his own mythography, a landscape he carried inside himself, folded small as a treasure map, right in the centre of his heart.

He barely hesitated. It was as if he had told this story many times. And yet it felt so new! Mint-new, each word coined glittering in their midst.

She didn't know about the others, but the boy made her feel as if she was the child, and he the ancient seer.

He took each one of them, and made them mythic. Every sentence came from the reality of who they were, right then, the way the boy had seen them. He took what they had given him and sprang away with it, leaping high into the air of fable. Between each of them and their mythic double he opened out a vast, singing space where they could walk and recognize themselves.

When he introduced the newcomer, the one who brings disease into the Land of the Well, she felt pricked all over by the needles of an exquisite pain.

The boy, who had known her only through the portraits painted by the others, made her the blighted heroine of his tale.

He made the king (whom he openly called Tiger, the poor deluded boy, did he not see where the real power lay, could he not have made Baby the king?) fall in love with her. He made the people of the land despise her, then honour her. He made Baby doubt himself, and Cracker break down. And after driving her like a wedge into the fissure that he had seen open up among them, he threw her down a well, destroyed the king and killed their fellowship for ever.

She should have hated the story, but instead she felt like hugging it to her, as if it were a breathing, living child.

Scourge, Blessed, Weakness—he called her names, each one like an arrow to its mark.

Baby was shaken. She could sense that in the mockery with which he said to the boy, 'So, the little myth-maker has spoken.' Baby always hid his weakness behind sarcasm. What must have rattled him most was that the boy had voiced what he already knew—his notebooks were a sham, an elaborate way of hiding behind other people's ideas. Baby felt exposed and it was the boy who had exposed him.

Cracker was so silent it was as if he was finally ready to drop the pretence of hilarity, shed the mask of the clown, and truly mourn, or truly celebrate, without laughter.

Suddenly, she couldn't bear to sit there a second longer.

She left. No one noticed because they were all too busy telling the boy exactly what they hated about his story.

She didn't go to her room. She was sharing it with Angie and she didn't want to talk to her, meet her. 'Fetishists'. The word Angie threw at the boy followed her as she hurried through the darkened lobby towards the gate. The night guard was dozing. She made a tiny gap between the metal gates and slipped out, making sure to close the gap behind her.

The road outside was lit only by starlight.

She thought of taking the little green lane that led to the river and sitting in the boat she'd seen the evening they arrived. The rest were following their luggage to their rooms while she sat in the lobby, reading, and when those loud men got too much to bear, she escaped and found the river. The others didn't ask where she had been when they met at dinner. On this holiday she realized how scared the others were of asking her anything, as if it might make her blow that final fuse.

On the left of the road there was an arcade of very fancy shops. She could tell by the size of the enormous glass windows that the things displayed behind them would be utterly beautiful and ridiculously expensive. She decided to investigate.

There was no one to guard the windows. She stopped at the first shop, pressed her face to the glass and, cupping her hands like brackets around her temples, looked straight into the face of a woman sitting on a chair with a scarf knotted around her neck.

The fright almost made her heart stop.

One second later she realized it was a mannequin and began to laugh. Christine's. Scarves, handbags, stoles, skirts. The next window had heads in it. Dark expressionless heads that ended just before the bust. Each narrow neck was adorned by heavy necklaces, studded with stones the colours of which she could not see in the starlight, even though by now it seemed as bright as electricity to her keen night-vision eyes. Next to the heads were arms cut off at the elbow, jutting up from the display stand, as if buried in it. Each arm wore more bangles than any woman could bear. And finally there were the hands, sliced neatly at the wrist, slender sculpted fingers flaunting their overpriced rings.

She flitted from shop to shop, peeking in, admiring, rejecting, a picky connoisseur, a fickle moth.

It was when she stared at the deep leather sofa and the queen bed strewn with cushions that she realized how much her body yearned to sleep.

If she had been a cat burglar, she would have found a way to creep past the glass, past whatever security devices undoubtedly took the place of human guards, and curled up on the sofa until morning.

Were they still ragging him, ripping his tale to shreds?

Why could she not have said something in his defence, protected him from their collective assault?

Because she was too tired, too feeble. And because she knew the boy could defend himself.

In his story, she had died.

She had been questioned by the Deity of the Well and had answered Her questions (had the boy said the deity was male?). She had answered so well she was allowed to drink. The acceptance of the Deity made her blessed and accepted among the people, and then the king made the mistake of holding her hand, for all to see that he was not alone, his heart was not unattached any longer.

The next day she died.

Would anyone drink from a well in which a corpse had been?

She wished she had asked the boy that question before she left. Why could she not have thrown herself in the river, since there was one so close by? Why the Well on which the whole land depended?

She had been thoughtless in her death, and irrational. That was not like her. Why would she want to die, now that everything was well again? The people loved her, the king loved her, it was only the king's companions who were bitter and unforgiving.

Maybe it was they who pushed her into the Well.

Maybe it wasn't suicide at all, but murder. Punishing her, punishing their king for breaking an unwritten pact, punishing the people.

Maybe that is why they disappeared, because they were guilty.

Lies, all lies.

A story in which she was reading too much, not that night, oh of course not on that balmy blameless night when she wandered off to rub noses with mannequins and slip like a shadow over the stones.

Now. Only now that some of it had come true.

It had been a long time since she slept outdoors. She was, had always been, a city girl. She liked her bed, her creature comforts. But that night, the idea of her bed in the cottage, the idea of her room-mate, the suffocation that would overwhelm her when she saw them all together, a many-limbed animal moving sluggishly through the night—she could not bear it.

She left the enticement of the windows, the interlocking tiles of the promenade punctuated by slender lamp posts, each holding an old-fashioned elaborately carved unlit lamp, and got back on the road, whose tarred surface felt rough under her thin-soled chappals, hurtful. She scurried back onto the promenade.The bench she chose was smooth and wooden. She lay down on it and slept. She didn't notice the sky clouding over, blotting out the stars, for by then she was asleep and dreams were stories being whispered in her ear.

Once, in happier times, she had walked down two hundred and fifty-five steps into the dark heart of a step well.

The others were up at the fort hotel, drinking. Each part of the restored fort came from a different century, and they found great joy in moving through the centuries by camping in a different room each afternoon to drink. They began in the fifteenth century, a tiny room tucked under the steepest staircase. They had reached the twentieth century by the time she discovered the step well.

Laxman—the thin man in jeans and black T-shirt, both ears pierced, who had silently materialized at her elbow and walked her all the way from the gates of the hotel through the village on to the road that led to the step well—decided not to climb down with her.

'I will wait here for you,' he said, in perfect English with a slight accent of American.

'You don't have to,' she said. 'I can find my way back on my own.'

'No, I will wait here,' he said, and sat down on a rock, the sand at his feet marked by the curiously star-shaped footprints of birds.

She left him there and started her descent. The steps were crumbling, and the lower she went, the narrower the steps seemed to get. She stopped and turned around to look at the sky she had left behind. Against the light, she could see Laxman, standing and talking to another man. They looked tinier than she had expected. Half-turned on a narrow step, suddenly confronted by the idea of scale, she felt the dark corkscrew behind her eyes, a small rising nausea. The steps were too crumbly, too narrow, too littered with feathers and droppings to sit down on. She turned around, slowly, afraid a sudden movement might pitch her headlong down the steps. After a minute, when the only darkness was from the walls around her, she began climbing down again.

This step well had been built by the king in the eighteenth century during a great drought, Laxman had told her. From all across the land, caravans came here for water. They stayed the night in the little door-less rooms that rose around the step well in tiers. They camped, they cooked, they exchanged news, and in the morning, their water carriers full, they went home. Now the tiers were like so many hollow eyes, watching her as she went deeper and deeper below the ground.

The air changed, again.

Walking through the village, the air had been hot and pungent with living. At the top of the step well, it had felt light, uncomplicated. Here, as close to the bottom as she could get, in this dryness of stone and sand and mouth, the air suddenly condensed, gathering to it a thickness that was neither merely smell nor temperature, but sensation. She could sense the ancient presence of water. It wasn't the significantly cooler temperature that spoke to her of water, it wasn't the smell that she could have defined as musty or dank, had she wanted to. She ran through the words that came to her, and it was like running through a forest full of trees she saw but could not name. Bark, she could have said in that forest of words. Leaf, trunk, nest. But not teak, sal, sandalwood, not even eucalyptus or mango, tamarind, gulmohar, jacaranda.

It was a sensation that refused her language.

All the words for water except *water* fell away from her as she stood at the bottom of the step well. All the words for the smell left behind when the water had gone, along with the people who drew the water, and the voices that celebrated its return and lamented its vanishing.

She stood in a great emptiness and listened to the silence. The water welled up in her eyes.

Climbing out, she noticed the great arch she had come through, like a gateway, the arches everywhere, the windows, the frames of the niche-like rooms cut into the wall, a repeating pattern that made her think of the gouging of stone by sharp instruments, the involvement of hands.

When a flock of tiny green parrots rose shrieking above her, she was grateful to them for breaking that frightening symmetry. For not turning voiceless like she had. Their screaming was of this moment, no other. They claimed their present completely.

'Come,' Laxman said the moment he saw her, 'I will show you where the water came from.'

She followed him as he walked along the uppermost tier, past the 'rooms' with fire-stained floors, smoke-darkened walls and chalk-bright etchings of lovers' names. They walked around the veranda-like passage to the furthest end of the rectangular structure, and there in the wall was a single window, that familiar arch cut into the stone. A blue light came through it and fell on the ledge, emphasizing its thickness, its age.

'Behind that is the well,' Laxman said. 'The water came from there into this step well. Why don't you have a look?'

Not wanting to disappoint him with her cowardice, she stuck her head through the window. The cylindrical shaft plunged so far below her she couldn't see the bottom. The surface of the well was surprisingly smooth, damaged only in a couple of places at eye level. The stone was a colour she had never seen. At times she was certain it was pink, at others brown. The patches that seemed grey could very well have been blue. Greyish-pink, bluish-brown, what stone was the well made of? Laxman did not know.

She stared and stared and wondered how long a falling body might take to hit the bottom.

It never occurred to her to look in the opposite direction and see how close, or far, the sky was.

When she pulled herself back though the window, she found the spiralling nausea inside her, the word *vertigo* outside.

On the broad bridge of stone connecting the tiers on the left to the ones on the right, she saw scattered grain.

'In the mornings,' Laxman said, following the direction of her gaze, 'villagers bring their sick children here. The flight of the parrots over their ill bodies brings them back to health. They scatter the grain to make the parrots come. Grain, seeds, chillies. The breeze from the parrots' wings cures the fevers of the little ones.'

And what about the big ones, she wanted to ask, why are they not brought? Who will heal the parents of the little ones?

She said nothing, and followed Laxman on to the road.

He didn't take her back through the village.

'Short cut,' he said, waving across the scrub where several brown sheep and one fat black goat were grazing intently. The sky, which had been a cloudless pale blue when she left the hotel, was now filling up with a swiftly moving grey.

'Rain,' he said. 'If we take the short cut we will arrive before it rains.'

She followed him through swathes of scrub, sudden patches of bright green grass, dry burnt brush, through acres of dust, and finally along a bumpy uphill slope where a narrow path seemed to have been scratched in among thorny bushes with a sharp and spiteful stick.

'Where's the hotel, Laxman?' she asked him. 'This way seems longer.'

'This is the short cut,' he said, calmly. 'There.'

And sure enough, they had just left the thorn bushes and got back on the road when the fort hotel rose out of the land, as if it too had grown out of it like the scrub, the grass, the bramble, as if its roots went as deep as the shaft of the well.

Behind the fort, the sky was full of cloud, and she could hear that the thunder had come closer.

She walked alongside Laxman, too breathless to talk.

At the hotel gate, he refused to take any money and walked swiftly away just as the first drops of rain began to fall.

Interrogation

I already told you!

I was in my room that night. No it wasn't a single room, I was sharing it with Angie. I didn't hear her come or go because I was sleeping. Why would she have woken me before leaving? Angie knows I hate goodbyes. Besides, even if she had tried, she couldn't have woken me up. I was dead to the world. That night, I took a sleeping pill. Yes, I have a prescription for them, would you like to see it? No? How nice to know you can actually take my word for it!

I am not being sarcastic.

I have no idea what the boy was doing there all alone. The night before, he was with his parents. I don't think there was any sinister *drug-related* motive, as you put it, behind his staying back. He just wanted to have a good time without his parents breathing down his neck. Is that so surprising?

What was our motive in befriending him? Are you kidding me? Motive in befriending?

Excuse me while I get a bit hysterical.

Perhaps this is news to you, but you don't make friends for a *motive*. Acquaintances yes, business associates yes, but friends, nope. Friends you make because you like a person, and you want to know him or her better. Isn't that frigging obvious?

Why did we like this person?

Well, he was sweet. He was shy. He seemed lonely.

No, we did not take pity on him.

You want to know the real reason?

Because he looked like he needed some friends.

I cannot explain what kind of look that is! But you know it at once when you see it. It's a sort of hankering, a sort of aloneness that is not the same as solitude. When you see a person sitting alone, you can always make out whether that person needs company, or is happy being by himself.

Yes, I think the boy needed company.

No, I never said he seemed unhappy! I just said that he looked like he could do with some company.

There are people like that, you can spot them a mile away.

Do *I* smoke and drink? What are you, my doctor?

Did the boy smoke and drink? I haven't a clue.

I know of no such cult.

I don't care if it's written in the boy's notes! How do you know he wasn't making it up? Just because he wrote it down doesn't mean it's true!

No, how can I trust someone I barely knew?

I am not contradicting myself.

I said I hardly knew him. It's the others who looked like they were really thick with him. I was away all day, remember? I barely spoke two words to him. Okay so maybe more than two words, that's an exaggeration, but apart from those questions I asked him because Cracker made me, I hardly said a word to him. So how can I know what he was really like?

Just because I said he was sweet doesn't mean I should take everything he wrote as gospel truth!

So what if it's written down in great detail? I never heard of it, and they were my friends before they were his.

He accuses Baby of *what*?

I never heard a funnier thing.

Why don't you cross-check this with Baby, since he is the supposed leader of this supposed cult.

No, I did not bring someone called Abhimanyu to our group. No, of course he wasn't my cousin! I don't even know anyone with such an absurd name.

Did he actually write 'Abhimanyu *also known as Christmas*?' And you still want to believe him?

He was obviously on substances!

Joke. I meant that as a j-o-k-e, joke.

You cannot take this delirious child's notes seriously! He was suicidal, he was in no state of mind to think clearly, he made things up!

Look, my friends are normal, successful, hard-working, stressed-out yuppies. They barely have time to worry about their EMIs and their receding hairlines and their failed relationships, forget about running around trying to get strangers to kill themselves.

Yes, that is exactly what you have been suggesting.

Yes. He made it all up!

How do I know why?

He was obviously seriously troubled. He needed professional help. Not our kind of childish let's-be-friends, he-looks-lonely type of help, but serious professional help. A shrink. A head doctor. I should know!

Yes, I have had that honour. No, I will not tell you what the problem was, and neither will my shrink, *if* I give you her number, because what goes on between a patient and her psychiatrist is confidential.

Of course one can change one's opinion!

If I had known he was writing malicious lies about us, do you think I would still call him sweet?

He was what?

He wrote that?

Oh the poor fool, the poor, poor little fool.

Tejaswini
aka Momo

That night she made herself run away.

She had the feeling that if she didn't get away from them, from the synthetic blue of the pool, the venom in their voices as they attacked the boy, if she didn't get some space around her head that wasn't filled with voices, she would go over the edge.

If she had stayed, maybe she could have prevented something. Maybe not.

And now this new knowledge, like a blow.

The boy, in love with her.

Suicidal manic-depressive old her.

And then the heartbreaking thought—was that why he stayed on?

There seemed no reason why he should have stayed on, friendless creature that he was. No one came to meet him the minute his parents were out of the way. He was all, all alone.

Suddenly she would have given anything to get her hands on his notes.

He was convinced her disappearance meant she had come to grievous bodily harm. Molly and Dodo said so, he had been frantic.

And all this time she thought it was Angie and Poka he was besotted by. Calling them the River Goddesses, blushing when they spoke to him, over the moon when Angie, or was it Poka, danced with him, wooing them with his words, cringing when Angie made her pleasure or her scorn known, that extra edge in her voice betraying—at least to her ears—that she was more than a little interested in the boy. Angie had a thing for younger men, always did.

The boy never looked straight at her, not once. He had laughed with, talked to and looked at everyone, however blushingly, but her.

Oh god. Oh god oh god oh god.

It seemed Baby had told the boy things she had never heard of. *A stab of jealousy, no less painful for being so fleeting.* Who Dares to Die—had she even heard the name right? Was it for real? And if it was a secret cult, as the cops would have it, why did Baby talk about it to a boy he had just met?

Oh but of course. Baby had a thing for holding forth. Especially to people he wanted to impress, people he liked, people he cared for, felt close to. Or so she liked to believe every time she was the beneficiary of one of his lectures. You could be sitting anywhere, doing anything, reading, having a cup of coffee in someone's messy living room, and he would start feeding you facts like, 'Listen, do you know an average-sized person in a sitting position consumes almost half a litre of oxygen every *minute*? Can you even imagine that?'

He would study you, the person next to you, be sure he had everyone's attention. He would observe whether the windows were open or shut and he would continue.

'What if you're sitting in a stuffy room? Are you getting your half a litre per minute? What if the stuffy room is crowded? How many other hateful people are snatching away *your* precious half a litre per minute? How long before you get less than half, less than a quarter, less than quarter of a quarter? How long before you find it difficult to breathe? Two minutes? Five minutes? Ten?

'Five minutes, and that's a fact. Five minutes of not getting your half a litre per minute and you die of hypoxia. Oxygen starvation. Call it what you like but the result is the same. You stop breathing and you die.'

It wasn't anybody's idea of normal conversation. Only Baby's. Someone like Cracker could weather it, performing a dumbshow while Baby talked, making absurd grimaces and clutching his throat as he enacted what it might be like to die of hypoxia. When she was at the periphery of those conversations she felt as if any minute, everything Baby said would come true and Cracker's death grimaces would cease to be funny.

'Do you know,' Baby would begin, chattily, in the middle of dinner, 'in a village in rural Bavaria, previously incredibly healthy people began dying of cancer and heart attacks six months after the telephone, television and radio came to their remote homes? Maybe they were just horrified at being invaded by civilization. Maybe they died because their precious isolation had ended forever. Maybe this was their way of saying no. It would have been far too gruesome if not for one other little fact. The luckier ones—those who survived the telephone, the television, the radio and died peacefully in their beds—got off lightly with cavities in their teeth. Can you imagine, cavities!'

And he laughed out loud, then stopped as abruptly as

he had begun. How easy it was for her to understand why. In his mind he would have seen the skulls found centuries later, a stack of carious smiles.

Or they would be travelling in a bus, or someone's car, packed in like sardines, knees, elbows, thighs squeezed tight, and Baby, who always made sure he got the best seat, next to the driver, or by the open window, would say, as if continuing an interrupted conversation, 'Anything that creates variations in the field of cosmic and solar radiation—I hope you're with me—disturbs the natural equilibrium of living cells. Which means that your living cells do not vibrate in their natural frequency. Which means they leave gaps through which disease-causing mechanisms enter and cause a breakdown in what had once been perfectly healthy systems. Do you see? And these interferences aren't science fiction, buddy. They can happen anywhere.

'You're taking a bus for example, as we are right this minute. It's a big city and you have a long way to go. It's hot. The sun beats down on the metal body of the bus in which you're sitting, breathing in smoke. But there's another kind of pollution you're breathing, and that's the one you can't see, hanging around you in a smog of electromagnetic waves. The people in the bus talking on their mobiles are causing it. The TV tower you're passing is positively radiating it. The plane flying low for landing is adding to the broth. The electricity poles on either side of the street are humming with it. The policemen's walkie-talkies as they communicate from that police van to the police station are loaded with it. The radios playing in the cars huddled around the big bus are cranking it up. And the bus that you're in is trapping *everything*.

'You're dozing as you travel, hoping to catch up on

some of the sleep you lost when you set off so early this morning, but you arrive an hour and a half later completely drained. And it's not because of the odd posture you slept in or the bumps on the road. It's because the bus you rode was a powerful antenna that picked up every last particle of electromagnetic radiation that hung around you as you slept. Transformed into a hot metal antenna, the bus vibrated until your own particles stepped out of time and you became a receiver. Exhausted by all the vibrations that entered you, you became weak, too weak to put up a fight when the real diseases came looking for you. You could catch a train, a plane, or not go to work, but they would still catch up with you. *That's* how helpless you were.'

And they would be silent, because what he said was true, they knew it in their tired bones, their shallow breathing, their zero immunity, their early ageing.

He relished that sort of thing, the silence that followed after he had spoken. Baby, their sweet, psychotic spiritual father, who had found himself another little acolyte in the boy who worshipped him, the boy who was in love with her, and who now lay upon her conscience like an immovable weight, dragging her down.

But even Baby was not invulnerable. He may have seemed utterly self-sufficient, unassailable, every time he opened his mouth, no, every time he walked into a room, that small, perfectly put-together body, that adorable face that looked so innocent of time but was secretly so ravaged by what time can do. Nobody would have guessed what terrors he spent his life seeking, as if by knowing the worst, the rest would be easier.

The one thing Baby needed was an audience. Perhaps it was the only thing he really needed. One night, everyone else had gone to sleep, it was past two in the morning, and only she was awake, because her asthma wouldn't let her lie down. That was the night Baby, for the first and only time, spoke to her, and her alone.

Her asthma got worse the minute everyone drifted off to sleep and she became aware that only the two of them were left in the room. It was April, the windows were wide open, the night was still and sultry. All she could hear was her own rattling breath and it magnified the silence, magnified the presence of this man not four feet from her in an armchair, looking away.

When he began talking, she first thought someone else had walked into the room. But no, there was no one but her, and Baby was talking to her. No, that would imply that she was important, that he was saying things he could only have said to her. He was simply talking to himself, with her as the ruse, the other body in the room that would listen and not interrupt.

She listened and did not interrupt.

'I went to Hiroshima once,' he said.

His usually precise, low-pitched, yet strangely carrying voice sounded hesitant. He sounded like he was finding his way tentatively through a dream.

'I stood at the base of the bombed dome and looked at the skeleton of the building. I stood in front of the eternal flame and looked at the mound of brightly coloured paper cranes that children had left in front of it. I stood inside the museum and looked at the videos on little TVs and the letters written by the mayor to all the countries that had tested nuclear weapons. I cringed to see we had a letter to our name. I looked at a girl skating down the broad clean paved pathway in the garden outside. She wore red pants and a black singlet and skated with effortless grace. Her wrists were strapped in leather and her hair was jet black. I sat on the steps and looked at the river. It barely moved. I looked at my hands and tried not to acknowledge that my face was wet with tears, had been all this time.

'That night I drank enough beer and saké to make me as cheerful as the people around me and I called home from a phone booth plastered with pictures of girls. When I told my mother I was calling from Hiroshima, she gasped, as if I were mad or in danger. At that moment, perhaps I was.'

She thought of him looking at the river and crying, and it hurt incredibly, a pain almost like pleasure, knowing that he too could cry.

'I imagined strange things those days, when I was still learning how dangerous living could be. I imagined sharply dressed executives with giant cauliflower ears. I imagined housewives with scaly lizard hands. I imagined lonely-hearts-club online sweethearts with lidless eyes that never blinked. I imagined teenagers with radioactive lungs glowing through their sheer T-shirts. Babies had X-ray skin, and when their mothers fed them, their mouths turned blue. Men hid their scorched-black testes in fluorescent nylon shorts. Women carried their cancerous breasts in diaphanous designer bags.

'No one smoked or drank. Too addictive. Instead, they hooked up to a little gadget that told them just which part of their body was currently diseased. It told you everything, that little toy, it measured millimetres of decay and degeneration, and it showed you pictures. Pictures of your insides, more gripping, more tantalizing than any movie ever made, the insides that had so far been mysterious except in doctors' labs and dissection rooms. Your insides, which you had so blissfully ignored, now occupied every waking minute. And when you slept the gadget worked on, taking pictures of everything, the sluggish heartbeat, the rapid eye movement, the grinding molar, the bursting spleen. The pictures were radiant. Every colour under the sun. Every mad fantastic swirl, every vivid pulsating detail. People sold pictures of their insides on the art market. No one painted any more. The blood the juices the fluids were doing the painting, spurting obscuring darkening swabbing engulfing.

'It was all so monstrously beautiful that people couldn't turn their eyes away. It was reality TV turned inwards, waiting for some final implosion.'

If only it would come. She sensed Baby's terrible impatience, his desire that it would come, the cataclysmic end of his world.

'I thought I was dying that year I got typhoid. I survived the dreams, the fever, the tortured days in bed, the terrifying pain that made me weep, I survived it but the tiredness that followed the fever almost killed me. I was fifteen and I felt like a very old man. I was helpless before that little squiggly organism that entered my body through the water I had drunk, and I realized how feeble we are, us humans. When we're ill we're reduced to nothing, just machinery for an alien being's growth. Forget typhoid, even a simple flu makes us feel like it's the end of the world. An alpha virus will be the end of the world, we all know that.

'Terror is not being able to see it, grasp it, know it until it takes your shape, enters your blood your saliva your cough your spit your secretions. You see it when it's too late, and then it looks like you. Your eyes turn bloodshot, your skin turns pale. You are not yourself. Suddenly the virus is you.

'Sometimes it got so unnerving I would do anything to provoke the horror rather than have to wait for it. My nasty tongue helped. I filled my mind, my time, my sleep with a jangle of thoughts too extreme to be voiced. It was comforting to know that I could provide my own little jolt, a little dose of self-administered, precisely calibrated shock treatment.

'And why not? After all what was my body but an "electrochemical instrument of exquisite sensitivity"? I was sensitive to everything. All the teeming electromagnetic impulses I was surrounded by sparked and tingled through me. There is a name for it. EHS. Electromagnetic Hypersensitivity. I was a conductor of nervous energy, I could sizzle, scorch or explode at any moment. In school it wasn't like that. In school, I was protected from my own electric instabilities by the clear mountain air, the dizzying isolating height, the sweat and gristle of other boys neutralizing me. But not any more. On the plains everything crackled. There was too much to be absorbed, everything jostled for attention, there was flatness, and I was a tree standing alone in that flatness, waiting to be cut in half by a bolt of lightning.'

If it had been anyone else, she would gone closer, held his hand, one living breathing neutralizing body next to another. But not with Baby. The wheezing had gone but now the tears flowed down her face as she listened, like a river that had changed course, summoned out of his story into hers.

'Do you know that radiation is everywhere? It leaks out of microwave ovens opened and closed by manicured hands helping themselves prettily to their own slow deaths, women who would rather be dead than seen slaving over a stove. I wonder what they would say if they knew where those machines came from.

'"The Nazis developed them, darling, they needed some quick-cooking methods before they invaded Russia. You know how it is, armies moving from place to place, they get hungry you know and if cooking takes forever, they're not going to get very far, are they? So, my dear, microwave cooking ovens to the rescue. Fast, efficient and oh so convenient."

'"Oh really? How fascinating! How do you know all these things, my dear? You're amazing!"

'"Oh no, not really! I've been reading that's all..."

'"Oh reading! I love reading..."

'And so on and so forth at the once-a-month kitty party in a plush flat or bungalow, everyone smelling of perfume and sweat in their embroidered saris and salwar suits while dish after microwaved dish kept coming to the table to the accompaniment of ooohs and aahs. Even if someone showed them the facts in a scientific journal, they would have pooh-poohed it as a male conspiracy against the little blessings that made a woman's life easier.

'"They'd rather see us tied to the kitchen, the brutes!"

'Anything to avoid knowing the truth.

'I'd have liked to tell those poor rich bitches the truth. What you're eating, ma'am, is basically damaged food. It's decayed. Those microwaves you adore hit the food particles so hard they get deformed. All that bombardment—1 to 100 billion times a second if you want the gory details, ma'am—knocks the poor food molecules into pathetic mutilated ghosts of themselves. It's spooky, isn't it, ma'am. You think you're taking out what you put in, the same lovely preparation of dal-gosht or vegetable pulao, looking as mouth-watering as ever, but in reality it's changed completely. It's like those science-fiction movies where a person looks like someone you know but is actually someone else. A sort of Terminator on your table. And I'm making light of it, ma'am, so as to not scare you any more than is necessary, but really the facts are a lot grimmer.

'When you put that irradiated food into your mouth, ma'am, you're going to pass the damage on. Instrument of exquisite sensitivity, remember, that body of yours. (And yes, exquisite in other ways, too, ma'am.) Your blood is altered. Iron drops. Immune cells die. You feel tired for no reason. You feel pale. Your doctor suggests a blood test. Nothing seems to be wrong, yet, but the luminescent bacteria in your blood glow brighter than they ought to. You're turning luminous with radiation. It sounds pretty, but believe me, ma'am, when the little tumours start sprouting along your stomach walls, it won't be pretty at all.

'Then there are those other little signs—signs your husband puts down to what he calls your "woman's problem"—aren't there? The headaches, irritability, nervous tension, the inability to concentrate on anything you do, the low blood pressure, the slow pulse. The hormonal changes. Your brain is shorting out, ma'am, you'll burn out like a fuse one of these days, and not because you're angry or lonely or sad. Simply because the food you're eating is eating you. You look like the woman you were, but really, you're someone else.

'Sounds like fun, doesn't it? Let me tell you another really funny thing. You know the lens of your eye? If you were to expose it to the radiation from your microwave oven guess what would happen to it? It would fry like the white of an egg! Egg white where your eye should've been. Sounds comical, doesn't it? But don't laugh so hard, gentlemen, your lovely ladies aren't the only ones to take the consequences of all this technological wizardry. Your sperm bags, gentlemen, they need to be kept cool if they're to be sufficiently productive. Blast them with a gust from your micro and boom—temporary sterility lands on you like a ton of bricks, worse, much worse than temporary insanity or amnesia and not even something to talk about when it's all safely behind you.

'And so what if you listened to my words of caution and threw your micro out screaming that your husband was trying to kill you? You still wouldn't escape. We live in a sea of radiation. And we don't even know it.'

The tears had stopped flowing. She felt weak, as if she had walked too much, or eaten too little. She couldn't have got a word in edgeways, even if she had tried. Now there was a pause, a long pause, and she could have said something, anything, but she didn't, she couldn't. Baby was looking away. And then he began again.

'It wasn't that I suddenly turned conspiracy theorist cum environmental activist. No! I was merely a person afraid to walk through the air surrounding me for fear of what it would do to me. I was open, you see, no insulation. I was a walking time bomb, only no one had set the timer. It could happen in three seconds or three decades. But every instant I was open and aware that surges of electromagnetic radiation were penetrating me pitilessly. When I spoke on my mobile phone, I felt the radiation pulse through my ear, warming it, piercing my head, probing a few inches into the brain, and staying there. In my brain I now had a hotspot, many hotspots, each a radioactive site where a cancer might decide to erupt, or a fatal loss of memory. My DNA strands were breaking. If they didn't self-repair, my cells would die, one by one.

'And yet I couldn't let go. I knew that after two minutes of talking, the waves entering my head would disable the defence mechanism that kept the harmful toxins in my blood from entering my brain. My brain was now a sizzling cesspool of toxic radioactive waste and I still went on talking on my cell because that's what big boys did, they didn't run screaming to their mammas, throwing gadgets out of their windows, they accumulated them, and used them compulsively. And so, I let that little mobile monster cook my brain, day in, day out, testing my invulnerability, knowing I had none.'

She remembered every word. She could barely remember what she read in books, but when someone spoke, especially someone she loved so much her teeth hurt, she remembered every word.

That night, when Baby said more than she had ever heard him say, she knew that listening would be the closest she would ever get to him. Listening like this, with no other pair of eyes on him, no other ears, no other body in the room but hers. It made her feel weightless. And then he said, 'If someone were to try and grab hold of me, they couldn't. Their grabbing hands would go right through me as if through air. Shiva's third eye, all of me a gash that opens in the head, one dreadful pupil swimming to the surface of an angry curdled white. Lashless and staring, light had no place in it, except at the cold core of its marble sheen, where something old and forbidden still burned. The image of the world was forever imprinted on it, one uninterrupted swathe of shape and colour, a mural without end. The moment the eye opened, the one it looked at would fade into nothing under the corrosive heat of that glance, like those ancient underground paintings that crumble at the first touch of intrusive unwelcome air. And still the eye would gaze, implacable. It was an eye without tears.'

Except that one time, she thought, in Hiroshima, by the river, holding your head in your hands.

'And anyway, what reason did I have to weep? Everything we dread comes true. Why else would a person terrified of traffic die while crossing a road? Or a person traumatized by the idea of not looking impeccable at all times get struck down by a disfiguring skin disease that destroys the only garment we're zipped into for life? People don't die of disease or old age! They die of emotion. Give me any emotional type and I'll tell you how he'll die.'

For a moment she thought he was asking her. But no, he wasn't. He had both the questions and the answers, he always did.

'Stingy bastard, anal-retentive, too proud to consider anyone else's feelings or thoughts as remotely valuable? Clear as crystal. Colon cancer. Next.

'Talks too much? Blather blather blather. Laughs too loud? Will tell you everything you never wanted to know about everyone, including himself? Self-confessed case of VD or verbal diarrhoea? Say aah. Bingo. Mouth ulcers, chronic, repetitive. Next.

'Fluttery, can't sit still for a minute, flits from topic to topic and room to room, waving hands airily? Speech one long melodious slightly high-pitched note, besotted by pretty things, preferably shiny? A tough case, eh? Not for me. Asthma! Stumped you, didn't I? You would have thought paranoia or jitters but no, an airy person is troubled by the problem of taking in air. All that flitting about is just an expression of longing for that one easy uncluttered breath.'

This was when she started getting angry. Airy fluttery person indeed! He had no idea what it meant, not being able to breathe, he had no frigging idea. If it had been any other person, she would have interrupted, argued, left. But it was him and so she sat, a slow anger simmering in the place of her weak-kneed pleasure in his voice.

'Smoke too much? Lung cancer. Drink too much? Cirrhosis of the liver and a wife who leaves you.

'Something vengeful about the whole business, don't you think? Illness as retribution. Something old-fashioned, old testament about it. I loved it. Disease as religion. Disease the path of repentance for sin, the holy book in which you read about your own destruction. Disease the cure for your ingrained vices, bringing them into the open, exorcizing them until you felt wholly cured and cleansed for the rest of your vice-free life.'

He sounded like an evangelist. He scared her.

'Except the only wholly cured state would be death. You moved into another body, you lived on in some superior ether-world bathed in neon, you crossed bridges that grew narrower or broader as you walked, or you escaped it all and became elemental, part of air, water and earth, never to be born again.

'If I am right, and I know I am, the world has never been more religious. And all without any evangelizing, preaching or praying. Just by being the emotional neurotic psychotic creatures that we are...

'My mother had never been very religious. At least, I never remembered her doing things that sounded or smelled religious. No incense, no little brass bells. Did she regret it? Did she, when her body denied her the normalcy of being two-breasted, wish she had a god to cry to? I don't think so. My mother was too strong. Not hard, but strong. It might have made her terribly lonely, but that was the price one paid for being courageous.

'Maybe it was loneliness that made her tend towards the figure of one. The comfort of two was not hers. One child, one breast, one lonely woman in a large empty house. Why had I never told her I knew and understood this? If I had been her daughter I could have.

'But even *she* was religious. Hers was the religion of the stifled sob, the unfulfilled hope, the eternal regret. What made my mother so sad? I never dared ask her, and even if I had, I don't think she would have replied.

'I used to have the same dream those days in boarding school, over and over again. I'm walking up a sloping gravel road. The gravel slips under my feet as I hurry, trying to keep up. I'm trying to keep up with the woman walking ahead of me with long strides. She is tall, and in a robe of some kind. I must catch up with her. My legs hurt, they feel heavy. With a sudden burst of speed, I catch up. I tug at the woman's robe, knowing now that she is my mother. She turns around impatiently. It is my mother but she has another woman's face. She knows it's me but she chooses not to. She tugs her robe free of my clutching fingers and she walks on, leaving me behind.

'The dream would never vary except for small details. Sometimes the woman, when she turned around, had no face at all. Sometimes she had my mother's face but when she turned around and saw me she laughed a loud, reckless, mad laugh. It would always arouse the same sickening fear in me, the same desperate urge to catch up before it was too late, the same numbing certainty that it would be her and she would not know me.'

He had forgotten she was in the room. She had never heard Baby talk about his mother, his father, anyone close to him. No one except Yanky, who was dead. He had slipped into it so seamlessly she almost didn't notice what had changed. His voice had become hesitant again.

And then it hardened, became almost coarse, as if Baby was willing himself to be vulgar, the way he was when he spoke of other people's diseases, the uglier the better.

'I never forgave her for sending me away. She tried to make up for it. The first winter holiday I came home from boarding school, there was a cute little Apso waiting for me. I fell in love with him on the spot and spent three glorious months potty-training and feeding and cuddling and walking my pup until it was time for me to go back up the mountain. We both cried, Pup and I, we whimpered into each other's faces. I reassured him with promises of a mid-term return, but it was another winter before I saw him again, not a pup any more, but still as crazy about me as I was about him. Three winters went by, and the fourth winter I went home to find he had gone.

'"He ran away," my mother told me tearfully. "We looked and looked."

'I was by then too old to cry. One night towards the end of the three months, I heard a scratching at the door of our flat. I knew it was Pup come home. I knew my parents were asleep. I knew all I had to do to change that heartbreaking whimpering into a joyous bark was get out of bed, walk to the door and let him in. But I didn't. I didn't get up. I lay there like a plank, a stone, a corpse, and I listened to him scratch and utter little whimpering howls, as if he were a baby again. And then worse than the sobbing, came the quiet.

'I lay stiff and cold on my bed, and pretended I had been truly asleep, pretended that Pup had never come back.

'Who knows the labyrinthine ways by which the human heart punishes itself? I wasn't rejecting Pup, I was rejecting something I had no name for. By not getting up, I was taking revenge on him for running away. I was taking revenge on *myself* by not getting up. It was obscure, my revenge, and it hurt like a thorn in my heart. I never told my mother, "Do you know that Pup came back, and I didn't let him in?" How could I? I would never find him again nor would he ever come looking for me again. By that one small inexplicable action, I had closed infinite doors.

'No one made me do it. I did it all by myself.'

Her heart twisted with something so sharp she lost her breath again. She wanted to cradle him in her arms, soothe it all away.

But he would reject her violently, bite her like a poisonous snake if she reached out her hand. She stayed where she was and everything ached and still Baby spoke as if to his shadow.

'Time I turned that eye on myself. What turned my bones brittle and my neck stiff? My weakness and arrogance, my envy, my fear, my guilt. I abused my best friend's girl and he grew white-hot with rage and called me names and cut himself off that lifeline. Climbing frayed spirits as much as boots and ropes. I shouldn't have chosen that moment to express my reservations about that bimbette girlfriend of his. What was I, his mother? No, I should have waited until afterwards, and told him, if at all, in the warmth of trip's end, in the glow of that wonderful aching tiredness. Bad timing. A guy dies because of my bad timing. Bravo! I caused a man's death with my burning envy and distorted charity, and instead of killing myself, I lived, my bones turning to chalk.'

He stopped, and without looking at her, without even one small acknowledging look, he left the room.

If she were to judge Baby by the boy's standards, that not-looking at her would have been a sign. But Baby could not be judged by anyone's standards, least of all a boy she didn't know then, now, or ever.

He vocalized for her. The more Baby talked, the less she needed to. Every fear that she might one day have, Baby had already anticipated, analysed, dissected. It changed nothing, and yet without it, he would only have been half-alive. She had never seen him so full of self-doubt and loathing as that night when he left the room abruptly. Something inside him was badly hurt, mangled, afraid. He tried to keep himself whole, gathering his friends to him, other mangled, frightened people. *It's not as if we were stronger when we were together. Just readier to face how weak we were, how fraught and unable.*

He must have sensed in the boy some weakness like his own.

Her weakness was him.

One day, some months after that night, everyone was talking about love. About their hearts, the way they lost them, gave them away, broke them, a silly conversation in which everyone made light of this thing that beat inside them, kept them alive, trivializing it as if it were a trinket. That was the day Baby had said, in her general direction, 'But even in my heart I am sardonic and never innocent.'

However cold he had been, however consistently cold, she had never given up hoping that there might be a chance he would stop looking behind him, and look straight ahead—at her. *Here I am.* But that day, when he said 'even in my heart I am sardonic' she heard the sound of a door slamming shut. No, how could it have slammed shut when it had never been opened, the door she had been waiting outside in all kinds of weather. She was a tramp, despised, despicable, standing there in her skinny self, ragged, eyes bright with emotion, unable to control her breathing just because she knew he was on the other side.

That day, for the first time she saw it for what it was, saw the heavy immovable weight of the door, saw that it was shut.

Interrogation

Yes, I have read the boy's notes, thanks to your generosity in sharing what you were previously treating like classified information, top secret, for your eyes only. I spent the whole of last night reading them. Can't you see I have dark circles under my eyes?

So what?

It doesn't change a thing.

Can't you see what he wrote was an act of spite, of childish revenge?

He says so himself. 'I will be their accuser.' So dramatic. No, melodramatic. Attention-seeking, that's what it is!

Yes I know what he accused them of. Of killing him. How can you take that seriously when it is clear he committed suicide? No one made him drown himself, he did it all on his own initiative!

Of course I'm sorry. My heart is bleeding.

But we didn't do it.

He was lonely, he was depressed, he killed himself. It happens all the time. Twelve suicides last month. All around his age. Sometimes there is no reason.

The autopsy should tell you what he died of, why ask me?

The father will not allow an autopsy? Why on earth?

None of my business? After all the trauma you're putting me through, you have the gall to say none of my *business*?

The father says the reason is clear? Wonderful, why don't we all go home now!

If you insist.

Oh.

So the father thinks I am the reason his little boy killed himself.

Wonderful. I drove him to his death. I was his secret girlfriend whom he stayed back for, who caused him so much heartache he killed himself. I was the despicable older woman who used him and discarded him and drove him to his death.

He couldn't have come up with a more outrageous way of avoiding the truth. The *many* truths.

The boy was lonely, the boy didn't want to go to Princeton, the boy had no friends, male or female, the boy was too shy to give me even the slightest hint about the way he felt, the boy was so desperate to make friends he allowed himself to be ragged, he wanted their admiration, their friendship, and he had no idea how cruel—

No, I never said that. I never even implied that.

No, I have nothing else to say.

What do you mean, there's more? Are you trying to trap me? More lies?

Baby's notebooks?

Ah, so you seized them too. The long arm of the law.

I'm sorry, I'm not laughing at *you*. I wouldn't dare.

No, I am not being sarcastic.

So why didn't you tell me that you know everything already and spare me the trauma?

Baby's notes corroborate what the boy wrote, there was such a cult? Great, case solved. Can I go now?

There is no case?

I could have told you that and saved us all a lot of time!

Look, Baby may have been a bit strange, but he was no murderer. I can swear to that. He was a great talker, that's all. He wouldn't actually ever *do* anything, leave alone plot that poor child's death. Or Abhimanyu's, or anyone else's, for god's sake.

Are you serious? Dated the night before? You mean that first night, when we didn't even know the boy?

Go ahead. I'm listening.

You'd rather I read it out? What is this, an audition?

Fine. As you wish.

'I think I have found him, at last. He was sitting at dinner with his parents like a lonely little pup, wishing he were someone else, somewhere else. He has what Abhimanyu had, without the arrogance. That same milksop desire to be liked. But he has something else. A core that will hold him back from impulsive, thoughtless bravado. I think I can play him any way I like. Half a day and he will be eating out of my hands. I will not let this one slip away.'

Tejaswini
aka Momo

Some things are best left in the dark. Some things must be told. The boy told lies, yes. He was angry, yes. He distorted facts, yes. She was never the one in their group who lost clumps and clumps of hair, the one Baby claimed to be worried for and frightened by. If only she had been. She had never been part of Baby's previous life, that weird cultish improbable life the boy wrote about.

She had wanted to believe it was all, *all* a lie. But how could she, after reading Baby's words out loud, the words that he himself had written? She had laughed it off, he's writing a novel, didn't you know that, always wanted to, these must have been his notes, why ask me, why don't you ask him. But behind the pretence, behind her defence of the man she thought she knew and loved, the growing horror of what he might have done.

The poor child, tapping out that last document, more confession of his love and his loneliness than the accusation he wanted it to be, losing the wonderful articulacy of the story he invented around the pool, sounding garbled, frantic, as if he had a gun to his head—his own fear.

The boy had been prescient in the story he told while he was still unafraid. He spoke of a death, a disappearance and a falling apart. All three happened. He died. She disappeared. And they fell apart. He wanted to twist his love for all of them—for Baby, for Cracker, for her—into a sharp metal object with which he could give back some of the hurt, and the weapon that took shape in his hands was a tale.

Perhaps he knew the saying—there are three sides to every story, yours, mine, and the truth.

Perhaps he wasn't sure any more if it had all really happened, if he was dying because of what the needle held, or because his own death wish had grown irrepressible.

They found these words in his laptop, not part of his accusation but on a single separate page, untitled, as if the beginning of a book he would never write.

It was bigger than me. It was bigger, darker, and in its unnamed terrors I saw a glimpse of what can only be called pleasure. I wanted it. I wanted it without knowing what it was I wanted. It was powerful, the thing they exuded. The seven. There were others, but it was the seven who mattered. I romanticized them. They were just people. Sick people, poisonous and charming. I adored them. No. Correction. I worshipped them.

And so I threw myself at their feet, a male virgin, seventeen years old.

My name? Sometimes a name is important. But sometimes a name is a pitfall. A fall into a pit of fork-tongued secrets. It pulls you down down down and when you land, you gasp at the ground slithering beneath your feet. Nothing is certain. That much I learnt from them.

Names are sand flung into eyes. Names are cruel.

They did not ask me my name. They gave me one. It was cruel, like everything they did. I took the name gratefully, a fish swallowing a hook. The tearing of the throat as I swallowed. Death began that day but to me it felt like the beginning of a new life.

Another monsoon has come and gone.

In between, she has met the boy's fine-boned, slender mother who held her close and wept with the force of a woman whose heart has been utterly broken and whose only reason to be alive was that she could not bring herself to do what her son did.

The boy's father refused to meet her.

The cop who asked her so many questions, a lean young cop, who seemed to believe that questions were a more effective form of torture than any other method, waves to her every time she cycles past the station. She never knew they made cops like that, except in movies. Maybe he watches those movies.

She has learnt how to laugh again. She feels better than she ever has, as if the water in the well the boy threw her into was the water of life, not death.

She wishes it didn't have to be either/or. She alive, he dead. There was a time when the idea of both dead would have been more appealing than both alive.

Her home-stay in Goa has extended longer than she planned. She plans to make it longer still. She is ready, finally, to start living here with all of her—her eyes, her ears, her heart. Ready to start seeing the place—how beautiful it still is, how ugly it could become. She senses how important it will be for her to live here like she means it, remembering the road names, the names of the people she buys food from, seeing the faces that smile at her instead of those she has left behind, hearing their conversation, the simple exchange of words that can feel so rich when the voices are familiar and the feelings warm. Soon she will begin looking for a house that can really be hers. If this were a fairy tale, she would have asked the boy's mother to live with her. *She who lost her only child, I who lost my only mother.*

Instead, she will live alone and learn to be happy. She will love, again, or not. The ailments will come, or go. She will write poetry again, or not.

Acknowledgements

To Karthika V.K. and Shantanu Ray Chaudhuri, my grateful thanks for persistence, patience and meticulousness.

To Mita Kapur and Neeta Gupta, thanks for continued faith and hand-holding.

To my young friends, Anshumani Ruddra, Mohini Gupta and Arjun Rajkhowa, thanks for readings and revelations.

To Gearóid Mac Lochlainn, thanks for letting me use lines from his poem 'Too Much'.

To Prasanna Sankhé, thanks for a fabulous cover, once again.

To Laura Bonner and family, thanks for thoughtfulness, warmth and a beautiful quiet room to work in.

To Pauline McGonagle and Richard Hooton, thanks for friendship and every kind of emotional and practical support.

To my parents Rina and Chandak Chattarji, my husband Kiran David, and my brother Subarno Chattarji—my debt is eternal.

One person I wish to remember is my Mama, Udayan Banerjee, who died tragically in February 2011. He took great pride and joy in everything I did, and the celebration of my second novel will be incomplete without him.